THE
HOUSE
OF
LOST
WIVES

Rebecca Hardy was born and raised in London, England and has lived between Sussex and London all her life.

Writing since an early age, she is a regular contributor to photographic publications and blogs as well as short works of fiction, and shares love for books on her Instagram profile **@Rebecca_readsbooks**. She now lives in West Sussex with her two lively boys, two equally lively cats and her husband. *The House of Lost Wives* is her debut adult novel.

THE
HOUSE
OF
LOST
WIVES

Rebecca Hardy

ACCENT

First published in 2022
by HEADLINE ACCENT
An imprint of HEADLINE PUBLISHING GROUP

Cataloguing in Publication Data is available from the British Library

ISBN 978 1 4722 9352 7

Typeset in 10.5/14pt Sabon Std by Jouve (UK), Milton Keynes

Printed and bound in Great Britain by Clays Ltd, Elcograf S.p.A.

HEADLINE PUBLISHING GROUP
An Hachette UK Company
Carmelite House
50 Victoria Embankment
London EC4Y 0DZ

www.headline.co.uk
www.hachette.co.uk

For Mamgu
Who taught me to love ghosts, books and history
Not necessarily in that order

Chapter 1

ജ൝

The bell rang.

Only later did I find that odd.

I didn't expect their kind to ring the doorbell and announce their arrival. The sort of people who wore crinkled suits and carried cudgels in mallet-sized fists. The men who came to call in a debt, or beat their debtors into senselessness when they couldn't pay.

Two of them marched into our house as though they owned it, and thinking about it now, they almost did, considering the amount of money my father owed them.

I sat at the pianoforte in the front room, my sister at the harp, while the men crashed through the house searching for my father. It wasn't the first time, but it was certainly the worst. Footsteps sounded past the door and up the stairs, the assailants somehow knowing that their quarry was up there rather than in the parlour. I looked at my sister uncertainly, but she only raised her eyes to the patch of damp on the ceiling, her lips moving as she prayed soundlessly.

He couldn't pay them. We knew he couldn't. We'd been scrounging lunch from the tea room for the past week because Father hadn't paid for groceries, having gambled a month's wages on a very, very bad horse.

1

Esme was a year older than me and far better at getting free food from unsuspecting tea room managers. All it took was one of her disarming smiles, a little charm and her renowned humour to acquire us sandwiches and hot tea with heaps of sugar. That she could do the same thing the next day, and the next, was a miracle. By contrast, no one looked too closely at me, or talked to me for long. I had a tendency to speak my mind in a way that displeased people – not that it bothered me. Esme was put in charge of finding us things to do, sneaking us into museums and finding new places to venture on foot during the warmer months. She had even convinced the local bookseller's son to allow us hours of uninterrupted browsing on afternoons when his father was out, in exchange for the elusive promise of a kiss from her that would never come to pass. That we had not been turned out on the street by him time and time again was a miracle, but I imagined he found the view of her devouring books, bundled up in her winter coat and tucked into the corner between shelves, too alluring to turn away.

'It will only be like this for a little while,' Esme had continued to reassure me as we went hungry for weeks. 'Father will think of something.' She was never wrong.

There was a resounding *thunk* from the floor above. I cleared my throat gently as the light fixture swung precariously. 'Whatever you do, don't say anything,' Esme urged as the men now tore through the upstairs floors where my father was no doubt hiding in his study.

I glanced from my sister to Brisley, the house ghost, who stood in the corner in his usual tatty attire. I didn't know why I could see him and no one else could, but he had been there for as long as I could remember. As soon as I had realised he was invisible to all but me, I had kept him a secret – not that he was particularly thankful for it. Unfortunately, he wasn't a pleasant

2

companion at the best of times, and at that moment he had a particularly worried look on his face.

'Don't let that mouth of yours get the better of you,' he said unhelpfully, adding to my sister's sentiments. 'You'll only make things worse.'

I glared at him, then looked back at my sister, hoping she hadn't noticed.

Her cheeks were hollowed, like mine, through not quite eating enough, her arms and frame wiry where before she had been fuller, but she still held herself as though she was completely in control.

My mother wailed from somewhere in the back of the house. The door to the parlour where we sat burst open, and she threw herself on the floor and beat it with her fists. She was drunk, as usual, and didn't seem to understand what was happening, or if she did, she was handling it very poorly.

'Get up, Mother,' Esme said through gritted teeth, just as the men shouldered in behind her, gripping my father's arms, dragging him into the room. The two of them were roughly the same height, with scars on their faces and hands from so many beatings inflicted. Their heads were shaved under their caps, which were askew but still firmly affixed to their heads, and both had red-brown eyes that reminded me of foxes.

'You say you have no money, Mr Dawson, and yet this pretty little lady sits at a perfectly good pianoforte that would easily cover a quarter of the debt you owe Mr Canfield.' His accent was coarse, with no consideration for consonants.

'No,' I blurted before my father could answer, splaying my hands across the keys as if that would protect them. 'Please, no.' Esme shot me a warning look. Brisley muttered something that even I couldn't quite make out but that was disapproving enough.

I watched my father's stricken face, his head already bleeding from being dragged down the stairs, his suit now as rumpled as his assailants'. 'Lizzie, I'm sorry, but they have to take it. I have no other way to pay.' No sooner did he say it than he was thrown onto our last remaining rug, arms flailing as he landed next to my mother, who was slipping in and out of consciousness, her eyes trying to focus on what was going on around her.

'Take this,' Esme said, getting up from the harp and waving an arm over it as though she were a hawker in the market. I wanted to tell her not to. The music was the only part of us that hadn't been taken away or sold to pay off debts. She couldn't let the harp go. But before I could protest, she shook her head at me, as though knowing what I would say. 'It's worth almost as much as the pianoforte and will be far easier to carry.'

'This one is clever, Mr Dawson,' one of the men said as he walked over to the harp to inspect it. 'She understands the value of loyalty, don't you, my dear?' he added, standing uncomfortably close to Esme and running a finger down her arm. I imagined his breath hot on her face, smelling stale and rancid. She hid her revulsion well, and only I, and perhaps our ghost, noticed the flicker of distaste in her eyes.

'Take the harp. That should buy him some time,' Esme offered.

How much time we didn't know, but it would keep them off our backs for hopefully another month.

They manoeuvred it out of the house with difficulty and loaded it onto their cart outside before coming back in to beat my father in front of us. As a small reminder, they said as something snapped in his jaw, echoing in the near-empty room. We watched, too afraid to look away. My mother threw up unhelpfully on the floorboards.

When they finally left, Esme tended to his split lip, cuts and bruises, while I bundled my mother onto the downstairs settee and wrapped her in a rough-spun blanket, propping her up so that she wouldn't choke on her own vomit, then cleaned the floor.

Two weeks later, a letter arrived. Lord Blountford of Sussex, distant cousin to my grandfather, had asked for Esme's hand in marriage. That he was older than our father didn't seem to matter to her.

'What are you doing, Esme? You can't marry a man old enough to be our grandfather,' I admonished her as we sat in her bedroom, packing what few things she had left. Brisley avoided Esme's room whenever he could, but now he watched from the corner with interest.

'I can and I will. He's *ridiculously* rich.' She smiled at me craftily. I rolled my eyes and Brisley snorted, trying to cover his laugh with a feigned coughing fit.

'Money isn't everything, you know. What are you going to do with your life all those miles away from London?' *From me?* I didn't add. I knew I sounded desperate, and I hated it, but I couldn't imagine surviving in the city without her.

'I will host extravagant parties and run the household. I shall take long walks in the countryside and have a dozen children to keep me busy,' she answered. 'The country air will do me good, and being surrounded by all that farmland, I imagine the food will be *superb*.'

I sighed and nodded, allowing my mind to wander to three meals a day, high tea with scones and sandwiches; things we hadn't enjoyed in an awfully long time. I told myself that she would be happy out there, away from the life my parents had created for us here. I just wished I could go with her.

'I'm pleased for you,' I managed. 'You deserve a better life than this.'

'We both do, Lizzie. And as soon as I've established myself at the house, I will invite you to stay, I promise.'

That was the end of the matter as far as we were concerned. She was bundled into a carriage and took a piece of my heart with her as it turned at the end of our street and disappeared from sight.

'Don't look so forlorn,' said Brisley, brushing an imaginary speck of dirt from his threadbare smoking jacket. 'At least you still have me.'

A week later, Esme was married. A fortnight after that, my father received a large sum of money and paid Mr Canfield every last penny he owed him. Where the money had come from, I didn't ask, but I suspected Lord Blountford of Sussex had a large part to play in it.

Letters came from Esme every few weeks telling me of her exploits as Lady Blountford, yet still I waited for the invitation to visit her manor. Twelve months to be exact. And then what arrived was something quite different.

An invitation to her funeral.

Chapter 2

☙ ❧

'Lizzie, we must tighten that corset. No man will want a sloppy wife with a wide waist. Besides, Lord Blountford won't wish to see you untidy,' my mother chided as she fussed over me in my once-shared bedroom. It was an hour before noon but I could already smell the sherry on her breath, and her eyes in the reflection of the mirror we both stared into were glassy and withdrawn.

I wanted to tell her that Lord Blountford wouldn't care if I wore a potato sack. He was probably too old to notice the difference, and I wasn't trying to impress him anyway. Corsets were also out of fashion, but she didn't seem to notice or care.

'And that hair,' she tutted, after stringing me up until I could barely breathe. 'It requires more attention than I can give it. I don't know how you ended up with a knot of curls like this. Your sister—' She stopped herself short, the words catching in her throat. My sister had thick hair, dark as coal and straight as a poker. You could do anything you wanted with it and she often allowed me to brush it, plaiting or weaving it through my fingers. The softest hair I'd ever touched.

I glanced at my mother's reflection as her cheeks tinged pink with the threat of tears. She chewed the inside of her mouth as if to bite back what she was about to say. I turned towards her and wrapped my hands around hers, the comb still clasped firmly in her grip.

'She had beautiful hair, Mother,' I said softly, prising the comb from her and beginning to detangle my hair as best I could. It was about as sentimental as we would ever be.

She cleared her throat and left, no doubt to strengthen her courage with another glass of sherry. I managed to clasp my wayward curls into some semblance of a style and straightened out my dress. With the powders Esme had left behind I dabbed my cheeks and reddened my lips, hoping that I hadn't gone over the top. I stared at myself in the mirror and attempted to look a little more confident, but failed miserably.

'You look melancholy,' said Brisley, stepping out from the wardrobe as if he'd just gone in to have a look around and had conveniently finished his tour as my mother left. Brisley did not much like my mother, but neither did I, so we had that in common.

'How astute of you to notice,' I replied acerbically as I dabbed some lavender water behind my ears and on my wrists. Maybe it would cover the scent of nervous sweat. Perhaps not.

'It is your birthday after all, Lizzie. Surely there must be some cause to celebrate?' Brisley feigned concern as he perched himself on the trunk at the end of my bed and pretended to inspect his nails, removing some invisible dirt from underneath them.

I sighed heavily, regretting it as soon as I felt the corset tighten around my ribs. I was fairly sure that one of my bones would stab me in the lung if I breathed too hard. I stared again at my reflection in the mirror; at the bitterness behind my eyes that only I knew to look for.

The last time I had allowed myself to be dressed up like this, I was wearing red. It had been one of Esme's old dresses that she'd passed along to me when she went away, with lace cuffs, and tiny pearl buttons running up the back. An image of another party pressed at my mind.

The echo of tiny pearls clattering to the floorboards, of stale breath on my neck and hands on my waist turned my stomach to acid.

'It's too much of a reminder, Brisley. Of . . .' I closed my eyes and swallowed. Now was not the time to get emotional. If nothing else, I'd pass out from the tightness of the corset.

'Are we referring to young Lord Darleston's twenty-first-birthday festivities?' Brisley enquired, knowing full well that was exactly what I was referring to. I flopped back onto the dresser stool, resting my elbows on the table and pinching the bridge of my nose.

'I cannot do this,' I said quietly, feeling a wave of anguish rise up, threatening to consume me. Perhaps I could lock my door and stay in my room all afternoon. My parents could entertain the guests; most of them were only coming to see if we were still poor, after all.

'I think you should go down there,' said Brisley, with a secretive grin. 'Just to prove to them that nothing can break you.'

My eyes shot open. I stared at my spectral companion in the mirror, although his reflection was always little more than a faint outline of his true form. He rarely, if ever, tried to comfort me. I was used to his teasing, his jibes and his general indifference towards the only person who could actually communicate with him. This was something altogether different.

'If I didn't know better, Brisley, I'd say you want me to have an enjoyable birthday,' I said, feeling better for drawing the attention away from myself.

'Hmm, must be getting soft in my old age,' he said non-committally, gesturing towards my hair. 'You may wish to pin that up lest someone mistake it for a bird's nest.'

I scowled, but it made me smile when my back was turned to him. It was easier when he mocked. Then I could forget that my only friend – if you could call him that – was actually dead.

A rap of knuckles at my door stirred me.

'Lizzie, the guests are arriving,' my father said through a crack in the door, with no further need for instruction. I pushed my nerves down and checked my face once more in the mirror. I was no Esme, but I would have to do.

As I crossed the room, I paused by the chest of drawers nearest the door.

'You're going to take the knife, aren't you?' Brisley asked rhetorically.

My fingers hovered over the open drawer, the glint of metal in amongst the bric-a-brac. The knife was a talisman, and although it was little more than a cheap piece I had acquired from an ironmonger, it would do the job or protecting me from those who might try to . . . take advantage. With a confirming glance at the ghost, I retrieved the weapon in its sheath and hid it in the pocket in the folds of my skirt. If nothing else, it would be a comforting weight. Reassurance. Nothing like that would ever happen to me again.

'Lizzie?' my father prompted, and I opened the door before he had a chance to rap his knuckles on the wood once more.

'Thank you, Father,' I said as he offered me his arm.

I studied him from the corner of my eye, the man who had caused his family so much pain. The lines in his face were deeper than I remembered, but he had made the effort to look the part: a banker and investor (although the horses he 'invested' in usually lost him more than they gained) wanting to prove to his colleagues from the bank that he was still of good repute. His favourite pastime was not only responsible for our near-destitution on multiple occasions, but I suspected it was not ntirely within the confines of the law. There were legal games, f course, but so many had been banned after the players had ost their fortunes, and only the more mundane had been left ehind. That did not stop the clubs from inventing new ways or people to squander their money, nor did it prevent the illated patrons from playing. It was like a disease, a sickness that fflicted my father in the most unfathomable way.

Today he had cleaned himself up, trying to convince his soalled friends that he was still a gentleman – that he didn't break he law at least once a week and fritter away his pay. But for all he effort he'd made, this party was supposed to be for me. My ineteenth birthday present. Find poor broken Lizzie a husband nd take her mind off the fact that her sister is dead and the family fortune is being squandered away on gin, horses and debt.

I would have protested about my parents' matchmaking if it adn't offered me an opportunity to escape this place. The nife in my pocket would see to it that no man laid his hands n me without my permission, and my temper would likely do he rest, but if I could only leave this house, I might have a hance at doing something with my life other than stopping my nother from killing herself with alcohol.

I had asked my father to press charges against Lord Darleson. It was explained to me, as though I was a child, that young Richard had an estate worth over forty thousand pounds. No ne could argue with money like that, not even the police. Besides, my mother had added, no one would believe me. They vould assume I made the whole sordid incident up in order to obtain some sort of payout, and our family's reputation would e in ruins. There was also the small but significant fact that my ather looked after Darleston's investment accounts and might ave borrowed money for a wager. Probably a drop in the ocean o Darleston, but it was enough to buy their silence.

My only consolation had to be that nobody else knew m
secret.

I descended the stairs on my father's arm, the entrance ha
already filled with guests chatting and inspecting the state o
the house when they thought no one was watching.

That was the good thing about being the invisible sister.
had learned years ago to study people without being noticed
and now I could see every meaningful glance, every whispe
behind a lady's fan, every snigger at the cracks in the ceiling, th
age of the wallpaper or how the lampshades hadn't been duste
recently.

We still had a maid and a cook, and had hired three mor
staff for the party, but our basic staff were already overworked
We were barely scraping the middle class.

I'd said repeatedly that I didn't want the expense of a birth
day party, or any celebration for that matter, but it fell upo
deaf ears. *You should be grateful.* My mother used that line o
me whenever I acted up. If she had any idea how much it stung
I doubt she'd use it so often.

Or maybe she would use it more. She could be spiteful lik
that.

'Smile, Lizzie,' my father said through gritted teeth as h
squeezed my hand on his arm. I wished for a moment that th
party was a masquerade, allowing me to scowl at the gawker
from the comfort of a false face.

I knew that my parents wanted me out from under their fee
as soon as possible, so that I was no longer a burden to them
but I had to pretend, even if just for a few hours, that they reall
did have my best interests at heart. So I wandered the room
smiling, thanking the guests for attending, greeting my father'
colleagues and their bumbling sons who were destined to on
day be bankers themselves. I pretended to enjoy conversatio

with the daughters, who were busy making eyes at the bumbling boys, and tried to laugh at the terrible jokes, all the while forcing myself not to flinch at the touch of strangers.

A buxom girl with dusty blonde hair put a hand on my arm and wished me many happy returns.

'Thank you.' I gritted my teeth and smiled politely.

'Miss Dawson, I'm Jenny,' she said, still holding on to me. Even though my intention had been to continue threading my way through the crowd, something about her expression made me stop. She looked younger than me by perhaps two years, but there was a fierceness to her that gave me pause.

'A pleasure to meet you, Jenny,' I said, studying her. The downturned mouth, the anger in her eyes, all while she attempted to look friendly.

'You may have heard of me,' she said quietly. 'Jenny Miller.'

My heart pounded. I *had* heard of her. Jenny Miller had been the elite of the elite before becoming another unfortunate casualty of Richard Darleston's inability to keep his trousers on. A true socialite, rivalling my sister in charm and wit but beating us hands-down in wealth. That this girl had once had three separate proposals and now stood before me with unspeakable pain in her eyes only filled me with more hatred for Darleston. *You aren't the first, you won't be the last. Buck up.* That was what my mother had said one night in a useless attempt to console me. Needless to say, it hadn't worked.

I looked up to find that the other guests had put distance between themselves and us, the subtle meaning behind it causing my blood to sizzle in my veins.

'How . . . how can I help you, Jenny?' I asked, leaning my head towards her so that no one could eavesdrop.

'I'm sorry. I just wanted to know . . .' She frowned and looked away, searching for the words. 'I wanted to know how you stay strong. How you manage to look as though you own the room, even though you've suffered such . . . tragedy.' The words came out in a stream of frightened whispers, as though she was worried she might stop herself before she had the chance to say her piece. Her voice was high and querulous, and I worried she might burst into tears right there and then.

'Tragedy?' I said, knowing that my smile had faltered.

Nobody is supposed to know. That was my first thought. No one was meant to speak the unspeakable. Again I glanced around at the guests. The room became stifling. I knew people spoke about my family behind our backs, but was that night at Lord Darleston's party common knowledge?

A banker's daughter whispered something to one of her friends, and their eyes trained on the two of us as though they were hunting and we were the prey.

They knew? They *knew*. Panic rose in my chest like a wave.

I managed a weak grimace, but only for show, as I gently guided Jenny to the window, as though to point out to her something of interest outside.

'I'm sorry,' she said again, hurriedly. 'I only wanted to pass along my condolences.'

'Your condolences?'

'For losing your sister.'

I would have slouched against the nearest wall if my corset weren't holding me upright. She didn't know, and perhaps neither did anyone else. I calmed my breathing and smiled wanly at her.

'That's very kind of you, Jenny,' I replied a little breathlessly. The room really was awfully hot.

'*There* you are, Lizzie.' My mother had appeared out of nowhere. 'Lord Blountford is here, and you really must see him,' she slurred, pulling at my free arm. I wondered if she hadn't stopped drinking since before the party.

14

I gave Jenny Miller an apologetic smile and a short curtsey, relieved to have some excuse to leave the conversation, but she gripped my hand before I could go.

'I also wanted to say . . . I'm so sorry for what happened to the both of us.'

My stomach plummeted. The conversation had felt as though someone were repeatedly holding a hot brand near my face and then pulling it away teasingly. With this final statement Jenny had slammed it into my cheek with the word 'DAMAGED' searing my skin. I felt the instant impulse to run away.

But this girl I had only just met had more in common with me than anyone else in the room. I didn't wish to think about how she knew, or if anyone else was privy to this dark knowledge, but I felt I owed her something.

'You asked how I stay strong. How I cope,' I whispered as my mother continued to tug at me. 'Honestly, some days I don't. Oftentimes I can't let anyone touch me beyond a handshake. But I also carry a knife. I promise myself every day I will *never* allow anything like that to happen to me again.' Most of that was true. Some of it was a lie I told myself, and now Jenny, to make myself feel better.

'You make it sound easy,' she said, looking at me with watery eyes.

'Not easy, Jenny, not at all. But if you let what he did ruin you, shred your soul and break your heart, then he's won.' She nodded, blinking away the tears and sipping her drink thoughtfully.

I wanted to tell her the truth. That every day was a struggle for me of fighting with painful memories. That losing my sister days after that party had nearly sent me over the edge. More than once I had wanted to lock myself away, never speak to anyone again or feel human companionship. I'd cried myself hoarse many nights and woken in a cold sweat from nightmares of leering women in saffron dresses and men smelling of stale elderflower wine. But that wasn't what she needed to hear.

'He's already taken a part of us away that we'll never get back,' I said, giving her shoulder a gentle squeeze. 'Don't let him take the rest.'

'Lizzie!' my mother brayed when she realised I wasn't following her. 'Stop standing there chatting and come *now*.' I squeezed Jenny's hand by way of goodbye and scanned the crowd.

Across the room, an elderly man with a walking stick glanced over the guests until his eyes rested on me. I forced another smile and made a beeline for him. I hadn't seen Lord Blountford since Esme's funeral, and he'd aged greatly, and poorly, in the past few months. The only entourage he had was a young man perhaps in his early thirties, who stood behind him with a faraway look on his face. My mind flashed back to the afternoon of the funeral, standing alongside my weeping parents at Esme's graveside. Lord Blountford had been alone then, facing us as though on the other side of a battlefield. He hadn't cried, but he wore a look that I couldn't place at the time. It was only after I'd replayed the day in my head that I realised what it was: disappointment.

I hadn't found it in me to forgive him for that, though in any case it wasn't my place to offer him any sort of redemption. I plastered the smile on my face even harder as I approached, fighting my desire to slap him across the mouth.

There was a shadow of that same disappointed look even now, as he stared me down.

'Lord Blountford, thank you for taking the time to travel all the way here for my birthday,' I said, trying to sound as grateful as I could. I really didn't know why my parents had invited him, or why he had agreed to come, but it didn't seem right to tell him he shouldn't have bothered.

'Ah, I'm afraid my attendance is both business and pleasure, although I am grateful for the invitation to such a . . . quaint party,' he replied, looking around the room with a slightly bemused expression on his face.

'You'll be wanting my father then,' I said, piecing the puzzle together. Of course he wouldn't have come all this way for a birthday party, I thought stupidly. 'Would you like me to take you to him?'

'Don't trouble yourself,' he replied, waving his walking stick at me. 'I'll find him myself. There aren't too many rooms to get lost in here,' he added, looking around, taking in our meagre trappings.

'Indeed. I'm sure your country home is twice the size of our humble town house,' I said, trying to sound polite.

'Oh, three times the size I would say,' he said without an ounce of irony.

He turned to the young man beside him before taking his leave. 'Charlie, behave yourself while I'm gone.'

'We haven't been introduced,' I said to Charlie, who looked at me intently.

'No, we haven't.' He glanced down at my proffered hand warily, and I suppressed a laugh.

'I don't bite, you know.' As soon as it came out of my mouth I felt foolish for saying it, but he took my hand anyway and bent to kiss it. At the last minute he seemed to think better of it, and it turned into something halfway between a brush of his lips on my knuckles and a handshake. Perhaps I was getting used to all these strangers touching me, but I didn't feel the desire to flinch.

'How do you know Lord Blountford?' I ventured, taking a moment to admire his dark green eyes, high cheekbones and golden waves of hair. He would have looked like a picture-perfect noble from a famous painting if it weren't for the fact that his nose had obviously been broken at some point and the tip of his left ear was missing.

'I'm his nephew,' he replied, looking over to where the old man was drinking with my father at a table in the corner. He didn't venture any further information, making me feel like I was being a nuisance.

'I see,' I said, feeling that this awkward one-way conversation had gone on quite long enough, and that there might be a better place for me to be right now.

'Well, Mr . . .'

'Charles,' he supplied.

'I do beg your pardon, Charles, it has been delightful meeting you.'

'That is unlikely,' he said, and I raised an eyebrow at his candidness. Something that looked almost like sadness passed across his features. 'I'm afraid it won't be the last you see of me either,' he added cryptically, before giving me the slightest bow and turning to stalk over to his uncle, leaving me speechless.

I was used to being ignored and shunned, but that was ridiculous. As I watched him thread his way across the room, I found comfort in the fact that he didn't ease up in the presence of his uncle, but seemed to stiffen even more, if that were possible.

'Miss Lizzie.' The maid scurried over, interrupting my need to feel affronted. 'Everyone is here. Are you ready?'

A surge of nerves ran through me. Somehow in the arrangements for the afternoon I'd been roped into playing the piano for the guests. I think my mother intended to use it as yet another ploy to find me a suitor. As this was apparently all I was good for, the more impressive I seemed to those attending the party, the better.

I made my way to the parlour and took my place just as someone tapped a glass for attention. My father's voice, booming and resonant when he needed it to be, could be heard from two rooms away.

'Ladies and gentlemen, my most esteemed colleagues and our honoured guest, Lord Blountford, my daughter will be performing for us presently, so please make your way to the parlour as swiftly as you can.'

I flexed my fingers over the keys and rested them gently on the ivory as people spilled into the room, taking their seats. The piano was the one thing I wouldn't let my father sell when times had become hard, but he'd warned me I would have to make good use of it. I knew he'd already been offered a price for it, and if I didn't play for our guests, he'd more than likely sell it tomorrow, given the chance. Besides, practice had provided me with a much-needed escape in the recent months, even if I missed Esme accompanying me on the harp.

I played one of Bach's preludes and fugues, followed by a Beethoven sonata, barely glancing at the sheet music I had long since committed to memory. Muscle recall and hours of scales and arpeggios had paid off. My final piece, the 'Devil's Trill Sonata' by Giuseppe Tartini, was over fifteen minutes long. I had read that Tartini had written the piece after having a dream where he made a deal with the devil for his soul. Back when we had still been able to afford a music teacher, she had arranged the piece for piano instead of the original violin, and somehow it had always felt familiar when I played it. From the soothing lull of the first movement to the wild and erratic climax, it was dramatic and sombre and often suited my mood. To play it for others was almost as if I was allowing them a glimpse into my very being.

It was as though the piece had been written for me alone.

I poured my heart into every key stroke. Every cadence was an outlet for all the emotions I wanted to feel in public but couldn't. I fought angry tears as I hit the crescendo and forced my features instead into deep concentration so that no one would see how much it hurt to open myself up like this.

As the final notes died away, I received applause the likes of which I had never experienced before. A thrill of exhilaration ran from my fingers through to my very core. I looked up, suddenly remembering that there were people in the room, and curtseyed. In the sea of smiling faces, a pair of green eyes stood out amongst the rest.

Chapter 3

ഔരു

When the last guests had left, my father called me into the study. I was surprised to find Lord Blountford sitting in the seat opposite his desk, with my mother nervously wringing her handkerchief from the settee by the window. Charles was nowhere to be seen.

'Lizzie, sit down, please,' my father commanded. I hadn't seen his face this grave since he lost at the Epsom Derby, so I complied.

I took the other seat opposite him, next to Lord Blountford, who openly studied me as I sat. He seemed to take in everything from my posture to the way I folded my hands on my lap, and he didn't avert his eyes when he caught me watching him. I felt like I was being sized up. For what, I wasn't sure, but the skin on the back of my neck prickled with a sense of foreboding.

'Lizzie,' my father said seriously after clearing his throat loudly for a full minute, 'Lord Blountford has been very generous to our family over this past year.'

Oh yes, very generous, I thought. He practically bought my sister as a wife, used her up and left her to die after a twelve-month. My stomach roiled at the thought of it.

It wasn't strictly fair of me. In all her letters, Esme had sounded happy at Ambletye Manor, the earl's estate, but I couldn't shake the fact that she had died while with him. I held my tongue and instead nodded at my father amiably.

'As you know, things are . . . difficult at the moment,' my father continued, selecting his words carefully. 'Difficult' meant that he had once again bought an unsound horse. Or placed a bad bet. Or owed someone money. No matter how many payouts he might get, he would always find a way to lose. 'Lord Blountford has overwhelmed us by extending his generosity even further, and has offered to take you for a wife. Without a dowry,' he added swiftly as my mouth dropped open.

I stared from my father, to Lord Blountford, to my mother, still wringing her handkerchief and gazing out of the window, unable to look me in the eye.

A dozen arguments fought their way through my mind, but not a single one came out of my mouth. A deep shock, the feeling of being slowly lowered into an ice bath and held under, had settled over me. There were no words.

'You seem a little surprised, my dear.' The earl reached across the space between us to take my hand. I recoiled instinctively, but a warning look from my father reminded me that it would be terrible etiquette, and I allowed him to touch me.

'I . . . I'm sorry, Lord Blountford, I'm a little confused,' I managed to say, looking furtively at my mother, who seemed to be finding the pattern of the settee very interesting all of a sudden.

My father forced a laugh. 'It's been a long day, your lordship. My apologies for my daughter's surprise. The excitement of turning nineteen combined with possibly a little too much wine seems to have addled her mind.'

'Is she prone to confusion?' Blountford enquired, as if I wasn't sitting there with my warm hand in his bony clasp.

'Not at all. But you know how women get, easily overwhelmed and excitable,' my father replied awkwardly.

I was neither overwhelmed nor excitable, I wanted to protest. I was possibly the least excitable person in the world. I could have argued. I could have told Lord Blountford how disgusting I thought it was that his late wife, my own *sister*, had barely been buried six months and now he wanted to marry me. I felt myself sinking in the chair as their voices washed over me, uncomfortable heat pricking at my skin once again. A thought occurred to me then.

'Is it not illegal?' I blurted, scrambling for an escape. 'You were married to my sister after all.'

'That has been taken care of,' the earl replied smoothly. 'And I have a special licence already,' he added with a twist of his mouth, as though he were surprised at my objection. If this was one of the games my father so loved to gamble on, Lord Blountford had the winning hand.

Are you all completely insane? was what I wanted to scream at them.

But what would have been the point? I had no voice in this transaction.

I thought of the other girls at the party whispering behind their silk-gloved hands. Of Jenny Miller. Of our family's reputation. The anger inside me fought against my cooler, logical side.

I had no illusions that this was nothing more than a transaction; just another deal that my father had struck, no different to the hundreds or thousands of others he had arranged as a banker. Lord Blountford had somehow made an offer my parents couldn't refuse, and their crippling debt and probably a certain amount of selfishness had forced their hand. In the quiet recesses of my mind, I fumed.

'I hope some country air will clear her of any peculiar notions and calm her nerves,' my father continued, ignoring the angry heat creeping up my neck and into my cheeks.

'It's been a very trying year,' my mother finally said, looking up at me for the first time. Her eyes were wet but I could see her attempting to hold it together, for the sake of appearances.

'Indeed it has, for all of us,' Blountford replied, a hint of sadness creeping into his voice. He masked it quickly with a stomp of his cane on the carpet. 'Our coach will leave in an hour. There is space for your daughter's belongings, and I hope that gives you enough time to arrange everything,' he said to my father.

'In an *hour*?' I blurted, and I felt the hand on mine stiffen.

No one bothered to answer, instead carrying on as though I hadn't said anything.

'Come along, Lizzie,' my mother said with a strained quiver of her voice. 'Let's get you ready.'

Lord Blountford released me, glancing in my direction for no more than a second before he turned back to my father to continue discussing the finer points of their deal.

'Did you know?' I asked my mother as soon as we reached my bedroom.

'Did I know what, Lizzie?' she asked, pulling a trunk from under the bed and beginning to throw clothes into it.

'That this was going to happen? That Esme's husband was going to ask for my hand and that Father would use me as a bargaining chip?' I said, allowing the fury to finally reach my voice. 'Did you agree to use me as some kind of currency? Marry me off to the highest bidder like you did with her?'

'Quiet your venomous tongue, girl,' she hissed.

'I inherited it from you, Mother,' I spat back.

The slap caught me off guard, and I was thrown to the floor, her handprint stinging my cheek.

'How dare you. You should be grateful. You and your stupid mouth, with your useless quips and insults. We are doing our best! You need only cooperate as your sister did and everything

24

will be well. Do you have any idea what we went through after we lost her?' My mother turned from angry to pleading in a heartbeat. She wasn't usually a violent drunk, but I didn't think the alcohol was helping her temperament.

'Have you suffered memory loss, Mother? I was *there* for it all. Everything you went through, every bottle you lost yourself in, I was there to clean up your vomit and tuck you up on the settee when you couldn't climb the stairs. Before Esme was sent away, we both did that. She would always be the one to make sure we ate while you and Father squandered our money on drink and bets.' I wanted to scream at her.

She opened her mouth to protest or defend herself, but I didn't let her. If another slap came, I'd bear it.

'Heaven help you if you had birthed two sons.' I threw up my arms dramatically. 'You would not have been able to palm them off on some wealthy women. But we were girls and able to be paraded and sold and made to work like maids while you drank yourself stupid.'

All the anger I'd suppressed over the years came flooding out of me, and I was going to let her have every last bit of it. I tore into her with vitriol, throwing words she had used on us straight back in her face. She tried to shush me, but I didn't care if the whole neighbourhood could hear. I blamed her and Father for everything bad that had ever happened to us, and as a last resort, when I had no words left to weaponise, I wailed.

And then I cried.

'No one else would have you, Lizzie,' my mother finally said when my tirade had ended. I had dropped to the floor, my gown spilling around me like a puddle of tears, the corset digging in in all the wrong places. I covered my face with my hands, knowing what was coming next. 'No one would have you with no dowry, and . . . already soiled.'

Soiled. Broken. Damaged. The words used to describe what had happened to me always made me sound like I couldn't be fixed.

And why had charges not been pressed? Because Richard Darleston had paid my parents to keep quiet. So that he could do it again.

I wanted to know how you stay strong. Jenny Miller's words rang in my ears. The truth was, I didn't, not really.

I picked myself up off the floor and began shoving things into the trunk, paying little attention to what was already in there.

'You'll need warm clothes. It's always colder in the country,' my mother said, finding a wool dress and stockings. I stopped with a summer blouse in my hand and shook my head.

'Leave me alone,' I said quietly.

'Lizzie, we don't have much time. If I could only—'

'Get out!' I shouted, refusing to look at her.

She left without another word and I packed alone.

Maybe I was excitable after all.

Chapter 4

ೞഐ

The coach ride had been long. We'd stopped for fresh horses once, but otherwise Lord Blountford had insisted on travelling through the night. We reached Ambletye in the early hours of the morning.

No chaperone, I'd noted as Charles offered his hand to assist me into my seat, never quite meeting my gaze. Perhaps Lord Blountford had taken care of that as well, along with his special licence and his ability to waive the law. I hadn't said a word the entire way, pressing my lips together and folding my arms so that my hand stayed trained on my hidden knife for comfort. I had dozed off once or twice, but every time I stirred, I found Lord Blountford watching me, those milky green eyes trained on me, so I tried to stay awake and look out of the window at the inky landscape.

Charles had sat up with the coachman for most of the journey, coming down into the carriage for an hour to sleep but saying nothing. For some inexplicable reason he had trouble looking at me, and it didn't help my mood.

When I did close my eyes, I would see visions of Brisley, his sombre face as I had packed angrily.

'I shan't miss you, you know,' he'd said, but I could tell he was lying to make me feel better.

'I'm not in the mood, Brisley,' I'd replied, throwing the contents of my armoire onto the bed.

'I'm certain you'll miss me, though. I am by far the best companion for a discerning young lady such as yourself.' He prattled on as if I hadn't spoken. It was secretly comforting to hear him speak, and I realised with a pang that I would indeed miss him. 'Besides, I bet all the ghosts in Sussex are terribly boring.'

I had stopped then. What if Esme lingered in the place of her death? What if I could see her again? Or worse, what if I couldn't?

The thought had fixed itself in my mind as I dragged my belongings down the staircase. As I said my goodbyes to Brisley. Even when I refused to speak to my parents as we left. I spent the entire journey with it gnawing at me.

Now dawn broke like a scalding slash across the sky, streaking the horizon above the treetops with orange and saffron yellow. It was a cloudless autumn morning, and grudgingly I admitted the landscape was breathtaking. When I first glimpsed the house as we emerged from the surrounding copse of fir trees, I thought the brickwork was on fire, the sandstone bathed in blazing sun pouring from the east.

I forgot my anger for a moment and leaned out of the carriage window to take it in. The air was crisp and sweet with the smell of turning leaves and harvest. Mother was right, it was colder down here.

When the coach pulled to a stop at the door, there were staff lining the entrance to welcome their employer, who stepped out of the carriage without looking back at me.

'Charming,' I muttered, as a footman stood by to help me down. I stretched the tiredness out of my limbs and tried to look as ladylike as possible. I didn't care what Lord Blountford thought of me, but I didn't want the staff to immediately assume

I was some city rat he had dragged out to the countryside, lacking manners and decorum.

'Turner, this is Elizabeth Dawson, my fiancée.' The earl addressed the steward, who cleverly disguised any surprise by bowing so low I thought he was picking something up off the floor.

'Madam, it is a pleasure to be of service,' he said, righting himself and signalling for staff to retrieve my trunk from the roof of the carriage.

I was introduced to every one of them. First the maids, with names such as Mary and Annie, in identical uniforms with wisps of hair escaping from their caps, their aprons starched and white. Then came the housekeeper, and the cook, with her dark hair and darker eyes. There were footmen and stewards, lined up like toy soldiers, and a grizzled-looking groundsman. Finally a cheery-looking stable hand, whose lopsided grin was the only smile amongst the workforce. After spending years with only two house staff, it was a struggle to keep up, but I did my best. Fatigue from the long journey and lack of sleep threatened to crush me with exhaustion, and I barely registered the presence of Charles by my elbow until he interrupted his uncle.

'Lord Blountford, your bride-to-be is dead on her feet. I think the tour and full introductions could be saved for later,' he said abruptly.

I glanced up to thank him, but he wasn't looking at me, instead fixing his gaze steadily on his uncle, his jaw clenched.

'Very well,' replied the earl, waving at one of the maids to escort me to my room.

Or rooms, as I soon discovered. My bedroom consisted of an expansive space, twice the size of my bedchamber in London, with a private bathroom. The four-poster bed took up the far wall, a dressing table and wardrobe flanking it, while deep Persian rugs and velvet armchairs occupied the area near the door. It was larger than some of the entire floors of poorer London town houses. If I hadn't been so tired, I would have commented on it, but almost as soon as I laid eyes on the bed, I flopped onto the mattress, dropping into a deep sleep before the maid could take her leave.

I woke up just after noon. Clean clothes from my trunk had been pressed and laid out for me, and a bath had been drawn in the bathroom. The water was tepid but I didn't care – I needed to wash the sleep from my aching body and get my wits about me.

After I'd dressed, I took a moment to study my surroundings. Large windows looked out onto the rear of the house. The grounds were well tended, the grass was trimmed and there didn't appear to be an autumn leaf out of place.

Had this been Esme's room? I wondered. Had she stood in this exact spot when she arrived and felt the unfamiliarity of not being able to see another building anywhere? No dirt or steam, grease or oil, no throngs of people walking past on their way to work or home, no clatter of horses and carts, no children playing on the cobblestones outside.

The grounds beyond the low-walled garden seemed to stretch right up to a line of trees, with a lake glittering just at the edge. Beyond appeared to be a forest, and then farmland. No other living soul could be seen, and there was a certain unreality about it all. If I weren't so certain that the nightmare of the last twenty-four hours had happened, I would have pinched myself.

A chill ran across my shoulders even though the windows were firmly shut, and I spun around half expecting the spectre of my sister to be standing behind me. My breath curled in front of my face as I exhaled, and I rubbed my arms, barely noticing the goosebumps raised there.

A creak from the bathroom had my heart thumping in my chest.

'Esme?' I said into the empty room, annoyed at how timid my voice sounded.

I would *not* be afraid of ghosts.

Part of me wanted to see what was causing the noise, even though my body screamed at me to run. As I crept across the floorboards and the rugs, I heard it again: the distinct sound of someone opening a door.

'Esme, are you there?'

What if it was some other, less friendly ghost? Who knew what had happened in this house before my sister had arrived. Bracing my hands against the bathroom door, I flung it open.

The room was empty, but a small window above the basin had been left ajar, the hinges creaking in the wind. No wonder it was cold.

I slammed it shut and cursed myself for letting my mind run wild and wondering why I hadn't noticed it before. I couldn't know for sure that Esme's spirit was still here. For all I knew, she had died peacefully and moved on to whatever it was that came after death. It was selfish of me to hope that this mightn't be the case, and I knew it. I wanted to call her name again in the hope that she might appear, but something told me that if she was a ghost, she wouldn't be the sort to come at my command. Brisley wasn't, so why would Esme be any different?

Retrieving a shawl from my unpacked luggage, I left the bedroom, and it was only when I smelled the scent of freshly cooked bread wafting up through the hall that I realised I was famished. I padded down a long corridor, my footsteps and the growling from my belly echoing in the otherwise deserted halls.

A maid appeared from somewhere and directed me where to go, curtseying politely when I thanked her. I followed her instructions until I reached the colossal double doors that led to the dining room. I'd been hoping to find it empty, and my stomach dropped when I saw that Charles was sitting at the table eating in silence.

Although the long dining table easily seated twenty, the steward pulled out a chair opposite Lord Blountford's nephew and brought me food without me even opening my mouth.

'Good afternoon, Miss Dawson,' Charles said abruptly, standing up until I took my seat, flicking a glance at me before returning his eyes to his meal.

'Good afternoon, sir,' I said, uncertain as to whether I still had permission to use his given name. Much had passed since that first conversation and I didn't want to presume how I should address him now that I was in his home.

'Please do call me Charles, if the informality of it doesn't bother you,' he said. The cool demeanour of yesterday hadn't completely disappeared, but it had softened slightly. Still, I was infinitely suspicious of noble-born men, and narrowed my eyes at him. It was improper, but I knew better than anyone that there was nothing proper about my being here.

'It does not, and in which case, you may call me Lizzie,' I replied, taking a knife and fork to my own food and savouring the roasted lamb as it melted in my mouth. I allowed a quiet moan of pleasure to escape my lips before I realised I was being watched.

'Not Elizabeth?'

I shook my head. '*Never* Elizabeth.'

'Very well,' Charles said, subtly raising an eyebrow when he saw my obvious satisfaction at the meal. 'You rested well, I hope?'

'As well as I could,' I replied, knowing that the dark circles under my eyes betrayed me.

'Excellent. I hope that in time you will find it more comfortable here, although I realise that at present it may be . . . distressing,' he added. At least he had the decency to notice my unease, I thought, which was more than I could say for his uncle.

I shrugged and kept my eyes on my plate. The meal really was divine. Our cook at home had been acceptable when she'd had the ingredients to cook with, but whoever had created this meal was a true master. Perhaps it was because the produce was fresh from the nearby farms, I thought as I devoured the lamb with rosemary and boiled cabbage, forgoing any attempt to be ladylike about it.

I glanced up at my mealtime companion only after I had cleared my plate, and found that he was still steadily eating, the corner of his mouth twitching all the while.

'Is something the matter?' I asked.

'Not at all,' he said, finally breaking into a smile. It transformed his face and made the slight unevenness of his nose a more gentle feature in his tanned face. 'Only I've never seen a lady enjoy her food quite so much.'

I frowned at him even as I felt the heat creep back into my cheeks. That I hadn't eaten well in some months was obvious from my thinning arms and face, but I'd forgotten that here in this new house, my every move would be watched. My body itched to leave, wanting to be away from prying eyes and taciturn nephews for a while, but Charles must have sensed it, as before I had a chance to slide my chair back, he spoke again.

'If you don't mind waiting just a moment, I would be delighted to give you a tour of the grounds,' he said earnestly, making me feel that I had little choice in the matter.

I stiffened, wondering if perhaps he'd been told to keep an eye on me.

'I really am quite tired,' I managed.

'Of course. I only thought that as my uncle is away for the afternoon, and the weather is still fine, you might wish to take a turn around the garden. See for yourself what Sussex has to offer.' The smile that came with that sentence was softer than the last, and changed my mind although I knew not why.

'Th-that would be lovely,' I said, trying not to sound over-joyed at the news that Lord Blountford was away. 'Your uncle has much business outside the property?' I added, leaning back in my chair and taking a small sip of the dark, sweet wine I had been poured. I noticed the tic in Charles's jaw as I asked the question, and filed it away for future reference.

'He has . . . business in town. I've been helping him with his affairs but he wanted to deal with this alone,' he replied cryptically. I didn't bother pushing him, as talking about Lord Blountford evidently made him uncomfortable, and he appeared to be finished with his meal.

'I shall have one of the maids fetch you a coat and boots,' he said, giving the instructions before I'd had the chance to tell him I hadn't packed any boots. Within minutes a young woman had brought me a heavy wool overcoat and a pair of leather riding boots that appeared to be roughly my size. I wondered if they had belonged to Esme.

'Shall we?' Charles asked, once we were ready, holding his arm out for me to take. I almost rejected it, but explaining why I didn't want to touch him would have been harder, so I placed my hand in the crook of his elbow and tried to keep my body turned away from him.

If he noticed, he said nothing as he led me out through the

French doors and into the midday sun, which hung high and bright in the blue sky above. Bushes of buddleia climbed up the walls either side of us, the last of the purple blooms still holding on, their heady aroma lingering in the air, which smelled better than any perfume.

Carved stone steps led downwards, with sculptures of naked nymphs standing sentinel at the bottom, pouring water from their urns into the round ornamental pond below. The path we walked cut straight through the middle, a flat bridge over the surface rather than a pathway between two ponds. I spied a large goldfish swimming underneath us, and couldn't help but smile as I spotted a frog jumping between the lily pads that covered the surface only a few feet away. Even the wildlife seemed to be happily ignoring us as we threaded our way along the path and into the rose garden beyond. The whole thing was idyllic, and almost Mediterranean in its style.

'My uncle spent some time in Italy as a young man and took inspiration from the villas he visited there,' Charles commented, as if in answer to my thoughts.

'How long was he there for?' I asked.

'Oh, only for a year, back in '56, if what he tells me is true,' he replied calmly.

I tried to disguise my gasp by taking a deep lungful of country air. 1756 was more than twenty years before I was even born. Of course I knew that Lord Blountford was old, but it was only now beginning to hit me how much of an age difference there was between us. The meal in my stomach felt leaden at the thought, and I quickly pushed it away.

Charles led me through a gap in the box hedge that bordered the rose garden and along a gravel walkway that weaved its way down a short hill. From here I could already see the small lake

I had spotted from my window earlier. Although it was still a fair distance away, I could make out the white shapes of swans on the water and a small red boat moored by the bank.

We stopped at a point where a stone bench had been constructed, as if to allow one to sit and read or take in the view. I didn't wish to sit, but I did stop for a moment and take big lungfuls of fresh air, closing my eyes as a gentle breeze brushed my face.

When I opened them, I found myself studying Charles, who had respectfully kept his eyes on the distant woodland and hills. He was interesting in his own way. I'd thought him capricious at first, but now that I began to see the pattern of his moods, it was almost too obvious that the cause of his unrest was his uncle. Whatever their relationship, Lord Blountford and his nephew were not happy with each other.

Other than my father, the men I'd encountered had always been loud and boisterous, keen to be the first to give their opinion and have the last word in a conversation. Having spent so much time listening to them, I was surprised that I had barely heard Charles speak. He didn't seem to have any of the qualities of those other men. But I'd been wrong before.

'My uncle doesn't walk very far even when he's here. He spends much of his time dealing with estate matters from his study, rather than venturing out into the wilds of Sussex. He would likely be opposed to losing his bride on her first day, so it might be an idea to get your bearings,' he said, giving me the faintest of smiles. The word *bride* felt like someone was hammering a nail into my heart every time it was said, but I tried to turn my grimace into a look of feigned interest.

'The stables are over there, to the west of the house,' he explained, pointing back towards a low cluster of outbuildings to our left. 'Do you ride?'

I scoffed before I could stop myself. 'Absolutely not. I can't stand horses,' I retorted, turning away from the stables and back towards the lake.

'That might cause some difficulty here in the country. There are very few ways to get around,' he said, and there was that smile again.

Looking up at his slightly weathered face, his tanned skin offset by those green eyes, the broken nose only truly visible when he was in profile, I felt the sudden need to know.

'How did you break it?' I said, feeling impudent as soon as the question had left my mouth.

He lifted a hand, his finger tracing the bridge of his nose. 'Is it that obvious?' he asked bashfully, making him seem suddenly much younger.

'Not at all,' I said hastily. 'In fact it has been set and fixed rather expertly. I have a tendency to notice things about people.' That he hadn't become angry at my question told me something else about him.

'Good to know,' he replied, giving me a sideways look. 'To answer your question, I was breaking up a fight between two of my men, one of whom had cheated the other in a game of rummy.'

'Your men?'

'In the Royal Navy. I was stationed in Egypt, Africa and more recently the Mediterranean, but was honourably discharged four months ago due to injury.'

'They discharged you because you broke your nose?' I asked, confused.

He laughed. It was much lighter and heartier than I had expected, full of genuine mirth and pleasure. It was a satisfying sound.

'No, not at all,' he replied, but didn't explain what further injury he might have sustained.

'Did your men fight often?' I asked, noting that he didn't wish to speak of his discharge.

'I'm afraid so.' The humour left his voice as suddenly as it had arrived, and a shadow passed across his features. 'On this occasion I was intervening in a fight that had broken out during a game of cards. Gambling,' he huffed with a shake of his head. The word had me recoiling instinctively, though if he noticed my revulsion he didn't show it.

'You gamble, then?' I couldn't hide the hint of disappointment in the question.

'Absolutely not,' he answered quickly, something bordering on anger in the flash of his green eyes. 'No, I've seen it ruin more men than I care to recall. But the conditions on board ship almost encourage it. Drinking, gambling, brawling. That's the problem with war. Men train for combat, and when it's all over, they find they're still fighting something. Usually themselves. Or their demons,' he added quietly.

He began to walk again, gesturing for me to follow as we wended our way slowly down the hill towards the lake.

'I hope you don't mind me asking, Charles, but how old are you?'

'I'm twenty-five, believe it or not.' He laughed wryly. 'I know I look older.' His cheek dimpled when he smiled, transforming his face so that I could believe he was only a few years older than me. I wanted to ask why he'd matured so quickly, but he seemed to sense the question. 'Fighting in a war and losing two parents along the way will do that to you.'

'I'm so sorry, I had no idea,' I floundered.

'No need to be. I've only been back from sea these few months, but I think being *here* has aged me ten years.' He shook his head, and there was that smile again.

'You work for Lord Blountford?'

'I . . . assist him, I suppose. He was my father's older brother and automatically inherited the title and estate, but even after four wives, he has no heirs, so I have an interest in making sure the place doesn't fall apart,' he said.

'Four?' I almost choked on the word. I felt as though I'd learned more about Lord Blountford in one sentence than in all the time my family had been acquainted with him.

Charles stopped abruptly by a large oak and rested his hand on the trunk, looking at me apologetically.

'Now it's my turn to say sorry. I meant no disrespect to your sister—'

I cut him off with a wave of my hand and slumped to the ground among the roots of the tree. I was to be wife number five. The lamb and cabbage in my stomach churned at the thought of it.

'Do you know how the others died? How my sister . . .?' I didn't want to finish the question. No one had told me what had become of Esme. The last I had heard from her was a letter telling me that she had news and that she was making plans for me to visit Ambletye. A few weeks later, she was dead. Everything had changed after that.

'I'm afraid I only arrived after she had passed,' he said softly, doing me a kindness by sitting down next to me, perching himself on a large tree root.

'My mother thought she must have been ill,' I said quietly, examining the patterns and shapes of the bark. I traced a finger over its rough lines, resting my head against the trunk. 'The way she said it, I don't think she knew herself what had happened. The coffin was closed,' I added, my voice breaking. I had shed enough tears to fill an ocean when my sister had died, but I could never stop more from coming.

Charles seemed to hesitate, but then came the weight of his

reassuring hand on my shoulder. I flinched at the sudden movement, but surprised myself by not pulling away.

'So you never met her?' I asked, looking up at his furrowed face.

He paused before he answered. 'No, although my uncle spoke of her often. I think her death shocked him as much as it did anyone. She sounded wonderful,' he said encouragingly.

I laughed bitterly. 'Oh, she was. She was soft and kind, witty and eloquent. She knew what to say in any given instance and could wrap anyone around her little finger after one conversation,' I said, failing to hide the anger that lurked in the depths of my heart. If Esme's ghost was listening in as I praised her, she made no appearance. The half-hearted hope that I would see her again crumbled and faded. 'She didn't deserve to die.'

'I can assure you, Lizzie, that those we love are rarely deserving of death,' Charles said, taking his hand from my shoulder. His voice had dropped and I snapped my head up to see him looking away. He'd lost both parents and had been fighting in foreign lands for who knew how long. How many deaths had he witnessed? My careless mouth had run away with me again.

'That was insensitive and inconsiderate of me,' I said, eyeing the hand that rested on his knee. His knuckles were scarred and his fingers callused. Not noble hands. Not the hands of a man who had stayed clear of danger and ordered his men around from a distance.

His dark emerald eyes looked away from me, through the trees and towards the lake beyond, although I doubted he really saw what was there. His mind was somewhere else: perhaps back on his ship, or beside his parents' graves.

He sighed and shook his head, standing up and offering to pull me to my feet as he did, my fingers soft in his rough grip.

'Death tries to make strangers of us all, whether we are on the giving or receiving end,' he said, turning towards the house and gesturing for me to follow. 'The real trick is not to let it tear you apart.'

He let go of my hand as he walked away, and my palm felt cold where his had been.

Chapter 5

ও৵৶ ৻৵

The tour of the house had been cut short by the return from town of Lord Blountford in the late afternoon. I was summoned to the drawing room, where Charles left me alone, making a hasty and somewhat suspicious excuse that he had paperwork to attend to. My indoor shoes were presented to me and my coat was taken by a maid, then I was swiftly whisked away and led to the first-floor landing, as though whatever it was could not wait another moment.

'Enter,' Lord Blountford commanded when a steward knocked on the large door that stood between myself and my future husband, ushering me in before closing it behind me.

He was sitting at a desk twice the size of my father's, the dark wood polished to a mirror-like shine. I examined the items on it with little interest; nothing looked as though it had been used more than once or twice. A wooden box sat open by his lamp with a dozen or so small keys inside, undoubtedly for different drawers or boxes of records. Indeed, on the shelves behind him there were locked cabinets alongside papers and tomes, organised with military precision. The door of the nearest cabinet was open, the key still in the lock. A large space on the shelf inside must have housed his ledger, which now sat open on the desk in front of him. It was the only item in the study that appeared well used, some of the pages yellowed with age and the spine almost crumbling from wear. Lord Blountford hunched over it, making notes on a separate piece of paper with a pen and ink.

I took him in as he studiously ignored me: the sagging skin, the thin lips set almost permanently into a scowl. What was left of his hair might once have been dark blonde, perhaps, like his nephew's, but was now a snowy white, combed tidily to match his generally neat appearance. I wondered if he had been handsome as a young man. There was still a hint of good looks – or there would have been if his face was not weighted with anger and, I realised slowly, grief.

He seemed to be struggling with a particularly difficult sum, and I almost offered to help him but swiftly changed my mind. As the daughter of a banker, I knew my way around numbers well enough, but no man I had met liked to be bested by a woman, and I doubted the earl was any different. I cleared my throat, thinking he had forgotten me.

'Miss Dawson, I have seen the vicar,' he said without so much as a hello, not even removing his eyes from the page in front of him. 'He has agreed that the wedding shall be held next Thursday. There will not be any guests, although my nephew will act as witness. I will have to arrange for a second upon my return to town tomorrow, but you will be pleased to know it is all in hand.'

Pleased? I reined in the terror that had embedded itself in my stomach, squashing it until it solidified, turning into something more akin to anger. 'Thursday seems rather soon, does it not?' I began to protest. Only then did he glance up from his book to give me a sharp look that made me close my mouth.

'We have no need for a grand affair, and the sooner the deed is done the sooner we can get on with our lives,' he said, picking up a letter from his desk and reading through it as though we were talking about nothing of more import than the weather. I wasn't entirely sure what to make of his attitude. As a girl I had entertained the idea of being married for love. Esme and I would sneak into our mother's bedchamber and try on her wedding veil, which she kept in a chest at the end of her bed, imagining that we would each meet a young, rich and handsome man with whom we would truly fall in love. Growing older, I knew the likelihood of finding love was a fantasy, and resolved to be content with marrying for convenience. No amount of resolve had prepared me for this, however. A quick marriage to a man thrice my age, a ceremony performed almost covertly, so that we could 'get on with our lives', as he put it. Get on with our lives indeed.

'And what will that entail?' I asked sharply, unable to hold my tongue.

He didn't appear to have heard me at first, but he eventually glanced at me over the top of the paper.

'Pardon?'

'The rest of my life. Here. With you. What will that entail exactly?' I failed to keep the edge out of my voice. He spoke about this marriage as if it were exactly what I knew it really was: business. I had no illusions about where the money had come from last year that staved off the creditors. My marrying Lord Blountford allowed my parents to continue their pretence of being upper middle class while getting rid of me and potentially providing them with some tenuous claim to his land and titles. To all intents and purposes I had no right to feel so angry. But still my clammy fists were clenched in my lap and I found myself unable to calm down. I had known that this would happen, and yet I still felt a sense of betrayal. A loveless marriage was to be my lot, and all at the behest of my parents.

'You are not a prisoner, Miss Dawson, so do not elect me as your gaoler. You may wander the grounds freely. You may ride nto town as you wish. Your duties as my wife will be minimal and you need not even run my estate if you do not desire it. You are as free as any other noblewoman in the county,' a slight change in his tone then, 'provided you play your part.' Those words weighed heavily on me. I knew what 'playing my part' would involve.

'And what if I can't?' I asked tentatively.

'Can't what?'

'Do my duty to you. As a wife. In bed.' The last word came out as though it were drenched in acid. The thought of allowing a man to touch me in that way made me both terrified and incensed.

'There is no "can't", Miss Dawson. Biologically speaking, there is very little you need do in our marriage bed. I was not informed of any medical problems you might have, and I would have thought that perhaps someone would have educated you as to what is involved—'

'That is not what I mean,' I interrupted him, wishing that the ground might open up and swallow me at that very instant. 'What if I cannot allow you to touch me. To be . . . intimate.'

'You have one duty, my dear. I have been more than generous with your family and I require that the favour is returned, however difficult a notion you may find it.' His tone had taken on an edge of its own, as though he were chiding a small child and not his future wife. Although perhaps in his eyes I was both.

Good Lord, I was going to be sick on the carpet just thinking about his papery skin on mine. His lined hands on my body. As I closed my eyes to fight the wave of nausea, a brief expression of confusion passed across his features.

'You look quite ill, Miss Dawson. Perhaps you should lie down,' he said, ringing a bell.

'And . . . will I have any further functions besides . . . providing you with an heir?' I managed, swallowing hard against the anger and sickness in my gut.

'I have become quite used to arranging the affairs of the household, if that concerns you. You may do as little or as much as you like, and if you require company, I will arrange for a lady to sit with you and do whatever it is that you enjoy to pass the time.' He waved a dismissive hand.

'You will pay someone to sit with me? And do what for the rest of my days? Needlework?' I sneered. Good. The anger felt better than the fear at least.

'I had worried that you might be like this,' he replied almost to himself.

'Like what?'

'Just as your sister was. Restless. Always in need of something to do, some way to occupy her mind. Like a mare that hasn't been broken in yet. It took her weeks to settle in,' he said, shaking his head.

'But she did? Settle, I mean?'

'Oh yes. The house became hers. She decided she would enjoy being its mistress and claimed all that was mine for herself. Esme owned it more than anyone else.'

Something in the way he said it forced the question out of me before I could stop myself.

'More than your other wives, you mean?'

I regretted it as soon as I had said it, watching his jaw clench beneath his jowls, seeing him narrow his eyes at me.

'How dare you.' The coldness in his tone had me on my feet and ready to flee from the room just as the steward entered to collect me.

I should have apologised, but somehow that seemed harder than keeping quiet and watching his anger unfold before me.

'Miss Dawson, do not mistake my generosity towards your family for charity. You have a part to play in this. If you refuse to hold up your end of the bargain, I will not hesitate to send you back to London.'

Images clouded my mind at the thought of returning home: of my mother on our threadbare carpet, passed out with an empty bottle under her arm; my father beaten into senselessness by a creditor's thugs.

If I thought that living here would be unbearable compared to life in London, there was something very wrong with me.

I nodded, now feeling too ashamed to say sorry.

'A wedding next Thursday sounds acceptable,' I acquiesced, giving a curtsey before taking my leave through the door the steward had left open. Lord Blountford hadn't told me I could go, but I didn't want to say anything else I might regret. He didn't stop me.

The conversation with the earl had left me feeling more lost than before, and I briefly wished I knew where Charles might be so that I could speak with him. Given time, I hoped we would become friends, although the strained relationship with his uncle might prove to be a challenge.

I couldn't face returning to my room immediately. Instead I began to explore the first floor, searching for nothing in particular but knowing deep down what I hoped to find. The manor consisted of ground, first and second floors, plus no doubt an attic and a basement that I didn't think much about. I knew that my room was located on this floor, but the sea of doors, many of them locked, left me intrigued and a little lost.

Wandering a house that was not yet fully mine made me feel much like a tourist shut in a museum after hours. Glass cases filled with carvings and sculptures from all over the world lined the first-floor landing. Stuffed animal heads were nailed to the walls at various intervals. There were decorated muskets and ornamental swords that shone, though upon running my finger along their blades, I discovered they were blunt. My betrothed seemed to have spent much of his long life travelling, or perhaps merely collecting.

I reached a part of the house that looked unfamiliar. I didn't recall seeing an antelope head or a stuffed pelican on my way down this morning, but these objects bordered the nearest door to me, and I tried the handle to find it unlocked.

The bedroom inside was . . . . purple. West-facing, the expansive windows caught the setting sun in all its glory, illuminating the walls and furnishings. Mauve silk draped over the four-poster bed that took up a large portion of the room. Lilac cushions and curtains offset the hand-painted wallpaper, patterned with lavender flowers and peonies. A large wardrobe stood to one side, while the other held a lilac armchair and a shelf of books.

But it was what sat on the polished dark-wood dresser, with a velvet stool tucked under it, that made my heart thud heavily in my chest.

I stepped lightly on the deep carpet and stared at the contents of the table.

My sister's hairbrush.

It seemed like such a small thing, but it was so much a part of who she was that I found my cheeks wet with tears before I even realised I was crying. This was a part of her life. A part we had shared, which she had then brought to this strange place where she had made her home.

A present from an aunt, the ceramic brush had been painted with her name on the back, surrounded by tiny pink roses. *Esme.*

I picked it up and clutched it to my chest, as if somehow I

could sense her through it. A few errant strands of hair still clung to it, dark like my own, but straight and long.

Untucking the stool from under the dresser, I sat before the large mirror and looked at my blotchy face, the dark circles from my few hours of sleep. My eyes were my mother's, grey-brown, the colour of ash. Esme's were the darker brown of our father's, but their shape, and the pout of our mouths, the high cheekbones and sharp eyebrows, were all shared between us. I unpinned my unruly curls and held out a lock of my hair, brushing it absent-mindedly with her brush the way she used to when we were younger.

I could almost see her behind me, sparkling in the shafts of light from the window. A quiet sob racked my chest as I brushed my hair, remembering the conversations we'd had. Things that had at the time seemed banal and unimportant, but that now I wished I could commit to memory, word for word. The ache in my chest spread through my body as another stream of tears ran down my face.

'Strange girl, crying over a hairbrush.' A gentle mocking voice interrupted my grief.

I turned, startled, clutching the brush to my chest. Behind my stool, only feet away, stood a beautiful woman in an indigo day dress, cinched at the waist, her hands folded in front of her as she studied me. Her blonde hair fell in ringlets around her face while her eyes were the pellucid blue of cornflowers, accentuated by the colour of her gown.

But her face gave her away. That luminous sheen, so light it was almost translucent, made her skin glow ethereally. A ghost.

'N-no,' I replied shakily, standing up and facing her. She blinked in surprise.

'How fascinating. You can see me,' she said, turning her head in a way that seemed almost feline.

'I can,' I supplied, pinning my hair back up and placing Esme's hairbrush hastily on the dresser. I sniffed the tears away and wiped my cheeks with my sleeve, trying for all the world not to look like I had been doing exactly what she had accused me of. 'My name is Lizzie. Might I have the pleasure of knowing yours?'

'How charming. Lizzie. Lizzie, Lizzie . . . short for Elizabeth? Or Eliza? Or Elspeth? No, silly me, then you'd be Ellie, not Lizzie.' The ghost appeared to be talking to herself as she walked around me in a tight circle, looking me up and down. 'You look just like the last wife, but she couldn't see or hear me. Why was that? Why are you so special?' She spoke rapidly, her voice high and soft.

'She was my sister, but she didn't—'

'Ah, a sister! How interesting. So Eggy has himself another spirited young thing and a sister no less. Goodness me. I wonder how long you'll last, dear, considering that your beloved Esme was the shortest-lived of us all.' The ghost shook her head sadly.

'Eggy?' I ventured, ignoring the barb. She was clearly quite mad.

'Edgar. Your fiancé. The man who owns all of this.' She waved a hand at the room in general.

'Ah, Eggy. Of course,' I said, doubting very much that Lord Blountford would ever let anyone refer to him by that name. 'And you are?'

'I am Persephone, the third wife, but you may call me Pansy. Everyone else does. Or did. I still find it very confusing not being able to speak to people,' she added, and I wondered how long she had been like this. Had being a ghost made her insane, or had she been that way before she died? She wandered over to the bed and hopped onto it, stretching out so that her legs dangled over the edge. 'It's been so *boring* being unable to speak to anyone, although scaring Cook has always been highly entertaining,' she added, tilting her head towards me with a mischievous grin.

'Pansy, have you seen Esme? Is she . . . like you?' From my experience with Brisley, very few ghosts liked to actually be told they were dead, and it seemed best to play it safe with this beautiful madwoman.

'Oh, I don't think so,' she sighed, and I tried to fight off the disappointment at her reply. 'Your sister had so much fight in her. Strong-headed. Competent. She'd probably be bossing everyone around even in death,' she mused, and I thought of Esme as Lady Blountford, giving orders and running the house. No doubt she would have done very well at it. 'You know why we become this way, don't you, Eliza?' she said, waving a translucent hand in the air as if to demonstrate.

'Actually, I've never known why some people end up . . . like you while others seem to pass on,' I admitted, although my experience with ghosts was really only limited to one particularly grumpy middle-aged man. The others I had encountered were never able or willing to hold a conversation.

Pansy shot up from the bed and faced me, pinning my body in place with those crystalline eyes of hers.

'Lies.'

'Pardon?'

She blinked once, twice, the waning afternoon light twinkling in her dark pupils. 'Lies keep us here. If there were no lies, we would have no reason to stay. It is up to the living to find the truth and set us free,' she said gravely. A shiver ran its way up my spine, causing my arms to goosebump under my sleeves. 'But you can help us, dear Eliza,' she went on, her face breaking into a grin again. A stunning, terrifying grin.

'How can I help you?' I asked, frowning.

'By finding out the truth, of course. Head for the summer house. That's where you need to start,' she added, turning her back on me and walking away.

'Wait! Where is the summer house? What am I looking for exactly?'

She glanced over her shoulder at me, that glint of crazed cunning sending another pang of fear straight through my already shattered nerves.

'Beware, little Eliza, of the truth you might find.' And with that she walked through the wall and disappeared.

I released an exasperated breath, wondering for a moment if my strange encounter with Pansy was merely a figment of my imagination, caused by stress and lack of sleep. As if my body agreed with the thought, I felt my eyelids droop and knew I would have to find my way back to my room as quickly as I could.

I pushed the stool back under the dresser so that it would look untouched, but found that it wouldn't tuck in all the way. Stooping down to see what was blocking it, I noticed that a corner of the carpet, close to the skirting, was slightly raised.

Suddenly nervous that I had damaged it when I had sat down, I pulled the stool out all the way and got down on my hands and knees. But as I pushed the lifted carpet down, my hand met with something solid. Frowning, I peeled back the edge and found a tin box, the sort that biscuits were kept in, wedged in a hole in the floorboards. It was an almost perfect hiding place.

With trembling fingers I prised it out, and my heart stuttered as I saw the grinning face of a child staring back at me. The tin had been my mother's, back when we were little and she used to bake sugared dainties and pound cake, Esme's favourite.

'Esme?' I asked the empty room, wondering if the box might conjure her ghost. When only silence replied, I shook my head at my foolishness.

'Pansy?' I ventured. Nothing. Ghosts had an awkward penchant for disappearing when you needed them.

A noise in the corridor outside stirred me, and I shoved the stool back into place and clutched the tin to my chest, hoping I could sneak back to my room without being asked about it.

Exhausted and slightly disoriented, I eventually found my room, which faced east on the opposite side of the house to where Esme's had been. In fairness to Lord Blountford, this room was far larger than my sister's, but I wondered if he'd used up all the bedrooms on his other wives and had had no choice but to give me this one. The shadows had already lengthened on this side of the house and lamps had been lit, but the shades of green, red and pale gold in here were a stark contrast to the brightness of the lilac room.

Purple, the colour of passion, of play and of summer, seemed so fitting for Esme's personality. The dark greens and reds, representing envy, anger and blood, were somehow suited to me even if I didn't like them.

I settled onto the bed and lifted the lid of the tin. The first thing I saw was a bundle of letters tied with string. Flicking through them, I realised that they were from myself and my mother. At the bottom, though, the unfamiliar writing on a loose letter caught my eye.

It was a gentleman's hand, spidery and not particularly well formed, but still legible.

Lady Blountford,

I have the information you requested and the records of proof. It is much as you expected, although some aspects

*may surprise you. I invite you to attend me at my home
on Thursday should it please you.*

*With sincerest wishes for your health,
Price*

My chest felt constricted. What proof had Esme been looking
for? And who was Price? It was odd for someone to sign only
with their surname, but I wondered if perhaps he didn't want
his title to be known. Or hers. Perhaps Price was a woman despite the inelegant hand.

I wanted to investigate the box further, but a gentle knock
on the door forced me to close it and shove it under my pillow.

'Miss? Dinner will be served in half of the hour. May I help
you dress?' The quivering voice of a maid.

My first instinct was to send her away, but I thought better
of it. I had barely been here a day and I needed to make some
sort of effort.

I beckoned her in and allowed her to select clothes for me to
wear. I managed to prise her name out of her – Marie, a mousy
girl with ash-blonde hair tucked under her cap and eyes that
sparkled with innocence.

She selected a simple evening dress of dark green fabric that
I didn't recognise, and the thought skittered across my mind
that perhaps it had belonged to one of the other wives. Maybe
even Pansy. I tried not to squirm when she laced it up at the
back, thinking that it was a little like sleeping in someone else's
bed. Or coffin.

After rearranging and pinning my hair, she escorted me
down to the dining room, where Lord Blountford and Charles
stood at the vast table, awaiting my arrival.

I gave them both a smile, a cursory one to Lord Blountford

and a more genuine one to Charles, but both returned it with nothing more than a slight incline of their heads, waiting for me to sit before they took their own seats.

Any moment of understanding I thought I had had with Charles earlier, any sliver of hope that I might have found a friend, or at least some connection in this new and unfamiliar place, seemed to be gone. He was stiffer than ever, and a small vein pulsed at his temple.

I endured the meal in relative silence, only speaking when I was directly asked a question.

'I was told you are yet to learn to ride, Miss Dawson,' Lord Blountford said after a particularly long stretch of silence.

I paused mid mouthful.

'I cannot deny it, sir,' I said, feeling childish, as I often did when people asked me about my fear of horses.

'Well, that is something we must rectify at the earliest opportunity,' he said, looking pleased with himself. 'I have an excellent stable, the finest purebreds in the county. It would be remiss of me not to have you taught.'

Although I had the impression he thought he was doing me a favour, perhaps to atone for our earlier conversation, my heart sank. How could I tell him that the very prospect of going near a horse was terrifying to me?

'Well, what do you say to that?' he persisted. I glanced at Charles beseechingly, although I didn't know why I bothered. He was studying the food on his plate as though it were the most interesting thing he'd encountered since leaving the East.

'Fine, sir. That would be fine,' I said, resting my knife and fork together on the side of my plate. I'd lost my appetite. The little girl inside me who had been half starved for years was furious at the waste of food, but I ignored her.

I turned to the steward and said in my most authoritative

voice, 'Please thank the cook for the marvellous meal and apologise for my leaving so much over. All the travelling has made me quite queasy.'

He seemed surprised to have been spoken to, but quite pleased. The earl stared at me in a way that made me think he was unaccustomed to other people speaking to his staff. Charles didn't even blink.

'I'm very sorry, gentlemen,' I said to the men at the table, who made to stand as I did. 'No, don't get up. Thank you. I find myself quite faint.' I gave a subtle curtsey as I fled the room and made my way back upstairs.

Horse-riding. On top of being married to a man old enough to be my grandfather, the widower of my sister, I was expected to learn to ride. I tried to explain to myself as rationally as I could that the worst that could happen was that I'd be bitten again. Or trampled on. Or thrown from my mount. Perhaps I would die before the wedding. I wasn't doing a very good job of convincing my fears to abate, so instead I changed into my nightdress and pondered on Charles's stand-offishness.

He was a different person when next to his uncle, that was for certain. But why? Was it because of the sordid history of the earl's previous marriages, or something to do with the mysterious business that they conducted together?

The only thing I was absolutely certain of was that Charles did not want to be my friend; not in front of his uncle, at least.

Too tired and deflated to open Esme's box again, I stowed it in the gap between the headboard of the bed and the wall, hoping that no one would be diligent enough to clean down there, and fell into a fitful sleep filled with nightmares, devoid of the usual sounds of the city and accompanied only by the eerie hoot of an owl somewhere in the distance.

Chapter 6

ഇരു

I awoke to the sound of birds singing. This would not have been all that unusual if there hadn't been quite such a number of them. I had never heard a chorus like it before, as though all the birds in Sussex had gathered outside my window to wake me.

'Good morning, miss,' a nervous voice said from beside my bed. Marie drew back the curtains, casting bright dawn light onto the bed and directly into my eyes. 'Lord Blountford has requested that I dress you in riding clothes this morning in time for your first lesson.'

I bolted upright, my curls a tangle around my head. The riding lesson. I swallowed drily as the maid fetched a riding dress and jacket from where she had hung it outside the wardrobe.

'There are clothes made especially for such torture?' I said hoarsely, stumbling out of bed and washing my face at the basin, not daring to look in the mirror. I had tossed and turned most of the night, too tired to plait my hair as I often did before bed, and knew that I would look no better rested than the day before.

'I wouldn't call it torture, miss. It's only a horse, after all. Can't get about the countryside without them, I'm afraid,' Marie said mildly, a bemused smile on her face as she guided me towards the dresser. 'Besides, the earl insisted that you learn to ride. It's only proper that you wear the correct clothes both for your safety and so you don't get any of your . . . nice dresses dirty.' Something in the way she said it made me wonder if she didn't approve of my existing wardrobe. I didn't blame her, if she was used to the clothes of wealthy country aristocrats.

She proffered the dress to me; it was made of a thick-spun wool of the finest quality in a simple but loose cut, allowing the rider to look elegant while being able to stay mobile.

'Does the earl realise that I don't want to be within a square mile of a horse?'

Marie hesitated, and then started explaining that the stables were only a few yards from the house, and thus they were already within a square mile of me.

'I know that. It's a figure of speech,' I complained, snatching the dress from her and scowling.

'Do you need help, miss?' she asked worriedly. It was clear from her expression that she hoped I'd say no.

'I've been dressing myself for nineteen years, Marie, I think I can manage,' I said, trying to take the hardness out of my speech and failing. 'You might be able to help me with this, though,' I added, waving to my hair.

Her eyes brightened and she allowed me to don the clothes before sitting me in front of the dressing table and carefully taking a comb to my tangles. Everything about her reminded me of a mouse. Even her deft little fingers as she teased the worst of the knots apart and began plaiting my hair. Within twenty minutes she had braids looped around each other and set into a tidy bun, pinned to the back of my head with copious amounts of hairpins.

'Goodness, Marie. You're a genius,' I breathed, admiring her handiwork in the mirror.

'Thank you, my lady,' she said with a curtsey as she beamed

with pride. I didn't bother to point out that I wasn't a lady yet as she bobbed again and left the room.

I pulled open the bedside drawer where last night I had tucked my knife. There would be no easy way to conceal the blade in this outfit, and I almost left it where it was, but in a final moment of deliberation I took it out, belt and all, and strapped it to my leg under the swathes of fabric. I had no intention of doing any riding anyway, so I hoped it would continue to go unnoticed.

Still in slight disbelief that I was going near a horse without being dragged kicking and screaming, I wandered downstairs, directed along the way by busy servants. It was only when I reached the west entrance to the house, nearest the stables, and the smell of hay and horse filled my nostrils that I realised I had skipped breakfast.

Cursing under my breath, I trudged across the cobbled yard towards the sizeable stable entrance, hoping my instructor, whoever they were, wouldn't show up.

'Not the usual language I hear from a lady.' A chipper voice came from somewhere in the depths of the stalls.

'I'm not a usual lady,' I retorted, my mood still sombre. Maybe I should have had breakfast after all.

He laughed, a bright sound that pierced the shadows like a spark, and emerged from the darkness of the stables leading a horse behind him.

I vaguely recognised the grinning, gangly boy from my arrival. He could have been no older than sixteen, tanned and freckled, with a crop of curly red hair and eyes the colour of shining conkers.

'Miss.' He bowed, still holding the reins. I took a step back when the beast got too close to me. 'My name is Jordie. I'll be teaching you to ride this fine lady,' he said, suppressing another laugh when I took another step away from the mare.

'She won't hurt you,' he added encouragingly.

'That's what they all say.' I rolled my eyes and crossed my arms over my chest. The scar from my childhood horse bite was hidden under layers of clothing, but I imagined it tingling on my shoulder all the same.

Jordie didn't seem perturbed by my reaction, explaining that he'd been riding since he was a boy.

'Have you ever ridden before, miss?'

'Not successfully. I had a . . . horse-related injury as a child and have been terrified of them ever since,' I admitted, eyeing the beast he held in case it decided to take a chunk out of me. He nodded, but if he felt any sympathy for me, it was short-lived.

'Everyone has a few mishaps when they first deal with horses, miss, as is to be expected. It's like learning anything,' he said chirpily, guiding the horse towards me. 'This here is Gwen. She's a gentle lass, tolerant of beginners, so she'll go easy on you.'

I stumbled backwards and found myself by the rear outer wall of the house, covering several feet before I had realised it, my back pushed up against the rough brickwork, my fists bunched at my sides. This time Jordie didn't laugh; instead he gave me a flat look of neither sympathy nor malice. Why had I even come down here?

'All right, all right,' he said soothingly, and I wasn't sure if he was talking to me or the horse. 'I was told you came from London, miss. Lots of horses in the city?' he asked casually. His accent was soft, countrified. It was hard to place, but he both sounded and looked as though he could have been raised in the stables, with the ease he showed around Gwen.

'Well, yes. They pull carriages and carry people around,' I said. Surely he knew that, though. 'My father is an investor – a banker,' I said, noting his confusion at the first word. Whether he realised it or not, I was desperately trying to change the subject.

'Ah, mine was a farmer before the sickness got him,' he said, smiling sadly.

A small pang of loss pulsed in my chest. Everyone lost people they loved, I had to remind myself. My sister was just one of hundreds – thousands – dying all the time. But it didn't give me much peace.

'I'm sorry for your loss,' I said, frowning sympathetically, my hands relaxing by my sides slightly.

Jordie shrugged and gave me another one of his crooked smiles. 'Part of life, I suppose.'

'And your mother?' I ventured to ask. I didn't want to talk about my own family, but I could quite happily ask about his to avoid having to ride.

'I've got five brothers, so she keeps her hands full. I'm the second eldest, so myself and Grayson work to bring some coin home for her and the younger ones,' he said proudly. He was only two or three years my junior, yet he was already support-ing his family.

'That's . . .'

'Sad?' he ventured.

'I was going to say admirable.' I pushed off the wall and took a step towards him, knitting my now less shaky hands together in front of me. I felt undeniably humbled. 'What does your brother do?'

Jordie smiled and patted Gwen absent-mindedly. 'He works a farm on Lord Blountford's lands, just a few miles from this one. We see him most nights except during harvest.'

'So he's not home at the moment?' I thought about the time of year, about fields being tilled and wheat and whatever else they grew in the country being harvested. I had never before considered that someone had to actually *do* these things until I imagined Jordie's brother, a larger version of him, out in the fields with a plough and horse.

'That's right. Long work days at this time of year,' he replied. 'And you, miss? Are you from a large family yourself?' I knew he was trying to distract me, attempting to make it seem like he wasn't inching towards me, but every hoof clop, even if discreetly made, brought him, and Gwen, nearer to where I stood.

My hesitation must have been palpable. The quick down-turn of my mouth, the sudden sting to my eyes that I rapidly blinked away. 'My only sister died,' I replied quietly. 'Here, on this very estate, in fact.' I wasn't certain as to why I had told him that. We were only just acquainted, after all.

'I'm sorry for your loss.' He echoed my sentiments from earlier.

I waved a hand at the look of sympathy in his eyes and raised a corner of my mouth. 'Part of life.' I quoted his words, even though the reminder of Esme cracked something inside me every time she was mentioned.

He gave me an understanding smile, and I couldn't help but return it genuinely. Whatever he was doing, whatever magic he was weaving over me to calm me down, it was working, and that scared me almost as much as the horse that was a few feet from me now.

'Can I let you in on a secret, miss?' he asked conspiratorially.

I nodded. I wasn't sure I wanted to hear it, on top of everything else I had to worry about, but his face was so open, his manner so relaxing that I felt I needed to let him confide in me.

'Between you and me, if I get you to ride, the earl will give me a bit extra. Enough money to support my brothers and mother for a *year*,' he whispered, and I had to step closer to hear him.

My heart plummeted. The thing standing between this boy and the income to look after his family was me learning to ride.

'I said I can't make no guarantees, of course, but I'd like to try, if you're willing.' There was a question in that final statement.

He was my height, and as I looked into his russet eyes, at the untarnished sincerity there, I decided I had to at least attempt it, if only for his sake. I nodded again, my chest pounding at the prospect of going near the horse, which still stood patiently waiting for me. Jordie broke out into an even bigger grin and exhaled deeply, as though he'd been holding his breath for my answer.

'That's grand, miss,' he breathed. 'Why don't we start by giving her a pat on the nose, eh?'

My mouth automatically opened to protest, but he reached out, grabbing my hand and placing it firmly on Gwen's muzzle, my palm flat against her soft nose.

I froze.

'That's it, miss. Just like that,' he said softly, clasping my wrist firmly in his strong grip, preventing me from pulling away. 'Now let her get used to the feel and smell of you. Can you take a step closer?'

I shook my head slightly. I didn't want to move. My feet seemed glued to the cobblestones as I stared Gwen in the eye. Her hoof clopped on the ground, but as I moved to back away again, Jordie was behind me, steering me closer with his free hand, the reins and his body barring my escape. She was inches from me, sniffing my clothes, her mouth nudging my riding jacket.

'There we go, Gwen, Miss Dawson doesn't have any treats for you today, but she'll remember for tomorrow, won't you, miss?' he said, moving around to Gwen's side and placing her reins in my other hand. I was touching her without any guidance from him at all.

I broke into a smile, and Jordie gave me an encouraging wink.

'I did it?' I asked him, and he nodded in reply.

'Yes, miss, all by yourself. Do you want to lead her around the courtyard just once?'

Emboldened by his lopsided grin, and his reassurance, I led Gwen slowly in a small circle. She went willingly and didn't pull on the reins or suddenly attack me as I'd expected, but came to a stop when I did.

Although my heart had levelled out into a steady rhythm, no longer pounding as it had been when I'd first touched her, I still hopped away once when her face came too close to me. Jordie only made soothing noises, more than likely for my benefit, and urged me to go on.

'What's next?' I said when we'd made a full turn.

'Keep going,' he said approvingly.

Emboldened, I led Gwen around the yard again, then a third time, before Jordie asked me to make a figure eight, getting used to the feel of leading her by her reins.

'What do I do now?' I asked when I felt I was confident enough to move on to the next step.

'Nothing until tomorrow, miss. You did very well,' he said, taking the reins from me and handing Gwen a carrot from his pocket.

'That's it?' I replied, oddly disappointed.

'For today, yes. Same time tomorrow we'll have another lesson,' he replied, giving me another slight bow before leading the horse away.

When I returned to the house, I noticed that an entire hour had passed. No wonder Jordie had ended the lesson. I'd spent an hour swallowing my fear only to lead a completely docile horse around the courtyard. It wasn't exactly progress that I was proud of, but I still entered the dining room for breakfast with a skip in my step.

The earl sat in his usual spot at the head of the table with a newspaper in front of him. A place had been laid for me and I gratefully accepted the hot tea and fresh rolls served for me as soon as I sat down.

'Good morning, Lord Blountford,' I said politely, unable to see his face and resigning myself to speaking to the front and back pages of the morning news.

'Miss Dawson,' he said simply, not bothering to lower the paper.

'No Charles today?' I asked, buttering a piece of bread and munching on it contemplatively.

The earl deigned to look at me, lowering his paper just enough to peer at me with his rheumy green eyes, the colour of lichen on a forest tree.

'My nephew has been called away on business,' he said gruffly. 'It is unlikely he will return until later.'

Something in his tone deflated the happy bubble in my chest that had come from my riding lesson – or rather, my horse lesson, as I hadn't actually ridden anything yet.

'You both seem to have a lot of business to attend to. Do you have other enterprises aside from the manor and estate?' The question was innocent enough, but it didn't seem to please him.

'I run a small overseas trade. Mostly spices. Occasionally horses for breeding. Charlie has contacts overseas from his time there, and from my brother, that are best dealt with by him.'

A trade in what? I wanted to know, but I felt I'd already asked my limited quota of questions for one mealtime and resigned myself to eating the rest of my breakfast in silence.

*

After a sullen morning meal I retired back to my room to change out of my riding clothes and don a simple knitted dress that I wore frequently in London during the colder months.

I retrieved Esme's tin and took out the letters. There was a small ornate key in the bottom of the box, and a leather notebook I hadn't noticed the night before. I opened it to the last entry, and my heart fluttered to read my sister's familiar handwriting.

I have decided to stow all of my discoveries in the summer house. When Lizzie visits I think it will be her favourite part of the estate. A place for us to talk about secrets and drink cool lemonade on warm days, or hot tea with honey on the cold days. It is certainly a happy place, untouched by the sadness of the house, and although Lord Blount-ford has been kind enough to give me a bright room, I cannot shake the darkness I feel here.

I shivered. Esme loved stories. Ghost stories, mysteries, romances. She was an avid reader, who relished learning about people's lives. She must have known about Lord Blountford's three wives before her, and perhaps her imagination had run wild while she lived here with the idea of dead women walking the halls at night. What was the darkness she felt, I wondered, aside from being hauled from our home and married off to a man more than thrice her age?

Perhaps she had sensed the presence of her predecessor, Pansy, watching her from whatever realm it was that ghosts inhabited.

I may have been the expert at keeping my head down and observing people from the shadows, but Esme had been able to prise information out of anyone. Unsuspecting colleagues of my father, the boys and girls she gossiped and went to parties with.

She was never short of secrets and tales, and she wouldn't have been here five minutes before finding out about the previous Lady Blountfords. No doubt she would have taken it upon herself to investigate their pasts.

I allocated the rest of my day to finding the summer house, as it seemed no one had any interest in me aside from ensuring that I attended meals and rode a horse in the morning. Provided I turned up to my wedding, I'd probably be allowed to disappear and no one would pay any heed.

It occurred to me to ask a servant for directions, but the idea of exploring the grounds alone was somewhat liberating, so I donned my coat and most comfortable walking boots and set out into the autumn morning.

The sky was the blue of forget-me-nots; cloudless and clear. No wind rustled the turning leaves, and the crisp air woke me up and made me walk faster to keep warm.

I found the route that Charles and I had taken yesterday, following the path down as far as the bench we had stopped at, and then further. We had turned back before we had reached the lake, and now I noticed a bridle path that appeared to lead all the way around it through the woods I could see from my bedroom window. It occurred to me that maybe the summer house was located on the water's edge, or set back from it in the woodlands, so I followed the path where it took me.

The lake was just big enough for boats to sail across, with a small island in the middle where ducks, moorhens and swans made their homes, chittering and quacking away, blissfully unaware of my presence. A keen mallard followed me a short distance, hoping for breadcrumbs, but when I showed him my empty pockets he soon lost interest and returned to the others.

The path around the lake seemed little used. Early falling

leaves had begun to carpet the earth, and it seemed I was the only person to have walked this route in a while. I kept my eyes open for the telltale signs of another trail, or a pathway leading to a hidden building, but it was only when I reached the other side of the lake that I found a track that led off from the one I'd been walking.

I turned to look at the view from where I stood, the house some way off in the distance but clearly reflected in the water, the sky a softer mirror image of the real thing on the surface. This would be the perfect spot for a bench, I thought to myself, my position obscured from view if anyone were to walk by on the other side of the lake. I allowed the sounds of the woodland to envelop me: the songs of blackbirds and sparrows, the angry caws of magpies and crows, a horse whinnying from a pasture some way off, and the splashing of the ducks and swans on the other side of the lake. A world away from the cacophony of the city.

I could understand why Esme had decided to make the most of her predicament; why she had turned her sorry situation into an adventure with her secret letters and hiding places. Why, indeed, she had 'owned' the place, as Lord Blountford had said. It was, in its own way, quite beautiful. Far more so than the city of our birth.

I turned towards the other path, the one that would take me away into the woods, hoping to spot the summer house set back from the banks of the lake.

The oaks and aspens were thick here. The track twisted and turned away from me, so that I had to be careful not to lose my way or trip over hidden roots, until it suddenly opened out into a clearing.

I came to a dead stop, my blood chilling in my veins. The

canopy of trees above blocked out the sunlight in all but the centre, illuminating it like a spotlight on a theatre stage. There ahead of me stood four graves, a murder of crows perched atop their worn and weathered headstones.

I took a tentative step forward and the crows took flight, their wings flapping like the capes of a dozen grim reapers in the wind, their disapproving caws setting my nerves on edge. I calmed myself, telling my overactive mind that they were just birds, and this was just a burial ground. I had dealt with ghosts before. What was I supposed to be afraid of?

Regardless of that, my fingers still trembled, my breakfast threatening to rise up from my stomach.

Then I realised that a fifth grave stood open to the right of the rest, but when I crept towards it and peered over the edge, it was empty.

My mouth had gone dry and my breathing felt heavy. Why were there five graves? And why, oh why, were they here on the edge of the property and not in a churchyard somewhere?

I wanted to run. My mind told me repeatedly that I shouldn't be here, that I had no business seeing who the graves belonged to, but my legs walked me over to the first one heedless of the warnings. My hand flew down to my thigh, where my knife was strapped under my skirts, feeling for its reassuring weight, although it wouldn't do me much good in a fight against the dead. I made a sign of the cross over my body as I approached the first grave. I had been raised modestly religious, but I felt it was the right thing to do all the same, as if God might forgive me for sticking my nose in where I likely shouldn't.

The tombstone was faded, the writing worn but still legible. Ivy had grown over much of it, curling around the edges towards the space in the middle that left the writing mostly visible.

MARISA
Amore mio, mia moglie
1750–1777

This must have been Lord Blountford's first wife, I surmised. *Marisa*. There was something exotic about the name, the way it was spelled. And the inscription beneath . . . Italian, perhaps? *Amore mio*. I knew from my French lessons as a child that it would translate into something along the lines of 'my love'. My love, my . . . wife?

Charles had mentioned his uncle spending time in Italy, and I quickly did the arithmetic. Edgar Blountford could have met his first wife over there, a young man destined to inherit this estate from his father falling in love with a dark-haired Italian beauty. Although it was purely a guess, my imagination gladly filled in the gaps.

I pictured him bringing her here, designing the gardens in the style to which she would have been accustomed, planning a life together. The first Lady Blountford.

But she died at twenty-seven. My heart hammered a little harder in my chest at the thought that she had lived and died before I was even born. I crossed myself again and turned towards the second headstone.

ANNE
Vitae lumen, stellae mortis
1760–1785

A test of my linguistic skills, this wife's epitaph was evidently in Latin. *Vitae lumen, stellae mortis*. I committed the words to memory, their meaning impenetrable to me. Perhaps I could find someone in the house who knew enough Latin to be able to translate them. That Anne had died eight years after Marisa was a sign that perhaps in his youth Lord Blountford hadn't remarried every year, as he was apparently trying to do now.

I expected the next grave to be that of Persephone, but instead it bore a man's name.

JAMES
Quamvis brevis temporis est semper memoria
1785

I tried to translate it in my head, recognising that *brevis temporis* could perhaps be translated as 'short time', only because there were similar words in English and French. I looked back at Anne's headstone and saw the correlation of the dates. Perhaps the two of them had been in some terrible accident together, I thought morbidly. Or – that horrific reality that faced all women – they had lost their lives in childbirth. My mind quickly jumped to conclusions and I pushed them all away. Pansy might be able to explain, if she deemed it necessary to reappear to me.

The fourth headstone was Pansy's, but she had no epitaph, no words of parting. Only her name and the dates she had lived, 1767–1802, indicating that she had died at the age of thirty-five, ten years before Lord Blountford had married Esme. Mental arithmetic quickly worked out for me that she had been more than twenty years his junior.

Another spirited young thing. That was what Pansy had called me, as she and Esme had been.

That there were no loving words, no inscription, made me wonder if that marriage had not been a happy one. Or if Lord Blountford had tired of burying his wives and had finally refused to find a suitable platitude. I could not bring myself to acknowledge it, but something akin to sympathy stirred in my chest for the man who had been so very unlucky in love.

The empty grave at the end would have likely been for my sister, but she had been buried in the cemetery near our house in London. Instead of being filled in, it had been abandoned, leaving this small cemetery of lost wives looking even more forlorn.

The sickening thought that I might end up buried there wormed its way into my mind like a parasite, and I backed away from the yawning hole. A whimper escaped from my lips. What was I doing here? Why had I come?

A twig snapped loudly behind me and I turned around to find a grizzled figure staring at me through the trees. Coal-black eyes in a bush of beard that ran all the way up his cheeks. He seemed momentarily just as surprised to see me as I him. But his shock was quickly replaced by a scowl as he let out a roar.

Fear paralysed me for only a second. I could have tried to unstrap my knife before he attacked, but I had no idea what I'd do with it once it was in my hand. I needed distance.

Better to run, to live to fight another day, than to make a stand in the middle of the forest where no one could come to my aid.

Without so much as a scream, I took off in the opposite direction to the one I'd entered the clearing by, calculating in my head that it would take me around the near side of the lake and back towards the house.

The man called to me, his low voice disturbing the birds from the trees and rabbits from their warrens as he crashed through the undergrowth behind me, far more certain of his footing than I was.

I could only make out a few words, and one of them was certainly a curse, which only drove me on faster. My heart hammered in my ribcage as I kept my feet light, eyes on the ground to avoid tripping over roots but failing to spot the branches that clawed at my face and dress.

What had I been thinking, trespassing where I didn't have any right to be? And who was this man I had antagonised enough to make him give chase?

I dared a glance over my shoulder and found him some way off, still cursing and shouting; far enough that I could lift up my skirt and release my knife in case I needed it.

I scanned the trees, hoping for some sign that I could make it to the lake, to a path back to civilisation. But everything looked the same. I had no idea where I was going, and I didn't seem to be getting any nearer to the house. I would *not* let a man hurt me again. *Never.*

I pushed off from the nearest tree and sprinted faster, tripping only once but otherwise staying upright, ignoring the prick of cuts on my skin, the tears on my sleeves from bushes.

'Wha' in the devil's hell! Come back here!' The voice was unearthly, filled with deep ire and rage. It spurred me on, my eyes stinging from the frigid air as it whipped my face.

I stopped once again, trying to get my bearings, my chest burning as I gulped huge lungfuls of oxygen. There were only trees and more trees as far as the eye could see. Something hot and wet slid down my cheek, and when I pressed my palm to it, a smear of blood tainted my pale skin.

I must have hit a low branch harder than I'd thought.

The guttural sound of my pursuer's voice, only a few yards away, forced me to run again, hoping to heaven I'd stumble across the lake or the stables or something that would point me towards home. Another shout erupted across the woods. Was that Gaelic? It didn't sound like English, for sure, though the fact that he was almost as out of breath as I was likely didn't help.

One word, however, rang out clearly across the distance between us: '*Stop!*' Followed by a stream of curses.

I gritted my teeth and kept going, clutching the knife harder.

A road up ahead had me almost sobbing for joy, and I sprinted the final distance. In my blind panic, I didn't notice the huge grey stallion, and I slammed into its flank, my head meeting with solid muscle, causing the horse to rear up above me, its hooves coming down only inches from my body.

I didn't get a chance to look at the rider before I blacked out, my knife clattering to the earth.

Chapter 7

ളൽ

I was jolted back to awareness by the feeling of strong arms lifting me up, the steady rhythm of walking soon following. I couldn't have been unconscious for more than a few minutes, but the murmur of two men speaking had me keeping my eyes firmly shut. If I were in any further danger, I wasn't sure I'd be able to run or fight even if I wanted to.

'What do you mean, you found her in the graveyard?' Charles said, the rumble of his voice in his chest vibrating through my body as he carried me. I tried not to stiffen at the recognition of it.

'She was snoopin' about where she dinna belong,' came the gruff response. I opened one eye a crack and stifled a scream when I spotted the grizzled face of my assailant.

'She is soon to be your mistress, Mr McMannon. She's entitled to go where she likes and you scared her half to death by the looks of things,' Charles chided. I could almost feel the anger rippling off him. 'You are the groundskeeper, not a watchman. I suggest next time you want to approach the future Lady Blountford, you don't go chasing her through the woods and cursing in Gaelic.'

So it *was* Gaelic. The sudden realisation that I'd been a complete fool for running away from a man I was introduced to yesterday sent a flush of embarrassment creeping up my neck to my cheeks. I'd completely forgotten both his name and his face overnight. Knowing that the heat in my face would give me away, I opened my eyes slowly.

'Put me down,' I said quietly, looking up at Charles's stern features. He glanced down, surprised to see me awake, and those features softened slightly.

'Miss Dawson, I don't think that would be wise. We've still a way to go to the house, and you're injured.' He wasn't unkind, but he showed no sign of letting go of me.

'Serves me right for being a fool,' I retorted. 'Now put me down, please.'

He didn't protest when I asked the second time, allowing my feet to drop gently to the road but keeping his other arm across my back in case I should stumble.

Although my legs shook in the aftermath of so much exertion, I wasn't as out of shape as they likely thought. My head throbbed and my body ached in places I couldn't name, but nothing seemed broken. I turned towards the groundskeeper with my head held high, bunching my fists at my sides to stop them from quivering. I couldn't imagine what I looked like – a scarecrow or worse, no doubt – but I mustered what dignity I could as I addressed him.

'Mr McMannon, I would like to apologise,' I said, hating the way my voice sounded, so small and quiet in the face of such a large, weather-beaten man. Like a mouse staring into the face of a bear. He was the same height as Charles, his skin wrinkled and tanned from being outdoors so much, while his dark beard and hair concealed most of his features. 'I didn't recognise you and I should not have run away like that. If I had realised who you were, I can assure you I would not have made you work so hard.' I gave him a weak smile.

He seemed not to know what to do with himself at that, but he smiled in return with a small bow.

'Nee bother, m'lady. Ach, I realise I'm not a pretty face. Nee doubt I'd be scared shitless if ah saw mahsel' in the mirror,' he replied.

Charles stiffened at his language, but I only laughed, an uncontrolled and impulsive giggle that caused the grounds-keeper to almost crumple with relief.

'Very good, Mr McMannon, I think that will be all.' Charles nodded at him. 'Please see to it that my horse is tended to.'

McMannon gave a cursory salute and turned in the opposite direction.

Without another word, his hand still around my shoulders, Charles guided me down the drive and back towards the house.

'I fainted,' I said. It wasn't a question so much as a statement.

'Actually, you hit your head on Hurricane's flank and passed out,' he said, eyeing my forehead. I touched it gingerly, finding a small bump to go with my cuts.

'Hurricane is your horse?'

'Yes, and not usually so easily startled, but you shot out of the brush like a wild animal,' he said, his voice turning hard. 'You're lucky he didn't trample you to death.'

My cheeks flushed again and I looked down, resisting the urge to pull away from him. I felt like the idiot I was. My theatrics could have got me injured or worse if I'd been trodden on by his horse.

'I'm sorry,' I muttered, feeling his hand stiffen on my shoulder as I said it.

He sighed and stopped walking, turning towards me and placing his free hand on my other shoulder, as if holding me at arm's length. I was tempted to wrench free of his grip but thought better of it. There was every possibility that his firm hands were

77

keeping me upright at that moment. His eyes roamed over my face, lingering on the spots where I knew the cuts and bruises must be showing.

'No, I'm sorry,' he finally said. 'I should have told you about the graveyard yesterday, but I didn't think it would be tactful of me to bring it up when you had only just arrived.' He sighed. 'If you had known, at least you might not have been frightened senseless.'

A short bark of a laugh escaped my lips. 'The dead don't scare me, Charles, only strange men chasing me through the woods,' I replied defiantly.

A quirk of his eyebrow was his only indication of surprise.

'Besides,' I added, shrugging out of his grip and turning away, 'worse things have happened to frighten me than Mr McMannon and a few graves.' I took a step in the direction we had been walking, but my legs quaked beneath me and he was quickly there again, an arm around my shoulders. I maintained some dignity by keeping my eyes firmly ahead.

'That may well be, but I realise that this must be a shock for you. Coming here, upending your life, finding out that your . . . my uncle has . . . an interesting history. One that he's not fond of sharing. Most of the staff here have been with him for the best part of two decades, some longer, and they're fiercely loyal because of it. They don't like people looking too hard into his past.'

'And what about the women he's taken such pains to hide?' I retorted, the words sounding harsher than I had intended.

'I beg your pardon?'

'Those women buried there. How would they feel to know that their graves are untended? That his only thought of them now that they're gone is to keep them away from prying eyes, lest someone find out about them?' My cheeks flushed for an entirely different reason now, the anger impossible to hide.

'The dead are gone, Lizzie. They don't care what happens to them afterwards or that their graves are in the middle of a forest,' Charles replied, exasperated. He sounded as though he were chastising a child, and I hated it.

'I don't believe that. And neither should you,' I replied, just as the house emerged from between the trees.

'Regardless of what I believe, I would recommend that you refrain from mentioning this to my uncle. I'm not certain that he would take kindly to your opinions on the subject. I don't know what you were doing wandering around in the woods, but no good can come of it.'

I scowled at him as we rounded the drive, but he ignored me, instead waving to a servant to open the door for us.

'I was going for a walk. As you keep reminding everyone, I'm soon to be Lady Blountford. If I'm supposed to run this estate in the not-too-distant future, I should probably know my way around,' I added, hating the haughtiness in my tone.

'Please ensure that someone attends to Miss Dawson's injuries, Elsie,' he said to an older maid as she rushed to meet us, before turning back to me. 'Lizzie, I can only beg that you stay out of this whole business, for all our sakes,' he said quietly.

'And I can only suggest that you don't tell me what to do,' I snapped, allowing myself to be handed off into Elsie's waiting arms.

I risked a glance back at him as I ascended the staircase, and wished that I hadn't. From the look on his face, I might as well have slapped him.

'As you wish, Miss Dawson,' he replied stiffly, sketching a bow and turning abruptly on his heel. I immediately despised myself for putting that steely barrier back up between us.

Marie came to my rooms with bandages, warm water and a

salve. A bath was prepared, and I stripped off my knitted dress, now ruined, and glanced at myself in one of the large bathroom mirrors. A bruise was forming on my forehead and my cheeks were scratched, as were my legs where the low branches and brambles had cut through my clothes.

I sent Marie away as soon as the bath was ready, before she could offer to clean me up, and sank into the hot water, sucking air through my teeth as my body stung in new places.

I ran through the incident in my mind, wondering how I'd managed to be so stupid. I had met the groundskeeper only the day before and yet had not recognised his face. It seemed as though whenever I felt the slightest stress or fear, everyone I saw became a predator.

Yet it wasn't the idiocy of running from a member of my own staff that had my stomach roiling, but the conversation with Charles afterwards. Something about his behaviour had rattled me. He was so cool and commanding in front of others, so distant and indifferent in the presence of his uncle. Yet when we were alone, he became someone else. It felt as though I could see under the armour he wore to a softer version of him. And I had no doubt ruined that by being so rude.

He intrigued and irritated me in equal measure.

Where his uncle's character was wintry, like a layer of ice on a frozen lake, ready to drown me with one false step, Charles was like the autumn, warm in the sun, quick to turn cold without warning.

Perhaps years of being at war and the tragedy of losing his family had made him that way, causing him to put up his barriers and only lower them when he was alone.

As I washed my body and hair of the dirt I'd picked up in the woods, I had to wonder: what else was the armour hiding?

*

I was surprised to see Charles at dinner, expecting him to have made some excuse to avoid both me and his uncle after this afternoon. But the earl sat at the end of the vast dining table in his usual spot, with Charles and me sitting opposite each other on either side of him.

I said very little as I dipped into the stew, savouring the flavours as they erupted in my mouth. I broke a piece of bread and admired how it steamed, fresh from the oven, all while my mind worked and wondered how I could broach the topic that I so wanted to, without needlessly angering Lord Blountford or Charles.

'Charlie tells me you went for a walk and ran into his horse this afternoon,' Lord Blountford said, barely looking up at me. If he'd noticed the angry bruise on my head, he hadn't commented on it.

'Yes. I wanted to acquaint myself with the grounds,' I replied steadily, glancing at Charles, who caught my eye before returning his to his food. The run-in with the groundskeeper had been kept quiet then, it seemed.

'You should take one of the staff with you next time, so you don't get lost,' the earl said gruffly.

'Indeed I will, sir,' I replied, tearing off another piece of bread. 'On the subject of finding my way around, I'd very much like to visit the nearest village if at all possible,' I added nonchalantly.

'Certainly that can be arranged. Is there something in particular you require?'

'I was hoping merely to get my bearings. It is so different to London here, where there are shops and markets around every corner. I only thought it might bring some familiarity to me.'

'Indeed. The village is a far cry from London, but there are certainly places that might interest you. Esme was forever going off there to meet friends and purchase things that we had no need of but that she wanted.' He waved his spoon in the air, flicking a spot of stew onto the table, which was swiftly wiped away by an attending steward.

'She mentioned a friend in one of her letters,' I said, trying to sound vague while secretly delighted at the opportunity that had been presented me. 'It would mean much to me if I could perhaps introduce myself to someone who obviously enjoyed her company,' I added, choosing my words carefully.

Lord Blountford's spoon remained poised above his food as he studied me, stew dripping back into his bowl as his hand quivered over it.

'Did this acquaintance have a name?' he asked, the normality of his voice betrayed by the glint in his eyes. Fear? Or guilt, perhaps.

I feigned a puzzled look, as if trying to recall something from memory.

'Price, I think? Or Page . . . I honestly can't remember, it was so long ago.' I smiled disarmingly.

'The doctor.' Lord Blountford went back to eating. 'I hadn't realised that Esme and he had become such great friends.'

The hair on the back of my neck rose. 'Why was she visiting a doctor?' I asked, the question sharper than I had intended, but the earl only shook his head.

'Who knows? Your sister went where she wanted and did whatever she felt like. Some days she would be out all afternoon, only returning for dinner. Always gallivanting.' He sighed, as if recalling some painful memory. 'I never stopped her, for all the good it did me.'

He sounded weary, and I wondered if my sister's vibrant personality and headstrong ways had worn him out while she lived here. Or whether it had kept him alive. He certainly looked greyer than usual, his lichen-green eyes dull and drawn, set deep in the hollows of his face.

Had she died during one of her visits out? I wondered. It seemed like the wrong question to ask, but it burned in my throat. I opened my mouth to say something further, but Charles interrupted me.

'I shall take you to the village tomorrow morning, Miss Dawson, if you'll allow me to escort you? I have some business to attend to myself and it would be no trouble.'

I gave him a meaningful look. Perhaps he was trying to make peace with me, but the innocence of his expression gave nothing away.

'That would be most appreciated,' I replied. 'Though I have my riding lesson first thing.'

'You're sure that's wise? After today?' Charles asked.

'She only bumped her head, Charlie. Let her have her lesson, for goodness' sake,' Lord Blountford interjected. For once I was grateful to him for speaking on my behalf. I wasn't about to let what had happened today stop Jordie from making the extra money he'd been promised; with winter coming, I could imagine that the pay would come in handy for his family.

Charles stiffened at his uncle's tone but nodded, agreeing to have a carriage ready at eleven.

Dinner was finished in silence, and I excused myself as soon as it was polite. I wanted to search Esme's little journal for any mention of the name Price before my visit, but not before visiting her room again for any further clues.

The hallways were blissfully quiet as I retraced my steps to the purple bedroom, seemingly undisturbed since yesterday. Esme's hairbrush still sat on the dresser where I had left it, and when I took the time to look, there were even some clothes left in the wardrobe. I pulled out a familiar dress – one that we had shared between us on more than one occasion.

'Most of the rooms are like this, you know,' Pansy said, materialising beside me, her head to one side as she studied the dress in my arms. I blinked at her, wondering if she could sense my alarm.

'Like this?' I asked, gesturing to the open wardrobe, the clothes still hanging inside.

'Yes, half empty, kept mostly clean, but often with our effects just where we left them. Except Marisa, of course. She was the *special* wife. Was married to him the longest of us all, and had a whole wing to herself,' she said, pulling an unladylike face at the name.

'There's a wing just for her?' I asked incredulously, wondering how I could have missed it.

'Well, not any more. Everything of hers is in the attic now,' Pansy said, flopping to the floor theatrically and picking at some invisible lint on her dress. 'But I know she was the one he loved the most. Can't blame him, I suppose. He used to tell me that he found his heart in Italy.' She rolled her eyes and gave a disapproving groan. 'Any sign of that sister of yours, Liz?' She changed the subject, preventing me from questioning her further on the topic of Marisa. I didn't point out that she seemed to have a different name for me every time we met.

'No . . . sadly she hasn't appeared,' I replied, returning the dress to the rail and closing the wardrobe door.

'Perhaps that's not such a bad thing.' She lay on her back on the carpet and splayed her arms and legs out like a starfish. 'At least then you know that her death was a peaceful one. Mine was *terribly* dramatic,' she said, waving her limbs as though she were making a snow angel on the rug.

'Can you talk about it?' I asked, sitting down beside her, avoiding her flapping arms.

'Don't be silly, of course I can't. But you can work it out, with the right clues. That big head of yours must be good for something,' she said, prodding at my forehead, her finger passing right through it. I shivered at the coldness of her touch but ignored the insult.

'I'm visiting one of my sister's friends tomorrow,' I said. 'A doctor by the name of Price. She had a letter from him that indicates he might have had some information for her while she was alive. I wondered if she had gone looking for answers too; if maybe it caused her downfall.'

Pansy flickered like an exposed flame. 'Your sister was very nosy. Bossy too. I can't help it if that got her into trouble,' she replied, sounding defensive.

'You were watching her, though. Perhaps she angered Lord Blountford and he retaliated in some way for her meddling.' My experience with Brisley had told me that the direct questioning of a ghost was usually useless, but I hoped that Pansy might reveal something less cryptic than merely sending me on a wild goose chase to find a summer house, which had ultimately been unsuccessful.

'Oh ho ho. Such morbid thoughts for a young thing. Yes indeed, Eggy has a temper, but I wouldn't begin to suggest that there was any foul play in your sister's death. That would make me a very bad wife indeed,' she said, watching me from the corner of her eye, a knowing look on her face. 'He wasn't the cause of my death, if that's what you're thinking.'

I hadn't been, but now the idea was firmly planted in my mind.

'Poor little Eliza-Beth, clueless as you are, I do feel sorry for you,' Pansy said, picking herself up off the floor and wandering towards the wall she seemed to favour exiting through. 'I really don't know how long you'll last . . .' Her voice grew fainter as she began to vanish.

'I found your grave today,' I blurted. It was enough to delay her, and she gazed at me with a forlorn sadness. It pulled at something inside my chest to see her suddenly at a loss for words. 'It should have been better looked after. I can put in a word with the groundskeeper if you like?'

The sadness in her eyes dulled, her mouth turned down.

'Don't bother. It would be a waste of time.'

The words, coated in bitterness, echoed in my head as she walked through the wall and disappeared.

Despite rummaging through her drawers and searching under the bed, Esme's room revealed no further secrets to me, and Pansy, thankfully, didn't return.

I hurried back to my own chamber to reread Price's letter, but my mind kept returning to Pansy's words.

I didn't need or want the peculiar woman's sympathy. In fact I couldn't help but think that her mood swings and quickness of temper might have driven her husband to want to be rid of her.

He wasn't the cause of my death, if that's what you're thinking.

Something about the words stayed with me while I got ready for bed, while I tried to take my mind off them by reading, even as I drifted to sleep.

Even though Lord Blountford hadn't murdered Pansy in cold blood, her death had been dramatic enough that her ghost still lingered in the house.

The way she had said it rang through my mind again. *He wasn't the cause of my death, if that's what you're thinking.*

Lord Blountford didn't kill her, no.

But someone did.

Chapter 8

❧

The following morning's lesson found us outside the stables once again, Jordie teaching me how to ready Gwen for riding. I still wasn't able to step into the stalls – being close to one horse was bad enough – and he didn't push me, particularly when I confessed that the purple blotch on my forehead was from crashing into Hurricane the day before.

'Don't be ashamed of the odd accident, miss,' he said kindly, showing me how to put a saddle on and strap it around Gwen's middle.

'This one was particularly stupid, Jordie. I was walking in the woods and got myself so utterly spooked that I ran from the groundskeeper of all people,' I confided. He was easy to talk to. Laid-back, unassuming and completely free of judgement. He seemed to take me for what I was, rather than what others believed I should be, mistakes and all.

'You're too hard on yourself,' he chuckled. 'Mr McMannon is a grizzly-looking man. If I'd spotted him staring at me in the woods, I'd likely have run away too.' He pulled down a stirrup and showed me how to adjust it.

'That's what he said.' I grinned, wincing as the scab on my cheek stretched.

Jordie tutted, pulling out a handkerchief and absent-mindedly dabbing my face with it. It came away with the smallest speck of blood. The action was so familiar I almost took a step back. No one usually tried to touch me without my permission. But if he noticed any hesitation on my part, he didn't show it, only putting the handkerchief back in his pocket afterwards.

'You'll have to be careful with those cuts. My mam uses witch hazel on cuts and bruises that she makes into a balm. I'll get you some when I visit tomorrow if you like,' he offered.

I looked up at him curiously; he was half a head taller despite being younger than me. 'That's very generous of you to offer, Jordie, but you don't have to.'

'It would be no trouble at all, miss.'

I felt a warmth spread through my chest and almost placed a hand on his arm, stopping myself and letting it rest on Gwen's flank instead. 'Please,' I said, 'call me Lizzie.'

I saw a moment of hesitation at the informality, and he deliberated for a second or two before giving me another one of his lopsided grins.

'Very well, Lizzie, but only when there's no one around to overhear it. Wouldn't want to be getting into trouble with the earl for not knowing my place. Now how about we get you to mount Gwen here? We won't go anywhere; I'll just show you how to get on if you'll let me lift you up.'

He guided me towards the saddle and instructed me to put a foot in the stirrup, but as soon as he placed his hands on my waist to lift me, I froze. The press of his palms on my hips drove fear through me like a lightning bolt and I was transported back to the party. The smell of alcohol and the grunts of Lord Darleston. The taste of tears and bile. Sweat and stifled screams.

'No,' I said sharply, pulling away from him, my hand flying down to my thigh where my knife should have been. Should have been, but wasn't, because I'd dropped it in the chase yesterday.

Panic bubbled inside me, the warmth I'd felt a moment before evaporating just as quickly as it had formed. I backed against the outer wall of the stables, putting distance between us.

'Sorry, miss . . . Lizzie, I didn't mean to startle you,' Jordie said, confusion and something that looked like sadness in his eyes. He reached out a hand tentatively, but soon dropped it when I didn't step forward.

I inhaled deeply, the smell of horse and hay tickling my nose.

This was not the party. Jordie was not Richard Darleston. I was in my new home in Sussex. My fingers trembled as I pressed them to my eyes, trying to push away the images that had forced their way into my mind.

'Lizzie?' Jordie enquired gently. 'Shall I get someone to take you back to the house?'

'N-no. It's fine,' I said, screwing up my face and forcing myself back towards Gwen. 'Just . . . just tell me how to get on without . . .' *Without you touching me*, I wanted to say, but he seemed to understand. He kept his voice quiet, low, as though coaxing a skittish mare into cooperation.

'Ladies ride side-saddle. It's tricky to get on without help, but if you can give yourself enough lift you can probably manage. Just pop your hands on the saddle and hold on tight. One on the front, that's it, and one on the back.' He kept his distance and I sucked in a breath, ignoring the shaking in my hands and arms. 'Foot on the stirrup now, there you are. On three you're going to lift yourself up and swing your body around to face me, all right?'

I nodded and swallowed as he counted. When he reached three, I did as he instructed but slid back off before I had managed to find my seat. He leapt forward and caught me, backing away as quickly as he could when he saw I was unhurt.

'This is ridiculous,' I said, my cheeks heating, either from my own incompetence or from my fear of him coming near me.

'Maybe you should sit astride her, like gentlemen do?' Jordie suggested.

'Is it easier?'

'I think so, although you'll have to hitch your skirt up a bit to get your leg over the top of her.'

I nodded. I'd seen men mount horses dozens of times. It certainly appeared more natural. If they could do it, so could I, even in a stupid heavy riding dress. Jordie explained how to swing my leg over Gwen's back and counted to three again. With my foot in the stirrup and my hands on the saddle, I lifted myself up and threw my leg across the top of her, nearly sliding off the other side as my weight tugged me over but righting myself at the last minute.

'You've done it, Lizzie!' Jordie said delightedly, beaming up at me as I sat nervously astride the mare.

'I did?'

'You did! Now take the reins like this.' He ignored my trembling and arranged the reins so that the strip of leather passed through the middle three fingers on each hand. I fought the instinct to pull my hands out of his grip, and allowed him to steer Gwen around the courtyard while I grew accustomed to the unnatural seat, the jolting of the horse beneath me.

After a few rounds, and satisfied that I had made my first steps towards riding, he walked us back towards the entrance of the stables.

'Getting you off her is going to be a little more complicated, because I don't want you to hurt yourself when you dismount,' he said, running a hand through his curls.

I thought the process through. I'd have to swing my leg back around without falling off or catching my foot in the stirrup as I did so. I could easily slip and break an ankle as I came down.

'You can . . . . you can help me down, Jordie,' I said, taking a deep breath through my nose. 'I'll be all right this time, I promise.'

He nodded with relief and held his hands out, telling me what to do. Dismounting *was* harder, but he caught me by the waist and stopped me from falling when my foot touched the floor, stepping back to a respectable distance as soon as I was safely down.

'I think we'll take the tack off and that will be it for today. If you'll be sitting astride, I'll make sure I've a new saddle for Monday,' he said cheerily, but I could tell he was forcing the smile that didn't quite reach his eyes.

We undid our work from earlier, my fingers unbuckling and removing the reins, committing the movements to memory. Other than offering to assist me in removing the saddle, Jordie said nothing.

I felt I owed him an explanation for my behaviour. My odd, unnerving reaction to him touching me. I must seem insane to anyone who didn't know what had happened to me. But what could I tell him? Nothing that wouldn't reveal my secret. Nothing that wouldn't put my position here, tenuous as it already was, in jeopardy. So I kept my mouth firmly shut, my lips pressed into a thin line as we worked and I attempted to come up with some reasonable excuse.

When it was obvious we were finished, I turned to him, my eyes burning at the sincerity and concern in his face. It was a look that confirmed what I'd already felt in my gut the moment I had met him, and I found myself wanting him to understand more than I felt the desire to keep any more secrets.

'I . . . I have to apologise,' I said, forcing the words out before I changed my mind, 'for my reaction back there.'

He shrugged casually, but I could tell from the stiffness in it that he was on alert, almost as nervous as I was. 'It's nothing to apologise for, Lizzie. Different things upset different people. We all have our moments.' Simple words, wise words from someone so young.

I closed my eyes and took another deep breath.

'But it appears I have more moments than others,' I said, unable to hide how much that fact annoyed me. 'Something . . . happened to me. I can't . . . I don't like people . . . I don't like *men* touching me.' I held his gaze, and the understanding, and then the horror, on his face broke something in my chest.

He took half a step forward and then seemed to think better of it, instead laying a hand on Gwen and shaking his head.

'You don't need to explain,' he said with more anger than I'd expected to hear from him. 'Just know that if you need to speak, need someone to talk to or anything, I'd lend a willing ear.'

I blinked the threatening tears away. I didn't know if I wanted to cry because I'd finally opened up to someone and he hadn't looked at me with judgement or disdain, or because this gangly boy with his red hair and kind eyes was actually the first honest friend I had found since Esme died.

'Thank you,' I whispered hoarsely, turning towards the house.

I had nearly reached the door when he called after me, and I turned to see him standing where I'd left him.

'Lizzie, I hope whoever he is rots in hell.'

I nodded. 'He will,' I replied. 'He will.'

Chapter 9

ಬಿ ಞ

'How is your riding progressing, Miss Dawson?' Charles asked as I stared from the window of the carriage at the countryside rolling past.

I was mulling over the mystery of Pansy Blountford's possible murder. Morbid thoughts for a Saturday morning, for that was what today was – not long to go until my wedding, as small and unceremonious as it was to be.

'It is going quite well, thank you, considering that before yesterday I wouldn't have dared touch a horse and today I managed to mount one,' I replied, smoothing out the skirts of my dress. Not one of my own, but one that Marie had selected for me, in a shade of deep blue that I particularly liked. I hadn't asked where it had come from, and had hoped Pansy wouldn't walk through the wall of my bedroom claiming that it was one of hers. Thankfully she did not.

Marie had also left my hair in the tidy braids I was growing fond of, covered with a navy hat that matched the coat she had found. The latter, warm enough to withstand the cold autumn morning, complemented the outfit perfectly, affirmed by the long gaze Charles had given me when I stepped out of the house to greet him. I had not missed the way he appraised my outfit,

93

nor how he studied the bruise on my face, which we had tried to cover with a little powder.

'That young stable hand must be quite the teacher if he has you riding already,' Charles now said as he sat opposite me in the carriage.

'It has as much to do with his method of teaching as it does with the fact that he will be able to feed his siblings and mother this winter should we prevail,' I said, giving him a smile. 'I understand that Lord Blountford has offered him a considerable bonus when we succeed.'

'Ah, so it is not just for your own benefit that you've progressed so admirably.' Charles grinned back, the expression lighting up those spring-green eyes of his.

'If it had been up to me, sir, I would have remained blissfully incompetent,' I said with a laugh.

'Ah, but a true lady of Ambletye would have to learn to ride eventually, else how would she cover the vast lands that are soon to be in her possession?'

Although he had said it in jest, the truth of it chilled something in me. He noticed my smile falter and was quick to try and salvage the conversation.

'Miss Dawson, I cannot imagine how you must feel having all of this brought on you so suddenly. Moving into your sister's position, and a sister so beloved to you, must be distressing to say the least.'

I inclined my head in gratitude for his sympathy. He had yet to call me by my Christian name since our argument yesterday, but I held out hope that by the end of our trip we might recover that familiarity. Until then I would follow his lead.

'Mr Blountford, it is not only moving into my sister's position that troubles me, but the fact that I still have no idea how or why she died. I think of her frequently, wishing that I could have another conversation with her. Just one more chance to see her smile, to tell her all that has happened since she left. And to find out if she would give this marriage her blessing,' I added, dropping my voice to a murmur so that Charles had to lean forward to hear.

A frown creased his brow as he nodded in understanding. 'It is . . . difficult, to say the least. As you know, I never met Esme, but my uncle spoke of her often.' He leaned back on the seat and glanced out of the window, the high sun hooding his eyes so that I couldn't read them, or any emotion they might hold. 'I would not presume to know the happiness of their marriage, but it seemed my uncle was very fond of her. Had she not died, or had she provided him with an heir before that unfortunate fate, I believe your circumstances would have been quite different.'

Who was this sailor who spoke like a poet? Every word was careful, considered, even as something like pain passed across his features.

'And yours? What would your circumstances be if Esme were still Lady Blountford?'

Would you be here, or still fighting in the war? Would we ever have met?

Yes, there was far more meaning to my question than whether or not he'd be sitting in this carriage with me now.

'It was my father's dying wish that I return to England if I were ever to leave the navy, to assist Lord Blountford, whether my uncle agreed or not.'

'And why, if I might ask, would your uncle not simply bequeath his estate and fortune to you in his will? It seems a far more agreeable solution than marrying for a fifth time.'

The quirk of his eyebrow was the only indication that he sensed the ire beneath that statement.

'Indeed, it was what my father wished, knowing that his

brother had been . . . unsuccessful in producing an heir for so long. They were not close as siblings, being ten years apart in age and from different mothers themselves. Lord Blountford never took to my father as they grew up, never saw him as an equal, and unfortunately, despite their own parents' wishes, they never became close. I was brought up in Kent at my mother's family home, only visiting Ambletye once or twice as a child. I never thought that life would lead me here, and even when it was apparent that this was to be my fate, I had no inkling that it would be so . . . complicated.'

He grew quiet, and I imagined him playing out his alternative life in his mind's eye. Perhaps he had been due to marry some admiral's daughter, or had hoped to inherit his mother's estate after his parents died.

'But I must tell you that I came here knowing how difficult my position might be. I do not wish you to think that I am somehow vying for my uncle's fortune, or that I moved to Ambletye for any other reason than my father's instruction to help his estranged brother. However much in vain that might be.' He fixed me with another of his intense stares and I forced myself to hold it.

'I would never believe you capable of such duplicity, sir,' I affirmed, and something relaxed in his gaze. There was so much I wished to ask him, but any further questioning was cut short by the slowing of the carriage.

The driver brought the horses to a stop outside a pretty cottage, single-storey with a low thatched roof. The path leading from the gate to the cheery yellow door was flanked on either side by tall rose bushes, late blooms still appearing here and there. It was as though the building had been plucked out of a painting of a country house, complete with geese waddling around the courtyard at the back and a single-stall stable jutting out of the side.

Charles knocked twice, loud enough to be heard throughout the house and along the otherwise quiet country lane.

'Do you know the doctor?' I asked as we waited for an answer.

'Only that he lives here, but otherwise I've never had cause to meet him. I wonder why your sister made his acquaintance?'

The statement was meant innocently, but it gnawed at me. Why *had* Esme befriended the doctor and shared letters with him? Had there been something wrong with her?

'I do not know, but I hope to find some answers here at least,' I replied.

That seemed to give him pause.

'Miss Dawson, whatever we might learn here, I would only advise that you keep it to yourself and not speak of it with my uncle or anyone on the estate,' he said hurriedly as footsteps sounded somewhere in the house.

The door was opened before I had a chance to ask what he meant by that, and a plump lady in housekeeper's attire smiled with surprise, although her expression faltered when she looked at me. Her hand gripped her chest as confusion contorted her face.

'Madam, I am Charles Blountford, Lord Blountford's nephew.' Charles introduced himself hastily. 'And this is Miss Elizabeth Dawson, Lord Blountford's betrothed.'

The housekeeper's relief was visible. 'Of course,' she replied with a relieved sigh, relaxing a little. 'My condolences for your loss, my lady. We were very fond of your sister here,' she added, curtseying to us both and ushering us into the house.

'I must apologise for not making an appointment,' Charles went on, saving me from replying to her. 'Would Dr Price be available to see us? It is purely a social call, so I understand if he is busy.'

'I'm sure he can spare some time for you, Captain. I shall fetch him immediately, if you wouldn't mind waiting in the sitting room.'

She led us through the cottage and into a comfortable-looking space surrounded by musty bookcases and battered but serviceable furniture flanking a large hearth. She bobbed another curtsey before disappearing the way we had entered.

'*Captain?*' I hissed at Charles in surprise. He had never used his official title in my presence before, and although I was not privy to how much a commission of that status might cost, I knew it to be far in excess of the total of my father's gambling debts.

'I don't use it very often,' he said shyly, inspecting the room.

'Well, apparently your reputation precedes you, sir,' I said, feeling a little disgruntled that a housekeeper he had never met knew about his rank when I hadn't even thought to ask. He remained silent, studying the wall of certificates hanging over the fireplace.

'These certificates are in French,' I said, joining him by the fire for warmth.

'I'm afraid my French is in need of rather a lot of improvement, so I won't be of any help,' he replied, seeming happy enough to change the subject.

The bookshelves were crammed with various volumes in both English and French, mostly on the subject of animals, birds and similar.

'Studying someone's bookshelf is like peering into a person's mind, don't you think?' a bespectacled man in his late forties said by way of announcement. 'Sorry to keep you waiting,' he added, looking as though we'd perhaps interrupted something rather important, his sleeves still rolled up to his elbows.

'Dr Price, I presume?' Charles said, holding out his hand, which the doctor clasped.

'Indeed, indeed. Captain Blountford, welcome to the village. My apologies for not visiting the manor to introduce myself earlier – duty calls at the most inconvenient of times,' Price said with a smile. I liked him immediately.

He turned towards me and smiled in delight.

'And you must be Miss Dawson,' he said, taking both of my hands in his own and squeezing them gently between his warm, leathery fingers. This was a man who worked outdoors, I observed, with his calluses and sun-weathered skin. Nothing at all like I had expected.

'I am indeed, Dr Price. It is a pleasure to meet you,' I said, and felt it deep in my bones. This was Esme's friend. A confidant, perhaps. A little thrill of exhilaration that one mystery at least might be solved ran through me.

'Judith!' the doctor shouted excitedly, startling me. 'Judith, bring some tea for our guests, please. And the best biscuits,' he added. I heard the housekeeper reply from another room, and the sound of the kettle banging onto the hearth was followed by the clatter of crockery. 'Try not to break the best china, please!'

I smiled, and found Charles doing the same. Dr Price was, it seemed, wonderfully eccentric and down-to-earth. A far cry from the doctors I had met in the past.

'I am sure you've been told that the resemblance between the two of you is quite remarkable. I was very fond of Esme – the fourth Lady Blountford,' he corrected himself quickly as he gestured for us to sit on the dilapidated sofa. He took up the armchair closest to us and folded his hands over his lap, studying me as I replied.

'I think I frightened your housekeeper, I'm afraid.'

'Worry not about Judith, Miss Dawson. She's a wonderful but horrendously suspicious individual,' he replied with a grin that put me at ease. 'I can only imagine that the similarity between you gave her pause. She did love Esme so very much.'

'Everyone did,' I replied without thinking. 'You knew her quite well, from what I gather?'

'I like to think she honoured us by considering us friends. She only visited perhaps once a month – once a fortnight if I was lucky – but the longer she lived at the manor, the more her time seemed to be consumed by business there.'

I thought about what Lord Blountford had said. How Esme had quickly taken to her role of running the household.

'We were both keen lovers of animals,' he went on, 'and at first I think she just wanted an excuse to get away from the estate. She assisted me with a few deliveries, a few tricky operations.'

'Deliveries?'

'Oh yes, horses mostly, but also cows, sheep and even dogs if they were complicated,' he said, waving a hand to the wall adorned with paintings of such animals.

'You're an animal doctor,' Charles said, breaking his silence for the first time since we'd sat down.

'That I am. Certified by the veterinarian school in Lyon,' the doctor replied, pointing proudly towards his certificates. Esme's visits here suddenly felt much less sinister than I had previously suspected.

'Of course,' I said, shaking my head.

His bright, intelligent eyes met mine, reading the relief in them. 'You must have so many questions.'

Judith brought in a tray with tea, and biscuits laid out haphazardly on a plate, almost tripping on the worn carpet on her way in but catching herself just in time. She poured from the chipped teapot and offered round milk and sugar, but I caught her looking at me more than once, averting her eyes quickly each time. It was as though she had seen a ghost, and the irony of it wasn't lost on me.

'I do have a few questions, Doctor, if you don't mind my candidness,' I said, taking my cup and saucer from the housekeeper.

'Please, miss, do call me Price. Everyone else does,' he said, taking up a biscuit and dipping it unceremoniously into his tea.

'Very well, Price. How did you and my sister first become acquainted?' I asked, wondering at the unlikely partnership.

'Ah, an excellent question. I settled here at the beginning of last year with the idea of establishing myself in farming country. I have offered my services all over England and France, and this cottage felt idyllic in comparison to the hustle and bustle of city life. Little did I know that I would be as much in demand in the countryside as I was in town. Sometime last winter, one of the horses up at the house fell ill. They had me there at all times of the night and day treating the poor thing, and your sister would often send refreshments down to me while I worked, or spend an afternoon keeping me company. She seemed to be finding her footing in her new station, and as I was relatively new to the area myself, we found kinship. Our discussions were a welcome distraction for both of us, I think.'

I imagined Esme sitting in the stables that Jordie now occupied, listening to Price's calm tones while he worked. It would be just like her to stand vigil with a near-stranger.

'She and I spoke of all sorts, and you came up in conversation regularly, Miss Dawson,' he said with a smile. 'I know she was looking forward to inviting you up to the house, but it took me very little time to ascertain that she was troubled.'

'She had found something out,' I supplied.

Price gave me an appraising look, perhaps wondering how much I already knew. 'Indeed she had. There had been rumours in the village when I first arrived about the house, the tragedies that seemed to forever occur within its walls and – forgive the observation, Captain Blountford – the ill fortune the earl appeared to have with his late wives.'

I turned to Charles, whose expression remained stoic aside from a small vein that had begun to pulse at his temple. I knew it was a sensitive subject, but my need for information outweighed my guilt. After all, if I was to marry Lord Blountford next week, I was entitled to the truth, surely?

Price finished his biscuit and selected another from the plate while I chose my next words carefully. 'I found a letter of yours to Esme when I happened upon some of her belongings. Although it was rather vague, it hinted that you might have found some clue for her. I wondered what it was that you had discovered and whether it might be . . . related to the previous Lady Blountfords.'

Price raised an eyebrow and paused mid dunk, but smiled at me as he did so, almost as though he had been expecting the question.

'It was a topic your sister and I visited often. She thought that perhaps there was something untoward about the goings-on up at the house before her arrival, and as I was an unbiased friend with no ties to the family, she singled me out as her confidant for her investigation.' His gaze slid from myself to Charles as he said it, and I held my breath a moment while I waited for him to continue.

'The very same thing has come to my attention,' I said when there was nothing more forthcoming, inching forward in my seat. I felt Charles stiffen beside me a fraction. 'I wondered if she had confided anything to you about . . . the nature of her predecessors' demise?'

Although I felt I was being more than considerate in my

questions, Charles chose the moment to clear his throat noisily, as if that alone would steer the conversation in a different direction.

If Price sensed his discomfort, he didn't show it, getting up to retrieve something from the bureau as he said, 'It was almost as much of a hobby for her as helping me with my practice.'

I risked another glance at Charles, whose expression was unreadable, his eyes trained on the doctor, who rummaged for a few minutes before finding what he was after.

'Ah, here it is,' he said, bringing a small packet of papers over to the low table, tied with brown string. 'This is all of the correspondence from your sister to me.' He pulled at the knot until it unravelled and thumbed through the letters. I could see Esme's familiar handwriting from where I sat.

'This one was particularly interesting,' he said, handing it to me. It had a red blotch of ink on the top corner and I ran my thumb over it. 'At first we wrote each other short, cryptic notes, but when they began to get tangled up with my other paperwork, I placed a red mark on them whenever they had something to do with the lost wives.' I looked up at him quizzically. 'That's what we called the previous Lady Blountfords,' he explained.

The term sent a slight shiver down my back as I nodded in understanding. Was that what Esme had become too? Another one of the 'lost wives'? Unsettled, I scanned the letter.

Dear Price,

I've discovered the graves. Although no one would tell me how many wives he'd had before me, there are four graves there – three women and a boy – all engraved save for one with only a name. The locked rooms in the house finally make sense. I have tried to memorise the dates on the

*stones, enclosed, in the hope that we can find out more. I
shall visit a week Monday if I'm not-so-subtly confined to
the house as punishment for all my snooping.*

*Sincerely yours,
Esme*

Her dark sense of humour and way of writing emanated through
the paper, and if it were possible, I missed her even more. The
number of things that had been left unsaid in those few lines
called to me. No one had told her she'd been the fourth wife and
she had not been pleased. There was also the indication that
there would be consequences to her finding her predecessors.

I risked another glance at Charles, whose face was imperceptibly blank. The thought that perhaps he had saved me from
a similar punishment by keeping my escapade quiet yesterday
crossed my mind.

'You both knew about the graves then,' I said, peeking at the
accompanying sheet of paper, which bore the same information
I had discovered on the tombstones yesterday.

'I'm afraid they came as quite a shock to your dear sister.
Unsurprisingly, she knew nothing of them until that day, but
after we obtained the names and dates, it became relatively easy
to find information.'

'You didn't tell her yourself?'

'Quite honestly, I didn't know for certain. Having arrived
only ten months before her, I had heard rumours but never felt
it my place to enquire as to the number of women who had
occupied the position prior to Esme. At least until she directly
involved me.'

'And did you find out how they died?' A mixture of fear and
exhilaration ran through me.

'No, not all of them,' he said, and I failed to hide my disappointment. 'But at least one mystery was put to bed, as it were. Perhaps the easiest one to solve, as there were several records available for poor Anne and James.'

Charles's face was shuttered. He knew something, I could feel it, but chose to remain silent for reasons I didn't understand.

'They died in the same year,' I said, deciding to plough on. Taking a sip of tea, I inspected the copy of the inscriptions in Esme's neat writing.

ANNE

Vitae lumen, stellae mortis

1760–1785

JAMES

Quamvis brevis temporis est semper memoria

1785

'Mother and child.' It wasn't Price who answered, but Charles, his voice subdued as though he was disturbed by his own words. I shuddered, and Price stoked the fire for some warmth even though the chill had nothing to do with the temperature of the room.

'I'm afraid the captain is regrettably correct.' Price nodded sadly. 'That the dates of death matched and there was no age for James indicated that he did not live long. Unfortunately, it was too easy to discover that the terrible pneumonia that had infected so many that year had also claimed the lives of Lord Blountford's wife and newborn son, per the parish records.'

'How awful,' I said, putting my tea down, the taste now sour in my mouth. 'He must have been devastated.' I didn't want to look at Charles, suddenly struck by regret that I had pried into what was obviously a very personal matter. He *did* know more than he was letting on about the deaths, but had stayed silent despite my ignorant questioning.

'It was a painful subject for the entire family,' he finally said. 'I only know from what my father told me, for it happened before I was even born, but my uncle became quite the recluse for a number of years afterwards.'

I swallowed the lump that had begun to form in my throat and nodded at the paper. 'And the inscriptions?'

Price replied, his tone gentle. 'Ah, yes. Anne's would translate to "In life a light, in death a star", or words to that effect. James's would be along the lines of "Although your time was brief, you are forever remembered".'

'Beautiful,' I said, my voice cracking. Lord Blountford had clearly loved both of them dearly, and the loss of two people so close to him echoed within me. Without truly thinking about it, I stretched out a hand and found Charles's resting on his knee. I didn't want to meet his eyes, knowing that he could see the tears lining my own, but I was content to provide comfort with a slight squeeze.

'The other wives, I'm afraid, are still a mystery to me,' Price said, clearing his throat and trying to bring some levity back into his tone. 'There were some horrendous rumours at the time, I was told, but I will not repeat them for fear that the good captain might consider it a slight to say such things when there is no evidence to their credit.'

If Charles had not been there I would have enquired further, but I understood Price's sentiments perfectly. Even that smallest grain of truth had changed the atmosphere in the room, and I felt it would be better to perhaps return another day, if the doctor were willing, to question him further.

'I almost don't wish to ask . . .' I said, glancing back down at the letter, tracing Esme's fine hand with my thumb. The pained curiosity must have been written in my face, as Price guessed my thoughts.

'How did your sister pass?' he finished for me.

I nodded and swallowed, thinking that he of all people must know the answer.

'I'm afraid I can't say for certain. She wrote to me telling me that she had some news. She wanted to come and tell me in person, but she was confined to the house and to her duties. I didn't see her for weeks, and I'm afraid she never did make it to me before it happened. I felt I had no right to ask anyone at the manor,' he said apologetically.

'Of course.' I understood, even if it didn't ease any of the pain I felt at not knowing.

'I will say, though, that she was a ray of sunshine in the village that no one could extinguish, a breath of fresh air that couldn't be stifled. I want you to know I considered her one of my closest friends,' Price said gently.

'Thank you,' I said, reaching over and placing a soft hand on his rough one. I wondered briefly if Esme would have had rough hands from working with him, and if Lord Blountford knew what she'd been doing.

'It is my pleasure, Miss Dawson. I am always here should you ever need an animal seeing to, or a cup of Judith's finest tea,' he offered.

'That is appreciated, but I meant for being her friend. For being there for her when I couldn't be,' I replied. 'And you can call me Lizzie.'

His face crinkled into the warmest smile I had seen anyone wear in quite some time, and it emboldened me.

'I would like to visit you again, if you don't object to being called upon when I can escape Ambletye,' I said, almost conspiratorially.

'My door is always open, Lizzie, and I can always use an extra pair of capable hands,' he added with a waggle of his bushy eyebrows.

Our conversation moved on to safer topics and I could have stayed for another hour at least, listening to Price's stories of Esme and how they had dealt with a particularly difficult delivery of twin lambs, or the recalcitrant goat that had got itself stuck in a fence, but eventually Charles gestured subtly that we ought to be leaving. Although he had relaxed once the subject had moved away from the lost wives, there was an unease in his manner, and I found myself not wanting to cause him any more discomfort.

I clasped Price's hands as I left, and then a slightly stricken Judith's on my way out of the door – the first contact I had volunteered in a long time. They responded with strict instructions to come back any time.

For the first time since I had arrived at Ambletye Manor, I felt I had found somewhere I wanted to be.

Chapter 10

ജ୍ଞ

'I have upset you,' I said as Charles and I meandered towards the heart of the village in contemplative silence. Although I had enjoyed the chittering of birds and the low thrum of insects working around us, I could still sense his unease.

He sighed, offering his arm to me as we walked, and shook his head. 'I am not upset by you, Lizzie.' A flicker of delight ignited in my chest at hearing him use my given name. 'I'm only distressed by the unhappy circumstances.' Something like regret tinged his voice and he didn't meet my gaze. 'I wish I could ask you not to pursue this business with my uncle's late wives,' he added wistfully. I opened my mouth to explain, or to make my own excuses, but he stopped abruptly in front of a clerk's office. 'I must run an errand whilst here. Would you mind if I left you for a few moments?'

'Not at all,' I said, letting go of his arm and looking around me. A bookshop sat opposite and I told him he could find me inside when he was finished. One could never spend too much time inside a bookshop, after all.

A brass bell rang above the door when I entered the dark interior, and the familiar smells of musty pages and leather greeted me. Walking into a bookshop anywhere, whether it was here or London, felt like stepping into a different world. If I closed my eyes, I could almost envision Esme roaming the stacks, a finger tracing the spines as she walked ahead of me.

Although it was a small space, the floor-to-ceiling shelves that lined the walls, with a winding staircase leading up to a mezzanine, gave it the air of somewhere much bigger. A wooden counter pressed against the back wall, lit by a solitary candle, and the proprietor bent over a ledger, absent-mindedly stroking the only other inhabitant: a great white cat.

'May I help you, miss?' he asked, peering from behind a pile of books to greet me. The cat looked somewhat disgruntled that I had interrupted the peace and cracked an eyelid open to appraise me.

'Oh, no thank you,' I replied, and then, feeling apologetic for wasting his time, and the cat's, I added, 'I am new to the village and wished to become familiar with it. Your fine shop seemed like a good place to start.'

As if my words had broken a spell, the shopkeeper leapt into action, straightening his waistcoat before greeting me with open arms. 'A newcomer! Well then, welcome, welcome to our humble village. This establishment is Grahame's Books, and I myself am Mr Graham Grahame – at your service.'

'Graham Grahame, sir?' I repeated, a little bemused.

'Indeed, the third of my name, like my father and grandfather before me. And my compatriot here is Merlin,' he added, waving towards the long-haired cat, who was now gently nudging the ledger off the counter, out of spite, no doubt.

'A pleasure to meet you, Mr Grahame. I am Lizzie Dawson. Soon to be Blountford,' I added quietly, with a perfunctory curtsey.

'Blountford?' he said with something like awe in his voice. 'Engaged to young Captain Blountford?'

'No,' I replied too hastily, ignoring the stutter in my heart at the suggestion. 'No . . . I am to marry Lord Blountford. Next week, in fact.'

Mr Grahame's eyes widened at the news.

'The last Lady Blountford was quite young, if I recall. You weren't related, perchance? Only the resemblance is uncanny,' he said with a telling look, one that I was familiar with from my time amongst the upper classes in London. The delight that certain individuals took in gossiping couldn't be mistaken, and the shopkeeper's eager curiosity was no different to the daughters of the aristocracy I had had the misfortune of meeting at social gatherings.

'My sister,' I supplied, hiding my discomfort by turning from him to study the shelves, if only to remove his look of interest from my line of sight.

'Goodness me, your sister!' he said with poorly concealed enthusiasm. 'She came to the shop once, a delightful young woman. Intelligent, quick-witted and charming to boot.'

I soaked up his flattery for Esme as though I could experience her once again through the accounts of others. 'I'm certain she loved it here,' I remarked.

'Well, she only graced me with her presence once. After that she would order everything on account, though I managed a word or two whenever she was in the village.'

Esme would have gladly escaped to the bookshop if life at Ambletye was ever too much for her, and I wondered if the change in book-purchasing arrangements had been her decision or Lord Blountford's.

'Such a sad situation in that household, I must say,' Mr Grahame continued as I pulled a volume gently from the shelf and thumbed it, pretending to be barely listening. 'Such misfortune for one man to have lost so many wives. It took him so long to put those murder accusations to rest, I am surprised he remarried at all.' I was grateful that my nose was within the pages of a book when he said it, for I felt my eyes might jump from their sockets at the words.

'Murder accusations?' I whispered, mimicking his hushed tones and leaning closer to him, as if we were merely two washerwomen discussing the latest scandal and not, in fact, talking about my future husband.

'Oh yes, miss. It was said that the third Lady Blountford drove him to murder her. I was only a young apprentice here under my father at the time, but I recall overhearing it from the butcher's wife. She told me that after the terrible infection that took his previous wife and child, he kept the next one on a shortened leash. Barely let her leave the house, would you believe? Although of course it was said that she was a little addled.'

The skin on the back of my neck prickled. Pansy's slight insanity could well be a result of being kept prisoner in her own home. And murder . . . well, she had already dropped that particular clue for me. But if she was right and Lord Blountford hadn't killed her, then who had?

I put the book back on the shelf and turned towards Mr Grahame, deciding I could use his tattling to my advantage.

'You must know a great number of people in the village, sir.'

'Oh, indeed, miss, and proud of it. I know this village and its denizens like the back of my own two hands,' he said, obviously pleased with himself. This could well have been the reason that Esme only ever ordered her books after her first encounter with him, I mused.

'I imagine, then, that you would know who was in Lord Blountford's employ all those years ago. The staff who might have seen things, or might have known my predecessors.' I narrowed my eyes and gave him a conspiratorial smile.

Just as Mr Grahame opened his mouth to respond, I was startled by the sound of the bell announcing a new customer.

'Sorry to have kept you waiting,' Charles said, touching my elbow gently by way of greeting. 'Good day to you, Mr Grahame,' he added with a shallow bow.

'Captain Blountford! It is marvellous of you to bring such a delightful newcomer to my humble store,' Mr Grahame said, all talk of murder and rumour forgotten. 'That book you requested arrived just yesterday,' he added, disappearing around the back of the counter and leaving Charles and me amongst the bookshelves. The space was cramped enough that I could feel his breath on my face, and as I looked up at him, I felt a twang of remorse. If he had known the subject of my discussion with Mr Grahame, perhaps he would not be looking at me with such affection.

'Here it is, as requested.' Mr Grahame returned, handing over a parcel tied with string. 'And should either of you require supplies of paper or any such thing, I would be delighted to assist.' He bowed low as we squeezed our way towards the front door, and I swallowed the disappointment of our conversation being cut short.

'Thank you, Mr Grahame, for such a warm welcome,' I said as Charles held the door for me.

'It is my pleasure, Miss Dawson,' Mr Grahame replied, taking my hand and pressing his lips to the skin. 'Please come back any time you wish to chat.' As he pulled away, I felt the rumple of paper beneath my fingers.

'He's an odd sort of man,' Charles said as he led me down the cobbled road, 'but his family has been here as long as the village and he's a good friend to have, provided you are not too . . . interesting.'

'It seems so,' I said, glancing at the small, hastily torn piece of paper. A name was written there in cursive script. *Mr Angus McMannon.*

Schooling my features into neutrality, I took Charles's proffered arm and thrust the note into my pocket, pushing the significance of it out of my mind. If I worried about it now, it would only ruin the afternoon, and I wanted so much to enjoy this new place and my present company.

'I can't say I know all the best places to purchase whatever it is that ladies require, but the butcher makes a remarkable meat pie. Or perhaps you'd prefer to visit the tea room,' Charles continued, oblivious to what ran through my mind.

There were no pushy hawkers or stall vendors thrusting their wares upon us as they did in the city, but rather laid-back gentlemen smoking their pipes and tipping their hats as we walked by, only engaging in conversation when I stopped to ask a question. It was a farmers' village by nature, and only the bare necessities were represented. Butchers, greengrocers and bakers, along with a tailor and a cobbler. People had access to everything they needed, but, other than the bookshop, perhaps not much else. I wondered what they did for entertainment.

'I've had my fill of tea for one day, I think, and I would be happy to eat when we return to the house,' I said to Charles as I pondered on how quiet and tranquil it was here.

The blasting heat from an ironmonger's shed had me stopping outside the open door, the interior limned in light from the furnace. A blacksmith hammered at a long piece of metal, red hot from the furnace, sending sparks flying with every blow. He looked up from his work to see me staring and threw the metal in a barrel to cool, making it sizzle and sending smoke billowing up to curl around his face. Bright, keen eyes observed me through the mask of heat as he wiped his giant hands on a greasy rag.

'Good day, sir, miss,' he said, touching his cap to us. 'Anything in particular that I can help you with?'

There wasn't really, and I wasn't sure why I had stopped. It annoyed me to be without my lost knife, but I couldn't ask for one in front of Charles, instead allowing him to speak for the both of us.

'I think the lady was drawn to your craftsmanship, sir,' he said smoothly as I moved towards a bench that displayed some of the smith's completed works – knives and swords, horseshoes and coat hooks. 'I had a trusty sword in the navy, but alas was unable to bring it back with me,' he carried on while I picked up a fine-looking blade. Small and discreet, with copper filigree on the handle and whorls and patterns etched from heel to tip, it was far more beautiful than the clunky thing I had lost, but I didn't dare ask how much it was. Unmarried as yet, I didn't have an allowance from Lord Blountford's estate, nor really a penny to my name.

'Well, sir, should you wish me to recreate it for you, I simply require a drawing. I am more than happy to make you an even finer sword than the original, if I may be so bold,' the blacksmith replied. I admired his unabashed pride in his work, and almost turned to ask him if he could keep the filigree knife for me for a week or so, until after I was married. But what would my husband think of me purchasing a knife as my first order of business after our wedding? I shook my head and placed it back on the table, feeling two pairs of eyes upon me – Charles, who turned away quickly when I caught him looking, and the smith, who had noticed my interest in his wares.

'And for the lady, perhaps a set of coat hooks wrought in the shape of roses?' he suggested pleasantly, and I smiled in return.

'I thank you, sir, but I want for nothing. There is no doubt, however, that your work is exquisite,' I added, gesturing towards his table of wares.

The smith beamed at the compliment, and Charles, seeing that I was edging back towards the street, made arrangements to send a sketch of his favourite sword in the next few days.

Outside, after the warmth of the ironmonger's shed, I instinctively huddled closer to Charles as he leaned down to say, 'You can have anything you want, Lizzie, you do realise that?'

'I wouldn't make such a bold statement,' I laughed, looking up at him from under the hoods of my eyelashes. 'You never know what a lady will ask for if you tell her she can have anything.'

His mouth quirked up in a half-smile as his eyes lingered on my face, but he said nothing.

'What?' I asked, wondering why he had not looked away.

'It is a most lovely sound hearing you laugh,' he said, his voice low, 'and I do not hear it often enough.'

I broke his stare and looked at the cobbled street. 'I have not had reason to laugh in quite some time, it seems.' And saying it aloud, I realised how true that was. I could not remember the last time I had truly felt light-hearted. Perhaps when Esme was still alive, but even then, it would have been long before she went away. Before my father was beaten by those men. Years perhaps.

'I have saddened you,' Charles said, stopping and touching my elbow so that I might look at him.

'No, not at all,' I said, realising that I was being poor company. 'I apologise. This is just as much a reprieve for you as it is for me, and I am being a complete and utter curmudgeon.' I forced a smile that he returned, tentatively.

'It *is* a reprieve, I must say, to be away from the house, and my uncle,' he admitted as we continued to wander. It was true that his mood was better, his eyes brighter, but I refrained from commenting on it. 'I imagine that this is nothing at all like the grandeur of London.'

'London is perhaps not quite as grand as those from outside might think,' I admitted, just as I spied a baker's wife standing outside her shop with a tray of sugared dainties.

'Care for a sample, miss?' she said, extending the tray towards me. Such dainties had been Esme's favourite treat, and I couldn't refuse, despite all the tea and biscuits we had already had. The fine sugar powdered my fingers like dust as I took one for myself and placed another in Charles's hand.

'Mmm. That is the best sugared dainty I have ever had,' I said as it melted on my tongue. 'Better than my own mother's,' I added to the grinning woman. Never mind that my mother hadn't made them since I was a child.

'Then we shall have a box,' Charles said, handing the woman a coin. She rushed into the bakery to prepare them for us.

I looked up at him and saw a dusting of sugar at the corner of his mouth. Giggling at the sight, I reached up to wipe it off with my thumb, not at all thinking of what I was doing.

Surprise barely registered on his face before it creased into a smile. My heart somersaulted of its own accord.

How many women had seen that smile he was giving me now? I shook the idea from my mind and tried not to blush as I gratefully accepted the box of treats from the woman, promising to buy more as soon as I had run out.

When we reached the end of the shopping street, we walked along the village green and back towards the carriage at a comfortable pace, with me holding the small box of cakes in the crook of my arm. He offered to take them from me, but I refused, stopping once again when I was sure there was no one within earshot.

'Why are you doing this?' I asked gently, because I wasn't annoyed, only curious.

His tanned forehead crinkled into a frown.

'I'm not sure I understand your meaning,' he replied, perplexed by what must have sounded like an accusation.

'Why are you being nice to me?'

He laughed – out of surprise rather than making fun of me, I felt. 'Lizzie, is it not ordinary for people to be nice to one another in London?'

'Not unless they want something.' I narrowed my eyes. I didn't want to be suspicious of him, but everything about the way I was feeling, the way he put me at ease, sent alarm bells through my mind. There was something dangerous about being near him, about how comfortable I was in his presence, and I both loved and loathed it.

'Well, my apologies that Londoners are not as amiable as us country folk, but I merely want to see you happy,' he said, taking the box from me and tucking it under his arm. He turned to continue walking and I kept pace with him.

I wanted to laugh too. Happy? Marrying a man old enough to be my grandfather, no matter his wealth, with a streak of bad luck with women who ended up dead? If he was trying to see me happy, he would be grossly disappointed before long. I changed the thread of the conversation slightly.

'Why are you so different, then, when we're at the manor?' The question was impertinent, and I knew it.

'Different how?' His voice hardened slightly.

'Colder. Diffident. Angry,' I said, putting a little more distance between us, 'whereas out here you're . . . softer.' I cringed at the word, considering it likely sounded like an insult to a military man six years my senior. What I'd wanted to say was 'nicer', but it hadn't sounded right.

Charles stayed silent for some time before he answered, leading me to think I'd hurt his pride.

'You are very outspoken,' he eventually replied.

'I'm sorry,' I fumbled. 'My mother tells me I have a tongue of venom and that my mouth should have been sewn shut at birth.'

He looked at me again, his eyebrows raised. 'That is rather drastic. I find your candour quite refreshing, actually,' he added, as if surprised to hear it himself. If my cheeks could have flushed any more they would have.

'My parents would disagree with you on that. Esme was the diplomat for us both. I chose not to speak, as I usually upset someone when I did.' I slowed down, kicking at a clump of grass on the path as I recalled unhappy memories. My mother had slapped me more than once for speaking out of turn, and I could at least be grateful that she'd done that for the last time. There were a great many things I owed thanks to Lord Blountford for, I realised bitterly.

'Lizzie,' Charles said softly, stopping a foot from me, his voice rough. I looked up at him again, the afternoon sun glinting off his hair, highlighting the golds and browns, a thrill running through my very core.

'Charles?' I breathed.

'Don't ever change.' He said it earnestly, not humorously as I'd expected, which made the ache in my chest all the worse.

'You didn't answer my question,' I said, giving him the slightest of smiles.

'About my taciturn disposition at the manor?'

I nodded, and he took a moment to reply, searching for the right words.

'My uncle and I . . . we disagree on many things.'

'Business-related things?'

'And other matters,' he said cryptically, and I got the distinct impression that my marrying his uncle was one of those 'other matters'.

'So your relationship at home is strained,' I inferred.

'That's one way to put it, yes. This business with his late wives will only make things more difficult, I feel,' he added quietly.

I felt wretched for dragging him into my investigations. If Esme hadn't been one of those women, I could try and will the mystery to stop pulling at me. If the ghost of one of those women would leave me alone – which, thinking of Pansy, was unlikely – I could pretend I didn't know any better.

We returned to the carriage in silence.

'I would like to promise you that I won't pursue it,' I told Charles during the ride back to the manor. He had been staring out of the window for the past ten minutes, either ignoring my glances or oblivious to them. It took him a while to look at me, and when his green eyes finally met mine I found a mixture of emotions behind them.

'Pursue what?'

'The wives. I want to tell you that I'll let it alone, but I would be lying, and I do not want there to be lies between us, Charles.'

He studied me, nodding just once, in acquiescence. 'I imagine that it is all the harder not knowing how your sister passed. I cannot blame you, even if it goes against my better judgement.'

I leaned forward and thought to take his hand, but stopped myself. 'I realise that this puts you in a difficult position with your uncle, so I won't involve you in any of my research, but I will ask you only once in good faith to tell me if you know anything. Anything at all.' I held my breath, seeing the pain in his eyes at my question.

I was not certain what I expected. A rebuttal. A denial. But I found him leaning closer to me and murmuring in such a way that even the coachman could not hear.

'I cannot tell you what I don't know, Lizzie,' he replied with a heaviness in his voice. 'I knew he had been married three times prior to your sister, and that each marriage had ended in tragedy, but my father told me very little, considering it to be the ancient history that it was by the time I was old enough to understand. Everything about Lord Blountford has been a closely guarded secret. He chose to be that way, and I have never succeeded in breaking his vow of silence on the matter. There are far too many secrets in this family,' he added cryptically.

I wondered what he could be referring to; was it just the lost wives, or was there something more?

'Do you believe he was involved in some way?' I persisted gently. I could feel myself growing quietly impatient. I believed he was being truthful, and that he didn't know how those women had died, but there was something more he wasn't saying. I wanted to push him until all the suspicions, thoughts, feelings and ideas spilled from him. I also realised that I didn't want to stop speaking with him. Despite how used to silence I had become, in his company I only wished to hear his voice. I tucked that thought away to examine later as I watched him, waiting for a response.

He sighed, dragging a hand through his hair. 'I wish to give him the benefit of the doubt. He is family, after all. But there are things my uncle does, business that he is involved in, that even I am not privy to. I am certain that he keeps them from me because he knows I would disagree with them. Whether that has anything to do with your sister's death, or indeed any of his previous wives, I have no idea, but I cannot shake the feeling that you and I will both be in a grave position if you pursue it any further.'

'And yet,' I said, pulling back from him slightly, feeling the danger in being that close to him, 'the fact that I'm going to be a part of this family makes me believe I have a right to know what went on before, even if no good will come of it.'

'No good will come of it at all,' Charles replied as if in

affirmation. He settled back in his seat and resumed his vigil out of the window.

'Something else is bothering you though,' I added, seeing that I hadn't fully appeased him.

He gave a wry chuckle at that, only a hint of humour in it.

'A lot of things are bothering me, but none of them are worth boring you with.' He waved a hand and pinched the bridge of his nose as he seemed to do when he was under stress.

'I don't think I could ever find you boring,' I said, unable to stop myself. I didn't know why I'd said it, or even really what I had meant by it, but a flush crept up my neck at the idea of what it had sounded like aloud.

This time it was my turn to look away. I could feel those green eyes on me, but thankfully he didn't ask me to explain. Instead, he said, 'I have another errand to run this afternoon. I hope to be home by dinner, but it may be a little later.'

'I'll let the cook know to keep something aside for you if you don't make it,' I replied, grateful for the excuse to change the subject.

The rest of the coach ride was spent without saying anything further, although it was a thoughtful, tender sort of quiet rather than the tense, brittle silence from before.

I thought repeatedly about what I'd said. *I don't think I could ever find you boring.* Stupid, stupid, I told myself. He undoubtedly wanted to know the meaning behind those words, and so did I. The wall between us had lowered part way, it seemed, but in its stead was something else entirely. A thickness in the air. Navigating whatever this was between us was like walking through quicksand, making a little progress in one way but still stuck, never quite sure whether I'd make it out without drowning.

Chapter 11

೩೦೦೩

When I returned to my rooms, Pansy was sitting on my bed.

Charles had requested his horse to be saddled as soon as we arrived back at Ambletye, giving me a brief but warm smile before I entered the house. A smile I returned, and still wore, right up until the moment the ghost wiped it from my face.

'You look happy,' she observed. 'Been out with the nephew, have you?'

There was certainly more to her question than the words suggested, and I felt the heat creeping into my cheeks.

'Charles was kind enough to show me around the village. He is proving to be a true friend,' I added, emphasising that our relationship was nothing more.

Pansy narrowed her eyes and made a disapproving sound.

'Be careful, girl. Your future husband does not like to share his belongings. He may be old enough to be your grandfather, but he can be as selfish as a child,' she said, watching me unpin my hair and allow it to spill over my shoulders.

'I won't belong to any man,' I retorted, glancing at her over my shoulder. She snorted in reply.

'Don't be so naïve. A wife belongs to a husband as much as his house, his carriage and his assets do. He will possess you and make certain that no one else comes close to you. If they do, they will suffer for it.'

The words were like shards of ice digging into my heart. Lord Blountford was old and miserable, most certainly, but I had not witnessed any cruelty in him, although what Pansy was telling me might account for some of the history with his wives.

And if what she was saying proved true, I would have to be very careful of how I acted around the earl and his nephew together.

'I met the proprietor of the bookshop today,' I changed the subject, 'and he told me that Mr McMannon is the longest-serving staff member here.'

Pansy stilled, flickering in and out of form for a moment before turning on a lazy sort of smile. I wondered if it was just a part of her taciturn nature, or if I might have hit a clue.

'Ah, Mr Grahame. I saw him once as a boy in his father's shop, before I was cooped up here. Worse than fishwives, that family,' she said with a grin that made me think she didn't entirely disapprove of them. 'He isn't wrong, though Mistress Damiani, the cook, comes in a close second. They began working for Eggy just months apart, from what I heard. She'd be able to tell you a horror story or two about his precious Marisa.' The jealousy in Pansy's voice was unmistakable.

'Why do you despise her so?' I asked, maintaining an air of amusement about it.

Pansy rose from the bed and bridged the gap between us. I found myself pressed up against the dressing table as she came near, the ferocity in her eyes sending a jolt of alarm through me. She ran a chilled finger down my cheek and let her hand rest on my neck, the touch nothing more than the gentle caress of cold air on my skin. I shivered involuntarily.

'Because, my dear, sweet lamb,' she whispered, her voice

taking on the sing-song quality it did when she said something particularly insane, 'she was as beautiful as you are wilful, as alluring as your sister, and as evil as the devil himself, but Eggy loved her more than any of us, and he still does.' She leaned into my ear, her fingers placed just where my pulse raced violently in my throat. 'And if you don't produce an heir, you'll die just like we did.'

I reared my head back to look her in the face as she began to fade. I caught the glint in her eyes, the unmistakable cruel delight in her smile. Then she was gone.

There was a gentle rap on the door and I shook myself as if from a dream, just as Marie entered with a tray of tea things and a few of the sugared dainties Charles had bought.

'Are you all right, miss? You look like you've seen a ghost,' she said as she laid the tray on a low table.

'Fine,' I muttered, disappearing into the bathroom so that I could scrub my face and neck where Pansy had touched me.

The roaring in my ears only died down once I was safely huddled up in an armchair with my hands wrapped around a cup of tea while Marie lit the fire. It was only mid afternoon, but the cold seeped through the windows, the wind rattling the panes in their frames. I shuddered again as Pansy's words echoed through my mind, recalling the sheer enjoyment she took in terrifying me.

Marie placed a blanket around my shoulders, no doubt assuming that I had caught a chill while out. But the cold inside me wasn't something a woollen throw could defend against. It was a deep and penetrating thing that came from the knowledge that I might be marrying a murderer, and that even if Pansy was insane and Lord Blountford was innocent, I would have to live with her haunting me for the rest of my life here.

I quashed the fear I felt and pretended that I had never met

Pansy, that she had never told me the things she had. After all, if I discounted the rumours and suggestions of a possibly mad ghost, what did I really know about my future husband? That he was unlucky? That he had lost more in a few decades than most did in a lifetime? Until I knew something more solid, I would play my part.

For the first time since I had arrived at Ambletye, I felt as though there might be some way out of this marriage, even if the hope was only a small secret kernel in the back of my mind. If Lord Blountford had been responsible for the deaths of any of his wives, could I make a case to have him arrested without doing my own family harm? Even if there was little more than a sliver of possibility, I had to try. For their sakes and for mine.

When dinner time finally arrived, Marie offered to bring food to my rooms, but I was glad to leave them even if it meant I was to eat alone with Lord Blountford. Charles hadn't yet returned, and I made good on my promise of asking a steward to set food aside for him. Lord Blountford raised an eyebrow at my request, or perhaps at the fact that I was beginning to treat the staff as my own, but I dutifully ignored him.

That was, until the topic of our impending matrimony arose.

'I believe that we have a dress that will fit you for Thursday's ceremony,' he said, his hands trembling arthritically as he tore into the roasted pheasant, keeping his eyes fixed on his meal.

'I have not been measured for one yet, sir.'

'No indeed, but you are the same size as your sister, and hers has been cleaned and aired.'

The clatter of my cutlery as I slammed it down made him look at me at last.

'I will not be wearing my late sister's wedding dress.' It was not a question, but he somehow took it to be one.

'It is too late to have one made for you, and it seems pointless to waste it after all the expense I went to for it,' he said, as though it was a reasonable argument.

'I find you insensitive, sir, if you believe that I would be willing to wear my dead sister's dress at our wedding. I cannot understand why you would consider this agreeable to me.' I spat the words out, wishing that Charles were present to take my side.

'Well,' he said, sighing, 'there are plenty of other dresses in the house for you to avail yourself of. I only thought you might like to have something of hers with you on the day.'

'Then you thought wrong, Lord Blountford. I will find something appropriate and will ensure you bear no cost for it, if that is what concerns you.'

If he heard the acid in my tone he didn't show it, but instead shrugged and returned to his food.

'What about my parents?' Now seemed as good a time as any to ask.

'What about them?'

'Will they be coming for the ceremony?'

He gave a derisive little snort through his nose and shook his head. 'Your parents will not be attending our wedding, Miss Dawson, and they have expressed no interest in leaving the city at this time.' He sipped his wine thoughtfully. 'Perhaps in a few months, or once they have a grandchild to visit,' he said, those final words laced with intent that made my stomach turn.

I gripped my knife and fork so tightly in my fists that my knuckles went white. Visions of thrusting the silverware into his eyeballs flashed through my mind. I had no room for fear of this man – only hatred and loathing.

My murderous thoughts were interrupted by a steward delivering an urgent letter, one that pulled the attention from me entirely.

'The messenger awaits your response, your lordship,' the man said, still bowing, as Lord Blountford read it. The earl's face grew redder by the second, and I desired very much to disappear into the depths of the dining chair I was sitting in.

'Ask the messenger to wait. I shall compose a reply to Mr Canfield from my study,' he finally said, flinging his napkin onto the table and leaving without so much as a glance in my direction.

Something itched in the back of my mind at the name, but I was so relieved to be left alone that I didn't spend any time thinking on it, instead finishing my meal in my own comfortable silence.

Perhaps whatever the contents of this letter contained, it would be enough to delay the wedding. It was doubtful, but I could hope.

I didn't see Lord Blountford for the rest of the evening; not when I sat in the drawing room by the fire reading for a time, nor as I walked back to my rooms, taking the long route along the first-floor landing, examining the ancestral portraits that hung in the gallery. The previous Blountford men and women looked down on me with various expressions of disapproval. The exceptions were a young Charles and presumably his mother and father. They appeared to be almost smiling.

I knew I was dawdling, waiting to hear the sound of the front door signifying Charles's return, but it was only when I was already in my nightdress that I felt, rather than heard, his presence in the house.

A small thrill ran through me, and I rang the servants' bell without thinking.

'Is everything all right, miss?' Marie appeared moments later, poking her head around the door.

'I'm well, Marie, but if Captain Blountford has returned, would you ensure that he has dinner. I believe he missed lunch and I asked for something to be put aside for him.' I put on my best 'lady of the house' voice in the hope that I sounded authoritative, but even I could hear the eagerness I was trying to hide.

'Of course, Miss Dawson.' She bobbed a curtsey and left with a somewhat mystified expression on her face.

I clambered into bed and pulled out Esme's green journal, reading her notes and thoughts about life at Ambletye. I was halfway through a story about a lame horse that Lord Blountford had threatened to shoot when there was a soft knock at my door.

'Come in,' I called, thinking Marie had returned to check on me.

'Lizzie?' Charles said, opening the door a crack. 'May I speak with you?'

My heart somersaulted in my chest. I thrust the journal under the pillow and snatched up my robe from the back of a chair, wrapping it tightly around me.

It would be improper to let him into my rooms. I knew it even without Pansy's words of warning echoing in my mind. *Your future husband does not like to share his belongings.* But if anyone were to see Charles loitering outside my rooms, it might be worse for both of us. Servants gossiped, and I didn't want to entertain the thought of what Lord Blountford might do if word got back to him.

'Come in, quickly,' I whispered, pulling him through the door by his hand.

He looked windswept and still smelled of fresh air from his ride. My own hair was wild and unravelled, and I had washed off the powder covering my bruises. Lord knew what I looked like, clutching my robe to me like a child with a precious doll.

'You were gone a long time,' I said breathlessly as I noticed him take in my face, my hair, my bedroom attire. I begged my heart to stop thundering. I was certain he could hear it from across the room.

'I, uh . . .' he cleared his throat and spoke in a low whisper, running a hand through his hair and sending it even more wayward, 'I had something very important to attend to. But I wanted to thank you for ensuring I had supper.'

My mouth quirked into a smile at seeing him so flustered and uncertain.

'That was all you came for?'

'No, I, uh . . . I have something for you. Something I didn't want to give you in front of anyone else, for reasons you will soon see.' He took a step forward and I forced my feet to take a slight step back.

The intensity of his gaze burned into me in a way I had never experienced. His eyes were dark in the candlelight, but he was looking at me. Not his uncle's betrothed. Not a victim or an idiotic girl running away from a groundskeeper in the woods. Just me.

'I hope you don't find it presumptuous,' he continued, 'but I didn't want you to be without it for longer than necessary.' It was then that I noticed the belt slung over his shoulder, which he removed and passed to me, placing it in my hands gingerly, not even allowing our fingers to graze.

I ran my hands over the supple leather, pliable but strong. It was a knife belt, I realised, as I spotted a sheath fashioned into one side; and within it, the filigree knife I had admired at the blacksmith's shed earlier. I gasped, not with fear as some girls perhaps would, but with delight.

'You bought this for me?' I asked.

He nodded. 'I remembered that you'd dropped a knife in the

woods yesterday. I went to retrieve it last night, but when I eventually found it, I noticed its poor workmanship. You were eyeing this one like a child in a sweet shop,' he said gently.

'I bought the old one from an ironmonger in London. It was all I could afford at the time,' I admitted.

'Well, a lady should have a weapon to suit her station, don't you think?' A smile tugged at the corner of his mouth and I found myself relaxing. He hadn't asked me why I had purchased a knife in the first place, or why I made a habit of carrying one with me.

'What did Lord B`l`ountford say?'

'He doesn't know,' he said softly, as something like guilt flitted across his face. 'Lizzie, I worry my uncle will take issue if he knows you carry it, but I'd be happier in the knowledge that you have some protection.'

'Protection from what?' The question felt heavy on my lips. If Charles believed I was in danger from his uncle, he had never hinted at it before now.

'From whatever it is you fear,' he replied.

I almost laughed. I was afraid of many things, and not all of them could be fended off with a blade.

'I don't know how to use it properly,' I confessed. I knew which end was the one you pointed at people you didn't like, but if it was life or death, I wasn't sure I mightn't hurt myself more than my assailant. I studied the knife and ran a thumb gently along the edge, careful not to cut myself. It was cold and beautiful, carved with an intricate pattern up the hilt. This sort of thing would ordinarily take days or perhaps weeks to create, and yet it fitted in my hand as though it was made for it.

'I can teach you, given time,' he said, his voice low and rough, causing something to stir in me. He was closer now, though whether I'd taken a step towards him or he to me, I wasn't sure.

'I'd like that,' I breathed. We didn't move. That quicksand I'd thought I was walking in earlier was consuming me. The air between us was thick with anticipation, neither of us wanting to interrupt it.

'Lesson one,' he said eventually. 'May I?' Without another word, he took the knife belt from me and showed me how to wear it, wrapping it around my hips, still managing not to touch me. The movement was deft and fast, but I watched him carefully. Only once it was in place did he take my hand, the touch sending a wave of exhilaration up my arm, and wrap my fingers around the carved hilt.

'If you hold it this way, with the sharp edge pointing upwards,' he breathed in my ear, 'you will do more damage, and your attacker will take longer to respond. But you have to be quick. A strong, fast thrust will give you time to get away.' Still holding my hand, he gently pulled my arm forwards and upwards, so that if there were someone standing in front of me, I would pierce their abdomen and then slide the blade upwards underneath a rib. I should have felt sick for picturing it, but instead I found myself feeling relief. I could actually defend myself if anyone came near me. What that said about me, I didn't want to know.

Ignoring the trembling in my core, I turned my face towards him and frowned. 'Do you suspect that I'm in danger, Charles?'

'I suspect that we are on dangerous ground,' he whispered. 'I wanted you not to be afraid.'

'I am used to being afraid,' I replied. 'Not from the sort of danger you are familiar with,' I added, remembering of course that he was a military man, more accustomed to death and destruction than I had ever been. But growing up with parents who didn't think anything of our safety had been terrifying in its own way; never knowing if our mother would wake up in the morning, or Father would find himself so badly in debt that his creditors would send someone around to hurt us, again.

He finally released my hand and stepped away, the warmth leaving me as quickly as someone opening a window to the night air. I made to unbuckle the belt, but as I did so, my robe slipped from my shoulder, revealing the web of scars peeking out from under my nightdress.

'What's this?' he asked, reaching out without thinking but pulling his hand back at the last moment. His fingers hovered momentarily over my skin, the heat radiating from them.

'Horse bite,' I said, grimacing at the memory. The thought of his touch on my shoulder was almost as bad, but in an entirely different way.

'That's why you never learned to ride?' He almost laughed at the realisation when I nodded in reply, the soft sound of an exhale through his nose. 'And that one?'

I didn't have to look at where his eyes had landed to know what he was looking at. The scar ran below my collarbone in a thin line, a reminder of my greatest fear. A reminder of what men could do when they didn't get what they wanted.

'That one is the reason I carry a knife.'

The image of Lord Darleston pulling me into a darkened room swam before my eyes, and I closed them to force the threatening tears back down.

'Lizzie,' Charles breathed, and I snapped them back open. His own eyes, though hooded by shadows, were full of concern and something else.

His hand came back up and he took one of my loose curls in his fingers, twirling it as if it were the most precious thing he had ever touched.

'For someone with so many fears, you are remarkably brave,' he said, almost to himself.

Something broke inside me then. I had never wanted some-one in this way, but the spike of desire brought with it another kind of fear. I knew at the back of my mind that I was playing a dangerous game, that I could be putting not only myself but also Charles in danger. If I were to tell Lord Blountford I didn't want to marry him, it would leave my parents destitute. He had made that perfectly clear. And if nothing came of my attempts to find him guilty, we were back to where we had started. As much as it hurt me, I couldn't selfishly lead Charles on.

I took his hand in mine and pressed it to my lips before let-ting go and taking a step back.

'You are a good man, Charles. You don't deserve the conse-quences that this will bring,' I said as firmly as I could.

If he was disappointed, he disguised it with a grim smile.

'I should let you sleep,' he said, walking towards the door stiffly, as though every step pained him.

I wish you wouldn't, was what I didn't say.

'Would you show me the summer house tomorrow?' I blurted, wanting any excuse to spend time with him.

He looked at me thoughtfully before nodding, then bowed and opened the door to leave.

'Charles?' I said to his back. He paused and turned his face to me, those green eyes shining like emeralds in the dimness. 'Thank you.'

With another brief nod he left.

Sleep only found me after what felt like hours of tossing and turning, my hand resting on the knife I'd placed under my pil-low next to Esme's journal, my dreams filled with him.

Chapter 12

ഗ൬ര

Sunday morning found me readying for church, only to find that neither Lord Blountford nor Charles was attending.

When I asked Marie why we weren't going, she gave me an uncomfortable reply, shifting her eyes from me as she said, 'I don't wish to repeat private information, miss, but I hear that the earl doesn't wish to draw attention to the fact that you are living in his home when you are not yet married.'

For once, I agreed with Lord Blountford's sentiments, relieved that I wouldn't have to endure the stares and whispers during the morning service. Knowing that Jordie had the morning off, I descended to the kitchens with more than just the intention of picking up a carrot for my horse. I had woken early with thoughts already dancing around my mind. How to spend more time with Charles without arousing suspicion. How to solve Pansy's death so that she might . . . move on. How to save myself from marrying a man I didn't love, with only a handful of days left.

I wondered whether those three problems might be solved at once, hoping, perhaps futilely, that there could be one solution for everything.

And then there was Pansy's warning. Esme had not produced an heir for Lord Blountford; was that why she had died?

Some mysterious 'accident' that would have got her out of his way? I shook those thoughts from my head as I wandered the servants' corridors.

The kitchen was a hive of activity, with maids bringing in baskets of vegetables while others cleaned and washed them, preparing everything before no doubt disappearing to church themselves. Girls of various ages did everything from preparing bread to scrubbing pots, and Mistress Damiani stood at the centre of it all, barking orders while she plucked a chicken.

But as if my presence had disturbed the equilibrium of the household, everything stopped when I approached the large cook.

'Mistress Damiani,' I addressed her as she studied me with small dark eyes. She was clearly Italian by birth, and had the girth of someone who had been cooking, and eating, for a number of decades.

'Miss Dawson,' she replied sternly, inclining her head. I immediately sensed her dislike of me, even though I had done nothing but compliment her art. I would have to tread very carefully indeed.

'I understand you must be terribly busy, but I was wondering if I could trouble you for a word?' I kept my voice light and pleasant, showing her the hint of a smile, mimicking something I had seen Esme do hundreds of times before.

The cook seemed to understand my meaning, and with a wave of her large hand had the staff scattering like a flock of London pigeons. I waited until the scurry of footsteps had petered out before I spoke again, pushing into my eyes all the warmth I could muster.

'Firstly I have to say that your cooking is far better than anything I have ever tasted in my life.' She must have been able to tell that the compliment was genuine, as a little of her stoniness softened. 'I was hoping I could trouble you to make some of these.' I held out my hand and unwrapped one of the sugared dainties from my handkerchief. 'They were my sister's favourite and I would love to have some at the wedding,' I added, feeling the word 'wedding' ring through every part of me.

Whether it was out of sympathy or the enjoyment of a challenge, Mistress Damiani nodded and took the small cake from me, placing it gently on a plate to one side.

'I was also told that you are one of Ambletye's longest-standing employees, is that right?'

'Yes, miss, second only to the groundskeeper. My mother and I moved here from Italy when I was just a girl,' she replied, still holding the half-plucked chicken between us, unwilling, it seemed, to let it go.

'Ah! Italy, I have always wished to visit. Lord Blountford's first wife was from Italy, was she not?' I asked the question casually as I picked up an unwashed carrot from a nearby basket. The older woman's eyes narrowed slightly, whether at my question or my cavalier regard for her vegetable supplies, I wasn't sure.

'Yes, my mother used to work for her family. It is how we got the position here.' She still had a hint of an accent, despite many decades in England.

'She must have been a good mistress to have you move all the way to another country.'

The cook shrugged, the chicken bobbing over the countertop as she did so. 'Lady Blountford was a true Mediterranean without a doubt. She was beautiful, but with a terrible temper. His lordship loved her dearly, though, and that is all that mattered.'

I nodded in acquiescence, choosing my next words carefully.

'Was she your favourite? Mistress, I mean.'

'It does not do well to speak ill of the dead, miss,' she replied, stiffening.

'Oh, of course not. I had no such intent,' I said, holding a hand to my chest. 'I only wished to understand how the women before me were viewed by the most loyal staff,' I gestured to her, 'so that I can ensure I fill their shoes competently.'

This seemed to appease her, and she nodded along thoughtfully before answering.

'If you do not find it too impertinent, miss, I would say that all of the earl's wives were a high class of woman, with the single exception of the third one. If you never hear about her it will be too soon.'

Oh Pansy, what did you get yourself into?

'I appreciate your honesty, Mistress Damiani,' I replied, filing the information away. I didn't want to push my luck, but there was still one thing that burned on the tip of my tongue as I changed the subject and asked her if I could take the carrot to Gwen.

As I was about to leave, however, I could hold back no longer, asking her quietly as I passed, 'Do you know how they died, Mistress Damiani?' *Should I fear for my life?* was what I thought but didn't say.

She turned to face me, her dark eyes shining, with grief, or possibly fear.

'Some doors are better left closed, Miss Dawson.'

'Sometimes, Mistress Damiani, the ghosts open those doors for us and we have no choice but to let them out,' I replied before sweeping out of the kitchen, feeling her eyes upon my back all the way.

Aware that I wouldn't have Jordie's reassuring presence to fortify me, it took me several moments to gather myself before entering the stables. Even a week ago this would have been impossible, I thought as I stood outside Gwen's stall and held the carrot at arm's length. I even managed to stroke her nose once, briefly, before retreating to the doorway to look out for Charles.

I kept to the shadows, just in case some servant happened to spy me waiting, knowing how they would gossip to each other. I had noticed Jordie speaking to Marie on the doorstep to the courtyard more than once. He would say something to make her giggle while he rubbed the back of his head, sending his red curls every which way. She would blush if I caught her looking out of the window at him too, and I was in half a mind to tell him to get on with it and ask to court her.

But if Jordie or anyone else drew conclusions about myself and Charles, that would risk starting rumours about us. Rumours I would have to deal with, and that could easily work their way back to Lord Blountford.

That all disappeared from my mind, though, when I saw Charles waiting for me at the end of the courtyard, a shawl draped over his arm in readiness for our walk.

A slight frown furrowed his forehead, while his face was stern, disinterested, even as he wrapped the shawl around my shoulders, murmuring that it was too cold to be out in just a coat. They were the first words he had said to me since last night, but they were as chilly as the autumn air.

Unperturbed, I gave him the smallest of smiles by way of greeting. Rather than return it, his eyes flicked to the house. Following his gaze, I noticed the curtains in one of the upstairs rooms twitch. His uncle's study, I presumed.

The cold that swept over me wasn't only from the crisp autumn air, and I schooled my own features into a semblance of seriousness, allowing Charles to lead the way.

The excitement I had felt this morning at visiting the summer house with him evaporated as we walked in silence, the windows of Ambletye peering down on us like dozens of eyes. He didn't offer his arm, nor say a word as we traced the route we had followed on my first day here. I pictured a map of the estate in my mind so that I could find my way again should I need to.

He led me down a path that ran past the rose garden, through arches of barren wisteria, before the wind picked up and tore my hair from its bun, sending curls flying into my face.

'I should have brought a bonnet,' I complained as I tried to reposition some of the pins Marie had carefully placed this morning, only making it worse.

'I will fetch you one if you like,' Charles said, the tension seemingly leaving his voice the further we were from watchful eyes.

'I don't want to trouble you . . .'

'It's no trouble at all. We've still got some way to walk and I wouldn't want you being blown away,' he said with the slightest grin before dashing back in the direction we had come, leaving me standing alone amongst the rose bushes.

But not alone.

For standing there among the shrubbery was the most beautiful woman I had ever seen. Black hair fell in a swathe all the way to her curved hips, her corset tightened to exaggerate her full breasts. Her clothes were some decades out of fashion, but they suited her perfectly. Large dark eyes seemed to look through me, while her full lips turned up into an almost-smile, as though she were keeping secrets. But her effervescent glow was the most telling feature of all.

The realisation was like someone pouring a bucket of iced water down my back. Marisa.

'H-hello,' I stuttered, checking to make sure there was no one nearby who might overhear me talking to a rose bush.

'Hello,' she replied in a deep, accented voice holding no hint of surprise that I could see her, let alone talk to her.

'You must be Marisa.' I curtseyed, keeping my eyes trained on her. After everything I had heard about her temper, it felt only right to remain polite.

'That I am. And you are?'

'Lizzie Dawson, my lady. Ambletye's newest resident,' I added, feeling it would be unwise to reveal my true reason for being here.

'Lizzie Dawson,' she repeated, like a curse coming from her voluptuous lips.

'Why are you not in the house, my lady?'

'Why are *you* not in the house, girl? Wandering the grounds with that young man,' she said, looking me up and down disapprovingly.

'I am taking some air. The young man is Lord Blountford's nephew, my friend.'

'Not your betrothed?'

The question left me breathless, if only because I knew deep down that it was what I wished.

'Not . . . exactly,' I replied. If this ghost did not truly realise she was dead, there was a strong possibility that she remained out here because this was where she had died. I had seen it once before at home. A flower seller who had been killed by a rampant horse and cart stood on the corner of the same street every day, ignored by those who couldn't see her, trying to sell her invisible wares. I had never spoken to her, but often wondered why she didn't move on to wherever ghosts went.

'Excuse my impertinence, but you didn't answer my question, my lady. I've never seen you in the house before, whereas I have seen . . . others.'

'I fell and am waiting for someone to come to my aid,' she said, and as she spoke, a trickle of blood ran down her pale neck.

'Fell? Where?' I asked, just as I noticed the scratches beginning to adorn her face, as though her ghostly form were only now remembering that she had been in an accident. She didn't reply, only pointed upwards with a slender finger. My eyes travelled to where she was indicating. Up the sandstone bricks, past the trellises where honeysuckle and jasmine grew, above the windows that looked out onto the garden, to a balcony some twenty feet over our heads. My breath hitched in my throat.

'You say you fell, my lady. How did you fall? Perhaps I can find someone to help you,' I added, the guilt of lying to her only slightly less than the desire to know the answer.

'Married men and women fight all the time,' she said with a wave of a hand. A hand that was bent the wrong way, as if it had broken and never been set.

'You fought with the earl?'

'It was stupid, nothing for you to worry yourself about, girl,' she said as though I were but a child – which I suppose to her I was.

'Of course,' I replied deferentially. 'Only I know your husband loves you more than anything in the world. I don't understand how he could have let you fall so far if it was something trivial.'

'Pah,' she scoffed. 'He loves me second only to his money and his business. That is why we were arguing. That is why we've always fought. I did not want him to bring my father's gambling house over to England. I thought I had left all that behind – the disgusting and debased desires of men,' she said fervently. 'But the money he could make was more important to him than I was. He and my father had already agreed to be business partners before he even proposed to me.' She spat exaggeratedly at the ground between us.

'Your father owned a gambling house?' A fresh wave of terror had passed over me at what this might mean.

'*Sì*, Il Ridotto. The biggest gambling house in all of Venice. All of Italy as well, if my father is to be believed.' She spoke with such hatred for it, I wondered if she had experienced the pain of what these games could do to a family.

'Did your husband . . .' *Did he push you?* I wanted to ask the question even as my stomach churned at the thought.

'I lost my temper, I slapped him, we struggled. It was an accident and he will have to buy me a very large diamond by way of apology,' she said ruefully. 'He's ruined my favourite dress.'

At her words, blood gushed from the back of her head over her shoulder. It wasn't fair to leave her here like this, having her believe that Edgar would come and save her at any moment.

'My lady . . . Marisa, I'm afraid—'

'Who are you talking to?' Charles said breathlessly, passing me a bonnet. He had jogged all the way to and from the house, it seemed.

'I, uh . . . well, you see . . .' I turned towards Marisa with an apologetic look on my face, but she was gone.

'Lizzie, are you well? If you're not, we can do this another day,' Charles said, his voice full of concern.

'No, I'm fine, really.' I gave him a wavering smile as I pinned my hair down and tied the bonnet below my chin. 'I just thought I saw something. That's all.'

Only partially convinced, he held out his arm and we continued our walk through the gardens until we reached a large trimmed lawn on the eastern side of the house, oak trees dotting the landscape.

We were walking in the opposite direction to the graves, I realised, the surface of the lake like a black mirror in the distance, and into a part of the estate I was entirely unfamiliar with. I tried to enjoy the songs of blackbirds and robins, the way the sunlight caught the dew on the grass as though someone had scattered diamonds across the lawn.

We entered a copse of trees, where the leaves were faithfully turning from their lush green to yellows and oranges, a few pulling from their branches and falling freely when the wind blew. In most places the paths had been cleared, but as we ventured further from the house, the grounds appeared less well tended. We walked in heavy silence, nothing more than the occasional crunch of leaves underfoot, but I knew that in a few days, if the rain came, this route would be muddy and treacherous, only suitable for navigating with heavy boots.

My thoughts continually returned to Marisa.

I lost my temper, I slapped him, we struggled. It was an accident.

There was no doubt in my mind now that Lord Blountford's first wife, no matter how much he apparently loved her, had been accidentally killed by his hand.

'Here it is,' Charles announced as a building emerged from between rhododendron bushes, smaller than a cottage but larger than a shed. The walls and ceiling at the front were made of glass, with heavy beams of dark wood supporting it. I could imagine sitting there in the summer with the doors open, inviting the warm air in, but there was also a red-brick interior with a fireplace at the back to sit around and read in the colder months. It was a one-room piece of heaven.

The doors were unlocked, and we opened them to let the stale air out before stepping inside.

'The chimney will need cleaning before you light a fire, and I would recommend airing it for a day before you take up residence, but as far as I know it hasn't been used in the few months I've been here, so I'm certain no one will protest,' he said, pulling dust sheets off furniture. Everything looked comfortable and well used, light-faded but functional.

'What a lot of books,' I observed as he pulled a sheet from the wall to reveal a bookcase spilling with volumes of all shapes and sizes. Some were on the floor in piles, leaving large gaps on the shelves. I ran a finger across the spines, reading the titles and noticing some in Italian and even Latin.

'I would imagine many of these belonged to your predecessors,' Charles said, coming up behind me. I turned to find him only a foot away, his eyes fixed on my face with that same intensity I had seen last night.

Leaves had blanketed the glass roof above, but shafts of sunlight peeked through the gaps and illuminated us, catching the glints of gold and copper in his hair, as though he were wearing a halo. My heart stuttered. He was by far the most handsome man I'd met. Not the arrogant, sickening looks of Richard Darleston, nor the comely youth of Jordie. It was as though time and experience had honed his features into something more genuine, more noble.

I realised I was staring and tore my eyes from his face reluctantly, but his hand came up to catch my chin, tilting it towards him, forcing me to look at him again. The frisson of desire between us grew taut, and I swallowed.

'Charles,' I breathed. Could it be possible to want someone so much that it hurt?

'Lizzie,' he replied, equally breathless, and I quivered to hear him say my name that way.

No one will know. No one can see us. Just a bit of fun.

Darleston's words slammed into me, a reminder of another time, another existence, and I pushed Charles away violently, the memories anchoring me to the past. 'I'm sorry,' I blurted, balling my fists at my sides. 'I'm sorry, I just can't . . .'

'No need to apologise,' he said, the look of surprise and hurt quickly replaced with embarrassment. He ran a hand through his hair sheepishly, making him seem younger. 'I didn't mean to startle you.'

I noticed vaguely that I hadn't reached for my knife, as if subconsciously I knew that Charles wasn't a real threat. And he wasn't. Not at all. I felt safe with him, whether we were at the house, in the village or here, alone in the quiet of the summer house. I would never have let myself come here with him if that weren't the case.

'Lizzie, you don't have to explain yourself to me. I mistakenly thought—'

'You weren't mistaken,' I interrupted him. 'You were far from mistaken.' I sidestepped him to sit on a worn chaise by the empty fireplace. 'Charles, there is so much I need to tell you. So much that I need to confide, but I worry . . .' I frowned. 'If you knew what I was really, you would have no interest in me, I fear.'

'I don't believe that could ever be the case,' he said, his voice hoarse. Could I really do this? Tell him my greatest secret, and with it my greatest fear?

'I've never breathed a word to anyone of how I got that scar, of why I won't let a man touch me. My parents forbade me to speak of it, understandably, for should anyone find out, my reputation would be damaged beyond repair.'

I wavered. What was I doing? For the first time I wanted to tell someone what had happened, and perhaps opening up to Jordie just a crack had made me realise that not everyone would judge me or shun me, as my parents had insisted they would. My hands trembled involuntarily and I sat on them.

'Whatever it is that eats at you, Lizzie,' Charles said softly, taking a seat in the armchair opposite me, 'I promise you I have seen far worse.' I could tell he took pains to move slowly, carefully, as though I were a frightened animal. This was the side of him that he didn't let his uncle or the world see. Sensitive, caring, open. That he had seen death a hundred times, sent his friends and brothers into battle and lost so much didn't seem to change that.

'It happened after Esme left,' I began, forcing the words out before I could think about them. 'My parents and I were invited to the birthday party of Lord Richard Darleston, who, having inherited his father's title after his death, decided to throw the biggest ball the West End had ever seen.

'The town house was five times the size of ours, and anyone remotely connected to the young lord was invited. I wore one of Esme's dresses that she had left behind, red with pearl button fastenings. I had never been to a party without her before and I worried that no one would ask me to dance or speak with me now that I wasn't accompanied by my charming sister.' I huffed a laugh. 'Instead I caught the eye of the host himself. My mother was plied with champagne imported from France, my father found himself at the faro table in his element, and I was so enthralled by the attention of the young lord I didn't realise I was in any danger.'

I closed my eyes and could still see it. The grand ballroom with its chandeliers that scattered glitter over the dancing couples, the small orchestra playing, the servants replacing our glasses just as soon as they were emptied. Amongst it all I stood terrified of being alone, only to find Darleston staring at me from across the room as though I were the only girl in it.

'He mistook me for my sister at first, but as I spoke, he realised I lacked all Esme's careful manners. He asked me to dance all the same, and again for a second and a third time, after which I was so exhausted and giddy from the drink that I had to sit down. He gathered a group of friends – the young upper-class men and women who hung on his every word and followed him like lapdogs – and told us that we were going on a grand tour of the house.

'My father was too busy playing his game to escort me and my mother was drunk senseless, but I assumed that in a large group it would be acceptable to leave them and go off with him. How wrong I was.'

I pulled my hands from under my skirts and clasped them in my lap, closing my eyes again and dropping my voice to a whisper. Charles remained so silent I almost forgot he was there, and there was something cathartic about saying it all aloud. A moment of panic gripped me that he would hear my story and leave in disgust. But if that were the case, I told myself, better to know now, before I became any more attached to him.

'We walked through the galleries and he showed us his late father's collections of pottery and sculpture. Halls and rooms and corridors all filled with art from ages past, yet he waved at them dismissively as if they were of no consequence. Only when we reached a dark room did I realise that the rest of our party had vanished, leaving myself and Darleston alone. I made my excuses to leave at once, not wanting there to be a misunderstanding between us, but he blocked my passage.

'"No one will know. No one can see us," he said, and I didn't understand his meaning at first. He took my glass and placed it on a bureau before pushing me against it and forcing himself on me. I shoved him off, but it only seemed to encourage him further. "Just a bit of fun," he said as he pinned me down, his breath heavy and stale with alcohol.' My stomach sickened with the memory. 'I reached for my glass and did the only thing I could think of: I hit him with it. His reaction was so fast I didn't see the slap until I was on the floor and he was on top of me, the broken stem of my glass held here.' I pointed below my collarbone, where, under my layers of clothing, the pale scar etched in my skin acted as a reminder of that night. A tear slipped down my cheek, leaving a cold trail on my skin.

'He did . . . the most unspeakable things. I only got away because as he ripped the front of my dress, he called me by Esme's name. Something shattered inside me then, as one hand held the glass to my neck while the other roamed my body. I managed to fight against him. I kneed him in a . . . sensitive place and ran from the room as fast as I could. I don't know how I managed to escape the party without anyone noticing, or with my dignity intact.

'When I told my mother, she swore me to secrecy. If anyone knew, I would become a pariah, sullied and unworthy of any husband.' My voice took on the bitter edge that came with the admonition she had given me. *You aren't the first, you won't be the last. Buck up.* 'So you see, Charles,' I looked at him, into those green eyes full of pain and regret, 'I would not be worthy of you even if our circumstances were different and I was not engaged to your uncle.'

With my soul laid bare, expecting only for him to leave in shock and disgust, I found him instead by my side, wiping the last of my angry tears away and taking my hands. His warm callused fingers pressed against mine as I waited for his goodbye.

'Lizzie,' my name was like a prayer on his lips, 'you have endured more heartache than any woman I know, have feared for your life more than many a man and are braver than most. You are more than worthy of my humble affections.' He swallowed, and the sincerity in his face made my heart want to fracture into tiny pieces. 'You are more than worthy of my love.'

Chapter 13

୬୦୦୯

No one had ever declared their love to me before, but I knew immediately, down to the very core of my being, that I loved Charles Blountford, and had done so for most of the little time we had spent together. Giddy joy tangled and fought with worried helplessness inside me. His uncle would never allow us to be together, of this I was certain. Even if we cast off our reputations and eloped, where would we live? What would happen to my parents? And what of his vow to his late father? All of this flashed through my mind in a moment as I stared into those deep green eyes, like pools of fresh water in a mossy wood.

I allowed myself an awed smile, unable to fathom how I had been so fortunate as to meet him, and yet how unfortunate the circumstances of that meeting were.

'You are uncharacteristically quiet,' he eventually said, callused thumb brushing my knuckles.

'You should not have said that,' I said, hearing the breathlessness in my voice, and the longing.

'I know,' he admitted. 'It was improper of me. Immoral. Downright dastardly, even. But I could not stop myself, even if I had wanted to,' he added with a wicked grin that set my insides on fire.

'You must know, Charles, I never imagined . . . I know not

what I have done to deserve you, or your love, but you must know that I return it.' I looked at his strong hands enveloping my own and felt a pang of pain. 'I must tell you something, though. I have a hypothesis. One you may not agree with but that I believe to be true nonetheless.'

He waited for me to continue, allowing me the space to gather my thoughts and words. 'Your uncle's business – how much do you know of it?' I untangled my fingers from his and stood, walking over to the bookshelf. I knew that whatever he told me would be true. There was no need for me to read his expression. I did not think he'd want to be so close to me considering what I was about to say.

'Very little, I'm afraid. He keeps his business meetings and correspondence private, leaving me to run the estate and deal with the more menial tasks, no matter how much I offer to assist him.'

'Do you think it may be because he knows you would disapprove?'

He cleared his throat. 'He knows that I would disapprove if he was involved in something illegal, certainly. But why do you ask?'

I paused a moment, selecting my words carefully. If my suppositions were correct, Lord Blountford was involved in something very illegal indeed; an accusation that could not be made lightly.

'If I told you he owned at least one gambling house, and that he is secretive because he knows you would report him, would you believe me?' I traced a finger down some of the spines of the books, wiping my dusty hands on my riding clothes. The silence hung heavy between us as he pondered this information.

'I would believe you, of course,' he replied, sounding troubled, 'but I would ask how you came to this information before I acted upon it in any way.'

A very good question indeed. 'I heard it from the ghost of his first wife' did not have the credibility I was looking for, and he would likely retract any declaration of love if he thought I was insane. I chose a different approach.

'Did you know that his first wife's family owned one of the largest gambling houses in Venice?' I answered his question with one of my own.

'I did not. May I ask how you found that out?'

'Mistress Damiani is one of the longest-serving members of staff here; she came over from Italy when Marisa and your uncle married.' It wasn't a lie, but it wasn't an answer either, though I knew the way I had said it would lead him to believe it was. 'If you were to find indisputable evidence of his endeavours, what would you do?' I didn't want to bring Marisa's death into it without some shred of proof – something that wasn't a ghost's own testimony. Besides, there were still missing pieces of the puzzle that I needed to find. It was as though I could feel them almost fitting together, and yet not quite, not yet.

'It would put me in a very difficult position,' Charles replied, his voice sounding far off as though he were deep in thought. 'If what you say is certain, then I cannot agree with the methods my uncle chooses to make his money, and yet it is ultimately not my place to challenge him. Provided he is breaking no laws, he has every right to run a gambling house or gentlemen's club.' He was correct, of course, but it did not stop the disappointment that curled in my gut.

'From my experience, gambling houses and illegality go hand in hand,' I said as images of my father's beating flashed through my mind. Of Esme's stoic face as her harp was hauled away. Of my mother sobbing on the floor.

'But if you know all this already, then what of your hypothesis?'

'I believe that he knows you would close his business down should you inherit it and he die without a legitimate heir.' I turned to find him with his hands braced on the edge of the seat, his gaze somewhere else even as I spoke. 'I believe that this is why he won't include you in his affairs and won't even acknowledge you as a candidate. And I think it's why he is so desperate to marry again despite his terrible misfortune in trying to have a family.'

They were ugly words, but even Charles could see they rang true as I said them. His father had sent him here as his dying wish to help Lord Blountford, not to fall in love with his fiancée and turn against him. I knew that his honour would exceed his need to fulfil his obligations, but even so, I hated forcing him into such a situation.

He rose from the couch and came over to where I stood by the shelf, taking my hand again, a gesture that was becoming so welcome and familiar to me I wondered how I had lived without it before.

'We tread a dangerous line, Lizzie. If your claims are true, this could . . .' He hesitated, as though he feared putting words to his hopes. But there were unspoken promises in the silence.

'It could change everything for us.' I finished the sentence, giving our desires form. He nodded, squeezing my fingers lightly before his expression turned serious.

'I must think on everything you have said, and make my own investigations,' he said, letting my hand drop from his, and I suspected that he wanted to go back to the house without me.

'I would like to spend a little time here alone,' I replied, relieving him of the need to ask my permission to leave. It bothered me not, now that I knew my way, and it would give me an opportunity to ponder now that the truth between us had been laid bare.

'Very well. But Lizzie,' he added, turning as he reached the door, 'please know this: I promise I will not let you marry him, if that is what you desire.'

The light caught him once more and illuminated the tanned planes of his face. My heart pounded, and I nodded.

'There is only one person I wish to marry, Charles.' I gave him a desirous look that made him smile, and he bowed and left.

My eyes followed him all the way up the path until he was out of sight, then I let out a huff of air. His presence was comforting and intoxicating all at once, and I wished, not for the first time, that Esme were alive so that I could talk to her about it. I was sure she would like the young captain, and no doubt would have encouraged something between us if our circumstances had been different. If she was not a ghost and was in fact in heaven, where I had to believe ghosts went when they passed on, I hoped she could see me now. She would shake her head with a smile and chide me for getting into trouble again.

Wanting to clear my mind of Charles and Esme just for a few moments, I looked at the stacks of books littering the floor and toppling from the shelves. Keeping my hands busy would help distract me, I was sure, and I set to work organising them as best I could. There were novels, plays and sonnets, journals and almanacs – books to suit every taste that had perhaps been indulged in by the women who had lived here before me.

Once I had a hefty pile of volumes, I started to put them back on the shelves so as to clear the space, although I didn't try to alphabetise them. That could wait for another day. Works of fiction came first, followed by historical volumes, almanacs and a few other oddities: an atlas, a set of encyclopedias, and an obscure cookbook that I almost set aside to give to Mistress Damiani but thought better of in case she took it as some sort of slight on her cooking.

What I was looking for exactly I couldn't say. I had been nudged in the direction of the summer house both by Esme in her diary and Pansy when we first met. I looked up at the dark rafters, the cosy fireplace, the comfortable furniture. Whatever this place had meant to the lost wives, there must have been a reason why I was led here.

Perhaps some of the journals would provide me with answers, I thought, although once I started placing them on their own shelf near the bottom of the bookcase, it seemed that most were inscribed with the names of people who had died more than a century ago and who seemingly had no relationship to Lord Blountford.

Until I found Pansy's.

The back of the bookcase had a loose board, I noticed as I pushed a book to the back. On my hands and knees I cleared out the space and moved the board to the side to discover two matching notebooks in red leather, the pages yellowed with age.

The first was clearly Pansy's journal; I could tell that from the inscription in the front. The diary itself was filled with large, looping cursive that sometimes overlapped itself in places and was nearly illegible. Half of it appeared to be written in some form of code, with numbers and letters appearing at random mid sentence, mismatching pages stuffed in that were smaller than the rest. It was like looking at a pen-and-paper representation of her addled mind.

There was a sudden dampness in the air that signified the onset of rain, just as dark clouds began to sweep over the sky above the summer house. Regretting not having a fire lit, my fingers beginning to numb with the cold, I stuffed the first notebook in the pocket of my coat and flicked open the other one in case it were any more lucid. But instead of the pages of writing I had expected, the book had been hollowed out to hold a key.

It was similar in shape and design to the one that Esme had kept in her box. Did it fit the same lock? I wondered. As a feeling of unease grew within me, I squeezed the faux-book into my other pocket and quickly placed the last few volumes on the shelf.

My stomach growled and I realised it must be past noon, my belly yearning for a cup of tea and a loaf of Mistress Damiani's fresh bread. My mind conjured images of Charles sitting at the table, a knowing smile creeping across his lips as he tried to keep his thoughts private. I would have to school my features into nonchalance whenever he was near or we would run the risk of being caught. A thread of doubt weaved its way through my mind even as I thought of it. My father had been paid, his creditors satisfied, all for me to marry Lord Blountford. If we undid my part of the arrangement, what would that mean for my parents? I could not expect Charles to embroil himself in my family's messes. And then there was the embarrassment of my mother and father themselves. Would an ethical man such as Captain Blountford want to be married to the product of a gambler and an alcoholic? He must have known some of this, for he had accompanied his uncle when he came to collect me, but did he truly understand the scope of what he might be involving himself in?

I shook my head, realising I would have to tell Charles everything before he did anything he might regret. With my pockets laden with secrets that would have to wait, I trudged back to the house.

My clothes were muddy, and Marie, having returned from church, refused to let me eat before I had changed into something more suitable for the dinner table, despite my protests that I was already late for lunch. My stomach rumbled noisily as I gathered up the skirts of the green gown she had chosen and hurried down the hall, my slippered feet slowly thawing. The fabric turned from jade to peacock in the shafts of light from the windows, catching the shell buttons and gold thread as I walked. It was far too grand a dress to wear just for lunch, I thought, but Marie had insisted. Despite her mousiness, she could be as stubborn as an ox when she wished.

The dining room was empty, the large clock on the mantel indicating that I was an hour late. I had been out far longer than I had realised, but a steward attended to me and swiftly brought me a bowl of soup and a roll, which I ate gratefully.

Where was Lord Blountford? And Charles? The thought that he might have confronted his uncle curdled the food in my stomach and I tried to push it from my mind. He and I were not alike in that way. He would not act on impulse or throw unfounded accusations at his closest living relative, no matter what he felt for me.

When I finished my meal, I found myself torn between returning to my room to investigate Pansy's journal and the mysterious key, and searching for Charles. The decision was made for me when the steward removed my bowl and plate, informing me that Captain Blountford was reading in the drawing room and had requested I be informed after I had eaten.

I found him sitting with a book in his lap by the fireplace, deep in concentration. My heart stammered and I silently warned myself to behave as he glanced up, surprised into standing and giving me a brief bow.

'Lizzie, I didn't realise you were back already,' he said, offering me the armchair closest to the hearth.

'My hunger told me I'd overstayed.' I smiled.

'Do you need anything further? I shall call a maid to fetch you a platter.' He made to ring the bell, but I held out a hand.

'No need. Please, I am more than satisfied.'

He settled back into his chair, his book turned upside down on his knee to keep his page.

'Don't allow me to disturb you if you wish to continue reading.'

He looked down at the book as if he'd forgotten it was there. 'Not at all. Your company is far more invigorating than the musings of Plato.' He placed the book on a low table by his chair. 'I have been puzzling our . . . situation and thought perhaps that the Greek philosophers might be able to provide me with some guidance.'

'And have they?'

'Sadly not, but do not think I have been idle. I have sent a letter to an old comrade of mine who is a member of the Jockey Club in London. If anyone knows of my uncle's business ventures, should they be of the gambling nature, I believe he will have the answers we seek. Including,' he added, as he poured me a cup of tea from the tray that had been set beside him, 'whether any of those ventures are of the unsavoury type.'

'There are three days between now and Thursday. That leaves little time for anything to be done,' I replied, feeling deflated already.

'I trust the messenger implicitly – he'll ride through the night to reach my associate, who in turn will surely come to our aid,' Charles replied with barely concealed fervour.

'It is possible that none of that matters, I'm afraid.' I took the tea gratefully, savouring the heat from the cup as it seeped into my fingers.

'What do you mean?'

'I mean we both know that Lord Blountford paid my father a hefty sum to move me here in order to marry him. Money that would have paid off my father's ever-increasing debts, and that could not be recovered even if I were to break off our engagement.' My voice lowered to a whisper. Just as I had begun to imagine that I could marry Charles and be truly happy, weaving a story in my mind of how we could live here, in this house too big for the both of us – him used to cramped navy living, myself to a town house that could almost fit into Amble-tye's dining room – the reality of my predicament had come crashing down upon me. For what could I do? Tell Charles that some thirty-six years ago his uncle had pushed his wife from a balcony but the only witness was the woman's ghost? Explain that I believed there to be foul play in Pansy's and possibly my sister's deaths?

'Lizzie,' he said, the sadness in his voice almost too much to bear. 'You are a human being. I cannot abide the thought of you being bought.'

'But this is the way of it, Charles. He bought my sister, and once she was gone, he bought me as a replacement. I don't know how to say it, but I am sure to the very depths of my being that the deaths of his previous wives were open to question. No,' I added as he opened his mouth to argue, 'no, I can't explain how I know it, but please believe me when I say that despite the tragedy surrounding him, I don't believe he is entirely free of blame. And he will do everything in his power to keep you, and the rest of the world, from knowing it.'

I held his gaze unwaveringly and his mouth pressed into a thin line. I was certain it went against everything he believed in, taking me at my word when all I had was hunches and feelings, and yet he knew, as I did, that time was running out.

'The measure of a man is what he does with power,' he said, leaning back in the armchair and pinching the bridge of his nose.

'Pardon?'

He gestured to the book on the table. 'It was Plato's idea that a person's actions decided their character, and I fear that my uncle has abused the power he has gained in ways I have been blind to. We have but days left, and I must act quickly if we are to stop the wedding.'

'This is too dangerous a topic to be discussed under this roof,' I said, shifting a little closer to him, dropping my voice again. It was impossible to know who might be listening outside the door, and we had already said too much.

'You are right, of course.' He sighed and stared forlornly into the fireplace.

A laugh slipped from me for which I received a puzzled look in return.

'What is so amusing?'

'Oh, nothing. The impossibility of our circumstance, the cruelty of fate, the fact that you are so handsome when you brood.' I chuckled again despite myself.

'I will never tire of your forwardness,' he replied with a grin of his own. 'I do wonder how you and your sister managed to be such delightful and open-hearted women despite the misfortune of your upbringing.'

There were many things I wanted to say to that, but I bit down on the words as my mind caught on what he had said.

'You told me you had never met Esme.'

'I didn't, but from what little I know of her, I would say she was only half as courageous as you.'

I gave him a pleased hum of amusement. 'You've travelled the world and fought in wars, while Esme set off to create a life of her own, and did a very good job of it as I understand. I've been the victim of unhappy circumstance at every turn. I find it difficult to call myself courageous in front of you.' I pulled at a loose thread in the armrest as I spoke.

'Courage isn't just about fighting, or leaving home to make a new life,' he said softly, a glint of admiration in his eyes. 'It's also about facing your fears, which you have proven to me time and again that you are capable of doing.'

The corners of my mouth quirked upwards at that. I wanted to reach out to him, to have him gather me up in his arms, servants and consequences be damned, but his face grew contemplative.

'Lizzie, there is something else I must tell you—'

He was interrupted by Lord Blountford bursting through the door in an explosion of fury, his cane flailing wildly as he stalked towards us. We both leapt to our feet, and I tried to wipe the look of guilt from my face.

'What is this?' he demanded.

'I-I was having tea,' I stuttered, despite Charles's talk of me being brave and courageous.

'What are you doing trying to seduce my bride?' he spat at Charles, waving his cane at him emphatically.

'Uncle, please, I think this conversation is best had when you have calmed down,' Charles replied, his voice taking on that edge that I had only heard when he suppressed his anger.

'You, get out!' The earl gestured towards me. I frowned and clutched my fist to my chest, unable to quite believe he was speaking to me in such a manner.

'I will not,' I replied defiantly, which seemed to give both men pause. His lordship's surprise was quickly replaced by an angry scowl.

'GET OUT!'

His roar was so loud that I fancied the pictures shook in their frames. A peal of thunder rattled off in the distance and rain began to lash at the window panes, darkening the room around us. I should have been scared of this man I knew to be an accidental murderer, but instead I was furious. My fingers itched towards the knife below my skirts. I was tempted to pull it out and press it against his flabby neck, imagining how it would feel to have power over him, even if just for a second.

Charles sensed something in the way I stared at his uncle and gave a slight shake of his head. *Let me deal with this*, his eyes seemed to say.

Words ran through my head. Arguments as to why I should be allowed to defend myself and stand my ground. But I knew that anything I might say in Charles's defence would only anger the old man more.

'If you do not leave us this instant, Miss Dawson, I will confine you to your rooms until the wedding. Do not test me.' He narrowed his eyes, spittle gathering at the corner of his mouth as he hissed the words at me.

I swept past him with as much dignity I could muster, feeling like a child who had been sent to bed for misbehaving.

'She is not your possession.' I heard Charles sling the angry retort at Lord Blountford as the door closed behind me.

'I paid for her. She's as much mine as this house, the land and everything in it, you ungrateful wretch,' Lord Blountford replied at the top of his voice. A maid scurrying past flinched at the noise, whimpering even as she crossed me on the stairs.

My cheeks were heated with humiliation, and I was grateful that Marie wasn't in my rooms. I could feel the crackle of argument permeating the air around me, filling the house with unease.

If I were truly brave, as Charles seemed to think, I would stand my ground and tell Lord Blountford that I didn't want to marry him. I would tell him his dead wives haunted his house and they did not forgive him for what he had done. If I was brave, I would tell him I loved Charles.

But I wasn't, so I sat on my bed, clutching my knees to my chest, and waited.

*

An hour passed, but no one disturbed me.

I flipped through the pages of Pansy's journal and found that I understood but one or two words. The only thing I could make sense of was a seemingly obscure reference to *Gulliver's Travels*, a novel that I was sure I had seen on the summer house bookshelf. Frustrated, I flung the notebook on the bedside cabinet and examined the two keys. They were almost the same, one a smaller version of the other but the grooves and notches aligned in the same way.

I would take the keys and the journal to Price tomorrow to see if he could make any sense of them. If the lost wives truly had been his and Esme's hobby, perhaps he could work out Pansy's peculiar code. Maybe I could ride there with Jordie, or even Charles.

I imagined Gwen trotting alongside Hurricane and smiled, but it soon withered on my lips as I realised that the conversation – or argument – happening below me might mean my situation would change greatly overnight.

I wasn't sure what I expected. For Charles to come sweeping in and tell me that we had to leave? Or that he'd arranged everything with his uncle and we were to be allowed to stay and marry? I was not so naïve as to believe that that would happen, but what I certainly did not expect was Marie, fighting back tears, her hands shaking at her sides.

'I beg your pardon, m-miss, but I wondered if you would like me to prepare you for dinner,' she said, her eyes lined with silver in the dreary candlelight.

'Whatever is the matter?' I asked, leaping up from the bed just as her face crumpled and a small sob left her throat.

'P-please don't tell anyone, miss. I could lose my job,' she whispered as tears silently slid down her cheeks.

I pulled her towards me and wrapped my arms around her.

It was not proper. I was her mistress and she was a servant, but what did I care? Her small body fitted perfectly into my arms, and comforting her while she cried reminded me of how Esme used to do the same for me.

'I'm ruining your dress, miss,' she mumbled into my shoulder.

'Tsk, not at all, Marie. Now, tell me the cause of those tears,' I said, holding her at arm's length and looking into her blue eyes. My mind quickly imagined the worst scenario. Lord Blountford had lost his temper and harmed Charles fatally. Or had disowned him. Or any number of horrors that I couldn't bear.

'It's really not my place . . .'

'You know I won't get you into trouble, Marie. Please, just tell me that Captain Blountford is well.' I could hear the desperation creeping into my voice, which she must have noticed too, for she dipped a shaking hand into her apron and handed me a folded slip of paper. My name was hastily scrawled on the outside, the ink not fully dried when it had been given over to the messenger, for the dots of the i's were smudged.

I pulled away from Marie to read it, moving closer to the lamp by the bed.

My dear Lizzie,

There is much that I need to tell you, but my uncle has sent me away. Accused of trying to steal not only you, but also his livelihood and his fortune, I must work to clear these accusations, quickly. Believe me, I argued. He threatened my life should I stay, and when I told him that would not deter me, I was horrified to hear him threaten yours. You are too precious, too important to me to endanger, so I have had to leave for now, on the condition that he will not lay a finger on you. Please know that I

*will do everything I can to make this right. I made you a
promise I intend to keep.*

*And I beg you, Lizzie, stay out of trouble until I can
find you again.*

Truly yours,
Charles

'The captain gave you this?' I asked her, folding the letter into
the smallest square and clutching it in my palm, as though if I
held it tight enough I could make it disappear.

'He gave it to me directly, miss, but please don't tell anyone,'
she said, the tears starting anew. I thought of the family she
must be supporting with her work here. Of course I wasn't
going to tell anyone.

My mouth was dry, my heartbeat erratic as I thought of the
things Lord Blountford must have said to Charles. To accuse
him of stealing. The most honourable man I knew? I would
laugh if I weren't so sickened by the idea.

I sent Marie away to fetch water for a bath, wanting to be
alone again for as long as I could, but even in the silence my
thoughts were loud and messy. All I could think of as I stowed
his letter in Esme's box, as I undid the dress I had thought
Charles would admire, as I combed my fingers through my hair,
was what a terrible thing I had caused.

Chapter 14

ෙන ග

I spent most of Monday in my room, unwilling to even leave my bed until after lunch. I had read Charles's letter until I was sure I would wear his words from the paper with my constant staring at them. I sent word through Marie to Jordie that I wouldn't be taking my lesson and ignored the tray of food she brought up to me, feeling too tired and uncomfortable in my own skin. She was in and out of my room every half-hour or so, checking on me and clucking like a mother hen every time she saw that I hadn't moved.

'Are you unwell, miss? Have you a fever?' she asked worriedly, trying to press a hand to my forehead, which I batted away. When I didn't reply she asked, 'Shall I send for a doctor?'

'No,' I blurted, my voice cracking from disuse, 'no doctors. I'm fine, truly.'

Unconvinced, she let me be for another hour, promising to return closer to dinner time and asking me to try and eat.

It was a lie, of course. I was not fine and I wasn't certain that I would ever be again, but sitting about feeling sorry for myself didn't seem to be helping either. I rubbed the burning unshed tears from my eyes and picked at the food she had brought, deciding that if I could train my thoughts to avoid Charles and Lord Blountford, ghosts and my future, I could pretend everything would be all right.

'It is a little early for supper, miss, but if you like, we can bathe and dress you now ready for this evening's meal,' Marie offered on her next visit, sometime past four o'clock.

It was too miserable outside to take a turn in the garden. I glanced out of the window to find the sky turning the light purple of a bruised damson, the rain clouds bringing with them a darkness that would now settle for the remainder of the day. It was that cunning twilight of late September, which snuck upon you like a thief and stole the daylight away, and it would only get worse as the days grew shorter. Would I become a caged animal desperate to be let out, or lose my mind like Pansy had? How would I survive years and years of this? I wondered as I watched Marie fetch water for a bath and lay out yet another dress for me to wear. The peacock one was now stained with the unhappy memory of Lord Blountford shouting at me, of Charles's departure, of tears. If I never wore it again it would be too soon.

I allowed a string of pearls to be placed around my neck, complementing the deep wine and white brocade of the bodice. I even permitted Marie to fashion my hair with gold combs so that it didn't sway haphazardly around my face, but after that, I sent her away again. Dinner would not be for another hour, and I had finally tired of languishing in my room. I did not want to wander the house aimlessly. I didn't wish to storm into the earl's study brandishing my knife, telling him to take it all back. That would only confirm what he already believed to be true: that his nephew had tried to steal me away. It was, of course, nothing as deceitful as that and I believed that we had fallen in love entirely by accident, but saying so to Lord Blountford would only be digging myself a hole to lie down in. A dark part of me considered the other uses for the blade that I now wore on top of my skirts rather than concealed, but I dismissed those as folly. I was no murderer.

My fingers itched for something to do and I wondered, for the first time, why Ambletye didn't have a pianoforte. I wasn't sure how much it would cost to have our piano brought from London, but now that I had thought about it, I would enquire, or perhaps find out if there was a secret music room that I had yet to discover. I almost attempted to conjure Pansy, if only to have someone to speak to, before quickly pushing the idea from my mind. I had had enough of ghosts for a while.

It was that spiritless agitation, my need for something to do after the plethora of emotions I had experienced these past few days, that led me to another disastrous discovery.

I was sitting at the vanity, Esme's box open alongside her journal, Pansy's diary and the matching keys. As I undid the bundle of letters, tugging at the coarse string, I suddenly realised that the pile consisted of not one but three sets of correspondence, each separated with their own ribbon.

I frowned at not having noticed this before. There were the letters from Mother and myself, which I looked through. None of them said anything surprising, but I still found myself disturbed to read my own words of hopelessness and longing from all those months ago. My tone was a little accusatory even when I wished Esme well. *I hope you are enjoying the comforts of country life.* Even that simple phrase seemed insincere to me now, and I pondered whether my sister had smirked at it. *You say you have such big plans. I cannot wait for you to share them with me.* They were useless words, not intended to make her feel happy but rather to surreptitiously beg her to include me in her life.

Mother's letters were no better and were certainly more threatening than mine had been. *You must provide children for your husband, Esme. It is your duty as a wife. You are being a good wife, I hope. An exemplary one. Make us proud after everything we have gone through.* Never mind that Esme had only been here a few months when Mother wrote that. I imagined I would get a similar letter before too long.

Then there were the rest of Price's notes, which were mostly simple arrangements to meet or visit, some of them with the red 'lost wives' marker. One letter, though, intrigued me because it mentioned arsenic, strychnine and cyanide, the merits and disadvantages of each. I shivered at Price's casual use of words such as 'painless death' and 'untraceable', and wondered why Esme would take a sudden interest in poisons.

He wasn't the cause of my death. Pansy's words rang through my mind again. Was she poisoned? I decided I would speak to Price about this at the first opportunity, and set the letter aside as a place-marker in Pansy's convoluted diary.

The final pile of letters made my heart stutter. I would not have known at first glance who they were from if I had not just seen the handwriting, if I had not read a letter from the same sender so many times today that the style of it was etched into my mind.

Charles.

'Lady Blountford' was written in the same hasty way he had written my own name, the letters slanting to the right, the L looped at top and bottom in cursive script, an echo of the way he had written 'Lizzie'.

Filled with a sudden unease, I sifted through the letters. He had told me he hadn't met my sister. It wasn't a lie, but the hesitation I had noticed and dismissed was presumably down to their correspondence. There were seven or eight letters here, and so I had to assume she had replied to each of them. Uncertainty prickled at me as I held the small pile in my hands, the sheer number of letters alone somehow suspicious in itself. Sick anticipation filled my gut. Unable to bear it, I opened the topmost one and began to read.

Dear Esme,

I hope we are safe in our correspondence. I beg you to burn my letters once read so that no one may happen upon them. The damage they could do to both of us if found would be irreparable. I write in the hope that the fact of you being my step-aunt will make it acceptable for a young man such as myself to commune with you directly this way.

As to your proposal, it seems you are a lady who does not hesitate at speaking your mind, albeit eloquently, and for this I am grateful. I am far too used to direct orders to adequately skirt around common etiquette, I'm afraid. My simple answer is, of course, yes.

That you would consider me for such without yet knowing me truly fills me with indescribable joy.

I dare say you would make me the happiest man alive if your desire is genuine. I realise there is the matter of meeting face to face. For this I bring you news.

I am in the rather unhappy circumstance of being in medical recovery berthing, which is why your letter took so long to reach me. To spare you the very gruesome details, I took a large piece of wood in the abdomen and am lucky to be alive. My men even jest that when the French failed to kill me, one of their boats made an attempt, for it was a piece of deck that nearly took my life.

I will be shipped back to England, no doubt, by the summer, when we can make more formal plans and finally meet.

Then there is the matter of my uncle. You say that you have it all in hand and I trust that you do, but please, my lady, I pray you are being discreet. He is a force to be reckoned with, and although I have not seen him for many years, it is his manner and ire that has caused the rift in our family.

I thank you once again from the bottom of my heart.

Sincerely yours,
Charles

I dropped the letter on the vanity, reading and rereading the words until my eyes stung, pricked with the threat of angry tears. I knew I must have misunderstood. Charles hadn't travelled all the way back here for Esme, had he?

Hoping for a better explanation, I scooped up the second letter, and the third, all as cryptic as the first. I read another – the last before Esme's death, I noted from the date.

Dearest Esme,

Your letter comes like a ray of sunshine through a storm at sea. I have been troubled of late that your plan will miscarry, and I admit I have felt like a coward, unworthy of your trust in me.

No words do justice to the portrait you sent me. You are beautiful. If it is even a hint of a true likeness, I would consider myself the luckiest man alive. You suggest an autumn wedding. I am now in the process of being formally and honourably discharged due to the extent of my injury. You'll be pleased to hear that I have recovered well enough but I would no longer be expected to go into battle. I retain my title as captain and I shall wear it proudly for the rest of my days. Days spent by the side of a beautiful woman, if you should make me so lucky.

And so an autumn wedding is most agreeable, should the tides permit me to arrive back in England in the summer. That will give us time enough to meet and arrange things, I hope.

I thank you, Esme, and I count the days until I return to home shores.

Sincerely yours,
Charles

I slid from the chair to the floor and sat there for a long time, the letters spread around me like fallen flowers, or broken promises. The one in my hand that spoke of Esme and Charles's wedding was already stained with my tears, the ink running in dark rivulets down the page. So much planning and preparation, scheming and devising in a few hundred words. Perhaps Esme had wanted all along to marry into this home, only to replace her old husband with a more handsome younger man. Or maybe she had happened upon Charles's existence and had concocted her strategy only then. Price's mention of poisons took on an entirely new meaning and I wondered if my sister, unlike me, had been brave enough to take her fate into her own hands and attempt to control her future.

I had felt the cracks in my heart, fissures that had been closing slowly with time but never fully healed, soothed over by Charles's words of love yesterday morning. But now they split ferociously apart, the pieces scattered until all that was left was a yawning hole, a great chasm of emptiness.

I think I wailed, or at least released a muffled cry, as I picked up the letters and one by one fed them to the fire, as my sister should have done in the first place. All except the last one, which I held on to to serve as a reminder of my naïvety. My stupidity.

I watched the edges of each one brown and curl, the words turning to ash as I allowed my grief to harden into anger.

I had been too trusting, yes, but what had I really known about him? The captain sent on a fool's errand by his late father to claim the family estate. Perhaps it was he who had instigated the affair between himself and Esme, in an attempt to inherit Ambletye and his uncle's business.

I searched my memories for the conversations we had had, recalling his expressions, his guarded solemnity around his uncle. But then the recollection of him offering me his arm when we walked, of gifting me the knife, of the intensity in his green eyes when he looked at me hurt too much to bear and I cast those thoughts away. I had been foolish indeed. So desperately in need of someone's love and attention that I had mistakenly believed every word he said. As I returned the remaining letter to Esme's box and tucked the rest of her memories away – her journal, the key – I also closed up a part of me, willing myself to face my fate. A new reality that was in fact old and completely unchanged, as if Charles had never been here.

I was to marry Lord Blountford in three days. I would be lady of the manor and would have to face bearing the old man's children.

Oh, how a few words on a piece of parchment could change one's feelings, as though it were as simple as the flip of a coin.

Marie called me for dinner and I walked to the dining hall alone, feeling like a spectre of myself when I found Lord Blountford there. I knew immediately that he was drunk. Perhaps he had not stopped drinking since yesterday – I hadn't left my room for almost twenty-four hours, and judging by the empty bottles at his elbow, he had kept himself occupied in my absence.

I wished I could make my excuses and leave, but he thumped the table loudly when I entered, making the cutlery rattle, insisting that I sit beside him. 'Future wife! Sit! Eat! Let us celebrate the removal of a scoundrel and cad from our midst,' he slurred as I seated myself. If he saw the knife at my side, he said nothing.

I ate in silence, ignoring the great slurps of wine he took between every mouthful, hoping I wasn't marrying a drunkard like my mother as well as a lover of gambling like my father.

'Where have you been? I've not seen you at all . . . today,' he said, as though he'd forgotten the word.

Steeling myself for conversation, I rolled my shoulders back and raised my head to look at him. He was a sorry sight to behold. 'I was not feeling myself so I decided to keep to my rooms,' I replied, repeating myself when his eyes became unfocused and I realised he hadn't heard me.

'You don't have some ague, do you?' His eyes drooped as he spoke, every other word obscured by lips that wouldn't obey him.

'Not at all, sir. I am quite well now. In fact I intend to visit Dr Price tomorrow, if you don't require me?'

'Of course, of course,' he said, realising that his glass was empty and motioning a steward to refill it. 'Just arrange a carriage with . . . Turner.' He stumbled as he tried to recall his manservant's name.

'Thank you, sir, but there will be no need. I shall ask Jordie to ride there and back with me. I believe I would benefit from the practice,' I said, hoping I could convince Jordie to agree to the idea. I wouldn't be able to handle Gwen on my own, but with his company and instruction I was certain I would be all right. It would do me good to get outside and be joined by a friendly face if nothing else.

'Excellent. Most agreeable,' he said. 'Your lessons must be progressing well for you to have such confidence,' he added.

'Indeed, sir, Jordie is a remarkable teacher. I have come along much quicker than I could have hoped under his tutelage.' I poked at my pigeon pie a little despondently, hoping that my progress with Jordie wouldn't encourage Lord Blountford to stop my lessons.

'You sound sad, Miss Dawson.' He grasped my hand suddenly, his lichen-green eyes becoming momentarily lucid. I looked up from his papery fingers clutching mine to see genuine concern. It was unsettling, and so unlike him to take my feelings into consideration that I said nothing. 'Are you not happy that the young rogue who tried to seduce you has left? Glad you can live your life free of him as I am, without him forever breathing down my neck?'

The smell of wine on his breath made me gag, and I leaned away from him while keeping my hand in his grip. He certainly seemed happier without Charles here, and I wasn't ready to share my sentiments yet, no matter what I had discovered about him and Esme.

'I do not yet know my feelings, sir, so I shall refrain from comment,' I replied tartly, and he slackened his hold, temporarily disappointed that I did not share his relief at Charles's leaving. 'But I am glad that the path ahead of us is clear,' I added, and he looked up sluggishly, swaying in his seat. 'Save for one delicate matter that we shall need to face before the wedding.'

'Oh yes, your dress. Well, perhaps you can visit the dressmaker in the village tomorrow, tell her to send me a bill.' He waved a hand and took another swig of wine. I pushed my own full glass as far away from me as possible, the scent of fermented grapes dizzyingly strong.

'No, not that . . .'

'Ah, your allowance. Well, you may send expenses to me through Turner should you desire anything, but if you require items from further afield, you will need to tell him before ordering,' he prattled on.

'No, Lord Blountford, that is not what I meant, although I appreciate the sentiment indeed and may ask for my pianoforte to be shipped from London if that is agreeable to you,' I said hurriedly.

'But we have a perfectly good pianoforte in the music room.' He looked befuddled. 'It might require tuning, but I can send for a man . . .'

'What I meant, Lord Blountford, was the delicate matter of your previous wives.'

He seemed to be confused, his eyes focusing on me and then somewhere else as he wrestled with my words. 'Well, I don't see what they have to do with our wedding or our future. What on earth could be so pressing that we must deal with it right away?' he spluttered indignantly.

'Well, the fact that two of them appear to be haunting your house.'

He had taken it rather well, I thought after dinner as I ascended the stairs to find the music room. Out of tune or no, I was going to play the piano tonight if it were the last thing I did.

Lord Blountford had blinked at me several times before shaking his head. I had repeated myself, noticing the steward shifting uncomfortably. His lordship had asked if I was a witch, and I told him that I most certainly was not. He dismissed my words as insanity then, and I told him I was not insane either. And then I whispered something to him that only he or his late wife would know, and watched as realisation dawned on him.

'Pansy refers to you as "Eggy",' I had murmured so that no one else could hear. I didn't want to confront him with Marisa's truth, not while he was drunk, but those few words were enough to have him almost leap from his chair in surprise. He had snatched the wine bottle from the steward and left, staggering on his way out and leaving me in peace.

It was peculiar to have a music room located so far from the common areas of the house, I was sure. Most hosts would have positioned it in pride of place so as to entertain guests or show off the household's many talents, but Blountford had relegated it to a far corner of the east wing. The instruments were draped in white sheets, like wraiths languishing around the room, illuminated only by the candle that I had brought with me.

I made straight for the pianoforte and felt something heavy in my chest lift at the sight of its polished dark wood. Yes, it was indeed out of tune, I noted as I pressed delicately on the keys, and certainly it did not have the vibrancy of our old upright, but it was also beautiful. The room, despite its dust sheets, had not been neglected. As I lit the fresh candles in the sconces and removed the coverings from other instruments, I could see that someone took the time to clean the room and keep it aired. There were chairs arranged for an audience, a stocked fireplace, a violin and a harp. The latter gave me pause. I wondered if Esme had played it, and marked how similar it was to the one she used to have at home. Perhaps she had even imagined me sitting accompanying her.

I placed my candle on the mantelpiece, not bothering to light the fire, and sat down to begin. The occasional harsh twang came from the strings as the hammers beneath the lid struck home, yet the action of pressing the keys soothed me, enveloping me in pieces that were as familiar to me as my own name, as the lines on my palms.

I played every piece I could recall from memory, and then discovered more stowed in a cupboard beneath the windowsill and tried to play those as well, allowing the imperfect music to ease my mind by forcing me to concentrate on something outside my own thoughts.

Tomorrow I would show Lord Blountford where Marisa had fallen. Tomorrow I would ride to Price's and uncover Pansy's mystery. Tomorrow I would try to forget about Charles entirely.

But today . . . today I would play.

Chapter 15

ଚ୍ଚ ୯

It is a peculiar thing to wake up after a night of storm, wind and rain to see the sun shining through one's window, illuminating droplets on the panes like thousands of tiny crystals, and feel nothing. I derived no pleasure from the birds chirruping happily outside or the stirring sounds of the household being readied for a new day. I had lain for as long as I could, almost marvelling at the emptiness inside me. One becomes accustomed to the feeling of being wholly alone, I suppose, when one is so used to losing people.

Even now, as I walked with Lord Blountford around the estate, him grumbling at the soreness in his legs as he wobbled on his cane, I remained silent, with only the sound of my feet crunching in the wet gravel to signify I was there at all.

'What in the name of the Lord has you dragging me out here before breakfast, Miss Dawson?' he demanded, not for the first time, as we ambled down the pathway.

'I told you last night, sir, that I wanted us to resolve certain things before we married. This is one of them,' I said simply.

I wasn't entirely certain of what I was doing, but I was fed up, absolutely finished with having men dictate my actions and moods. I had realised as I played the pianoforte to the sound of the storm raging outside the window that I could not control

my fate at this moment, but that I had to do something in orde
not to feel utterly helpless. So that was what I did now as
guided Lord Blountford around the corner and stopped short a
the rose bushes.

'Why are we here?' he asked suspiciously.

'Because I would like you to speak to Marisa,' I replie
looking around for her and hoping that she would manifest.
knew he wouldn't be able to see her. That was not the point i
this exercise.

'Oh dear God, no. I thought I had dreamt it, or that you ha
been jesting,' he said, stumbling back a step.

'I confess that I rarely jest, sir. I want only to help her, an
you,' I said quietly but firmly. 'Humour me in this if you wil
for it can do no harm if we stay here for just a minute or two.'

He sighed through his nose, making a loud whistling soun
that I was sure I would grow to hate, but then stepped forwar
so that we stood in just the place I had been when Marisa ha
last shown herself to me.

And what now? Well, I did the only thing I could think o
that might bring us some form of closure. I made him talk.

'Tell me what happened the night of your argument, sir.'
kept my voice soft and unthreatening. I was prepared if h
lashed out in anger. My knife was visible at my hip and I wa
grateful that I hadn't tossed it out into the night as I had though
to do more than once. It was my knife. I had chosen it, regard
less of who had given it to me.

'How could you possibly know about that?'

'Marisa told me. As I said, humour me. What happened tha
night? You argued about your business, about the gamblin
house, yes?'

Lord Blountford looked at me as though I had sprung a secon
head, but I kept my gaze unwavering, my body completely still s

as not to betray the nerves I felt. There was every chance he would walk away or lash out with the cane that he clutched in his arthritic fingers, but to my surprise, he gave another one of his long sighs and spoke.

'Why must we drag up the past?'

'Because, Lord Blountford, the ghosts are as much in your head as they are in this house. You need to move on, and so do they. It is for the good of everyone,' I said firmly. 'So tell me how it began.'

'She was angry,' he started, his voice little more than a murmur. 'So angry. She would have these fits of rage where I would be unable to console her. She was so beautiful when she was outraged. I once made a comment that we had broken more crockery than the kitchen when we fought. I was being facetious, of course, but she took it as an excuse to throw her teacup at me.' He gave a sad smile.

'But you loved her,' I said gently.

'More than anything in the world. She was difficult, but who is not? No single person is uncomplicated or unemotional. I constantly defended my decisions to her, which only angered her more. We had met through her father while I spent time in Italy and I knew she despised me for bringing his business over here. That night I had wanted to celebrate the acquisition of my newest premises, but rather than rejoice, Marisa was irate.'

'We fought for what felt like an hour,' a voice came from beside us, and I stiffened.

Blountford must have noticed it, as he paused and followed my line of sight. Marisa stood there, as beautiful and fierce as ever, her dress only slightly torn from the fall, her face unmarred as yet. He couldn't see her, I could tell, but my reaction alone must have indicated what had occurred.

'Is she here?' he asked with something like awe in his voice. I nodded once. 'May I speak with her?'

I looked at him, at the mixture of joy and fear on his lined face, and took his hand, squeezing it once in confirmation.

'Edgar, you look a million years old,' Marisa said in surprise, and I relayed her words. He gave a melancholic chuckle.

'I feel at least that old,' he said to the space I gestured to, sheepishly at first.

'I fell such a long way. Why has it taken you so long to help me?'

She pouted as I told him what she had said, looking all the more alluring for it.

'I am so sorry, my love. I didn't know you were still here. I have missed you so much.' His voice broke as emotions suppressed for decades came flooding back. 'I never meant to push you. I have regretted that moment every minute of my long, tortured life. I sometimes think that God has been punishing me for my actions that night ever since.'

My eyes stung at the guilt in his voice that he had been carrying for so long. Certainly in his position I would think it was a punishment to lose three more wives and a child. What he had done was unspeakable. Unforgivable. And yet I knew what I had to do to help them both. Perhaps this was why fate had led me to Ambletye in the first place.

'It was my fault too, Edgar. I wanted to hurt you, and you turned my own fury on me,' Marisa said, the blood from her injuries beginning to show as we stood there. 'I allowed you to push me. I realise that now.' She gave a gentle huff of a laugh as crimson ran from one of her ears and her nose. 'I think in fact I wanted to fall, just so that you would feel horribly guilty.'

Somehow as I pictured that night – the two of them arguing, Marisa falling – I could see it was true. How often did people make sure that the damage done to them was truly awful, just to make another feel bad?

'You are so calm, my love,' Edgar said when I relayed her words. 'Please, Marisa, will you ever forgive me?'

'I have had enough time to think on that night to know that it was an accident. I have waited so long for you to come to me, for us to be together again, but now that I see you, I know . . . I am not really here, am I?'

I didn't reply to her. I felt it wasn't my place – in this conversation I was the messenger, the conduit, and not a participant. Pansy's words from just a few days before, which may as well have been a lifetime ago, came back to me. *Lies keep us here.*

Edgar shook his head when I repeated Marisa's question.

'You have been gone some years now, my dear. But I keep you in my heart always.' He clasped a fist to his chest as the other rested on his cane, which wobbled with the strain of standing for so long.

'Then I forgive you, Edgar. I forgive you, and I will wait for the day that we meet again. I am very tired now and feel quite faint.'

The image of Marisa receded as I conveyed her final words. Edgar reached out a hand into the space where she stood and brushed his fingers against her fading face. I didn't know if he felt the cold caress of her skin, but he stared at the spot for a long time.

The wind picked up around us, causing the trees and rose bushes to sway, blowing at our coats and my skirts, and when it was gone, so was she.

Lord Blountford, or Edgar as I began to think of him more and more, was grief-weary when we left the rose garden, but I sensed a peace in him that I didn't wish to disturb. We did not speak at all, even when he parted from me at the bottom of the stairs, presumably to go and lie down or work. I bundled up Pansy's diary and Price's cryptic poison letter in my coat pocket and went straight to the stables to saddle up Gwen, telling Jordie of my plan.

'Are you sure you're ready?' he asked as I retrieved my saddle. 'It's quite a leap from a gentle trot around the courtyard.'

'I need to get away,' I offered by way of an explanation, 'just until the afternoon. I wouldn't ask if it wasn't important.'

He raised a sceptical eyebrow before finally nodding an agreement, saying, 'All right, but I'll be leading you the entire time, and if it gets too much at any point, you just say the word.'

Once I had agreed and he had helped me saddle Gwen, he brought another horse out of the stable: a white mare named Cowslip for her white dappled coat, grey speckles gathered like the tiny wild flowers on her back.

I volunteered little conversation as we rode, trying to memorise the route while Jordie happily chattered of his brothers, his mother and his aspirations as a great horse breeder. It was a comfortable sort of talk that I could easily listen to without reminders of how I felt inside. Even with the satisfaction of healing a little of Edgar's past and hopefully sending Marisa onwards, I struggled to ignore the ache in my chest. So Jordie's gossip about his brother's work on the farm and what breeds of horse he preferred was a welcome distraction.

I was not a graceful rider, although to be fair to myself it was my first true ride beyond the stable courtyard. My hips and thighs ached after only a mile, and I wasn't sure how I would walk straight when I did finally dismount.

Jordie knew the way to Price's, having fetched him for help with a sick foal or a lame horse once or twice, but when we finally arrived, he remained outside, leading Gwen and Cowslip to a water trough in the yard.

'It's not my place inside the house, Lizzie,' he said with an easy smile that was neither offended nor embarrassed.

'I'm sure the doctor wouldn't mind if you came in for some tea, Jordie,' I replied, frowning.

'Don't worry about me – I belong outside in the sunshine with the horses.'

Unable to convince him otherwise, I walked unsteadily across the lawn, my legs protesting at the movement, and knocked on the cottage door, hoping that my surprise visit wouldn't inconvenience anyone.

Judith opened it moments later and broke into a smile. My last visit had apparently eased her troubled regard of me somewhat.

'Judith, I'm sorry to trespass upon you unannounced, but would the doctor be in?'

'Oh yes, Miss Dawson. I shall announce you at once,' she said. I noticed her glance down the path as if she were expecting someone else, and my stomach dropped a little when I realised that it might have been the captain. I pressed my lips into a tight line as she ushered me into the familiarly worn sitting room, where Price found me moments later, examining his bookshelves once again.

'Lizzie!' he exclaimed as he pulled me into a light embrace. 'I did not expect to see you so soon, but I am glad you have come. Would you like some tea? Or breakfast?' he added, looking at the clock on the mantel. It was a little late for breakfast and early for lunch, but I settled for tea all the same and made myself comfortable on the shabby sofa as he took up his spot in the armchair.

'No Captain Blountford to accompany you today? I noted that young Jordie Blake escorted you this time.' He nodded out of the window at Jordie, who was brushing down the horses and speaking to the geese waddling around the yard in that easy way of his.

185

'I am afraid the captain has been dismissed from his duties at Ambletye rather suddenly,' was all I said, not wanting to speak of him for longer than necessary. Price seemed to read more in those few words than their simple meaning as he appraised me with a keen eye.

'I am sorry to hear that,' he said simply, before clasping his hands on his lap and brushing past the topic tactfully. 'So, to what do I owe this absolute pleasure, my dear?'

'I'm here on business, I'm afraid. Lost wives' business,' I added. The term that he had shared with Esme was becoming my reference to the ladies in question too. 'I was hoping you might be able to assist me with a little code-cracking.'

I pulled out Pansy's journal and handed it to him. 'I found this in the summer house on the Ambletye estate, along with a hollowed-out book that contained a key. It was hidden behind a loose board in the bookcase, and I assume it was put there by the lady herself before she died.'

As Price thumbed through it interestedly, his own letter slipped out. I picked it up from the floor and placed it on the table between us.

'I also wanted to ask about this,' I nudged a corner of the paper, 'and why my sister might have been enquiring about poisons.'

Price raised a bushy eyebrow and picked up the letter, peering at it through the reading spectacles balanced on the end of his nose.

'You have been busy in the last day or so.' He sounded quite impressed as he placed the letter back down and resumed studying Pansy's diary. 'Perhaps we should tackle one problem at a time, eh?'

I nodded as Judith brought in the tea things – a slightly more worn set – and some freshly baked bread, a creamy pat of butter and a jar of thick, light honey. My stomach grumbled at the sight of it and I helped myself at Price's insistence.

'The letter is a tricky one. Your sister mentioned that she had found some poisons somewhere on the property and asked me what they would be used for. At the time, I too wondered why anyone would have them outside an apothecary or chemist's laboratory, but when I enquired further, she said she had not located them within the house itself, but in a cabin in the woods. I did not hear any more of it after that, I'm afraid,' he said, taking a sip of his tea.

I pondered on this for a few moments as the warm bread and honey melted on my tongue. Were the keys in Esme's box and Pansy's book something to do with this cabin, perhaps?

'And the diary? Do you understand any of it?'

'Well, it seems to me that it is written in English, perhaps Gaelic and occasionally French, which luckily I understand, as well as a form of code . . .' He trailed off, balancing the book on his knee as he used his free hand to pop a crust into his mouth, chewing it thoughtfully. I hadn't known Pansy spoke French, or Gaelic, but then I supposed I didn't know much about her beyond the fact that she had lived and died at Ambletye when I was still a child.

'I noticed a reference to *Gulliver's Travels* in there. What do you think that might be about?'

When he came to whatever conclusion it was that he had reached, he raised his eyebrows and his eyes went wide, reminding me a little of a surprised owl. 'Ah, I think I have it. *Gulliver's Travels* is the book we need to solve this particular riddle!'

I slumped in my seat. I was sure I had seen a copy of it in the summer house but hadn't thought to bring it.

Price set the journal down and darted over to the shelf on the left of the fireplace. 'I am certain I have an edition of it here.

It may not be the same one she used, of course, but we can at least see if my theory is correct.'

I felt a little thrill of excitement as he brought both books over to the table and pushed the tea tray out of the way to make room. He then fetched some paper, pen and ink from his bureau to make notes. 'Perhaps you can be my assistant, dear Lizzie,' he said, and I nodded, taking up the novel while he opened the first coded page of Pansy's journal.

'I recall purchasing this edition from Mr Grahame some years ago, so there is every chance that our dear Lady Pansy owned the same one. All right, you see these page numbers, yes?' I nodded as I looked to where he pointed. 'Well, they are a little unusual in their sequence and placement, and there are odd superscripts interspersed with the writing. It is a simple method to hide a message, but it may well be the one we seek. Let us see if this is the sequence in which the code works, shall we? Page twenty-four . . . line seven . . . word three,' Price instructed, and I found the relevant word in the pages I held.

'"My",' I read aloud.

'Page seventy-six, line ten, word six,' he called out.

It took me a while to find it. '"World",' I replied, and he noted it on the blank paper.

We worked this way for ten minutes or so before he read out what we had translated.

'"My world is torn and my heart feels that it belongs only to him."'

I frowned. Could that be right? We attempted another passage from the diary.

'"It can only be right, and yet I am certain that I shall be sent to hell for my deed",' Price read from across the table. 'It all sounds very suspicious, does it not?'

'What do you think she did?' I asked, thinking of Pansy's

threats when I saw her last. *If you don't produce an heir, you'll die just like we did.* I suppressed a shudder at the reminder of the encounter.

'Something rather untoward by the sounds of it. Shall we continue, or would you prefer to borrow my copy and complete it yourself?'

'Oh no. If you wouldn't mind, I would be most grateful for your help, and your company,' I added with a timid smile. Price felt to me like the kindly uncle I had never had. Comfortable and unassuming, with that magical quality of being able to make one feel entirely at home.

'It would be my pleasure. I have only one call to make, a little later this afternoon, but perhaps most of our work will be done by then,' he said, picking up the journal and finding another passage to decipher.

We worked for an hour, Price adding French translations where necessary alongside our solved code. What we found astonished us both.

My world is torn and my heart feels that it belongs only to him. It can only be right, and yet I am certain that I shall be sent to hell for my deed. For my plans. We met today in the woods as we so often do, hidden from sight by all but the animals, who knew well of what ensued, and God, whom I must pray will forgive me for my sins. I have begged the earl that I might be with child. This will be enough to secure my position at the manor when Eggy is gone. No one shall turn the heir to Ambletye out on their ear.

For I love him, my darling Jo. His brown eyes like ripe chestnuts, the muscles that hide beneath his clothes, his skin that darkens so quickly in the sun.

Never mind my husband, who spends more time with his money than he does with me. He does not notice when I am gone for an hour or two, or when I return wild and dirty. And happy. For my Jo makes me happier than anyone ever has.

The maids call me 'lady'. I am anything but. And yet that is what I must be, for our plan to work.

This was what Pansy had been concealing? An affair? I gave a loud and disapproving huff as I read it. The sentiments were far too close to those of Esme and Charles's letters. Had Pansy intended to murder Edgar so that she could instead marry Jo, whomever he might be?

My mind spun and I leaned into Price's settee, pressing my pulsing head against the backrest. The headache had come on suddenly, along with the unwanted desire to cry again.

'Are you all right, Lizzie? You look rather pale,' Price asked, before shouting, 'Judith!' at the top of his lungs so that I jumped.

Judith bustled in as I tried to explain that I was fine, but was I really? Everything about this situation was too familiar and too painful. What Pansy had written stank like the disgusting plans Esme had been hatching.

'Shall I fetch the smelling salts, Doctor?'

'A marvellous idea, Judith.'

'I don't need smelling salts,' I protested.

'Some more tea then? Or perhaps something stronger?' Judith chimed in.

'All of the above, Judith, please,' Price ordered, and the house-keeper scuttled out, tripping on the loose carpet and shrieking as she stumbled into the corridor outside. 'Be careful!' Price added unnecessarily.

'I'm fine, really,' I said again, but he was already rummaging around in his drawer for something to give me.

'I don't suppose a horse tranquilliser would be of interest to you?'

'Price, please!' I said, standing up and sending another throb of pain through my temples. 'I do not want medicine, or smelling salts, or tea. I am merely alarmed to learn that Lord Blountford had such a number of plots contrived against him by his wives. I am overwhelmed by the similarities between Pansy's private thoughts and my own sister's intentions.' I knew my voice was rising now, so that possibly even Jordie could hear me from outside the house, but I didn't care. If I didn't scream, then I would cry, and I did not want to do that.

'I am disturbed by my own poor judgement and inability to see when someone is deceiving me for all I am worth, and no doubt laughing behind my back as they do so. And above all, I am tired. I am so very tired of the secrets and lies. I worry they will be the death of me, as they were my sister and Pansy.' I flopped back down on the sofa, my anger spent. It seemed the whole world had stopped and held its breath for my monologue. Even the birds and the geese outside had grown quiet.

Judith, unable to sense when the moment was right, came in with a tray bearing whisky, a vial of salts and another pot of tea along with hastily prepared sandwiches.

'Well,' Price muttered, sitting back down across from me and leaning forward so that his elbows rested on his knees, 'it seems to me that you have had quite a revelation since I last saw you, and I perhaps misjudged your reserved manner as something else. I apologise for not being astute enough to notice your distress, Lizzie.'

'No, I am sorry,' I said, feeling a fool. 'That outburst was quite improper of me, for neither of you is to blame for my anger.'

'I assure you, in my many years in this profession, I have seen far worse. I wouldn't even consider that a real outburst, would you, Judith?'

'Oh no, Doctor. Perhaps a minor frenzy, but certainly not an outburst,' Judith said kindly, nudging the plate of sandwiches towards me. 'Nothing that can't be sorted by something to eat and a cup of tea,' she added with a smile.

'If only all of the problems of the world could be remedied with a pot of your tea, Judith,' I said, gratefully taking a sandwich from the plate.

'I do not expect you to tell me anything at all, Lizzie,' said Price, 'but if you wish to talk, I am more than happy to be an impartial ear.'

I wanted to. Was desperate to, in fact, but I did not wish to mar my sister's memory in his eyes. They had been close friends, after all, and it seemed unfair to speak ill of her, no matter how much her actions had unwittingly hurt me. After all, she wasn't to know I would fall in love with Charles, or that I would end up living at Ambletye, engaged to her husband. Whatever her plans had entailed, I knew that her intention had never been to cause me distress. She had always had my best interests at heart.

When she had used her wiles and charm at the tea house to get us lunch. When she had insisted I accompany her to any party she was invited to. When she refrained from complaining if I caught her hair in a tangle while brushing it, or misplayed a note during a duet. When she had sacrificed her future to pay Father's debts so that we might never be tormented by another bailiff.

I had that sudden and catastrophic feeling of the ground opening before me, as though I had forgotten all over again how to live in a world where she no longer existed.

Price took my silence to mean that I would not, or could not, divulge what had led to my sudden tantrum, and instead pointed out of the window at Jordie, who was gratefully accepting his own lunch from Judith: an apple, a slice of bread and some hard cheese along with a jug of ale.

'He's a good lad, that Jordie,' he said as though nothing had happened before. 'I knew his father well, the poor soul.'

'He has a remarkably old mind for someone so young,' I replied, grateful for the change in subject. 'Although I've only known him a few days, I already consider him a friend as well as my riding instructor.'

Price nodded amiably. 'I think his wisdom comes from having so many younger siblings. Alongside his older brother he's become very much the man of the house. When his mother called for me to attend to their ailing donkey in the summer, she told me so herself.'

I thought of Jordie in a cottage filled with younger brothers. I could imagine that his easy attitude and calm demeanour around small children would do as much good as it did around the horses.

'I will miss him if he leaves,' I said, thinking of his dreams of becoming a breeder and wondering if the money he would receive for my riding lessons would be enough to start him off. Of course, I had no idea how much a horse cost, but no doubt it would be more than a year of a stable hand's wages.

'Why would he leave such a good employer?' Price asked.

'A number of reasons that I can think of. Perhaps he might wish to marry.' I thought of Marie's blushes whenever he spoke to her. 'Or run his own stables, as he has often mentioned.'

193

'I think it will be a number of years before that might happen, if at all.'

'Why so?'

'Well, unfortunately those born without a fortune rarely succeed on goodwill and charm alone. I know from what your sister told me that you don't come from an aristocratic household, but individuals born into servitude are unlikely to make enough to leave their employers. Particularly with all those mouths he has to feed already.'

It seemed wrong, somehow, for bright, intelligent Jordie to be stuck working as a stable boy just so that he could support his own family. Certainly the other boys would grow and begin to work and bring money in themselves, but I realised I had no idea how much a servant's salary was. That Jordie might never achieve his dreams saddened me, and I resolved to change his fate if I possibly could.

'Lizzie,' Price turned back to me, his tone gentle and serious, 'it is perfectly acceptable to be angry and upset. I only want you to know that because our society prides itself on keeping up appearances. One might imagine it is not respectable to have emotions, or to feel deeply as we humans do. You must know that here, in this house, you can be whatever you wish to be. Whatever emotion, whatever desire or notion you have, I will not judge you for it. And neither, might I add, will Judith, despite her outwardly disapproving disposition.' He smiled to take the seriousness from his voice. He and I both knew that he jested, and that Judith had a lamb's temperament.

I took a deep breath and exhaled between pursed lips. 'I feel like I will never stop thanking you, Price.'

He nodded in acquiescence and sipped his tea.

Unable to face translating any more of Pansy's journal, I

took my leave of Price, slipping both his translations and his original letter to Esme within the folds of the journal.

He showed me out to my horse, where Judith was chatting away happily to Jordie, and I embraced them both again in thanks for their hospitality.

'There you go, miss, we got some colour back in your cheeks, I'm glad to see,' Judith said as she popped a spare apple and a small cask of her home-made cider into Jordie's saddlebag.

'You do look better, Lizzie, even since this morning when we set off,' Jordie said, glancing at me from atop his horse as we rode down the lane at a gentle walk.

'I find that in the company of certain people I am able to be wholly myself,' I told him. 'I thought . . . I thought I had found someone I could share that feeling with, but I was mistaken, and it tore me apart a little. But I think I know who my true friends are now,' I added, and he returned my smile.

I asked him if I could stop in the village before going home, and he was happy to oblige. Remembering Lord Blountford's instruction to send my bills to Ambletye for Turner to take care of, I bought paper, pen and ink from Mr Grahame. I stopped briefly at the linen draper, who also served as the local seam-stress, to ask if she had a hat or shawl that might be appropriate for the wedding, so that even if I were to use Esme's dress, which now did not seem such an unwelcome thing, I had some-thing of my own too. She was more than happy to assist 'the new lady of the manor' and found the most exquisite shawl, which she had apparently been saving for such a moment as this. It was trimmed with lace and dyed a soft pink, which she insisted brought out my colouring perfectly.

As she wrapped it, I glanced across the cobbled street to the bakery, and that faint pang of heartache tugged at me again.

Was it only three mornings ago that I had stood there with Charles and wiped the sugar from his face?

'Are you all right, miss?' the seamstress asked as she handed me my parcel.

No, not yet. But I will be.

I didn't reply, but simply smiled and bobbed her a curtsey.

Laden with our wares, and knowing that I would have to face the house and Lord Blountford once again but unable to dally any longer, we made our way slowly home.

Chapter 16

ೞ ೦೩

The sky was the light blue of borage heads and cornflowers as we rode back to Ambletye. Although it was not yet October, the days were beginning to shorten incrementally, and in a matter of weeks the daylight would begin to steal itself away – a reminder that winter would be on its way soon enough.

When we finally arrived, Jordie told me it was just before three o'clock by his reckoning. My legs were chafed from the saddle, my thighs aching in places I didn't know I had, and I stumbled as I dismounted. A servant came out to meet us, expecting no doubt for me to foist Gwen off onto him, but instead I asked him to take my purchases into the house while I tended to her myself.

I helped Jordie remove her tack and brush her down, tasks that just days ago would have been impossible for me but that I now found myself enjoying. It wasn't my place as a future lady of the manor to be doing any such thing, I knew that, but anything that kept my hands busy was a welcome distraction from my thoughts.

When I had done all I could manage, I glanced towards the house, torn between heading back inside to clean up and face my future husband or staying away for as long as I could. Thinking about the edition of *Gulliver's Travels* that I was sure I had put away on the shelf in the summer house, I left Jordie to it and retraced my steps from two mornings ago.

The place was just as I had left it, although slightly darker now. Set back in the trees, it felt almost ominous, the glass reflecting blackly back at me like the still surface of a lake. I turned the handle and entered. The air was less stale than previously but still with the undertone of forest smells and mildew, so I left the door wide open, wishing I'd brought a candle or some matches with me. Without the morning sunlight pouring in, it was difficult to read the titles of the books.

I searched the mantel of the large fireplace for any sign of a matchbook or flint and tinder, eventually finding spare candles and a box of matches in the drawer of a small table in the corner. I retrieved an empty candlestick from the mantel, the heavy silver ornaments flanked by cobwebbed porcelain King Charles spaniels that gazed at me with mournful expressions as I disturbed the dust around them.

The candle brought no warmth but just enough light to read by. It took me several minutes to locate the volume I wanted, which had ended up near the top, and I had to stand on tiptoe to reach it. The worn print on the spine would have been invisible without the aid of the flame to see by.

I backed away and sat on the nearest chair, the candle in one hand as I flipped open the front cover of the book. I expected to see Pansy's now familiar handwriting there, but instead there was another's.

Mo Leannan,

Read and remember those nights we have spent together. My adventurer. My brave heart.

With my warmest love,
Your Jo

Jo again. Pansy's lover. I wondered what 'Mo Leannan' meant and assumed it was a nickname. Price had mentioned that her journal was in a mixture of French, English and Gaelic. I said the words aloud a few times: 'Mo Leannan'. It did not sound French on the tongue, so I assumed it was Gaelic. I would need to find myself a translator, then, in order to understand what it meant.

I snapped the book shut and placed it in my coat pocket, unwilling to read further until I was back in the house. The keen autumnal wind blew in through the open door and disturbed the flame of my candle, putting it out so that I was in darkness once again.

With the sudden loss of light, I could almost picture myself sitting in the same spot the day before yesterday, Charles's hands wrapped around my own, sincerity in his green eyes as he declared his love for me. A tear slipped down my cheek and landed in my lap, and I wiped it away angrily. A frustrated growl slipped from my mouth.

How could I have let myself love so freely, so quickly?

Because he had made me feel safe and valued, I thought to myself. Because he had not looked at me as though I was damaged, or less than him, but rather as if I was his equal. I sighed, my breath curling in front of me in the frigid air. And because I had wanted, more than anything, to be loved by him.

I teetered on the verge of tears, feeling them build up behind my eyes like the water behind a dam. I could just sit here in the dark and allow them to fall, but how would that help me? Instead I pushed them down, swallowing my grief.

As I trudged back to the house, I cared not if Lord Blountford would be there to greet me after this morning's reckoning, only wishing to return to the warmth and brightness. Tomorrow, I thought, I would take the mysterious keys I had found and go in search of this cabin that Price had mentioned. The one where Esme had found the poisons. I shivered at the idea of it. It would also be the day before my wedding. I didn't know if the cold that gripped me was from the wind picking up or the many messy thoughts running through my mind, but I was grateful when I finally reached the main building so that I might put it all out of my head for now.

I came in through the back entrance covered in horse smells and mud from my walk, glancing in a mirror in the hallway to find that my appearance resembled that of a London beggar. My eyes were red from those almost-tears and I had somehow got a smudge of dirt on my forehead, while my windswept hair had been pulled out of the tightly plaited bun Marie had fashioned this morning. My hands were covered in dust and my dress was filthy.

I raced through the house and towards the grand staircase as quickly as I could, hoping to avoid interaction with anyone except a maid who might fetch me some hot water to clean up with.

I was to be disappointed.

'I am grateful that you brought this news to me in person, Mr Canfield. The gentleman you discovered enquiring after my business would most definitely be working for my nephew. You made the right decision in halting his investigations.' I could hear Lord Blountford's voice as he rounded the corner of the corridor and began to descend the staircase with another man, presumably a business associate, in tow. I froze at the realisation that it was Charles who was the topic of their discussion. Had this Mr Canfield seen him? Though it shouldn't matter to me, something in Lord Blountford's tone had me worried.

I looked for somewhere to hide. There was nowhere for me to go. I could turn around and race back down the stairs, but by that time they would have already spotted me.

Lord Blountford looked taken aback at my dishevelled aspect.

'Miss Dawson,' he said, failing to disguise the alarm in his voice.

'Apologies for my appearance, sir,' I said, giving him a curtsey and standing aside to let them pass. 'I was not sure of the time and I have been out riding all day.'

I met Mr Canfield's gaze. He was fairly plain, with slick brown hair and unremarkable features. Someone you could easily forget after a single meeting.

'Not to worry, Miss Dawson,' he said, interrupting whatever the earl had been about to say to me. From the stricken look on my fiancé's face, it was no doubt something along the lines of telling me to disappear as hastily as possible. 'It is a pleasure to finally meet you,' the visitor added, stretching out a hand so that I was forced to give him mine. His fingers were dry and rough, his eyes filled with amusement as he brushed his lips over my filthy knuckles. He did not seem to care for the dirt that I left smudged on his hands when he released me. His accent was also distinctly London. Unmistakably working class. I wondered why the earl would be dealing with such a character.

'Miss Dawson was just on her way upstairs, no doubt,' Lord Blountford said meaningfully. 'And Mr Canfield was just leaving.'

'Such a shame,' Canfield said, placing his hand on his chest, 'for I have heard so much of you, miss.' I could not tell if he was mocking me or trying to irk the earl, but I felt that I was the butt of a private joke. His smile was perhaps the only remarkable thing about him, in that it slashed across his face to show his small yellowing teeth, reminding me of a weasel.

'Well, then I apologise that our first meeting finds me in such a state,' I said, gesturing for them to continue past. 'Perhaps next time you are in the area you might stay for dinner, where we can properly make an acquaintance.' For I would be lady of the house by then and certainly it would be my place to extend such an invitation. I looked at my fiancé, whose grim expression was otherwise unreadable.

'It would be my absolute honour, miss,' Canfield said with a brief bow before carrying on his way. Lord Blountford appeared visibly relieved that the conversation between us was over, although I couldn't think why.

It was then that I spotted two figures walking several paces behind them, blocking my way up the stairs. Personal guards, perhaps? They were large, brutish fellows with thick arms and bodies wider than tree trunks. I looked up at them to indicate that I would like to pass, and froze. Two pairs of russet eyes leered down at me, their faces twisting into smiles that had not an ounce of mirth in them. Fox-like.

'You,' I breathed, recognising them at once as the two men who had barged into our home. Who had beaten my father and taken Esme's harp to pay a debt for their master. I turned around to look down upon Lord Blountford and Mr Canfield. 'You!' I said again, this time to the earl's associate.

Mr Canfield only grinned in that weasel-like way. That was how he'd heard about me; not from my betrothed, but from his own lackeys.

'Lord Blountford, this . . . this man,' I spat as though the word were not insulting enough, 'is responsible for untold distress in my family. I demand that you dismiss him from the property at once.'

The earl looked uneasily between myself and Canfield, but said nothing.

'Sir,' I said, more forcefully, 'I demand that you tell him to leave.'

He looked again at Canfield, and muttered something I only caught the end of: '. . . have this conversation privately.' He nodded towards the entrance hall, his associate still grinning as he followed a step behind him.

'It was a pleasure to meet you, Miss Dawson,' Canfield called back to me when he reached the bottom of the stairs. 'Give my regards to your parents.'

I did not realise I was launching myself at him until my knife was in my hand and at his throat. How I had retrieved it from my waist in a matter of seconds was a mystery to me, and yet there it was, as sharp and violent as cut glass, pressing against the pale skin under his chin, so close that I could smell the alcohol on his breath. Lord Blountford paled and shouted something that might have been a curse, or might have been my name. I was too enraged to hear it.

It all happened in moments, and before I could contemplate how it would feel to have Mr Canfield's blood trickling over my fingers, my arms were wrenched behind me, my wrist gripped so hard that I gasped and dropped the knife. Hands that had split my father's lip and broken his bones had me pinned in place, my wrist already aching from where it was being squeezed.

'Unhand me, you devils!' I shrieked, pulling at them, which only made the two men hold me tighter.

'Oh ho ho, Lord Blountford, I did not realise that your future wife was so . . . . wilful,' Canfield said, touching the place where my blade had met his skin. I was grimly satisfied that a streak of blood came off on his handkerchief when he dabbed at it.

'Told you the other sister was the clever one, sir,' one of the henchmen remarked, and although I had my back to him, I could hear the sneer in his voice.

I was moments away from leaping for my knife again when Lord Blountford bellowed, 'Miss Dawson, we do not behave like savages in this household!' I didn't care that he roared at me at the top of his lungs, or that it was the second time in forty-eight hours that I had seen him lose his temper where I was involved.

'You accuse me of acting like a savage, sir?' I scoffed, wincing at the pain in my arms where the men held me back, their fingers like vices. 'And yet you invite criminals and thieves into your home. These are the men who beat my father and took my sister's harp. One of them even touched my sister – your late wife – suggestively!' This seemed to be the only thing that caused Lord Blountford to look at my captors with displeasure.

'I'm afraid Mr Weston and his brother do have some . . . unconventional methods for reclaiming the money owed you, Lord Blountford, but they are always successful,' Canfield explained.

I froze in my struggle.

'Wait. The money owed to you?' I looked at him with narrowed eyes.

'Miss Dawson, now is not the time for explanations.'

'Now is the perfect time for explanations, sir! I am to be your wife the day after tomorrow and yet you have omitted to tell me that you were my father's creditor? That you had men sent to my house to beat us and take whatever they could to repay the debt?'

Lord Blountford's expression answered the question for me. He looked befuddled, for once, and I could see him searching for an answer that would appease me. Canfield pocketed the bloodied handkerchief and rocked back on his heels, his hands tucked into his waistcoat.

'Well, this is an awkward predicament, is it not?' He sounded amused more than anything, and if I had not been restrained, I would have hit him. Lord Blountford looked as though he might do it for me.

'Miss Dawson—'

'No! You are *not* permitted to "Miss Dawson" me! What was my sister to you? Another payment for the debts my father accrued? Is that what I am? A substitute for an investment gone bad?' I knew I was screaming. I would not have been the least bit surprised if the entire household could hear me.

'I think it is best if I leave you to it, your lordship,' Canfield said, not even bothering to spare me a glance. 'Come along, gentlemen,' he added, and with that the Weston brothers released me. I had been pulling at them so fiercely that I almost sprawled on the floor, but caught myself in time.

'This is a discussion for another time, Miss Dawson,' Lord Blountford said coldly. 'For now, I suggest you go to your rooms.'

Turner appeared from somewhere, no doubt having heard the entire exchange, and murmured something to me that sounded soothing even if I didn't catch the words. His gentle grip at my elbow was enough to prompt me into motion, and I scooped up my knife as I glared at the four men who were now standing awkwardly in the entrance hall.

Lord Blountford appeared to be frustrated with Canfield for provoking me, but neither of the Weston brothers looked particularly affected by the events that had unfolded. Just another day of work for them, I thought bitterly.

'Allow me to fetch your maid, miss,' Turner said as we climbed the stairs. 'I shall send her to your rooms.'

'No,' I replied abruptly. 'I wish to speak with the earl as soon as those men have left.'

'But Miss Dawson—'

'Turner, I will have my explanation now, whether I wait here in the corridor or in his study, and I shall not move until I have spoken with him.'

Seeing that he would not win this battle, he nodded warily,

escorting me to the study rather than to my rooms. As I waited there, I could see my reflection in the darkened window. Still filthy, eyes red-rimmed and hair every which way, I looked as wild as I felt, still gripping the knife hilt and running my thumb over the pommel.

'Miss Dawson, I told you to go to your room,' Lord Blountford said, barely hesitating when he entered some twenty minutes later. Turner must have warned him I was here.

'And I told you that I wanted an explanation.' I turned away from the window and fixed him with a scowl.

He gave me a wide berth as he walked across the room to his desk and sat down. His chair was slightly higher than those opposite, I realised. A secret signal of authority, causing him to look down upon whomever he was entertaining. So it was that I chose to stand instead, stalking over and leaning on the back of one of the visitors' chairs, the knife balanced in my fingers.

He gave a long-suffering sigh, steepling his hands in front of him on the desk and pressing his forehead against his fingers. I noticed how much older he looked every time I saw him. It took a little of the fight out of me to see him so defeated.

'Yes, your sister's hand in marriage was payment for the debt your father owed me. It was proposed by those gentlemen as an elegant solution to your family's troubles.'

'But the harp they took—'

'Was not nearly enough to cover it. It ended up here, in this house, rather than being sold.' He waved a hand above his head as if gesturing to where it now stood in the abandoned music room. So it had been Esme's. One and the same. My already battered heart ached at the thought.

'And so I was a substitute,' I said flatly, already knowing the answer.

'Yes. When your sister . . . failed to produce an heir before she died, the agreement between me and your father was unfulfilled, and he offered you as a replacement. It was that,' he added quickly when I scoffed, 'or he would have to sell the house. All of your belongings. You would have been living on the street. I'm afraid he really is a terrible loser.'

I thought of them then, my parents, whom I had hated as much as loved. Possibly hated more than I had loved much of the time, if I was honest with myself. Yet they had given me up to this life to save us from destitution. It made my feelings for them no clearer, but for the first time in as long as I could remember, I wanted to see them. I wanted to embrace them and tell them I knew and understood why they had done what they did.

'And I have no choice but to marry you.' Again, more of a statement than a question.

'If you do not, Miss Dawson, you will be returned to London, where your parents will have to resort to the one thing they attempted to save you from.' He said it as though he was resigned to it. As though he wouldn't enjoy the wedding or what came after; it was just another part of business that required his somewhat reluctant attention. I thought of Charles despite myself, of how he had looked at me with love and longing. I would never have that kind of relationship with this man, I realised, and it hurt.

'Why did you let my father play if he was such a terrible loser? Why allow him into your gambling house at all?'

It was Lord Blountford's turn to scoff. 'I am a businessman, Miss Dawson. I would be considered a very poor one if I did not take advantage of my unfortunate players.'

My blood fizzled at the way he so casually dismissed my father as a luckless participant rather than a man with a wife and children to feed. These were people's lives he played with, and yet all he had consideration for was the money to be made.

'Besides,' he added with a shrug, 'I couldn't have stopped him playing even if I'd tried. You get your stubbornness from him, of that I am certain.'

If it was a compliment, it was well disguised.

'And my sister?'

'What about her?' he asked, confused at my sudden change of tone.

'Did you love her at all? Did you want her to be happy and fulfilled as your wife? Did she love you?'

He looked at me levelly, his lichen eyes flat and bored, as though my questions were tiresome.

'I believe we shared a mutual affection, and I allowed her every liberty as lady of the house. As for her feelings, I cannot say, but she certainly seemed joyous and busy when she was here. She was an easier woman to please than you are, it appears. Even when her pregnancy caused her difficulty or she was in pain, she bounced back with—'

'Her what?' I felt that sickening feeling of the ground gaping before me suddenly, as though I might be swallowed.

'Her pregnancy. She was expecting our child,' he said, as though he were speaking to an imbecile.

Had it become darker outside? The room dimmed until all I could see was his face in the candlelight, his sad, ancient eyes losing their patience with me. My pulse pounded through my body so that I could hear it in my head, my ears.

'She was with child when she died?' My own voice sounded hollow and far away, and I was certain I might faint.

'Miss Dawson, you look unwell . . .'

I did not hear the rest of what he had to say. I tore from the room, stumbling into the corridor where an alarmed-looking

Turner stood. He called out to me, but I ignored him, fighting the trembling that seemed to rack my body as I ran. Away from Blountford. Down the stairs and away from the memories of Canfield and his cronies holding me back. Away from the startled maids, who whispered to each other as I passed, my knife still gripped in my hand. As I tore out of the house, the wind picked up around me, loose leaves dancing feverishly in the air, whipping my hair into my face.

I didn't realise where I was going until I was there.

'Lizzie!' Jordie exclaimed as I ran into the stables, barrelling into him and wrapping my arms around his waist. The dam of tears I had walled up inside me broke free, burning my chest and lungs.

I felt Jordie's strong arms wrap around me as I sobbed into his chest, his hand cupping the back of my head and holding me to him. He smelled of wind and rain and horse, earthy scents that kept me grounded while he soothed me with the sound of his voice as though I were a distressed animal.

I hadn't trusted anyone to be this close to me in so long, drawing comfort from the presence of another. That I had enough faith in Jordie to let him envelop me like this only made my tears fall harder, with the realisation that I had been so incredibly lonely for so long.

We stayed that way for a long time, him not asking me any questions, my face buried in his shirt, the tears falling freely until my nose was blocked and my eyes stung.

'I'm sorry,' I managed to whisper, although I wasn't sure what I was apologising for. For making his shirt wet. For running into the stables like a woman crazed. For needing his solidarity and comfort where I could otherwise find none. 'Thank you,' I said instead.

'Nothing to thank me for, Lizzie,' he said, wiping the tears from my cheeks and giving me his handkerchief to blow my nose with. I sheathed the knife, which had somehow stayed firmly in my fist. It was a wonder I hadn't cut myself when running, or Jordie when I had bowled into him.

He didn't comment on the weapon, instead leading me out of the shadows of the stables to where a lamp was lit, kicking over an empty bucket with his foot and turning it so that I could sit down, all while holding my hand gently.

'Don't think you owe me any explanation,' he said, finding another bucket and emptying its contents into the corner so that he could sit beside me, 'but if you wish to talk, I'm happy to lend an ear.'

I wrung the handkerchief between my fingers and breathed deeply, hiccuping once or twice as my grief subsided.

'I don't know where to start . . .'

'The beginning is usually a good place,' he said with a soft lopsided smile. 'Oh no, I didn't mean to make you cry again,' he said as my face crumpled.

'I-I can't control it,' I stuttered.

'Well, there's nothing wrong with a good cry. My mam even says that boys should cry every once in a while. Lets it all out, you see.'

I nodded. It was true that I was finally beginning to feel like I could breathe again. As though the pressure that had accumulated behind my eyes and inside my head was finally spent, and perhaps I could face the events of the past few days.

'The beginning,' I croaked, my voice hoarse in my throat, 'feels like a lifetime ago. I suppose in some ways it is.'

He nodded encouragingly. His expression was open, easy, as it so often was. It was this that made me tell him everything, right from the start. My father's debts. The Weston brothers. Mr Canfield. The ghosts. He barely raised an eyebrow when I told him I could see them, only nodded and murmured something about his grandmother on his father's side being a 'seer', as he called it, like it was the most ordinary thing in the world. I spoke of Marisa and Pansy, of how I'd managed to help the former but that I had no notion of how to help the latter.

And then came Esme's arranged marriage, and my substitution. Charles and his declaration of love for me, and then the heartbreak of finding his letters to my sister.

We sat well past dinner time, but no one came to retrieve me and I was grateful for the lack of interruption.

'But I don't understand,' I said finally, when my tears had dried and my voice was almost normal again. 'If Esme was expecting Lord Blountford's baby, why would she arrange a marriage to the captain? Surely he would notice that she was with child when they met, and would not wish to go through with it?'

Jordie looked thoughtful for a moment, an unfamiliar frown creasing his brow. 'Perhaps she didn't know at the time. I hear it can take months for letters to travel overseas. Maybe when they first began arrangements she was not expecting, and she found out too late to tell him and call it off, for by that time the captain was already on his way back to England?'

And then she had died.

'When Esme passed away, I felt like I had lost a piece of my soul. Now, to know that her baby perished too . . .' I searched for the words but could find none. The ache in my chest was more than heartbreak, surely. It was as though I was being torn apart piece by piece, each new bit of bad news slowly taking away some fragment of me until I worried there would be nothing left.

Jordie cupped my cheek in his hand, his rough palm warm against the clamminess of my skin.

'There was nothing you could have done to change her fate,' he said firmly but kindly. 'Now you just need to decide what you will do with all of this.' He waved his other hand around the stables, to encompass the estate, Lord Blountford, the ghosts and everything else.

'What *can* I do? I have thought of running away, but then my parents would become beggars. I cannot refuse to marry him or bear him children for that exact same reason. I thought, foolishly, that he might grow on me over time, as I thought he had on my sister. Now it seems that even she could not stomach her marriage to him.'

He grimaced, knowing my words were true.

'Well, then you must look on the bright side,' he said.

I choked out a humourless laugh. 'What on earth could be the bright side?'

'You'll always have me to be your friend when all else seems lost.'

I gave him a rueful smile. He was making light of a horrendous situation and he knew it, but somehow it worked. I was warmed to know that even when I did marry the man responsible for my woes, I would have a friend nearby.

I stood and brushed down my skirts, proffering the sopping handkerchief back to him. He wrinkled his nose. 'Keep it. You might need it more than I.'

I laughed more sincerely this time as he stood and guided me out of the stables and into the courtyard.

'I'll help you if you like,' he added as we walked, 'to find this mystery hut in the woods and solve your sister's death once and for all, if it will put your mind at rest.'

I nodded gratefully, turning to him and throwing my arms around his neck. 'I have no words for how thankful I am to have met you, Jordie,' I mumbled into his shoulder as we embraced.

'Ah, don't mention anything of it,' he said coyly, letting go to hold me at arm's length and giving me another of his ready smiles.

A smile that froze as a shadow fell across us from the house. He released me abruptly, taking a step back, causing me to turn and see what had provoked his sudden alarm.

There in the doorway, silhouetted against the light, was Lord Blountford.

Chapter 17

ഗ

I awoke the morning before my wedding day with a bubbling worry deep within my gut. The windows were a colourless blanket, as though I were still in a dream, and my room was illuminated with dull white light.

I felt the presence of someone at the end of my bed and found Pansy there, staring at nothing in particular, her expression solemn.

'Good morning,' I said softly, breaking her contemplation as her attention moved to me.

'You helped Marisa,' she said quietly, very much unlike herself. I sat up in bed and rubbed the sleep from my eyes, not ready for this conversation so early in the day.

'I did what I could,' I said, clambering out of bed and washing my face at the basin. 'I don't know if I helped her, but I certainly tried.'

'But she . . . moved on?' There was something in her voice. A wonder, or curiosity, or perhaps longing.

'She does not appear to still be . . . haunting the site where she died, so I can only hope so, for her sake.' It was a surprisingly complex thing, trying to talk to ghosts about death. Harder almost, than discussing it with the living.

Pansy pulled at invisible threads in my bedspread, looking forlorn. 'Where do you think we go after we move on?'

The anxiety in my stomach twisted at the question. No, I was certainly not ready for this conversation.

I shrugged. 'I can only hope it is to heaven. That is where I wish for my sister to be, and Marisa, if God has willed it.'

'I do not think I shall be going to heaven,' Pansy said, brushing the blanket as though sweeping away her thoughts and concerns. She stood and twirled around the room, her seriousness gone for the moment. But not truly, for I could see it well hidden below the facade of carelessness she put up. Underneath it all she was worried.

'Because of your adultery?' I blurted, realising how unkind it was only a moment too late.

Her eyes flashed angrily and within a second she was inches from my face, as though she had crossed the distance in less than a blink of an eye.

'Because I so deeply loved a man who loved me in return,' she said bitterly. 'What would you understand of such things, child?'

I narrowed my eyes at her, unwilling to speak of Charles and what his betrayal had done to me.

'Nothing, apparently.'

A knock at the door, shortly followed by Marie entering to help me dress for the day, forced me to hold my tongue. The ghost sat back down on the bed and I ignored her, hoping that she would disappear of her own accord, but she was not done yet, it seemed.

'Would you help me?' she asked as Marie brushed and braided my hair.

I glanced at her in the mirror and gave a non-committal

shrug, which Marie mistook for me adjusting my position in the chair.

'If you help me, I might finally be at peace,' she continued, appearing by my side and forcing me to look at her.

'Miss, would you mind awfully turning your head so that I might finish this last plait?' Marie asked quietly. I mumbled an apology and resumed staring at Pansy in the mirror.

'If you can find him, I could rest at last.'

I frowned. Did she mean Lord Blountford? Did she really want me to bring him to her?

'Promise me,' she insisted. I glanced at Marie, who was just putting the final pins into place.

'How can I?'

'Promise me!' Pansy insisted.

'Are you all right, miss? Did you say something?' Marie asked, confused.

I sighed. Brisley had never been this demanding back home, although if I were honest with myself, I had never tried to solve the mystery of his death. Something I might want to rectify if I returned.

'I promise,' I replied, and with that Pansy vanished as though she had never been there.

'What do you promise, miss?' Marie enquired, taking a step back to admire her handiwork.

'I . . . promised Jordie I would bring a carrot for Gwen this morning. You wouldn't be able to add one to my breakfast tray to save me a trip to the kitchen, would you?' I recovered quickly.

'Would you like breakfast in your room, miss?'

'Yes, I think I would this morning.'

She nodded and curtseyed in reply, leaving to do as I asked.

I didn't wish to eat with Lord Blountford. I worried at his reaction to seeing me and Jordie last night, no matter how innocent it had been. He had barely said a word to me when I came indoors, although I had sensed a ripple of anger beneath his silence. I had caught him glowering at Jordie before closing the door and shutting him out, and something in the action had felt threatening.

When I ventured outside for my morning's lesson, a carrot in one pocket, Pansy's diary and the keys in the other, everything was cold and damp. Mist rose from the grass on the lawns and snuck over the walls, filling the cobblestoned courtyard with an impenetrable haze, cleaner but icier than in London.

It was too quiet, as though the fog had absorbed all sound. I listened for the cheery notes of Jordie chatting to the horses, or the familiar nickers from the stalls, but there was nothing. The apprehension that had started in the pit of my stomach took root and spread when I entered the stables to find no sign of my friend. Gwen stomped uneasily in her stall, and I handed her the carrot, no longer worried that she might try to take a bite out of me at the same time.

'Where's Jordie, girl?' I asked her quietly, the sound of my voice muted in the frozen air.

She of course revealed nothing.

I floundered for a few minutes, wondering what to do. I told myself that there was a logical reason for him not being here. Perhaps something had delayed him this morning. Or spilling my heart out to him last night had scared him off. Or . . . or something dreadful had happened.

Pansy's words from the other day rang through my mind. *Your future husband does not like to share his belongings . . . He will possess you and make certain that no one else comes close to you. If they do, they will suffer for it.*

My stomach clenched at the thought. But surely Lord

Blountford wouldn't have harmed Jordie? A strong young lad against a frail old man was a match that weighed heavily in Jordie's favour, I reasoned. Failing to calm my unease, I set out walking, away from Gwen and the stables and across the lawn towards the lake and the woods. Part of me wanted to saddle up and go in search of him, just to be sure that he was all right, but aside from not knowing where to start, the rational part of my brain told me that I would only make things worse. Instead I would keep my mind occupied, and perhaps by the time I returned to the house, Jordie would be back, tending to the horses and laughing that I had ever worried about him. Perhaps he had gone to visit his family, or taken the day off?

That was what I told myself as I trekked through the grass, my boots wet with morning dew, my gloved fingers thrust in my loaded pockets.

I only vaguely knew what direction to follow, and I kept my eyes on the ground so that I didn't accidentally slip, or fall into the lake without realising I had reached it. It was folly, really, to walk in this weather, but some grim determination to find the cabin Esme had discovered had me persisting. Perhaps I did get my stubbornness from my father, as the earl had said.

I wished that I had had the forethought to invite my parents to the wedding, overriding his dismissal of my request. I could have done it, I mused, simply by writing to them myself. But of course, I hadn't known then what I did now, and I didn't think I would have been brave enough to go against his orders even a few days ago. Every day that I spent in this place, I felt myself changing. Yes, at home I had been difficult and recalcitrant, but here at Ambletye, the mysteries of other women's lives unfolding around me, I had also discovered some strength, some resolve that I hadn't had before.

I found the lake, the swans floating ethereally on the surface like paper wraiths, and the path that led away towards the graves. I followed it, locating the bench that I had paused at before, but rather than turning away and into the woods, I continued all the way to the opposite side of the water, searching for an obvious break in the trees or an abandoned track. There was no logic to my searching, other than an internal compass telling me that when I'd run through the woods last time, I hadn't seen a cabin or shack, and that I was following a different route this time.

My internal compass was correct.

After half an hour, I caught the scent of woodsmoke before I saw its source: a single-room building set back from the path, well disguised by a copse of hawthorn and gorse. The almost cheery log cabin, with its smoking brick chimney and small flower beds by the door, was not at all the shack I was expecting. And it was occupied.

Hesitantly I knocked on the door, wondering if the keys I held in my pocket would fit the lock but not wanting to try. Whoever the occupant might be, I didn't think they would appreciate me barging in on them first thing in the morning.

There was the scrape of something heavy along with some shuffling behind the door, which eventually opened to reveal the dark, grizzled features of Mr McMannon, barefoot, in trousers and an undershirt.

His eyes widened when he saw me, as I was sure mine did too.

'I'm so sorry—'

'Beggin' yer pardon—'

We both spoke at the same time, and I averted my gaze, staring at the ground and taking a step back.

'My apologies, Mr McMannon, I did not realise there would be anyone here,' I said hastily.

He slammed the door and cursed, even though I was certain he didn't intend for me to hear it. He re-emerged moments later wearing a loose-fitting shirt.

"Scuse my appearance, miss. I didna expect any visitors this mornin'.' He failed to hide his ire, even though his words were pleasant enough.

'You have nothing to apologise for. It was I who intruded,' I said, peeking up to see that the view was truly safe. 'I didn't realise that anyone lived so deep in the woods. I was actually looking for a cabin, but I think I may have been led astray . . .'

'A cabin, you say?' His dark eyes gleamed with recognition and suspicion. 'What would you be out here lookin' for a cabin for?' His Scottish accent was thick, as of someone from the very highest lands, but I tuned my ears to it so that I could keep up with his words.

'I, er . . . my sister once mentioned she had found such a place. I only wished to retrace her steps, as it were.' It was not truly a lie, for although she had never mentioned the cabin to me, she had certainly discussed it in her letters to Price. The question was, would Mr McMannon cooperate, or would he grow angry as he had when I had discovered the graves? He had not seemed to like me looking around before.

Something that resembled relief settled in him at my explanation.

'Ah, I'm afraid the old cabin has been locked for years, but yes, there's one in the woods not far from here,' he said, pointing in a northerly direction.

'Not to worry,' I said brusquely, hoping to bring our conversation to a close. I was sure Mr McMannon was a nice enough fellow, but something about him frightened me slightly. I felt the reassuring weight of my knife underneath my coat, immediately chastising myself a little for being so untrusting.

'I can take you for a look at the outside if you like?' he offered, already unhooking his coat and cap from behind the door.

'That is very kind of you, but there's no need, really,' I said, turning away from him even as he slipped his feet into his boots and followed me out of the door.

'It would be no trouble. The least I can do for scaring you the other day,' he said, already taking off down the path in front of me.

I sighed through my nose, realising that there would be no way I could avoid admitting I might have a key to the old place now. It was that or come back later when he wasn't there, and I really did not want to have to make the journey again. As I moved to follow him, something caught my eye. 'Pansies,' I said, looking at the flowers that were still thriving in the beds despite the cold autumn. The yellows, whites and purples were a splash of colour against the browns of the forest.

'They bloom all year round if you know how to look after 'em,' he said with a hint of pride in his gravelled voice.

Something in my mind began to slide into focus, another piece of the puzzle that was just beyond my grasp, and I worried at it while we walked the fifty paces or so to a dilapidated-looking shack slightly uphill of the groundskeeper's own cottage.

There were no windows to peer through, and the roof was so sloped it looked as though it might collapse at any moment. The walls were made of grey logs that had split in places, and as we approached, I found myself peering through one into the darkness beyond. This was what I had expected when I had come looking for Esme's discovery.

'As I said, it's been locked for years now,' Mr McMannon said, his voice faraway and rough as he stared at the building with his hands folded across his broad chest. There was a melancholy, lost look on his face that I was slowly beginning to recognise.

Without another word to him, I pulled out the larger of the two keys in my pocket and approached the thick door, which, miraculously, was still standing and strong as ever.

'What're you doin'?' he asked as I forced through the resistance the lock offered. The key jammed, but I felt certain that with the right amount of pressure it would turn. Before he could stop me, I forced my weight onto the door and turned the key as hard as I could, feeling the bolts slide into place, screeching with protest. The final click was swallowed up by the mist.

'Where'd you get that?' he asked, aghast.

I turned towards him, right hand slowly reaching toward my left hip, where the knife sat under my coat. Just in case.

'My sister had a copy,' I said, watching his expression change from shock to fear and then to grief. 'And as it happens, Lord Blountford's third wife, Pansy, had one too.'

I didn't know what I expected him to do, or why I pulled the knife out from under the folds of my coat as he stalked toward me, but when he dropped to his knees by my feet, I felt a ripple of uncertainty.

His wail pierced the wall of quiet around us and he shuddered, prone on the ground, his cap fallen in the dirt. Then he began to cry.

'I knew you'd come,' he said as he sobbed.

'Pardon?'

'The avenging angel. I knew ye'd come for me one day. I jus' didna think it would take ya so long.' He beat a fist on the ground before sitting up on his haunches and looking at me with eyes so dark they might be black.

For the first time, I truly looked at his weathered face, disregarding the thick beard and the lines from the sun. He would have been very handsome in his youth, with his high cheek-bones and long aquiline nose.

'Mr McMannon, I am not an avenging angel,' I said firmly, sheathing my knife and bending down to where he knelt, his face streaked from weeping, his beard having collected debris and leaves. 'I am only a woman who wishes to find some answers so that a ghost can go to her final resting place.'

'Ye're not here to send me to hell?'

'Indeed not. Or at least it was not on my original agenda for the day,' I said lightly, placing a hand on his shoulder in what I hoped was a comforting manner. After all, I had just pulled a knife on the poor man.

He retrieved a handkerchief from his pocket and wiped his face, blowing his nose noisily, before stumbling to his feet and brushing his knees off.

His reaction had set my mind racing. His guilt, his anger when I found the graves, the flowers outside his cabin. The fact that he'd been here for decades, ever the faithful servant to his master. But there was something he was hiding. Something so awful that he thought I was there to kill him. Avenge someone.

Then there was Pansy's diary. The code. The Gaelic.

The puzzle in my mind began to shift and morph, pieces clicking into place. I reached behind me and turned the door handle of the cabin, heaving it open before he could protest.

The darkness within was barely illuminated, but as my eyes quickly adjusted, I could make out a room. A bedroom, it seemed, with a low mattress, a small wooden table and two chairs. A thick layer of dust covered everything, stirring in the air as I took a step inside, causing me to sneeze.

A shelf of decayed books and tiny glass jars sat in the furthest corner, barely three feet high. I stooped to look at them, noting how the dust had been recently wiped away from the labels on the jars.

Cyanide, one label read. I didn't need to examine the other jars to know what would be inside them.

'Pansy,' I said to Mr McMannon, turning to where he stood just outside the doorway. He flinched at the name as though I had struck him. 'What was she to you?'

He blinked at me once, twice, as though not really seeing me at all, but rather seeing someone else in my place. He said nothing, only gazing around a space that he had perhaps not been in for more than a decade.

I persisted. 'She is stuck in between, Mr McMannon, and I wish to help her. She is not a happy ghost and I need to find her peace. So please, tell me, what was she to you?'

I felt I might already know the answer.

'She was the woman I loved,' he said with a lamenting sigh.

'You are Jo,' I stated, pulling her diary from my pocket and holding it out. He reared back and looked at me with horror on his stricken face, as though I were proffering a dead animal rather than his lover's journal. I walked over and placed it in his grasp even as he shook his head fervently.

'I deciphered her code,' I said as he stared down at the red leather, tracing a line over the embossed cover with a pained expression. 'She loved her Jo very much, and felt conflicted, it seemed to me. I didn't realise at first why she had written in Gaelic until . . . well, until today. Because Jo spoke Gaelic, and you are him.'

'You're a clever woman, Miss Dawson,' he said, looking up at me. 'I was her Jo, yes. Jo is an old Scottish word – we use it the same way you might use "dear" or "darling" down here. I was trying to teach her Gaelic and she was trying to teach me the French she learned as a girl.' His mouth quirked up at a memory.

'And "Mo Leannan"?'

' "My love",' he said, his voice breaking. 'Where did you see that?'

'In a copy of *Gulliver's Travels*. The one she used to write her secret code with.'

He sighed again, all the grief and pain of memories summed up in a single breath. 'We wrote notes to each other that way, using numbers. We used to lie here and read together, and it was a book she particularly loved to hear me recite. I gifted her a copy the Christmas before she . . . passed.'

I looked down at the ramshackle bed, unable to stop images of the two of them together from flashing before my eyes. This had been the place for their secret trysts.

'I found Pansy's key in the summer house, in a hollowed-out book, but the other copy,' I produced the smaller version that had been in my sister's box, 'might have been yours.' I passed it to him and he looked at it thoughtfully.

'I lost this some years ago. 'Twas kept on the mantel in the summer house, underneath a little dog figurine, but I had no reason to come back here after Pansy was gone. It only brought too much heartache,' he said, stepping into the shack and sitting down on the bed, sending up a cloud of dust.

'You called me an avenging angel, Mr McMannon,' I said, glancing pointedly at the jars of poison on the shelf. 'I'd like to know what exactly it is I might be avenging.'

He wasn't going to answer, I thought at first as I watched his fingers fumble agitatedly with the key. When he did finally speak, his voice was deep and hollowed with grief.

'She wanted us not to live in secrecy any more. We spent almost two years sneaking out to this hut, only when neither of us would be missed.' There was a pause, and then, 'She wanted to get rid of him, so that we could be together properly. When it turned out she was barren, my master resolutely ignored her. She was no longer useful to him and yet he failed to see the bright, creative spirit that she was.'

My mouth went dry at the shock of revelation. Pansy had not been able to have children. I thought of the slightly mad, ever-candid ghost I had met. Perhaps finding out that truth had pushed her closer to the edge of sanity.

'I didn't care that we wouldn't have children. I only wanted her. I loved her and she loved me, I knew it. She spent months planning the poisoning, asking questions at the apothecary and experimenting with quantities by feeding laced food to the rats that would find their way into this cabin. I worried about her, but the promise of being married and living together made me blind.'

He didn't meet my gaze but instead looked at the room as though seeing it in a different time. I imagined Pansy, that slim, elegant woman, sitting at the table with vials and plates of food, concocting the plan to murder her husband. And then sharing a bed with her true love, all under the same roof. My stomach writhed, but I said nothing, unwilling to break the cocoon of confession that I had somehow created.

'She was certain that Mr Blountford, the earl's brother, would not turn her out on her ear, and we could take over the manor in his stead. If not, she had a plan to sell her jewels before we were ousted so that we could start afresh, perhaps venturing back to Scotland. And so it was that one Friday evening she invited me into the house to help her with the deed. She was going to ask the earl to give me a promotion and propose a toast with a poisoned drink.'

The words were terrible, horrible things. I should have been disgusted that anyone would entertain such a notion. That a woman might want to kill her husband so that she might be with her lover. And yet, after everything I had witnessed in these past few days, it did not at all surprise me. People were too complicated. Life was not all blissful marriages and happily-ever-after endings.

'What happened?' I asked, my voice barely a whisper.

He huffed a frustrated laugh. 'I . . . was a coward. At the last moment I tried to switch the drinks, but my master somehow already knew everything. Whether it was my own panic that gave it away, or that someone had seen us and reported it, he was already aware that she was being unfaithful. I swapped the glasses thinking that I had taken the one with the poison and would throw it out, but Lord Blountford had also rotated them. Pansy drank the poison that may well have been meant for me and died right there in his study while I watched.'

I blinked in shock. 'Lord Blountford knew the glass was poisoned, but he permitted Pansy to drink it anyway?'

Mr McMannon shook his shaggy head. 'I couldna say for sure. He appeared as surprised and distraught as I at the time, but even in my grief I could've sworn there was a glint of something in his eyes. As though he had suspected the outcome but was still shocked to see it unfold.'

Something in my stomach sank. The man I was marrying had 'accidentally' pushed his first wife from a balcony during an argument. His third had died by poisoning at his own hand. Another accident? A coincidence? I wasn't certain. Trying to quash my distress, I focused on the groundskeeper before me. 'And he kept you in his employ?' I said tentatively.

'If he knew I was her lover, he made no indication of it. Either he didn't think it was me because of my lowly station, or he knew and kept me here as a punishment, working and living on the land that I had lost her.'

It explained so much. Lord Blountford's tendency towards

jealousy. The lack of epitaph on Pansy's grave, no doubt because he felt her treason did not warrant one. Her dispassionate manner towards him. The truth was, she had been the cause of her own demise.

'I need you to come with me to the house, Mr McMannon,' I said firmly, giving the cabin a final glance before walking out.

'I don't belong there, miss. I'll be kicked out,' he said, following me and closing the door reverently behind him. I spun around.

'I told you that I have a ghost to put to rest. I wholeheartedly believe that it is you she asked me to find, not her husband, and she will not be at peace until the truth between you is laid bare.'

'This is no' a jest then – ye're serious? Her spirit still lives on?' He asked the question with some awe.

I was learning slowly that people were not so incredulous as I expected them to be about my peculiar abilities.

'Indeed, and she has been causing me no end of trouble. I would like you to speak with her.'

Without further explanation I led him away from the cabin and back towards the house, walking in silence the entire way. He still clutched the journal in one hand and the smaller key in the other, having left the larger one in the lock.

'Are ye a witch, Miss Dawson?' he whispered.

'Not that I know of, Mr McMannon,' I replied with a little severity. I certainly did not need that rumour being bandied around. 'I am merely a girl who occasionally sees unrestful spirits.' For what good it had ever done me, I thought with a grimace.

I hoped that we would not bump into Lord Blountford as we walked through the house, and for once my wish came true. A few of the maids gave us confused looks before receiving a raised eyebrow from me that sent them on their way.

I was heading towards my own quarters when a thought occurred to me. I had seen Pansy twice now in Esme's purple bedroom, so laying out a map of the house in my head, I led him there instead.

He looked uncomfortably out of place, his outdoor clothes somewhat inharmonious in such a feminine setting. I ordered him to sit at the vanity while we waited, and silently prayed that Pansy would be cooperative. I had never seen her out of doors, just as I hadn't witnessed Mr McMannon inside the house. She had possibly not seen him since the day she had been poisoned.

'What do I have to do?' he asked nervously.

'Nothing for the moment. She usually makes an appearance when I least expect it,' I replied, hoping I didn't sound as impatient as I felt.

I was not sure how long we waited. The clock on the mantel had not been wound and the white sky outside gave no indication of time passing, but I sensed it was an hour before either of us spoke.

'I don't think I should be here,' he said eventually.

'On the contrary, I think you are exactly where you ought to be,' I said from where I stood on the other side of the room.

'But what if she doesna want to see me, after what I did?'

I was about to open my mouth in protest when I heard another voice.

'Angus?'

I looked from Mr McMannon to the face that was slowly emerging through the wall beside me.

'Angus, is that really you?'

He must have sensed something in the way my expression changed, for he stood up. 'She's here, isn't she?' he asked breathlessly.

I nodded, waiting.

'You found him, clever girl,' Pansy said, sparing me a glance as she walked over to the man she had not seen in over a decade. 'You look older, my Jo, but no less handsome.'

I relayed her words as she stroked his face, her thumb tracing the shape of his lips. He closed his eyes as if he could feel the cold caress of her touch, then gave a small chuckle, which turned into a sob as she ran her hands down his arms affectionately.

'Oh, my Jo, don't cry for me. I've missed you so much; let's not waste these precious moments on tears,' Pansy said with nothing but warmth in her voice. I had never heard her speak so affectionately, and I tried to convey her emotions as I told him what she had said.

'Mo Leannan, I did a terrible thing. I was such a coward,' he replied with a shaky breath.

'Shush now, there is no need for regrets. You know that I could not leave until I saw you one last time,' she replied, resting her forehead upon his chest, her arms reaching around his neck in an embrace that he could not truly return.

They spoke for the longest time. I delivered her words as best I could, while he confessed what had happened that evening and how his actions had led to her death. It was longer and harder than with Lord Blountford and Marisa, the emotions deeper, so that I felt myself holding back tears at the loss they had endured. Or perhaps it was that I could see two souls so intricately interwoven that I felt an echo of my own sorrow within them. I had always felt that my sister was a part of me, and to have this gift, or curse, and not be able to see her was a form of torture.

When the stories had been told, the memories revived, Pansy spoke the words that needed to be heard, a sad smile upon her lips.

'I forgive you.' She held up a hand to show me that her fingers were starting to fade away.

I held back a gasp. 'You are at peace now,' I told her. 'It is time for you to go.'

Mr McMannon looked to where he thought she might be. 'I love you for ever.'

'And I you, my Jo,' Pansy replied. She turned to me as her dress slowly disappeared. 'Thank you for what you have done. I hope you too find peace.'

I nodded, blinking away the sting in my eyes as she looked back at him, his face the last thing she wished to see before she moved on.

A phantom wind passed through the room, stirring the curtains and twitching my skirts, as if blowing away the last of her spirit, until she was there no more. Mr McMannon and I sighed in unison, mine the relief of a promise kept, his the breath of someone who had had a weight lifted from his shoulders.

'I would like to repay you,' he said, reaching under his shirt.

'I require no payment, Mr McMannon. I vowed I would help her and I did.'

'All the same, I think she'd like you to have this.' He unclasped a chain from around his neck and took my hand in his rough, warm grip, dropping a necklace into it and closing my fingers around the pendant. I frowned at the glint of ruby between my fingers. It was as large as a quail's egg, and thrice as heavy.

'I cannot accept this,' I replied, astounded by what I held and what he had hidden all this time.

'You must. I insist. Pansy was given it as a wedding present, but bestowed it upon me for safe keeping. It was the most valuable of her belongings, enough to buy us land and a house in the Highlands if we needed to run,' he explained, taking a step back.

'Why did you not use it yourself?'

'I never had the courage. I couldn't leave her memory behind, and I suppose I considered my time serving Lord Blountford penance for what I had done to her. I couldn't live happily on the sale of it knowing that it had been meant for us. Besides,' he added, tugging his beard thoughtfully, 'I never wanted to part from it until now. I think she would be pleased that you have it.'

'I . . .' I stopped. Could this be enough to pay my father's debts? Could I escape my fate after all? My breath shortened at the realisation. 'Thank you,' I said instead, putting the necklace on and tucking it under my dress out of sight.

'It is the least I could do. Now, I had better get to my duties before I'm missed,' he said, straightening his coat and wiping his face a final time.

'I shall walk with you downstairs. Hopefully Jordie will have returned by now,' I said hopefully.

Mr McMannon stopped. 'You didn't hear?'

'Hear what?' The worry that had plagued me this morning returned in a fresh wave of panic. 'Where is he?'

'Jordie Blake was dismissed from his post last night, miss. He was sacked.'

Chapter 18

ഔൽ

With the briefest of directions from Mr McMannon, I tore from the house and down to the stables, grateful that I knew how to ready Gwen for riding myself.

I didn't think of anything beyond finding Jordie and making things right. He had been my only true friend since Esme, and it was entirely my fault he had lost his position. I had befriended and confided in him, and my jealous future husband had immediately removed him from my life. Just as I had been warned. My blood boiled at the thought. I would not allow someone to control me so easily. I would not end up like the other four wives before me.

I ran it through in my mind as I saddled the horse up, thinking of all I had learned so far, of everything Lord Blountford was capable of. Marisa had been pushed to her death. Yes, it had been an accident in the heat of an argument, but it did not make the fact any less than it was. Anne, well, she had died of an illness, but what if she, like the other wives, had grown suffocated and oppressed and it had somehow made her ill? It might have been cruel of me to think the earl the cause of her death, but I had begun forming patterns in my head and now they could not be ignored.

And then Pansy . . . She was not innocent by any means, but

233

if Lord Blountford was aware that she had been unfaithful, it was not such a stretch to believe he also knew it was her he was giving the poison to. Whether he had decided to play God and make her the victim of her own plot, or intended to poison Mr McMannon in front of her, the man was cruel beyond comprehension. He had taken a life out of his own selfishness, something that made me all the more worried for Jordie, and about whatever had happened to Esme.

I mounted Gwen by using an overturned bucket, finding it much harder with no one to help me but not impossible. Once I was safely seated, I nudged her into a trot, through the courtyard and on to the road that led out of the estate. I could not go any faster even if I'd tried – when I prodded her sides with my heels and she began to canter, I felt myself jostling and slipping from the saddle. It appeared my lessons were far from complete, so I slowed her down hastily. I did not need to fall and crack my head open on top of everything else.

The directions the groundskeeper had given me were simple enough to follow. Jordie's mother and brothers lived a mile east of the last cottage in the village, the first of a row of six houses on the lane. I thought of how long it might take me to get there. My legs had barely recovered from riding the day before, but I would persist for him.

It took me almost an hour at my slow pace, keeping to the main road and passing through the village, where I waved to a few locals who were busying themselves, completely oblivious to my distress. The morning mist cleared as the noon sun beat down above me, surprisingly warm for the time of year. The white blanket that had obscured everything from view now revealed yellow and brown fields of wheat, freshly harvested, and bare orchards whose fruit had recently been picked. Never before had I been so aware of the passing of time. Here in the country, things constantly changed, while in the city I had felt more often than not that I was stagnated, unable to move or alter the course of events happening around me. Here, surrounded by evidence of passing seasons, and knowing that I now held the key to my own fate, I was terrified and liberated in equal measure. The pendant that hung around my neck, pressed against my skin, was a reminder that I might now be able to truly undo everything once and for all.

I knew nothing of the value of jewels, but if Pansy had planned to buy her and Mr McMannon their freedom, surely it could cover my father's debt. The idea made me anxious with anticipation, like insects skittering around my insides. How I would put such a plan into effect with only a day before my wedding, I didn't know, but I began to imagine it as I rode.

I recognised the house as soon as I saw it, almost as though I had been here before. Two small boys played in the garden with sticks, both with the same red curls and freckles as their older brother. I dismounted awkwardly and went to tie Gwen up by the water trough at the side of the fence, feeling two pairs of eyes upon me.

No, not two pairs, but three.

Standing by the front door, pipe in his mouth, was a broad-shouldered man with light-brown hair, looking at me with a comfortable smile.

'Hullo,' one of the boys said, their game paused for the moment as they inspected me nosily, unaware that the ghost of their father had been watching over them.

'Good day,' I said with a painful curtsey to the three of them. My thighs would take a week to recover, I was sure.

'Who are you?' asked the smaller of the two, which got him a nudge from his bigger counterpart.

'He means "Who are you, miss?" don't you, Darry?'

'Oh yes, sorry, miss,' Darry said, frowning at his brother.

'No trouble at all. My name is Lizzie Dawson. I live up at Ambletye and I'm a friend of your brother Jordie. Is he here?'

They shared a wary look, but the older boy seemed to decide he would speak for them both.

'He's not well, I'm afraid, miss,' he replied awkwardly. My heart plummeted.

'Do you think I could see him? It's very important,' I added when neither boy seemed convinced. I glanced at Jordie's father, but he gave no sign that he knew I could see him.

The boy shrugged in reply and ran down the short path to the house, yelling for his mother at the top of his lungs.

'What's your brother's name?' I asked Darry, who had been left to supervise me.

'That's Crispin. He's ten, and I'm eight,' he said proudly. 'I'm the fourth oldest.' He puffed out his chest and gave me a wide grin, which I returned.

'Ah, so you must have two younger brothers then?'

His eyes widened and he nodded fervently. 'That's right! Peter is four and George is only one, so I'll be allowed to tell them what to do when they're older.'

I laughed, looking up at the boy's father and smiling.

'I'm going to grow the biggest vegetables in town next year,' Darry went on. 'Can I show you my watering can?' he asked eagerly. I nodded and he ran off to fetch it from the large vegetable patch by the side of the house.

'You must be very proud of your sons,' I said to the ghost.

The man pushed off the cottage wall and came over to the fence where I stood, switching his pipe from one side of his mouth to the other.

'That I am, miss,' he said, pleasantly surprised to be speaking to someone. 'They're good lads.'

'They truly are. Jordie has been the best friend I could ever have asked for. I imagine they get their kind hearts from you and your wife,' I said, studying him. Jordie certainly took after him in looks, but no doubt he got his colouring from his mother.

'Who're you talking to?' Darry asked me, running back with his watering can.

I flicked a glance at the ghost, who shook his head gently and rested a hand on his boy's shoulder, though Darry seemed to sense nothing of it.

'Ah, just the friendly spirit that watches over you,' I said, bending down to inspect the object that he had thrust up at me. 'That is a fine watering can indeed,' I said, just as the front door of the cottage opened to reveal a flustered-looking woman with a baby on her hip. Crispin stood behind her peering out, along with a small child I assumed was Peter.

'Mrs Blake,' I said, opening the garden gate and walking down the short path to meet her, giving her husband a nod of acknowledgement as I passed. 'I am so sorry to trouble you. My name is—'

'I know who you are, miss,' she said abruptly. It was as though she were speaking to someone she had to be grudgingly polite to but perhaps would rather avoid altogether. I was taken aback by the anger that she barely concealed behind her rosy cheeks. As I had suspected, Jordie had inherited her red hair and russet eyes; eyes that now examined me coldly from across the threshold.

'I apologise for intruding, but might I be able to speak with Jordie?'

'I'm afraid he's unable to receive guests at the moment,' she said, pulling back into the house and making to close the door in my face.

'Mam!' I heard a croak from within. 'Mam, let her in.'

237

'Have you not done this family enough damage, Miss Dawson?' she hissed even as she opened the door again to allow me in.

'Mam!' the voice chastised from within.

Mrs Blake spared me a disparaging glance before shooing the boys outside and retiring to a corner of the room, laying the baby in a cradle near the window.

I allowed my eyes to adjust to the darkness inside the cottage. The downstairs consisted of an open space comprising kitchen, dining area and living room, while a door to the left stood ajar with a neat row of small beds visible just beyond. A ladder jutted up from the middle of the room to a loft above that presumably served as a second bedroom.

Everything was worn but clean, used but in good repair, which I found a feat in itself with so many small boys around the place.

A hunched figure with a mop of curls sat by the fire, shirtless, with bandages wrapped around his torso. When he looked up from the flames, I gasped. Jordie's face was a swollen mess, his usual smile gone and in its place an ugly bruise that marred half of his jaw. One eye was blackened and closed, and as he leaned forward, I could see blood seeping through the bandages on his back.

'What did he do to you?' I asked, rushing over and kneeling in front of him, taking his hands in my own.

He stifled a groan as he shifted in his seat, turning the disfigured side of his face away from the light.

''Twas my punishment, Lizzie,' he mumbled, the effort of speaking too painful for him to manage more than a few words. I reached up and with the lightest touch brushed the side of his face that wasn't purple from bruising.

I heard a disapproving harrumph from the kitchen area and flicked my gaze over to find his mother emphatically kneading a ball of dough. There was no need to guess what she thought of me, the woman who had brought this upon her son.

'I'm so sorry, Jordie. You must understand I never wished for this. I am only just beginning to understand the extent of his cruelty.' I dropped my voice to a whisper, not wanting to be overheard.

He gave the smallest shake of his head, which was more than I could have managed if I were in his state.

''Tisn't your fault,' he replied.

'But it is, Jordie. Completely and utterly. If I hadn't confided in you, if I hadn't come straight to you last night when I was so upset, he would never have known of our friendship. You would still have your job and . . . and you wouldn't have had to endure this.' I gestured to his injuries. 'I am the worst kind of friend to have brought this upon you.'

'What about you, Lizzie?' He winced as he moved. 'I worry about you all alone in that big house. With *him*.'

I said nothing as I dragged a nearby stool over to sit in front of him.

Worry about me? He didn't know the half of it. Pansy's poisoning immediately came to mind. 'I know, I know. But you mustn't fret for me, Jordie – I can take care of myself.' I patted my hip where I kept the knife, as if that would be enough to solve all of my problems.

'What about the ghosts?' Jordie asked under his breath, glancing with his good eye across the room to his mother. I paused for a heartbeat, ensuring that I couldn't be overheard.

'Do you recall all I told you of Pansy last night? The third wife?'

He gave the smallest of nods.

'Well, when I couldn't find you this morning, I hoped you had been merely waylaid so I did some investigating of my own.

I found out who she was having an affair with – Mr McMannon, no less,' I said, and his brows rose in surprise. I continued, explaining how I had made my discovery. The Gaelic in the diary, the cabin in the woods, the poisoning, the guilt that Angus McMannon had shown and the flowers that he maintained year-round in her honour.

'Clever, Lizzie,' was all Jordie managed in reply, but I could see that he was impressed.

'I remembered what Mr Grahame, the bookshop owner, had said about Pansy being locked in the house all the time. I don't believe that to be the case, but rather that she never ventured off the estate because everything she wanted was right there.' I sighed, a sadness tugging at my insides. 'They loved each other so much. I think it was her plotting to poison her husband that sent her astray. Taking that upon herself must have been a great hardship, and then for it to go so very wrong . . .'

'She couldn't believe that her plan had gone awry,' he offered.

'Exactly. And it was that disbelief, that she'd failed her mission, that caused her to haunt the house.'

'But she's gone now?'

'Yes, I reunited them, and she moved on happily in the end.'

I should have been glad that I had managed to help her, but I still felt a strange hollowness inside me. One that had started even before I knew I would never see Jordie's smiling face around the estate again.

'So it's better that you aren't there,' I concluded, 'for I couldn't bear it if anything worse had happened to you. At least now you have a way out, a way to start afresh.'

I hadn't realised how loud my voice had become until Mrs Blake scoffed again from the other side of the room.

'There'll be no starting afresh for some months yet, Miss Dawson,' she said bitterly, 'not with Jordie's injuries. He'll not be able to get a job until after Christmas, and even then, the demand is low until the sowing of the crops next year. Winter will be lean in our household now. The money he was supposed to get from teaching you would have been enough to keep us for a whole year, but even that hasn't come through thanks to your antics.' She pummelled the dough against the table hard enough to make me flinch.

'Mam!' Jordie said gruffly, the angriest I had heard him sound.

'No, Jordie, she's right. I must take responsibility for what I've brought upon you.' I stood up and brushed my skirts off, addressing Mrs Blake directly. 'I will do whatever it takes to make this right. I will demand that he be employed to finish his lessons with me.'

Even as I said it, I knew that it was foolish. Not only was Lord Blountford too stubborn to take back the dismissal, but why would Jordie even want to return to an employer who had beaten him so badly? Mrs Blake's raised eyebrow confirmed my thoughts, and I quickly changed my tune.

'I shall write Jordie a reference recommending him for service anywhere he wishes, and I will personally make sure that any money owed you is paid.'

'With all due respect,' she replied, her tone indicating that no respect was in fact due, 'no one will take a reference from you, Miss Dawson. Not for the work Jordie wants, anyway.'

I looked back down at my friend, his expression glum. He knew that what she said was right, even if he didn't wish to make me feel worse for it.

I thought about what Price had told me – that servants rarely made enough money to start a business or fulfil their dreams. It had seemed wrong to me then that Jordie might never have his own stables, his own horses to breed. After the trouble I'd caused, I had made that goal more distant than ever.

The door burst open. 'Mam! We found a frog under a bucket in the garden! Come and see,' Darry said excitedly, pulling on his mother's apron. The look she threw in my direction as she wiped her hands and walked out into the daylight said that she didn't trust me an inch, but I tried not to take it to heart even as my cheeks heated with shame.

'Don't worry 'bout her,' Jordie said, watching me carefully. 'She hasn't smiled much since Pa died.'

I stilled, wondering if I should tell him what I knew, or if it were better to let Mr Blake continue his happy existence watching his boys grow without my interference. Perhaps he merely wanted to see his family were well? Better to leave it be, I thought as I sat back down on the stool.

'She's entitled to her opinion about me,' I said, trying not to look too hard at his bandaged back. How many lashes had he received? Ten? Twenty? I imagined what the skin must look like under the bloodstained dressing and shuddered. 'This is such an awful mess.'

I leaned my elbows on my knees, pressing my fingers to my eyes. My nerves and emotions were fraught, like the strings on a harp being overtightened to the point where every note was off key.

'It is what it is,' he replied, resigned. 'The money from your riding lessons would have been nice, Lizzie, but people like me don't usually see that kind of coin in their entire lifetime. Perhaps God willed it so that I would see he had another path for me.' The sadness in his tone was unmistakable, causing those strings to snap altogether.

'No. No, I refuse to believe that,' I exclaimed, standing up suddenly and throwing my arms out. 'You are a *good* person, Jordie. Your family don't deserve this. I want you all to be able to eat this winter, and every winter hereon. I want your brothers to receive presents at Christmas and your mother to smile again. And I want more than anything for you to realise your dream.' I clutched at the weight on my chest, my thoughts whirring.

It was wrong that he and his family had to suffer. For what? Because I had befriended a servant? Because I had not been a good little bride-to-be and just submitted to the pain of discovering my future husband had *bought* me and my sister before me? My resolve hardened as I looked at him, the firelight illuminating the bruises to a deep purple. Enough was enough.

'If I had a way to get you the money for your own stables, your own horses, and to feed your family for years to come, would you accept it from me? Hypothetically?' I asked him, my stomach tightening with the thought of what I was about to do.

His good eye widened. 'I could never ask that of you, Lizzie. I wouldn't want to get you in trouble, and I couldn't start a business on stolen money,' he said, even though the effort of so many words tore at a scab on his lip and it began to bleed.

'Not stolen money, Jordie. It would be my money, truly. But I want to know whether you would take this gift if I were to give it to you. If there were absolutely no consequences tied to it other than that I insisted you live a full and happy life with it.'

He frowned uncertainly. 'It wouldn't be Lord Blountford's?'

'I promise it would have nothing to do with him,' I replied earnestly.

Time seemed to stretch out between us, the crackle of the fire and the tick of a clock above it marking out the minutes as they passed. Jordie's lovely, kind face, usually so open, looked troubled and drawn, and not just because of the injuries.

'I suppose Mam wouldn't forgive me if I said no, but of course it's just a what-if, isn't it? You don't actually have that kind of money to give away.'

I gave him an awkward smile as I unbuttoned my coat and

unclasped the chain that hung around my neck. Holding the ruby, warm from my skin, I rubbed my thumb over its polished surface. In that moment, all the ideas I had conjured, the plans I had half made, vanished from my mind one by one. It should have hurt to give such a precious thing away, my ticket to freedom, but instead I felt a deep certainty. A small part of my mind screamed at me for allowing it to slip through my fingers, like grabbing sand from the beach and watching it spill out of my grasp. But I told myself this was how it had to be. This was right.

I took one of Jordie's hands and placed the precious stone, chain and all, into his callused palm, closing his fingers around it. 'It is yours,' I said, my voice low as I saw the shock and emotion in his beaten face. He began to shake his head, but stopped as pain rippled across his features. 'Before you object, this is rightfully mine. It was a gift, and one that I pass on to you gladly. Please don't make it difficult for me by refusing it.'

'Lizzie—'

'*Please*, Jordie. I want you to have it. Sell it for all it is worth and more and feed your family. Buy your own stables and horses. Perhaps buy your mother a new bonnet, or something that will make her happy again.'

Anyone would have called me mad for gifting something so valuable to a boy I had known for less than a week, but to me it was liberating to do something that could help not just one but seven people.

'Why?' It seemed to be all he could manage as he stared at the gem in his palm, glinting blood-red in the flames before us.

I knelt down in front of him so that he would look at me, my neck feeling light from where the necklace had been.

'Because there was a time not so long ago when I needed someone to do that for me. To help me when I was broken. You gave me something I hadn't had since Esme died – a friend I could truly rely on. And hope.' I smiled at him as I stood, brushing down my skirts. 'All the gold in the world wouldn't repay your friendship, Jordie. I think I knew it from the moment I met you.'

The side of his face that wasn't bruised went a delightful shade of crimson, and he stood, unable to stop the whimper of pain as he did so. I opened my mouth to chide him for straining himself, but his strong arms wrapped around me and he pressed his cheek against the top of my head. I returned his embrace, being sure to avoid the bandages on his back as best I could.

'Thank you,' he whispered into my hair, his voice hoarse with emotion. My eyes stung and I blinked back the threatening tears.

I looked at his kind, honest face and for a moment I envied the girl who would one day capture his heart. In another life, perhaps, I would have been content to marry Jordie. He was the best kind of person, and he would make someone very happy.

I didn't think about the fact that I had just given away my escape route from Ambletye and Lord Blountford. The plan to sell the ruby and pay off my father's debts had been so short-lived that it had barely taken root in my mind, and this felt more right than that ever had.

There was a displeased sound from the doorway, and I glanced over to find Mrs Blake with her hands on her hips giving me one of her scrutinising looks. Jordie and I broke apart, and I squeezed his hand in farewell before walking to the door.

'Be sure to book me in as your first student when your stables are open,' I said to him, giving them both a small curtsey as I left.

I made sure to say goodbye to all the boys playing in the yard, committing each of their names and their joyous faces to memory as I did so. I hoped more than anything that I would be able to watch those boys grow up and become young men in their own right. With the money Jordie could get from the necklace, their future would be brighter. Mr Blake gave me a wave, pipe in hand, as I untied Gwen and used the edge of the trough to mount her.

Squealed sounds of delight came from within the house, and I broke into a smile, finding myself holding back tears once again. I had done something good. Rather than just helping the dead, I had helped those who were truly living. My heart pressed in my chest, feeling so full it was fit to burst.

I blew out a breath as I set off back the way I had come, turning once in the saddle to find Mrs Blake at the door again, waving me off with a handkerchief, her face creased into a smile. A smile I recognised from seeing it on Jordie's face so often.

With a nod and a wave of my own, I made my way home, not bothering to wipe away the happy tears that slid down my cheeks.

Chapter 19

❧

By the time I reached the village, a thread of doubt had sewed its way into my mind. It had started small, like a piece of cotton tying my thoughts together, but by the time I reached the shops and cobbled main road it was as thick as a rope, binding each worry to the next until they were clumped in the forefront of my mind. How could I return to Ambletye now, knowing that Lord Blountford had been responsible not only for the deaths of two of his wives, but for beating Jordie so brutally? Only yesterday, I had resigned myself to the forthcoming wedding, but now, with all the new information I had about the man's character and temper, I struggled to see beyond the ceremony.

I did not regret my decision to give Jordie the necklace, however. That still felt like the responsible and right thing to have done, for what were my troubles compared to the lives of six boys and their mother?

I rode past the shops, waving to the baker and his wife, the blacksmith and the seamstress. I kept Gwen to a slow pace, narrowly avoiding a group of children playing in the street, their squeals of laughter and joy doing nothing to ease my troubled mind.

I found myself steering the mare towards Price's house,

seeking refuge and comfort, and someone to speak with without being overheard.

'I'm afraid the doctor is out, miss,' Judith said when I arrived, my brow so furrowed I felt the beginnings of a headache forming. My heart sank with the news. 'He was called up to the Smithsons' farm this morning to tend to an ailing cow, and I'm not sure when he'll be back.'

'Oh,' I said, trying to hide my disappointment. 'I had hoped to speak with him before . . . before tomorrow,' I finished, reluctant to say the word 'wedding' aloud. Judith's eyes shone with something like pity and understanding. 'Perhaps I can come back later,' I added.

She must have caught the lost look on my face as I said it, the realisation creeping up on me that I would have to go back to the manor if Price was not here.

'If you don't object to sitting in the kitchen, I'd be happy to make you a cup of tea while you wait for him,' she said.

I appreciated the offer more than I could say, and found myself nodding. I was undoubtedly being a nuisance, but she was too kind to admit it.

She ushered me into the house and through the entrance hall to a door at the back, behind a narrow staircase that must have led up to sleeping quarters. The cottage was bigger than Jordie's, smaller than my parents' house in London, but could likely have fitted into the dining room at Ambletye.

The country house kitchen was nothing like the one Mistress Damiani ran with brutal efficiency. Pots and utensils hung from hooks on the walls, a single counter running all the way around the room with a small wooden table in the centre. Two rickety-looking chairs sat at each end and Judith pulled one out for me, telling me it was the least likely of the two to collapse under my weight. Where the kitchen at Ambletye was order and strict planning, the food following a logical flow from one end of the space to the other, Judith's was more like a tangled and disorganised mess. It seemed I had interrupted her in the middle of either cleaning vegetables at the table, plucking a pigeon at the far counter, or boiling soup, with various other parts of the meal in stages around the room.

'Now, let me find a cup for you,' she said, bustling around and knocking her head on a low-hanging saucepan as she opened a cupboard. I winced at the crash of china from within as she hastily closed the door and risked a glance at me. 'Perhaps something cool to drink instead?' she suggested hopefully.

I nodded, feeling terrible for inconveniencing her. 'Do you cook as well as doing the housekeeping?' I asked, surprised to find no other help in the house.

'I do now. Our last girl married and left to start a family, and the doctor hasn't had the chance to find someone else, what with all his duties,' she explained, disappearing into the pantry to retrieve a small keg of what I assumed was her famous cider. She found a pewter mug, only slightly dented, that seemed to pass the cleanliness inspection, and retrieved another for herself. I wasn't a drinker, but it seemed almost rude not to partake after all the pains she had gone to. The drunken stupor in which my mother spent most of her time was enough to put me off the idea for life.

'Is there anything I can do?' I asked. 'Perhaps I could enquire in the village to see if anyone is looking for work?'

'Oh, that's very kind of you, miss, but there's no need. I'm quite happy . . . Oh dear.' Judith darted across the kitchen to where the soup had bubbled over, causing the flames below to sizzle. I rushed to help her clean the spill while she heaved the pot from the hook and set it on the counter, muttering something about burnt pans being impossible to clean.

249

With the immediate disaster averted, I instructed her to sit and join me for a moment, and sipped tentatively at the cider she had poured. It burned pleasantly in my throat, sweet on the tongue at first but leaving a crisp, sour aftertaste. Judith perched on the edge of her seat across the table, sitting as lightly as she could so as not to tempt fate and break the spindly chair.

Regardless of what the accident-prone housekeeper said, I would find a way to get her help. She might not want it, but I feared that if I didn't intervene somehow, the cottage would go up in flames, or worse.

'How do you like the cider, miss?' she asked as I took another gulp.

'Delicious,' I replied, feeling a comfortable warmth spread from my stomach down through my limbs. Not only did I rarely drink, but I also realised that I had not eaten since breakfast. Perhaps that was why the room felt like it was gently turning.

The brief quiet was interrupted by the sound of boots trudging up the garden path, shortly followed by the back door bursting open to reveal a rather muddy-looking Price.

'Ah, Lizzie! To what do I owe this immense pleasure?' he asked, unabashed to find me amongst the chaos of the kitchen rather than in the drawing room, which was actually only slightly more respectable in appearance. He shucked off his boots and slipped his overalls onto the floor, treading carefully over a mound of onions by the door and padding across the tiles in his socks.

'Can a friend not drop in unannounced simply for a mug of Judith's famed cider?' I said, raising my cup to him a little unsteadily.

'Of course, of course, although usually they at least pretend there is an ulterior motive,' he replied with a grin, turning to the kitchen sink. 'Judith, what did I tell you about leaving potato peelings in the basin where I wash my hands? They will only become covered in animal entrails if I have to remove them every time I come back from an operation.' His voice was pained, but there was no real anger behind it as he added, 'I suppose I'm to become accustomed to entrail and potato-peel pie. Perhaps it adds to the flavour.'

'It is not the basin where you wash your hands, Doctor, but rather the basin where I prepare the food that you insist upon washing your hands in!' Judith replied, getting up to fuss about him.

I stifled a chuckle as the two of them bickered light-heartedly about the best place to keep vegetable leavings, and why the doctor could not, perhaps, clean up before he entered the house.

'Apologies for my delayed return, dear Lizzie. Had I known you were waiting, I would not have involved myself with the goings-on up at the public house, or at least tried to extricate myself before I became witness to the fisticuffs.'

'There is no need at all to apologise, for I had no appointment but merely wanted to delay my journey home,' I replied, certain that he wouldn't miss the meaning behind my words. 'I have news that I wished to share, and would have been more than happy to lend a hand to your work if I had been early enough.' I remembered what Price had said about Esme helping him with his visits. I now understood why she had done it. The desire to have a purpose, to be useful and to work with one's hands was sometimes too great to resist, particularly when in good company. I could foresee myself slipping into the same habit quite easily. 'What happened at the inn?'

He dried his hands on a cloth and made to sit on the chair that Judith had just vacated, but thought better of it when it wobbled precariously under him.

'It seems that a small group of strangers from out of town

began a fight with a local lad. I only became involved because I happened to be riding past when they were all kicked onto the street by the landlord.'

'How dreadful,' I said, wondering if there was this much excitement every day in the village.

'Well, it could have been worse. Apparently the local boy had been sent by one of these strangers to deliver a message up your way, to Ambletye. It appears Lord Blountford refused not only to hear the message, but also to pay the lad, who came back to find those who had tasked him with the errand most displeased.'

'And they came to blows over such a thing?'

'Oh yes. Wherever money is involved, my dear Lizzie, men will fight. Well, money and love – usually the two obvious candidates,' he added as an afterthought.

Judith made an appropriately alarmed sound while I pondered this information. Who would be staying at the inn who might send a message to Lord Blountford? A message that might be turned away?

'You didn't get a good look at any of the gentlemen involved, did you?' I asked, my mind feeling pleasantly but worryingly foggy.

'I did indeed. I had to give a statement to the parish constable. There were three men in the party, two of whom could well have been related.'

'The foxes,' I murmured, before draining my mug.

'Hmm, funny you should say that. The notion did cross my mind. Two foxes and a weasel, I thought to myself when I saw them huddled together, defending their honour for all it was worth. They talked their way out of any consequences, of course, despite my intervention and attestation of the messenger's character.'

'Of course they did,' I said, feeling slightly nauseous, either from the alcohol or at the realisation that Mr Canfield and his compatriots were staying locally. 'Where is the inn?' I added, urging my mind to clear so that I could formulate a plan.

'Just to the east of the green, on the London Road. I wish I had taken another route home,' Price added wearily. 'Now, shall we continue to sit around in the kitchen like a group of fishwives, or would you rather retire to my more civilised room at the front of the house and Judith can perhaps make us some tea?' He waggled his bushy eyebrows in her direction.

'There was a problem with the cups, Doctor,' Judith replied vaguely.

'Somehow that does not surprise me, but I would be more than happy to have mine in whatever vessel you desire, provided that I can sit down and have *something*. I was called out before the cockerel this morning and I am quite exhausted.'

Despite the cosiness of the dishevelled kitchen I didn't want to keep him standing, so I allowed him to lead the way back to our usual meeting room, where he could rest his legs and listen to all I had to say.

'You mentioned you had news,' he said as he flung his jacket on the back of a nearby chair and took a seat in his favourite spot.

'That I do,' I replied, settling down on the battered sofa and leaning forward, willing my thoughts to arrange themselves into something coherent. I wondered blearily what vintage Judith's cider was, and whether it was always this strong.

It took me almost half an hour to explain all I had discovered of Pansy, with Price asking far more questions than Jordie had. I paused only when Judith came in with the tea things, resuming the story once she had left.

'Oh Lizzie, this is a most alarming development,' Price remarked once the tale had been told in its entirety, though of necessity with no mention of ghosts. 'I am not one to involve myself in the affairs of others so directly, but there must be some way to prevent your wedding tomorrow.'

I gripped my teacup until my knuckles were white. When I had discovered what had happened to Anne and James, I had felt sorry for my fiancé. When I learned the truth of Marisa's death and reconciled him with her ghost, I even convinced myself that he had suffered terrible fortune. But he had killed Pansy and had got away with it. That truth could not be exposed without also putting Mr McMannon in the crossfire, but though the groundskeeper was willing to let it lie, I didn't think I could. Especially after what had been done to Jordie. I only hoped that if I could solve Esme's death and lay the blame at the earl's feet, I might still have a way out.

Mistaking my silence for pained resignation to my fate, Price lightened his tone. 'I must say, I am most impressed that Mr McMannon confessed everything to you and was not worried that you would have him dismissed, but then you do have that sort of character,' he mused.

'What sort of character?' I asked, downing the tea in the hope that it would clear my head.

'Well, you're rather no-nonsense, my dear, and I mean that in the best way possible,' he added hastily. 'I believe that people have a tendency to trust you with their truths, as they did with your sister.'

The knowing look that came with that remark was all too close to the bone. Price did not know the half of it, and yet he had perceived something about me that I thought only the dead had taken advantage of.

'Oh, I don't know about that,' I said uncertainly, putting my cup back on the table. 'I think people are often lonely. It doesn't take much more than the ability to listen for them to want to talk. Besides, I have always found their stories fascinating,' I said with a shrug.

'If you don't mind me saying, your sister once told me something of you. She was sitting just where you are now, during one of our afternoons when we weren't delivering lambs or nursing pigs back to health.' He smiled at the memory and leaned back in his armchair, crossing one leg over his knee. 'She said that you were more perceptive than anyone she had ever known. That you saw things in people but that perhaps you also spoke your mind more often than they might like.'

I felt an uncomfortable blush creep up my neck. 'She always told me to let her do the talking,' I mumbled.

'Indeed, but she said it not as a criticism. She admired you for your ability to see things that other people ignored. Take the lost wives, for example.' He gestured to me with a wave of his hand. 'Esme pondered over her little discoveries, but in the year she was here, we made little progress in uncovering the truth. She was too busy planning dinners and fulfilling her duties as Lady Blountford, and it never seemed to bother her enough to persist. You, on the other hand, have already unearthed most of the story.'

'For what good it has done me,' I said, pulling at a thread on the fabric of my dress. 'I only set out to discover what had happened to her. I wish I had known nothing about the women before me. I wish I didn't know who it is that I am really marrying, and what he's capable of when crossed,' I added darkly. 'I wish that I was an oblivious idiot who was more than happy to swan around Ambletye without a care in the world.'

'Ah, but that's what makes you dangerous, my dear Lizzie,' Price said. I looked up from the fabric in my fingers and into his observant eyes. 'Your sister rebelled in her own little way, coming to visit me when she could and helping with my work, but she felt that her place, and her duty, was ultimately with her husband. You, on the other hand, could bring about a change to that estate the likes of which has not been seen in decades.'

I opened my mouth to question his meaning, but he leapt up from the armchair and walked over to the bureau, picking up an envelope and handing it to me.

'This came yesterday after you left. I wanted to give it to you as soon as I saw you, but I warred with my conscience a little. The news inside might be . . . upsetting. I did not want you to have it without fair warning.'

I looked at the envelope as though the contents might leap out and bite me, then flipped it over to find a familiar hand that sent my heart juddering within my ribcage. Charles's distinctive writing was hurried, as urgent as it had been when he wrote to me on Sunday night.

Dear Dr Price,

I must, first and foremost, apologise for putting you in this position. I would ask, if you would be so kind, to ensure that the message I enclose within this letter makes its way to Miss Dawson. I am unable to send a letter directly to Ambletye for my uncle has forbidden me from communicating with her, and I do not wish to put her in any further danger.

I am confiding in you as a fellow gentleman whom I believe cares deeply for Miss Dawson, for I understand her to be at great risk.

You may have become aware of the fact that my uncle dismissed me from his estate on Sunday afternoon. I spent the evening at the Hand and Plough, with plans to take a coach travelling by night to London, as I already have an ongoing investigation into some of my uncle's affairs that I wished to continue in person. However, upon speaking with the retired Dr Lewis, whom I did not know until now had been in attendance at Ambletye these past four decades, I discovered most distressing news. Information that has led me to conclude that Lizzie is in the gravest of peril should she be allowed to marry my uncle.

I am therefore entrusting you with this letter in the hope that you will not object to being a messenger for me, however improper it may seem.

I will, of course, understand if you refuse, but I believe that Miss Dawson would wish to hear from me, for my dismissal from the house was abrupt and allowed for no goodbyes.

If nothing else, it would put my mind at rest to know that my words are in her hands.

Sincerely,
Captain Charles Blountford

I looked up to find concern on Price's face.

'Why did you not bring this to me at the house?' I asked, a little sharply.

He shifted uncomfortably before replying. 'I did make enquiries yesterday at Ambletye, but you couldn't be found in your room. Your young maid was adamant that you be left alone, and I didn't know how else to pass the message along.'

I pictured him coming up against small, mousy Marie, who was proving to be a formidable ally.

'But what does he mean, that I am in the gravest peril?' The words came out as a whisper.

'That I do not know. I can only imagine that Dr Lewis told him something quite disturbing. The messenger who delivered this letter explained that he had been instructed not to give it to me until he was certain the captain had left the village. The letter for you is still in the envelope,' he added.

I felt guilty for even wanting to read Charles's note. My traitorous heart still surged at the sight of my name in his hand, even though I despised him for all that had gone before between him and Esme. From his words, I did not doubt that his feelings for me were at least a little sincere, but the idea that he was using me to get to his uncle's estate still itched in the back of my mind like a flea bite. I could not ignore his warnings, though, and so I unfolded the paper.

Dear Lizzie,

I will not say where I am writing from, or what I am doing, but please know that I have not discarded, nor forgotten, what I said to you. I truly meant it. I am searching for a way to secure your future, our future, with what little time we have left. I will contact you as soon as I can. If there is any way for you to delay the wedding proceedings without igniting my uncle's suspicions, I urge you to do what you can. If it is impossible, rest assured I will make things right somehow. Do nothing that will stir his anger.

With my deepest admiration,
Charles

My breath caught in my throat, the headache that had threatened before now beginning to pound in my ears. *Do nothing that will stir his anger.* Well, it was perhaps too late for that. I attempted to read the words he hadn't written, the clues between the lines. He evidently believed that marrying Lord Blountford would be perilous for me somehow, and aside from the obvious, I wondered what he could possibly be alluding to. Doubt and uncertainty warred with the hope and longing within me. There was only one way to decide whether his warning to Price was true.

'Where would I find Dr Lewis?' I said, folding the letter back into the envelope and leaving it on the table.

'He would either be at home or, more likely on a Wednesday afternoon, at the public house,' Price replied with a hint of distaste. 'But Lizzie, surely you don't mean to go there yourself?'

'Of course I do,' I replied, standing and taking my coat from where it lay on the back of the sofa. 'The captain has insinuated some rather serious allegations about the man I am to marry tomorrow. *Tomorrow*, Price. If I am truly in danger, I must know the nature of it.'

'Then allow me to accompany you,' he said, bracing his hands on his knees.

I stooped to take his rough hand in my own. 'Thank you, but no. You have been up since dawn and I would not want to be the cause of your exhaustion. I can look after myself,' I added as I saw worry cloud his face. As much as I wanted his support, I felt I might be better able to press this Dr Lewis for more information if I were alone.

Price did not seem appeased by my reassurance, but he nodded all the same, weariness winning over his concern that I make it to the inn in one piece.

With a squeeze of his shoulder and a goodbye called to Judith down the hall, I left the cottage, the mixture of tea and cider churning in my otherwise empty gut.

*

The Hand and Plough was a pretty building with whitewashed walls and black-painted beams that matched the aged dark tiles on the roof. It served both as the local public house and as a coaching inn, evidenced by the stables that stood to the right of the building, which were bustling with activity even this late in the afternoon. Travellers would undoubtedly stop here on their way to either London or Brighton, as there was little of interest nearby.

A boy took Gwen from me and I entered through the low front door, originally designed for those much shorter than I, for I had to stoop to enter. The smell of hops and pipe smoke hit me like a wall as soon as I stepped inside, my eyes taking several moments to adjust to the candlelit interior. The windows that should have let at least some daylight in seemed unable to compete with the shadows that fell upon every corner of the room, the benches and tables plunged into darkness, hiding their denizens as though the inn itself knew that people wished to lose all sense of time here.

The only true source of light was the lanterns suspended above a large bar across the far wall, manned by a middle-aged lady with a mass of blonde hair that coiled around her head and over her shoulders, grazing her generous cleavage, which seemed to be trying to escape from the top of her bodice.

Laughter ripped through the murk as men and women drank, smoked and did whatever it was that people did in pubs. My mother had always been more of a private drinker, rarely attending such places in London, but still, the sharp tang of alcohol and the glazed look on one or two of the patrons' faces brought unhappy memories to mind.

Who knew that a tiny village could have such a bustling social circle?

I threaded my way through the tables until I reached the bar, hoping to catch the server's attention. If anyone knew who Dr Lewis was, it would be her. I waited my turn, not realising at first that there was no particular queue, but that rather whoever shouted the loudest was served first. When eventually she glanced in my direction, I waved, hoping it would be enough to pull her away from the leer of a gentleman at the other end.

'What can I do for you, miss?' she asked, giving me a smile so dazzling I felt as though I could have been the only person in the room. No wonder the place was so popular.

'I was wondering if you could direct me to Dr Lewis? I was told he might be here,' I said as loudly as I dared over the raucous laughter of the man beside me.

She gave a slight nod to the far corner of the room. 'He always sits over there,' she said, her eyes flicking up and down in a quick examination. 'You're new around here?'

'Yes,' I replied before giving her hasty thanks and making my way to where she had indicated. I did not want to announce that I was from Ambletye, not here, when I was on a mission to get away from the place.

The man draped in shadow at the far table looked ancient, his salt-and-pepper hair combed back from his face in a way that accentuated the wrinkles in his skin. He was, perhaps, as old as Lord Blountford himself, I thought as I studied him, and looked just as haunted. I was about to slide onto the bench opposite him when a hand snagged my own, spinning me around, and I found myself looking at the broad chest of one of the Weston brothers, the other standing just behind him, blocking my view of the bar.

'Well, well, well,' said a voice that curdled my blood. 'Miss Dawson, I did not expect to see you frequenting such an establishment as this.' Mr Canfield stood up from the bench where he had been sitting.

'I am here on an errand, Mr Canfield, and I would appreciate it if you would tell your hound to let go of me,' I said abruptly.

'Ho ho, did you hear that, Mr Weston? You are my hound now,' Canfield said, giving the man a pat on the arm.

'Woof, woof,' Weston said before breaking into a dirty chuckle, but still gripping my wrist with enough force that I had to bite back a yelp of pain.

'I will tell the earl of your assault on me if you do not unhand me this instant,' I said, trying and failing to yank my hand free.

'Oh, be our guest, Miss Dawson. Why do you think we are here except to finish our business? Perhaps you can take word to him, seeing as he refuses to listen to our messages.'

My free hand edged towards the buttons of my coat. If I could only undo them and reach across my hip, I might be able to free my knife.

'What would you have me tell him?' I asked, narrowing my eyes at the weaselly man.

'For some reason he seems to be ignoring the immediate threat to his business in London. I would like you to advise him that we will be staying here, at his cost, until he gives us his approval to deal with the situation. Alas, I fear he is not taking this threat seriously,' he added, picking up his glass and sighing theatrically when he noticed it was empty.

'Why don't you deal with it yourself?' I asked.

'Well, the sort of thing I will need to do requires his consent, miss. I wouldn't want to be disposing of any Blountford family members without his express permission, now would I?'

My blood chilled, sending a wave of shock down my back. I recalled the conversation I had overheard between Lord Blountford and Mr Canfield last night. It seemed that Charles had made his way to London after all and was causing more trouble than I had realised.

'I can assure you that he will not give you his permission for such a thing,' I said, finally managing to pull out of Weston's grasp as his fingers slackened slightly.

'Don't be so sure, Miss Dawson. After all, you know what happens to people who interfere with the earl's business.' Canfield smirked, then signalled with a nod of his head for the Weston brothers to follow him. 'Tell him if he doesn't send us orders before the day's end, he may find himself with the constables on his doorstep. I'll wait until first light but no later before I take matters into my own hands. Better to sort it out now than to let that happen,' he said over his shoulder, pushing his way through the room until I lost sight of him.

I huffed a sigh of relief that they had left, but it was short-lived. Shaking the pain out of my wrist, I turned back to where the doctor sat, seemingly oblivious to the exchange.

As I slid in opposite him, several thoughts came to mind. I had no intention of relaying Canfield's messages to the earl, but in doing nothing, was I putting Charles in more danger? I certainly did not want Lord Blountford to order him killed. I felt a wave of dizziness and gripped the edge of the table.

'Are you all right, miss?' the doctor asked, his voice hoarse.

'I'm . . . fine, thank you. I simply need to eat,' I replied, taking in the man's face. He looked lost, empty, like a house with no lights on. A man without purpose. 'Dr Lewis, I presume?'

'One and the same,' he said with a nod and a raise of his mug. 'And you are?' he asked as an afterthought.

'My name is Lizzie Dawson. A young gentleman spoke to you the other night. A captain. Do you remember what you told him?' I had no time for niceties, and I didn't think he would notice, or mind my abrupt manner.

'Captain? Ah yes, the young naval man. I thought he was Lord Blountford at first. It was like seeing a glimpse into the past. He looked just like the earl when I attended Lady Anne and their son. I told him as much. I think that was how our conversation began, in fact.' He mumbled when he spoke, as though he had cotton stuffed under his tongue, making it difficult for me to understand him.

'You cared for the earl's second wife?' I asked, masking the surprise in my voice. Was this what had Charles so spooked? Something to do with Anne? Doctors learned more than they would often let on, being so intimately connected to their patients' lives.

'Yes, I'm afraid so. And his fourth. You remind me of her, actually,' Lewis said, peering at me with rheumy eyes.

'She was my sister, sir,' I said, in the hope that it would encourage him to tell me more. 'I believe she was expecting when she died, yes?'

He nodded vaguely, as though he were trying to piece something together.

'It is peculiar in my line of work, seeing how history repeats itself. Patients with similar ills. Babies with deformities. Families with the same conditions passed from parent to child. People who look just like their relations from generations before . . . That was what struck me when the captain came to see me. He was worried.' The old doctor sighed and swirled the ale in his mug. 'I think that was what made me mistake him for Lord Blountford. That furrow in his brow.' He narrowed his eyes, trying to recall something.

'Lord Blountford was worried for Anne, I suppose, when she caught the infection?'

'Yes, she was very ill, and the babe, already weak from his deformity, contracted the same sickness. But it was the bruises that struck me as odd . . .' He trailed off as if remembering some detail.

My mind snagged on the mention of James having had a deformity. This was the first I had heard of it, and darker thoughts crowded in. Lord Blountford would not have tolerated having such a child, if I was any judge of his character.

'Bruises?' I pressed, hoping the doctor would reveal more while silently hoping there wasn't anything else to know.

'Yes. I enquired after the bruises on her arms and neck. His lordship told me she was weak with the sickness and had fallen.' He shrugged. 'A perfectly reasonable explanation, of course, but they were the same . . .' His words slurred, and I struggled to make sense of them.

'The same as what?'

'The same as the ones on Lady Esme's body after she and the babe died.'

I barely felt the pain from my fingernails digging into the wood of the table, my other hand reaching across to grip the doctor's sleeve.

'And these bruises? They caused Lady Esme to miscarry?'

'Alas, no. The child was growing out of place and there was nothing that could be done for her. Blood all over the nursery in the attic. Horrible business. She was terrified for the fate of the child, begging me to do something. She died of heartbreak as much as the child's complication.'

My eyes stung as I envisaged Esme, beautiful, buoyant, lively Esme, discovering that she was dying, her child with her. What would that have done to her in her final moments? I knew what an out-of-place pregnancy meant. It meant that the child would have caused her agony. It was the babe itself that had killed her, not Lord Blountford. I didn't understand how that made me feel. Pained. Angry.

But why would Charles have worried for me so if all the doctor had told him was the sad tale of my sister's death?

'You mentioned bruises,' I croaked, trying to force the quiver from my voice.

'Yes, bruises,' he repeated vaguely, staring off into the distance.

'Doctor, what were those bruises?' I pushed, squeezing his arm gently to remind him I was still there.

'I think . . .' His gaze fell upon my hand gripping his arm before he looked into my face with a frown, and I could see that he was struggling with the idea of confessing his thoughts. I kept my expression as blank as I could, even though the knowledge he was imparting was cleaving my heart. He shook his head. 'Well, it is just as I told the captain. I don't think either woman fell at all. There were clusters of five bruises, like fingerprints, on their arms. I think they had been . . . maltreated.'

'You evil, pernicious man!' I screamed as I burst into the study. Lord Blountford rose to his feet as though I had marched into the room with a musket aimed at his head. I wished I had. 'What did you *do* to her? Why did she have signs of injury before she died?'

'Miss Dawson, I don't know what in God's name—'

'I spoke to Dr Lewis! He told me about Esme's injuries. The same ones on Anne's body. Fingerprints, bruises from mistreatment. He told me that your son, the one you lost to illness, had been born deformed. Was that why you lost your temper? Was that why you hurt Anne?'

'Stop it,' he said, horror upon his face.

'When you found out Pansy was barren, were you happy to have the opportunity to be rid of her?'

'I said stop!'

'And my sister? When you discovered that her pregnancy would not survive, did you take your anger out on her as well?'

I sounded hysterical, a woman gone mad from paranoia. But the truth of the evil that stood before me was indisputable.

'You will stop this at once!' he shouted, ringing the bell on his desk. Turner entered the room a heartbeat later. 'Restrain Miss Dawson and lock her in her room,' he ordered.

Turner hesitated only a moment before trying to take my arm. I lashed out and hit him, even though I knew he was simply following orders. Lord Blountford stepped around his desk towards me. 'RESTRAIN HER NOW!' His bellow was so loud it shook my very bones.

Two more servants appeared from the hall and tried to pin my arms to my sides. My knife was in my hand quicker than they could gain purchase. These were no Weston brothers. They were boys, used to polishing boots and pressing shirts, not fighting.

'Keep away from me!' I said, brandishing my blade at them. 'What is the purpose of all this, Lord Blountford? I will *never* have your child! I will *never* let you touch me!'

'You will.' His voice was a growl. 'For if you do not, I will seize your parents' assets and have the pair of them left for dead. I require only one thing from you, Miss Dawson. A legitimate child who can carry on my legacy. If I have to lock you in your room until that happens, I will.'

'Your legacy? Your legacy is corruption and death.'

I turned my head and spat on the floor at his feet. But I was too slow to see the brass weight in his hand, too slow to move out of the way. It hit me across the back of the head and everything went black.

Chapter 20
෨ ൬

My mother had said that my mouth would get the better of me one day. She was not wrong.

I cracked open an eye and stared at the ceiling of my room, only slightly comforted to find that I wasn't in some hidden dungeon in the house. Night had fallen since I had returned to Ambletye, and the room was illuminated by fire and candle-light, casting everything in a golden glow, so at odds with the feeling of dread that crawled upon my skin like dozens of angry spiders. A blackbird sang its happy evening song outside my window, and I damned its cheerfulness when I felt so sour.

How could I have been so stupid? I cursed myself silently, echoing my mother's censure. I should have gone back to Price and told him what I had discovered, should have allowed him to calm me and formulate a plan, but my impulsiveness had led me straight into the lion's den. There was something I was sup-posed to be doing now, I was certain of it, but my head felt as though it were full of syrup, my thoughts slipping away when I tried to grasp at them.

A pounding came from somewhere. My heartbeat, I real-ised, throbbing in my ears and sending a constant dull pain through the back of my head, but when I tried to reach up to feel the lump I imagined was there, I could not move my hands.

Seized with panic, I glanced down to see that a sheet had been tied across the bed, clamping my arms to my sides. I wriggled beneath the makeshift fetters, to no avail.

A shadow was cast across the bed, belonging to the disturbing figure of Lord Blountford, who stood by the window staring out into the darkness beyond. He must have sensed my struggle, for he turned to fix me with his milky green eyes. He looked about a hundred years old, the lines etched into his face like tree bark in the dim light.

'The restraint is for your own good, Miss Dawson,' he said solemnly. 'It was recommended by Dr Garrett, in case you tried to do yourself, or anyone else, harm.'

I threw him a look that told him exactly what I thought of Dr Garrett's recommendation. The earl had probably called for a doctor as soon as possible, claiming that I had flown into an inexplicable rage. I had heard of women being committed by their husbands for lesser outbursts. I supposed, grimly, that I was lucky I had not been sent straight to an asylum.

How long had I been out? Three, maybe four hours? My stomach cramped with hunger, my throat was raw from shouting, and there was a sour taste in my mouth that I could not identify.

'Water,' was all I managed to rasp.

He nodded, ringing the bell beside the bed. Its shrillness sent a stab of pain through the side of my skull. Marie entered a moment later and I managed to lift my head enough to see her glance worriedly from the earl to myself.

'Fetch Miss Dawson the food and drink that was prepared for her at dinner time,' he commanded. Marie blanched, but curtseyed before shuffling back out of the door. I wondered briefly if she knew what had happened to Jordie, although the thought was quickly pushed out of my mind by Lord Blountford sitting on the edge of my bed, his hand wobbling on his cane.

'You have vexed me most gravely, Miss Dawson,' he grumbled. 'I have half a mind to send you back to your parents and make good on my earlier promise.'

'Why don't you then?' I wheezed, the pressure from the sheet and the dryness in my throat making it difficult to speak. 'What is the point of suffering all this torment just to wed again?'

He shook his head angrily. 'I have never known such a recalcitrant, disobedient girl. It is as though you care nothing for your family at all. You would rather live in the gutter than marry me and bear me a child?'

The question was rhetorical, but I scoffed in reply. Opening my mouth for a retort, I found that no words would come.

Would I rather live on the streets than in the comfort of Ambletye, committing my parents to the same fate? I thought numbly that it must have been the choice Esme was given, and perhaps the women before her too.

'Is that why you killed them? Because none of them succeeded in providing you with an heir?'

'I beg your pardon?' His surprise was visible, but the expression swiftly twisted into a scowl.

'Marisa,' I rasped, 'headstrong and fearless, fought with you and died. Anne and her deformed baby died. Pansy, barren and unable to bear a child, found comfort in another's arms and died. Esme, with her unfortunate pregnancy, died. What will it take for you to see that *you* are the problem, not the women you married?' The accusation poured out of me despite the pain in my head and the roughness of my voice, all the anger I had felt earlier rising back to the surface.

'You do not get to say their names,' he snapped. 'You do not get to speak of them as though they meant anything to you at all, for you do not understand.'

'I do and I will. I will repeat them to you every day of your

270

miserable life so that you might never . . .' I felt nausea sweep over me, so sudden that I had to clamp my lips down.

He smirked, as though he were privy to some information that I was not.

I swallowed, the sickness ebbing like a wave. 'You killed them all,' I whispered, the fear in my voice betraying me.

'You would paint me as an evil man, Elizabeth,' he said, brandishing my full Christian name like a punishment, 'but you do not understand. So although I owe you no explanations, I will tell you of the torment I have suffered.' He looked away from me to the fire that crackled in the hearth.

I waited, a little dazed, to hear what lies he would weave for me this time.

'To lose Marisa so young, my first love . . . I changed once she died. I thought . . . I hoped I could put her death behind me when I met Anne. For a year we were happy, filled with joy when we discovered she was with child.' His voice was faraway, almost muffled, and I worried that I was losing my hearing. The sound of my own heartbeat seemed to roar above everything else and I felt uncomfortably hot. Was I ill? Feverish?

'But then when James came, his legs were . . .' His voice cracked. 'He would never walk, they told me. He would be lucky if he survived past his first birthday, even if properly tended to. He was always in so much pain, but Anne would never leave his side. It angered me that this bright, intelligent woman would give her very soul up for a child who cried all day and night.'

'So you hurt her,' I choked out.

'I never meant to,' he said quickly, as though he were defending himself in front of a judge, rather than a woman he had just tied to a bed. 'I pleaded for her to leave the house, to leave James with a nursemaid and walk with me. To go to the summer house,

271

or to see the children she taught in the village. I thought perhaps a change of scene might revive her spark. Perhaps I was too rough with her, leaving marks on her arms when I tried to prise the boy from her and make her leave him. The doctors suggested she be cared for at a hospital, somewhere they could treat her case of melancholy, but I refused. They came almost every day to give her concoctions that might cure her, but they only seemed to make her worse.'

Visions swam before my eyes of a woman roaming the house with a squalling child, unable to let the babe go, already a ghost of her former self. A shiver came over me even though it was stifling in the room.

'And then one day she picked up James and left the house in the rain. I had returned from London late that day and had no notion that she was out until at dinner time nobody could find her. We searched everywhere, but it was Mr McMannon who discovered her by the lake with no overcoat, singing to the boy. She had the most beautiful voice, even then.'

Marie came in and set a tray upon the bedside table, and Lord Blountford dismissed her with a wave of his hand. He picked up a decanter of water and poured a glass, bringing it to my lips. I gave him an astonished look, but he only said, 'I am not untying you, so you can either drink or go thirsty.'

I took a few sips of water until I could speak again.

'That is how they both became ill?'

He nodded, placing the glass back down. It was only when I dared to look him in the face that I saw the brightness in his eyes and the tears streaking down his lined cheeks. A pang of pity spiked in my chest despite my anger. That was, until I remembered the true reason for my distress, and why I was tied down like a crazed lunatic.

'Why did my sister have bruises on her arms?'

He turned his face away from me, spotting something on the vanity and hobbling over to pick it up. My knife, I realised with a start. He twirled it between his fingers, grazing his thumb against the point so that it scraped his papery skin but didn't draw blood.

'Esme was in pain from just a few months after we married. She hid it well, but there were times when she would become very faint. They told me later, after she died, that the babe had grown out of place, as they called it.'

That was what Dr Lewis had said. My parents had never been informed, I was certain of it, or they would have said something.

'She used to insist that I go for a walk daily, dragging me out come rain or shine to wander the grounds with her. Said it was good for my health even when I told her I was busy. Your sister was a very persistent woman when she wanted to be,' he added, and sadness rang through me like a bell. That was the Esme I remembered. 'One day while we walked a faintness came over her and she fell forward. I grabbed her by the arms so that she would not crack her head on the paving or cause herself injury, but it appeared that I held her too tightly, leaving marks on her.'

That familiar dark pain of loss opened up inside me like a chasm, stretching out until I thought it might swallow me. I searched for some indication that he was telling me an untruth, as he studied the carvings on my knife in the candlelight, but saw nothing that gave him away. I had automatically assumed the worst about him, which said nothing of my own character.

'Dr Lewis said that he suspected . . .' I trailed off, hunger making my words disappear like clouds being blown away by a gale. I looked at the tray Marie had set down and willed it to come towards me. Maybe if I ate something I could make sense of all I was being told.

'Ah, I see now,' he said, placing the knife on the bed and picking up a bowl. He dipped a spoon into what appeared to be cold soup and raised it to my mouth as he spoke. 'You believed the word of a man who spends his days drowning his sorrows in ale, who has no professional capacity any more and so fills his time musing over days gone by. You thought I had hurt your sister.'

I blinked, my cheeks heated with shame from the truth of his words.

'Why did you not tell me before?'

His look was impatient, as though he were speaking to someone of lesser intelligence than him. 'You didn't ask,' was his only reply.

I frowned, searching his face once again for a sign that he was spinning me a yarn.

'Believe me, do not believe me, Elizabeth, but I loved your sister, and I believe she loved me too, in her own way. Her death was a tragedy, but nothing more.'

The soup slid down my throat uncomfortably, bitter and oily, but it was better than nothing even if it tasted a day old.

'But why marry again?' I said, pulling my head back from the proffered spoon. 'Why not simply bequeath your fortune to your nephew? You are not ill, or dying. You are not too old to enjoy the comforts of what you have achieved. After so much heartache, does it not seem like folly to try again and hope for a different outcome?'

He looked down his pointed nose at me and slammed the bowl back down on the tray.

'Do you understand nothing?' He snorted derisively. 'Charles would not continue my legacy. He owes me no allegiance, and would only close down my businesses and squander the money on whatever it is that military men like. Women and alcohol, from what I've heard,' he added with indignation. 'I will not have everything I have worked and slaved for thrown away by a feckless young man.'

'I do not believe he is like that at all,' I blurted, the words sounding childish even as I said them.

'You wouldn't,' he retorted, not bothering to hide his disgust. 'I saw the way you looked at him. Young people these days have no loyalty, none at all.' I wondered to whom he was referring. Me and Charles? Jordie, perhaps, or even Pansy.

'Not to your nephew then. Why not change your will so as to pass everything on to someone who understands what you've worked for? Someone you trust?'

The question sat between us as heavy as if it had solid form. Perhaps it had not occurred to him. Or perhaps there was no one he trusted enough. He did not answer at first, the minutes stretching on until I thought he had fallen asleep. The room seemed to be gently rocking and I wondered why that was, even as something itched in the back of my mind.

'You would truly condemn your family so as not to marry me?' he said quietly.

When he put it like that, I could see that he might think me mad.

'What about you? You would allow Canfield and his men to kill your only living relative?' I blurted, remembering finally what it was that had bothered me so. If he deigned to reply, I didn't hear it, for my eyes began to close involuntarily.

'Ah, that will be the opium. Good,' he said, and as I blinked instinctively to stay awake, I saw him wipe his hands on a napkin as though his work here were complete. 'You have to understand, Miss Dawson, that after I lost Marisa, I never loved another the way that I loved her.'

'You drugged me,' I whispered.

'Only to keep you from becoming hysterical,' he said with a shrug. 'Doctor's orders.'

'Will you kill me too once I have served my purpose?' I said faintly, aware that I might be asleep before I heard the answer.

'I did not kill them. You must know that by now, with your witch's gifts. Tell me, did my other wives come and visit you too? Is that how you found out about Anne and James? And Pansy, that treacherous, sinful woman?'

'Pansy was not the only sinful one,' I slurred, my eyelids drooping. 'You discovered her plans and used them against her to end her life. You cannot possibly expect me to believe you innocent.'

'You know nothing of which you speak. You weren't there! How would you feel to hope that your suspicions were unfounded, that the woman you had brought into your home was not a duplicitous she-devil, only to discover that all your fears about her were true?'

'You didn't have to kill her to prove it,' I spat.

'Yet if she had succeeded in poisoning me, would she have been subject to the same chastisement as you are giving me now?'

I shut my mouth, grudgingly seeing his point. The room was stifling and I fought against my drooping eyelids as I said, 'What about your ill-gotten fortune? How many men like my father have you bullied and threatened into giving you what you want?'

'I am not the villain of your piece, Elizabeth,' he replied indignantly, avoiding the question. He was not expecting me to answer, for he stood and turned his back to me.

'The women were never the problem, Edgar,' I replied, hating how weak my voice sounded. 'The problem is that you are . . . cursed.'

'No,' he said quickly, although even in my drugged state, with my thoughts blurring into each other, I could see fear in his eyes.

I could say no more, for a wave of dizziness set the room spinning around me and I slipped out of consciousness.

My dreams were a mess of colours and shapes, faces swimming in and out of my vision. Or at least, I thought they were dreams.

A woman sang a lullaby somewhere nearby while rain beat the windows relentlessly, and I found myself standing on the bank of the lake, a squalling bundle in my arms.

'He will never stop being in pain,' a voice said beside my ear. I turned to find a pretty, slender woman with light brown hair and dark blue eyes sitting beside me, rocking slowly back and forth. I looked back down at the babe, but it had vanished.

'I'm sorry, but I . . .' I turned back to Anne, for that was who she was, my mind knew without further clarification. She held the bundle of blankets, humming to it until the crying stopped.

'I would sing for him until the end of my days if it would take the pain away,' she said, looking at me vacantly. The rain lashed at my face and I shivered, realising that I was in my nightclothes. I was vaguely aware that someone must have changed me while I was asleep.

'What can I do?' I pleaded. 'How can I help you?' I had to shout above the sound of the wind, despite rain pouring into my mouth as I spoke, cutting my skin like hundreds of tiny knives. A gust whipped the hair from my face and bent the trees with its force. Yet Anne looked untouched, dry, as though she were protected from it, with not a hair out of place. She smiled beatifically.

'Do? My dear, you must marry Blountford. It is your duty, as it was mine.' Although the words stung, I could hear the relief there, as though she were grateful to be bestowing this unwanted task upon me.

I blinked and I was in my bedroom again, dry and warm.

Esme sat at the end of the bed where Lord Blountford had been minutes, or maybe hours before. She picked up the knife that still rested upon the sheet and examined it as he had.

'Tell me, why do you feel it necessary to carry a weapon, Lizzie?' She sounded just as she had the last time I saw her. Sad and resigned, but still my sister. Shock and grief burst in my chest like an exploding star. I wanted to gather her into my arms, to hold her close and smell her familiar sweet, floral scent, but my body was still braced to the bed by the sheet.

She studied me with her dark eyes, just the way she used to when I had said something particularly uncouth to someone and she would have to make excuses for me.

I was dreaming, I thought. I squeezed my eyes closed, scrunching up my face, but when I opened them again, she was still there.

'Because of what happened after you died. Because of Darleston trying to . . .' I could not say the words to her even in a dream. 'I carry it so that a man might never hurt me the way he did.' My voice was that of an old crone with years of pipe-smoking behind her, the dry air tickling my throat.

'I wanted to protect you,' she said, getting up and sliding the knife onto the bedside table. Someone had cleared away the drugged soup but had left the water, I noticed. 'I never meant for it to happen like this.' She waved a hand at my helpless form, tied to the bed.

'I would have come to live with you if you'd only written to me, Esme. If I had known that you were in pain or unwell, I would have been here in a heartbeat,' I said, unable to disguise the hurt in my voice. 'But instead you always told me you were busy arranging things, or that you weren't quite ready for me to visit. Were you hiding?'

She looked at me sharply, her lips, the same as my own and

our mother's, pursing as they did when she did not wish to lie but also did not want to tell the truth.

'I suppose I was ashamed,' she said, looking away and pouring me a fresh glass of water, then raising the glass to my mouth and lifting my head gently so that I might drink. I was grateful for it and studied her as I sipped: her sombre expression, the smallest of creases between her eyebrows as though she had done a lot of frowning.

'Esme,' I said, incredulous, pulling away from the glass, 'you never have to hide anything from me. You know that. We are two different people, but you are a part of my very soul. And now . . . now you're gone, and I could not even say goodbye.' A tear slid unbidden down the side of my face and into my hair. She brushed it away, her thumb a little rough, as though she had been working outside.

'I tried to save you while I was here, you know. I had plans that would change your fortune once and for all and get you out of the city.' She sighed wistfully and placed the glass down, before reaching to where the sheets were tied to the bed. She loosened the knotted fabric deftly, the pressure easing from my chest, and I took a deep breath, shaking out the numbness in my arms and hands as I sat up.

'Did your plans involve Charles Blountford, by any chance?' I asked her, the question coming out sharper than I intended. I *was* wearing my nightclothes, and I hoped that it was Marie who had undressed me while I was unconscious, and not someone else.

'Why, yes,' Esme said with surprise. 'I corresponded with him—'

'I do not wish to talk about Charles,' I interrupted her, not waiting to hear her explanation. I had had enough of adultery for a lifetime. Heavens knew what Lord Blountford would have done had he known about their letters. Even so, I feared for Charles, and what might become of him if I didn't interfere.

'Did you love him?'

'Who?' she asked, puzzled.

'Your husband. As ridiculous an idea as that might be, I need to know. Did you love Lord Blountford?'

She rested her hand gently on her stomach, and I saw the slightest bulge beneath her dress there. Ghost or dream I could no longer tell, but the Esme in my mind was evidently still expecting.

'I loved the idea of Ambletye. I loved the countryside and being away from Mother and Father. I adored the idea of becoming a mother myself, and giving my child all the comforts we did not have.' She smiled and it lit up the room. 'But I missed you desperately, Lizzie. I missed you every day. I wanted you to live with us, but Lord Blountford wanted me to have the babe first. And then, when I thought I could not wait to see you any longer, I became quite ill. I could not walk in the grounds without fainting, and I did not want you to see me that way. When I realised that I mightn't live, it was already too late to summon you.'

I reached across the bed and twined my fingers into her cold ones, understanding even if I regretted not being able to comfort her when she was alive. I tugged her arm gently, and she climbed up onto the bed, her hand still in my own, until we both had our backs pressed up against the headboard, as we had done countless times before, staying up until all hours talking.

'You are not surprised that I can see you? That I can touch you?'

'Not really, Lizzie. You were forever talking to imaginary friends when we were little. I should have realised they were not imaginary at all. Brisley, was it? He was a regular, if I recall,' she said with a smirk. As if I could have hidden anything from her.

'I've seen all of them now,' I said, running a thumb over her knuckles, willing them to be real and warm and not cold as porcelain as they really were. 'The wives, that is. Marisa, Pansy . . . even Anne in a dream, I think. I have tried to help where I can, but it's not always easy.'

'It never is,' she said, resting her head on my shoulder, her straight dark hair cascading down and tickling my arm. 'But if there's one thing I know, it's that you never give up. You have always been persistent, wilfully so, even when I've warned you against it.' She lifted her hand and gave me a knowing look. A question stirred in the back of my mind.

'Your harp, how did it end up here?'

She looked down at her dress, plucking at the lace hem that was hitched up around her knees. 'Edgar ordered Canfield to buy it back for me. I think he was trying to make me feel at home here.' She gave a little shrug, as though she were shy of the fact that a man had given her such a gift.

'He cared for you then? He was not a monster?'

She laughed, although it was the kind of sound that had no humour behind it. 'He was not a monster, no. I worried sometimes that there was one underneath the surface, particularly when he became enraged, but he only ever showed care for me.'

I nodded, pondering this. I had seen so many versions of Edgar Blountford in the past few days, but a caring one who would buy my sister's harp back for her and who would try to stop her from hurting herself, this one I had yet to see manifest itself.

'People are so very complicated,' I said with a sigh.

'That they are.'

'I must save him, though.'

'Who, Edgar? I think he is beyond saving,' Esme replied grimly.

281

'No, Charles. He is in danger from Canfield. I have to stop him from getting hurt, even if . . .' *Even if he broke my heart.*

A plan began to form in my mind as we sat there speaking of nothing in particular and everything all at once. Every word shared felt precious, as though somewhere in the back of my mind I knew I would not have another moment like this again.

After an hour, maybe two, when the fire in the room had died altogether, I turned to her, leaning over and pulling her into a sudden embrace. 'I love you,' I said, breathing in her lavender and sugar scent as though it were a perfume. There was a coppery undertone with it too. Blood.

'And I love you, Lizzie,' she said, resting her forehead upon mine.

'Will you come back? When I wake up, will I be able to see you again?' I asked, secretly dreading the answer I felt I already knew.

Her frown was sad when she pulled away. 'I am here because you needed me, Lizzie, and because I needed to say goodbye.'

'But I *always* need you, Esme,' I said, gripping her hands in mine as if that would stop her from disappearing before my eyes.

'No, I don't think you do. I don't think you have done for some time now. Besides,' she added, extricating one of her hands from mine, 'I will always be with you, right here.' She laid her palm on my chest and I rested my own upon it. 'It is almost morning, dear Lizzie.'

'And?' I asked, not daring to look at the window, or the lightening room. I felt as though she would slip away at any moment, and I wanted to remember every feature of her face. Every line and beauty spot, the shine of her eyes as they gazed at me.

'And it's time for you to wake up.'

I shook my head. It was not true morning yet, surely? We had not been together that long.

'Wake up, Lizzie,' she said, more insistently, and I felt my body shake. '*Wake up, miss.*'

'What?'

'Time to wake up, miss!'

My eyes flew open and I saw Marie's concerned face staring down at me.

I blinked rapidly, trying to clear the cobwebs from my brain. Had any of that been real? I wondered. I looked down at my hands, which were unbound. My knife rested on the bedside table near my head, and the decanter of water was almost empty.

'We must get you ready, miss, or you'll be late,' Marie went on with some urgency, pulling the sheets from the bed and heaving me up. My limbs felt like they weighed a hundred tons, and I stumbled the first few steps to the bathroom.

'Ready for what?' I managed to say. The bitter aftertaste of opium still lingered on my tongue, and I resolved to scrub my mouth with soap to remove it.

'For your wedding, of course.'

My stomach tangled in an instant knot of nerves. I had wondered whether everything had been a dream, but alas, the thing I dreaded the most was real.

'What is the time, Marie?' I asked, my mind beginning to catch up with me.

'It is almost eight, miss, so we must bathe you quickly.'

I ripped myself from her grasp and ran out of the room, my nightdress tangling up in my legs as I raced through the corridors and down the stairs to the floor below.

'Where is the earl?' I demanded of a startled-looking maid.

'I . . . In his rooms, miss,' she replied, adding something that I didn't hear as I tore through the west wing of the house. I had never been to his rooms before, but I recalled vaguely where they were.

When I burst through the door, he was standing in an untucked shirt and trousers, a manservant buttoning up the front for him.

'You have to call off Canfield,' I said breathlessly, stumbling as I crossed the room to him.

'Elizabeth, what is the meaning of—'

'*You have to call off Canfield!*' I repeated, putting all the urgency I could muster into my voice. 'We may already be too late – if he does not hear from you before breakfast, he will travel back to London and murder your nephew in your name!'

Lord Blountford frowned, as if I had interrupted him for something trivial and not because a man's life was at stake. He opened his mouth to protest, but I interrupted him.

'I will refuse the wedding vows if I know a murder is taking place on my account. The only reason he went to London was because you dismissed him. Send a messenger to the Hand and Plough immediately, and I will never give you any trouble again. I swear it.'

My arms and legs quivered from the sudden exertion, but I could see that I had appealed to something in him as he considered my words.

'I very much doubt you will never give me *any* trouble, Elizabeth, for that is not in your nature, but,' he held up a hand to stifle my protests, 'I will do as you ask if it means that this wedding will go forward without any further difficulty on your part.'

I sagged to the thick carpet in relief, watching as he scrawled a note at his writing table and sealed it, sending Turner off to the inn almost as soon as the man had entered the room.

'There, are you satisfied?' he asked, holding out a hand to help me up from where I still sat on the rug.

I would never truly be satisfied from this day onwards, I knew, but at least I had saved an innocent man from his fate. I nodded, taking the offered assistance, surprised to find strength in the old man's arms as he lifted me to my feet.

'Excellent, then you had better hurry to your rooms and get dressed. The coach leaves for the chapel at eleven.' His mouth quirked and I realised that it was his attempt at a smile as he looked me up and down, delight and greed shining in his eyes. I suddenly felt very exposed and aware that I was wearing only a nightdress.

Shoulders hunched, arms folded across my chest in a vain attempt to cover myself, I left, feeling his gaze upon my back all the way out the door.

Chapter 21

ဆာ ღ

The chapel sat on a hill overlooking the village, the rolling Sussex countryside stretching out around us. As I stepped down from the carriage, I paused a moment to take in the view and suck in deep lungfuls of air in an effort to steady myself. Although the drugs had mostly worn off, I still felt a haze of unreality that I assumed was more to do with the occasion than anything else.

Worry pricked at the back of my mind that my soon-to-be-husband could have written anything in his note to Canfield; I had not thought to read it before he sent it off, so desperate was I to ensure Charles's safety. I wondered now if I had put too much faith in the earl's already questionable character.

I shook my head, looking down at the ensemble I was about to marry in. Marie had kindly found the nicest dress I owned, a silver satin frock with white lace cuffs, and tailored it, adding a blue trim around the collar and finding me some matching slippers for the ceremony. It had been too small, for in my fury and haste to pack I had not thought about what was going into the trunk, and I had been dismayed to find it short in length and tight around the bodice. But in the past few days she had taken it upon herself to fix it for me.

I was surprised to find that she had cut a slit in the side to hide my knife belt. When I had questioned why she assumed I would carry a knife to my wedding, she simply said that it was more a part of me than anything else I seemed to own, and that she had thought it only right. I knew not what that said of my character, that my own maid would think me comfortable carrying a knife under my wedding dress, but I certainly did not contest it. The weight of it was reassuring, like a talisman at my side. The shawl I had bought from the seamstress was draped over my shoulders, and in my quivering hands I held a posy of lavender and pansies that Marie whispered were a gift from Mr McMannon. I sniffed them, reminding myself that Esme was with me for every step, even if I could no longer see her.

In the hour that we had been given to prepare, my maid had done remarkable work, coiling my hair with flowers so that it looked like an effortless floral bun, though in reality it was being kept together with a small army of hairpins.

As Lord Blountford tottered down from the carriage after me, I gazed up at the cheerful pale-brick building looming above us, surrounded by evergreen bushes and roses. I would enter as Elizabeth Dawson, but I would leave as Lady Elizabeth Blountford.

Deep breaths, you can do this, a chorus of voices seemed to say in the back of my mind. Whether it was my imagination or truly echoes of the women who had gone before me, I could not tell, but it was fortifying to think that they might be with me, even if only in my mind.

There was a light touch at my elbow, and I looked around to find Lord Blountford appraising me. 'Shall we?' he asked casually, and not as though the impending few minutes would be irrevocably life-altering for both of us. I merely nodded, stepping into the cool darkness of the chapel behind him.

I wasn't sure what to expect. The very few weddings I had attended growing up had been relatively small affairs, the ceremony sparsely attended while the wedding breakfast was held in the home of the bride's parents. I had only been to one church ceremony. That had been the grandest of all, with friends and family invited along with anyone else in the area who happened to pass by and wanted to witness a moment of happiness and unity between two people.

The church before me was deserted, a line of fat pillar candles lighting the way to the altar. The high windows cast shafts of midday sun onto the stone slabs, illuminating the epitaphs etched into their surfaces. I tried not to look at them too closely, or think about the bones that lay beneath my feet, as Lord Blountford took one of my clammy hands in his and folded it over his arm.

'What did you write?' I asked quietly.

'Pardon?'

'In your letter to Canfield. What did you write?' I insisted, even though it felt wrong to raise my voice in church.

A crease formed between his eyebrows, adding to the dozens that were already there.

'I simply told him to leave Charles alone, and that we would discuss matters in London after the wedding,' he said impatiently.

I wanted to believe him, if only because I could not bear the alternative.

'Can we please put that out of our minds for today, Elizabeth?' It was barely a request, but I swallowed my questions and allowed him to lead me down the aisle.

The air felt as though it was being pressed out of my ribcage with every step, my heart desperately pumping like a drumbeat in my chest. I was acutely aware of every sensation: the scrape of my slippers against the flagstones, the smell of burning candle wax and musty bibles, dust and stale Eucharist wine. Even the feel of the wool of Lord Blountford's coat sleeve as I held unwillingly on to his arm, every row and weave of thread painfully coarse against my fingers. This was real. And yet I had never felt so much like I was walking through a dream.

The church wedding I had been to had felt grandiose, with flowers tied to the sides of each pew, the altar draped in ceremonial colours and a harp accompanying the bride, my mother's cousin, as she walked down the aisle. But where that had been cheery and romantic, this was . . . barren. No music played, not even the church organ, which sat bereft to the right of the pews.

I played a tune in my mind, picturing my fingers hovering over the piano keys. It was a simple but sorrowful melody chiming in the back of my thoughts, providing an accompaniment to our procession of two. If I shut my eyes for a moment, I could envisage people standing in the pews. My parents giving me nods of eager encouragement; next to them my sister, her face just as it had been last night, creased with worry and resignation.

I visualised Pansy and Mr McMannon arm in arm, their expressions a mix of warmth and concern. Anne cradling James, singing her lullaby in harmony with the tune I had created, the two weaving together in my thoughts. Marisa as fierce and as beautiful as ever, gripping the pew in front of her so hard that her knuckles were like stars bursting under the skin. Dissatisfaction radiated from her, and I forced my eyes open so as to clear the image from my mind, just as Lord Blountford tugged my arm hard enough to grab my attention.

The minister had materialised from somewhere behind a curtain and opened his arms to welcome us as we approached the altar, but I barely heard his words of greeting over the thundering of my heartbeat and the rattle of my breathing.

Rebecca Hardy

'. . . who shall be your witnesses?' I vaguely heard him enquire.

I hadn't registered the presence of two people behind me until I turned to find Turner and Mistress Damiani standing in the aisle. The cook gave me a grim smile before fixing her eyes upon the cross that hung from a rope above the vicar's head, Christ looking down on us with sympathy in his eyes. I stole a glance at Turner, whose face was as unreadable as ever, years of practice as a manservant, never showing a flicker of emotion or disagreement towards his master, paying off.

'We are the witnesses, Reverend,' he volunteered, his voice neutral.

'Excellent, excellent. And this is the lovely bride.' The minister attempted a warm smile, which soon grew fixed and awkward when I didn't return it. He cleared his throat noisily and continued, folding his hands together as though in prayer, 'You have acquired a licence, so we may proceed.'

He was younger than I had expected for a clergyman, but I supposed, in the way that one's mind manages to ponder on such things during a time of crisis, that his age might have been why Lord Blountford had been able to arrange a ceremony so quickly, forgoing convention.

Without further preamble, he began, and I closed my eyes again to listen to the words, pretending in a detached sort of way that they were meant for someone else. Each part of the ceremony would be like a piece of music, broken down into movements: the vows, the ring, the prayers, and concluding with the register. My stomach rumbled emptily and I realised that I hadn't eaten since the congealed soup yesterday, which meant that I would go hungry for another hour or two yet. Perhaps that was the cause of my light-headedness?

'Dearly beloved, we are gathered together here in the sight of God, and in the face of this congregation . . .'

What congregation? I thought bemusedly.

'. . . to join together this man and this woman in holy Matrimony.'

I let out a shuddering breath, feeling the blood slowly drain from my face.

Don't faint. Please don't faint now, here in the church.

But then a thought occurred to me that perhaps I should. *It would only delay the inevitable. You bargained, remember? You promised to cooperate.* I couldn't tell if the voice of reason in my mind was my own or my sister's, but what it said was true enough. I swayed involuntarily on my feet, small spots appearing in my vision like dust motes.

'. . . and therefore is not by any to be enterprised, nor taken in hand, unadvisedly, lightly or wantonly to satisfy men's carnal lusts and appetites, like brute beasts that have no understanding; but reverently, discreetly, advisedly, soberly and in the fear of God; duly considering the causes for which Matrimony was ordained,' the reverend continued, his voice high and querulous as though he were appealing to a church full of parishioners rather than this sorry excuse for a wedding party.

I considered my husband and his unadvised, wanton marriages. Could he truly state in front of God that he had treated the sacrament with reverence? If I did not feel so faint, I would have laughed in his face as though it were some sort of divine joke.

'First, it was ordained for the procreation of children, to be brought up in the fear and nurture of the Lord and to the praise of His holy Name.

'Secondly, it was ordained for a remedy against sin, and to avoid fornication . . .'

The piano in my mind played louder, drowning out the priest's words in an almighty crescendo as he spoke about the importance of marriage and its purpose, until the moment when I foolishly allowed hope to surge up inside me.

'Therefore, if any man can show any just cause why they may not be lawfully joined together, let him now speak, or else hereafter for ever hold his peace.'

I held my breath. Silence reigned in the church, no disturbance save for the birds outside with their complete disregard for what was happening within these walls. I shifted my weight from one foot to the other awkwardly. Nobody was coming to stop this wedding, I thought bitterly. Why would they? Not Price, nor Jordie, nor indeed Charles, for none of them had any just cause to halt the ceremony other than the fact that I did not wish to marry Lord Blountford. Mistress Damiani cleared her throat gently, but after that no other sound came.

'With silence heard, I require and charge you both that if either of you know any impediment why ye may not be lawfully joined together in Matrimony, ye do now confess it.'

I saw Lord Blountford set his mouth into a determined line at that, and I tried to mimic him. I couldn't speak up now. I had, as the voice in my head told me repeatedly, made a bargain for Charles's life, and my father had made one before me for mine. There was nothing more to do but carry on.

The reverend turned to my betrothed.

'Edgar James Blountford, wilt thou have this woman to thy wedded wife, to live together after God's ordinance in the holy estate of Matrimony? Wilt thou love her, comfort her, honour, and keep her, in sickness and in health; and, forsaking all other, keep thee only unto her, so long as ye both shall live?'

The minister's words were barely spoken before the earl replied, 'I will.'

I was going to be sick. I could feel the bile rising in my throat even as I chastised myself for being so dramatic. It was just a wedding. It was a means to an end. A safety blanket so that my parents could never be tormented again, so that Charles, despite his conspiring with Esme, could be safe and live out the rest of his days without the fear of someone trying to kill him. I stared at the minister, trying to hear what he said over the crashing of piano keys in my head.

'Elizabeth Anne Dawson, wilt thou have this man to thy wedded husband, to live together after God's ordinance in the holy estate of Matrimony? Wilt thou obey him, and serve him, love, honour, and keep him, in sickness and in health; and, forsaking all other, keep thee only unto him, so long as ye both shall live?'

I opened my mouth to speak, but no words came. Lord Blountford stiffened beside me, and I forced the words out even as they felt acidic on my tongue. 'I will,' I managed to whisper.

'Who giveth this woman to be married to this man?'

Turner stepped up from behind us. He took my hand in his, which was surprisingly soft and warm, and gave it to the minister. I resisted the urge to pull it away as he gave it to Lord Blountford.

'Repeat after me: I Edgar take thee Elizabeth to be my wedded wife . . .'

The earl repeated the words as I looked down at our hands, my own feeling like a stranger's against his leathery skin. I felt his eyes upon me, but I could not bring myself to look into them.

'. . . and thereto I plight thee my troth.'

'And now you, Elizabeth, repeat after me, please,' the minister said, not unkindly. There was an undertone of concern and gentleness in his instruction, as though he knew, could see into my heart and read what was written there. But he was young and ambitious, and no doubt the church had been supported handsomely in exchange for this small task, so he continued.

'I Elizabeth take thee Edgar to be my wedded husband, to have and to hold from this day forward, for better for worse, for richer for poorer, in sickness and in health, to love, cherish and to obey, till death us do part, according to God's holy ordinance; and thereto I give thee my troth.'

It was peculiar that a woman had to obey her husband but that the vows for the husband said no such thing. I pondered this as I repeated the words, my voice sounding dead and hollow to my own ears.

As a ring materialised from somewhere, a tarnished golden band that I feared might have belonged to one or more of the wives before me, I closed my eyes again, not wanting to see it being placed upon my finger. Panic rose in my throat at the feel of it grazing my fingertip. I had done almost everything that was required of me. This was the final task I had to undertake. But then there would be the rest of the wedding. And the wedding night after it.

Whether it was the sudden wash of sickness at the idea of it or something else that spurred me on, I did not know, but my eyes shot open and I yanked my hand away from Lord Blountford's.

'No.'

There was a startled silence as the reverend paused in his ministrations. 'I beg your pardon?'

'No. This is . . .' I shook my head feverishly. I could not allow it to carry on another moment. Even now I might be too late. My hand retreated from the ring, reaching towards the slit in my dress. 'This is *wrong*.'

'Elizabeth!' Lord Blountford choked. 'Stop embarrassing yourself!'

'Is there something the matter, my child?' asked the reverend apprehensively.

I could hear a clattering coming from somewhere and

wondered if my heart were about to give up, the noise was so loud. But no, it was not from within me, but footsteps outside. The next moment, the door opened with a resounding slam.

'Halt!' a voice called out, ringing across the church. 'In the name of the king, I must halt this wedding.'

There was a deathly silence as Lord Blountford and I turned in unison, him to find out who had the audacity to stop the ceremony and I to find out who my saviour might be.

Charles stood at the end of the aisle, breathless and dirty from riding, in the same clothes I had seen him in four days previously, a sword slung at his hip under his coat. His blonde hair was windswept and dishevelled, a shadow of stubble on his chin, but he looked to me like an angel. The light from the high windows caught his hair, giving the effect of a golden halo and illuminating his eyes so that they shone like emeralds.

Any anger I felt at his and Esme's colluding buried itself deep within my chest. There was time for anger and retribution later, but now . . . now I could do nothing but allow the thrill of seeing him to run through me, kicking my pulse up to an alarming speed.

'What is the meaning of this?' Edgar said, his own eyes ablaze with fury.

Charles caught his breath, his cheeks reddened with exertion. Had he come all the way from London?

'Uncle, the constables have raided your gentlemen's club and made several arrests. Witnesses have testified to your criminal acts and there is a warrant out for your arrest. It is over.' His hand gripped the pommel of his sword. I doubted he would unsheathe it here, in this holy place, but I could see from the set of his shoulders that he was prepared to fight.

He flicked his gaze to me, just for the briefest of moments, and I tried to ignore the thrill in my chest.

'Oh dear,' I heard the minister mutter, his prayer book still open in his hands. 'Oh dear, oh dear.'

Lord Blountford turned back to him. 'Finish the ceremony,' he hissed.

'B-but I cannot, for there is still the prayer, and the Eucharist to be given, not to mention the register—'

'I said *finish it*!'

I looked down at the ring still clasped between his fingers, just inches from my own, and snatched my hand away. But it was no use. He seized my arm, gripping it so tightly that pain shot through to my elbow.

'Ah, erm, repeat after me if you will,' the reverend stuttered. 'With this ring I thee wed . . .'

Lord Blountford almost shouted the words at me as he freed my curled finger and thrust the ring onto it. So intent was he on completing the ceremony that he did not notice my other hand reaching to the slit in the side of the dress.

'I said stop!' Charles called from the back of the church, just as surprised as I was that his uncle was ignoring him.

'With my body I thee worship, and with all my worldly goods I thee endow . . .' repeated the earl, even as the knife slid out of its sheath and I pulled it through the gap in my skirts, bringing it up to the loose skin of his neck.

The cold sting of metal against his throat stopped him mid sentence, his face a mask of shock.

'That is enough,' I rasped, wrenching my hand from his, the ring sliding off my finger and bouncing off the stone at our feet. 'He said it is over. I suggest you take heed.'

Charles was already striding up the aisle, barking accusations as though they were orders.

'Edgar Blountford, I charge you in front of these witnesses and in the sight of God for violating the Gaming Act of 1738, for running illegal games in your institution and for knowingly forcing your clients into excessive debt for your own gain.'

'I have no knowledge of such things,' his uncle replied, his surprise quickly replaced by the calculating menace I had seen only too often from him. 'You cannot charge me for something I have had no part in. Surely I am not expected to know everything that happens in my club? I merely own it, I do not manage it.'

'What about my father?' I asked, pressing the knife tip ever so slightly against his skin. He hid any discomfort well, even as the reverend muttered something and crossed himself, taking a step backwards.

'What about him? You cannot blame me for his addiction to the hazard table,' he scoffed.

'Hazard has been illegal for more than sixty years, Uncle,' Charles said, approaching us so that he was almost within touching distance.

'Oh, semantics,' Lord Blountford retorted dismissively. 'Whatever his *legal* game of choice, it was he who spent your family's savings, not I.'

'So you deny all the charges against you?' Charles pressed on, undeterred.

'Of course. I had no idea that anything untoward was happening in my name. Now, I will forgive you this gross intervention if you leave at once so that our wedding can continue,' he replied, as though I did not still have a weapon pressed to his neck.

'Who, then?' Charles asked. 'Who was in charge of deciding the games and permitting debts to go over the legal limit of ten pounds?'

'Nigel Canfield, of course. He runs all my affairs in London. He is the man to arrest, not I,' Lord Blountford said hastily, evidently seeing a path out.

Charles seemed to consider this for just a moment, his eyes

darting to the transept, where I caught the twitch of a curtain in my peripheral vision. 'You are telling me the man I should arrest is Nigel Canfield?' he said, his voice carrying across the church.

'Yes, of course. It is his decision as to what games are played at the club. I believe he is on his way to London as we speak. If you leave now, you might be able to catch him.'

'Actually, I decided to stay here a little while longer, your lordship.' The curtain moved aside to reveal the slender figure of Mr Canfield, a look of displeasure written across his weaselly face.

Lord Blountford stiffened. 'Canfield, I demand you come to my aid at once! Turner, deal with my nephew immediately.' The orders came out so rapidly, I had little time to register Turner moving towards Charles as Mr Canfield approached the steps where we stood. A muttering came from somewhere behind the altar; I realised it must be the reverend, in what I hoped was a prayer for all our souls.

'As it happens, Lord Blountford, the captain and I have already had a little meeting on the way here. Our altercation led to . . . an interesting understanding,' Canfield replied, looking pleased with himself.

I made the mistake of looking at Charles in horror. From here I could see a bruise forming under his eye, and a cut on his eyebrow that had been hastily tended to. As I watched, he spun around to meet Turner head on, drawing his sword with a metallic scrape that rang through my very bones.

Lord Blountford took advantage of my distraction, grabbing my hand and twisting it behind me far quicker than a man of his age should have been able to, so that I dropped the knife straight into his other outstretched palm. Within a breath he had spun me around, pulling my back against his chest with my own blade pressed against my throat.

'Canfield, where are your men?' he called.

'The Weston brothers, sir? Oh, they are just at the entrance to the church, awaiting my instructions.' Mr Canfield spoke as though nothing untoward had happened. My heart sank. I couldn't tell whose side this man was on – had he not heard the accusation levelled against him? Or was he so loyal to Lord Blountford that he didn't care?

'Tell them to be ready to escort us to my carriage at once. We must leave. Oh, and bring the priest.' The earl nodded towards the terrified heap that was our vicar.

'Charles!' I called out as loudly as I could, the pressure from Lord Blountford's arms around my chest stifling my cry.

Charles and Turner had reached an impasse, circling each other at the bottom of the steps, neither of them making a move against the other. The steward was unarmed and could do nothing against a naval captain with a sword, but even so, I worried that Charles would be no match for Canfield's men if they came in.

'Charles, you must run!' I wheezed as Lord Blountford dragged me with him down the aisle, the blade pushing into my neck so that I could feel the hot trickle of blood.

'Stop struggling or I might slit your throat, you stupid girl!' he hissed.

Canfield had managed to retrieve the reverend from his hiding place and was nudging him towards the door, the occasional 'Oh dear' and 'Good Lord save me' coming from behind us.

Everything was happening so quickly that my thoughts seemed painfully slow to catch up. Against Canfield and his henchmen, Turner and Lord Blountford himself, Charles and I were grossly outnumbered. I couldn't even think where the cook had gone to, not that she would have been much help other than to curse someone in Italian perhaps. As the earl kicked open the door, I expected to find the Westons and our carriage waiting outside.

Both were there; the carriage a little way off, the horses pawing impatiently at the grass, while the brothers flanked the pathway. But so were two dozen other people.

Men both in and out of uniform, a combination of local parish constables, naval officers and Bow Street Runners by their attire, had assembled themselves in a line, blocking the path between the church and our waiting transport. A further crowd stood beyond them, and I was startled to see Price and Judith among them. The baker and his wife, Mr Grahame and even the blacksmith were watching with expressions of awe and horror.

'What in God's name is going on?' Lord Blountford asked, his grip around my chest faltering just for a moment. Enough for me to regain my balance and stamp on his instep so that he reflexively dropped the knife. Even in my slippers I had managed to angle my heel into that sensitive part of his boot. I scrambled for the blade on the ground and hastened to put distance between us, holding the weapon up and backing towards the line of men, hoping that my faith in them was not misplaced.

'Ah, Lord Blountford,' Mr Canfield said, exiting the church behind us, the reverend quivering like a leaf in the wind at his side. 'You see, I could not cause you harm in a church, even if you did attempt to so grievously damage my character. It seems your nephew has some friends in *very* high places.'

The confusion on Blountford's face quickly twisted into fury at this sudden turn of events, even as he realised there was nowhere for him to run and no one he could order to save him.

The Westons swiftly moved in, the other men on their heels, pushing past me gently so that I was outside the ring of bodies that began to form like a human barrier around the old man. A hand rested upon my shoulder and I flinched, turning with relief to see Price at my back.

'It's all right, Lizzie,' was all he said as silent tears began to run down my face.

One of the Bow Street Runners had taken it upon himself to read out the charges again, in much the same fashion as Charles had done inside the church, but this time there was no escape, no excuse or passing of the blame to be made.

As if I had conjured him with a thought, Charles appeared in the doorway, his sword sheathed, Turner holding his hands up in supplication beside him. It looked as if he had managed to talk some sense into the steward.

'Uncle, you will be transported to London, where you will stand trial for your crimes. Your estate and assets will be frozen, unless you wish to speak now and bequeath them to me, either temporarily until this matter is resolved, or permanently in the event of your imprisonment or execution.' He spoke with no emotion, but I wondered if this was what he had wanted all along; if this was what he and Esme had been working towards even before he had returned to England, though he certainly did not seem to show any satisfaction that the tables had turned in his favour.

'You little parasite!' Lord Blountford screamed, his face just visible above the circle of men. The crowd gasped as a glint of metal appeared from somewhere, the earl's frail hand raising a dagger as if to throw it directly at his nephew. A scream caught in my throat even as the men jostled to prise the knife from his hand. 'You planned my downfall from the moment your father died,' he bellowed. 'My useless half-brother, unable to do anything but leech off me—' There was a sickening thump, the visceral sound of bone and blood, and his voice was cut off.

Unable to look away, I watched as the man who had bullied

me and my family, who had drugged me and bribed me into marrying him was bundled into our carriage. Canfield and the Westons climbed in too, no doubt to make sure that if he awoke, he would not attempt to escape.

I hadn't noticed the horses tied up at the side of the church, among them Hurricane, Charles's stallion, who seemed content to nibble on the foliage of the church garden. The officers and watchmen began to mount up now, one by one following the path their prisoner had taken until only a handful remained. Turner had been left in the care of one of the parish constables, and the baker's wife seemed to be giving him a piece of her mind.

I turned to Price and Judith in disbelief. 'It's truly over?'

They both nodded and smiled in reply, pulling me into an embrace that had me sagging into them with relief.

'Lizzie!' Charles's voice called across the lawn.

'We'll catch up with you as soon as you're ready,' Price said gently. 'Unless you'd like us to stay?' I shook my head, barely able to speak.

'It's all right, miss. Just send word to the cottage if you need us,' Judith whispered, giving my shoulder an affectionate squeeze before they broke away from me.

I was still gripping the knife, I realised, and had no idea what I must look like. I resisted the urge to fix my hair or do anything other than slide the blade back through the slit in my dress and stand still as Charles approached.

'You are bleeding,' he said, pulling a handkerchief from his pocket and pressing it gently to my neck. I ignored the tingle that ran across my skin at his touch and pulled away, taking the square of cotton with me.

'Thank you,' I said, not wanting to look up into those beautiful green eyes of his. Not wanting to see the tenderness I could feel was written across his face. Not wanting to remember why I'd fallen in love with him and to do so all over again. 'What you did . . . You saved my life,' I said, my eyes downcast, my pulse beating irregularly beneath my fingers where they were pressed to my neck. 'I don't know how I can ever express my gratitude for that.'

'Please, Lizzie,' he said softly, 'you never need to thank me for doing what I consider my duty. Besides,' he added, and I could hear the smile in his voice, 'you did a fine job of saving yourself, I would say.'

I studied the grass, the scuffs on his boots and how small my feet looked beside his. Anything to keep my mind off the fact that he was standing so close I could feel his warm breath upon my skin.

Taking my silence for something else, he spoke with concern. 'I'm so sorry I couldn't get here sooner,' he began, but I cut him off.

'Charles, please. I am half starved and exhausted. Today has been . . . difficult. Might I go home?'

'Of course,' he replied, sounding hurt but as understanding as always. I had little excuse really, for he must have been more tired than I. When he wasn't looking, I stole a glance at him. The dark circles under his eyes were prominent, as though he hadn't slept since the night he left. Considering the force of men he had managed to gather, it was more than likely he hadn't.

'Lieutenant Brisley!' he called to a young man who appeared to have been calming the poor reverend and Mistress Damiani.

The officer strode over to us, his face serious save for an undercurrent of amusement. Something about him was decidedly familiar. Brisley was not an uncommon surname, of course, but there were definite similarities between this man and the ghost I had grown up with, his expression open and warm with underlying mischief. I could not help but wonder . . .

'Lieutenant, I will return Miss Dawson to Ambletye. I trust you can ensure my uncle arrives to his trial in one piece?'

'Of course, Captain,' Brisley replied with a smile that was so known to me I couldn't help but gasp. 'Miss Dawson.' He bowed to me even as I stood with a bloody handkerchief pressed to my neck, pale and dishevelled.

'Lieutenant, I . . .' I stopped. What could I possibly ask him? *Do you know if the ghost of one of your relatives is haunting my family home?* Instead I settled for 'Does your family hail from London originally?'

He seemed pleasantly surprised by the question. 'Indeed, miss. I was brought up there, in fact, before I joined the navy.'

'In that case, I should like to speak with you, perhaps, when things are less chaotic. I believe we might have a mutual acquaintance.'

It was all I could manage before Charles escorted me gently towards his horse. The poor beast looked a little winded, but he allowed his master to lift me up and place me on his saddle.

'He has forgiven you for running into him the other day, it seems. I hope you don't mind riding in front of me? It will be faster than if I were to walk beside you.' Charles sounded almost nervous, I thought.

I nodded, allowing him to mount behind me and wrap his arms around mine so that he could take the reins. I stiffened at the familiarity, but when I looked around at the few people left in the churchyard, no one was taking any notice of us. Except, perhaps, Mistress Damiani, who seemed to catch my eye and give me a grin.

If there was ever a time I wished I didn't know about Charles and Esme's affair, and their letters and schemes, it was now. I wanted nothing more than to lean into the curve of his arms and press my back against his chest, feeling safe and secure in his embrace.

But that was just it. I *did* feel safe, I realised, his body keeping me in place as Hurricane broke into a canter.

And so it was that all the way home I pretended as best I could that I didn't know, and that I was the same Lizzie who had fallen for him, who had wiped sugar from his cheek and confided in him about my past. It was a lie, of course, for I had changed more in the course of a few days than most people did in a decade, and I knew now that whatever Esme had been planning before her death had involved the man I loved. But it was a lie that allowed me to relax, my head pressed back into his shoulder, his chin almost resting on the flowers pinned in my hair.

And that was how I stayed, all the way back to Ambletye.

Chapter 22

ജ ൝

I sat in the parlour and listened to the staccato of hailstones against the window panes.

I hadn't seen Charles in days. He had arranged for me to be fed and looked after before changing his clothes and riding straight off to London to oversee his uncle's trial, and he hadn't yet returned. Although saddened to see him leave, I had been deeply relieved that I did not have to confront him, however cowardly that made me. The days had dragged endlessly after the failed wedding, and very little news had come from London, leaving me at a loose end in a house that wasn't my own, moping and worrying over my future.

The tea in my still-quivering hands had long gone cold, and I placed the cup back on the low table with a clatter.

'Is it not as good as Judith's tea, Lizzie?' Price's voice broke through my thoughts and I looked up, having forgotten he was there.

'I'm sorry, did you ask me something?' I folded my hands in my lap and squeezed them together in an effort to stop the shaking that had plagued me all week.

His worry was clear upon his face. 'The tea. I asked if it was not as good as Judith's, but never mind that. Have you been eating?'

'Oh. Yes, I have,' I said, picking at a crumb on the side of a plate as if to demonstrate.

'And Jordie? Have you had any word from him?'

I thought of the sea of faces outside the church, and the fact that his had not been among them. 'No, not since I visited him last week. Do you know if his injuries are improved?'

'I believe his mother has been taking advantage of him being home. I'm sure he will fully heal soon enough,' Price said gently, as if to make me feel better for the fact that I was the cause of his condition.

There was a strange, hollow feeling within me that I could not explain. I felt as though I had won the top prize in a competition, only to find that the reward was something I did not want.

'Would you like to tell me what plagues you?'

Price's tone was so gentle I wanted to scream. I pressed my lips together to stop myself from doing just that. I could not tell him all of what bothered me, for there would be no good in burdening him with things that neither he nor I could change.

When I had asked Charles to bring me home after the wedding, I had meant Ambletye, but it had slowly dawned on me that this would not be home for much longer. Even if Lord Blountford did not willingly bequeath his estate to his nephew, it was unlikely now that there would be any other alternative. Perhaps the house would be sold to pay off fines, or maybe Charles had it in hand; after all, it was a part of his grand plan. He no longer needed to charm me in an effort to gain a foothold here, and he had left so quickly that I hadn't dared to ask him what would happen next. I did not wish to think of my return to London, and I was not ready to write to my parents yet.

All of that jumbled around inside my head, a bric-a-brac of dread and anguish, vexation and worriment, as Price studied me. Rather than speak of any of it, I told him what little truth I could, a fragment of my fears.

'I'm afraid I am quite embarrassed.'

'What on earth would give you cause for embarrassment, my dear?'

'All of those people from the village yesterday, they no doubt came to see the spectacle of Lord Blountford being arrested, but I . . . I can't help but think I looked a fool in front of them.' My cheeks flushed with shame even at the thought of it. People I had respected and very quickly warmed to staring at me in my distressed and still stupefied state, brandishing a knife.

'Oh, dear Lizzie, not at all,' he said, leaning forward and taking one of my quivering hands in his own. 'Those people were there for you, not to watch Lord Blountford fall from grace.'

I allowed a little relief to dampen the indignity I felt. 'You're certain?'

'Of course. As soon as word spread that the parish constables were off to the church to arrest the earl, the villagers began gathering. It was Mr Grahame who knocked on my door to tell me that everyone was making their way up there to ensure your safety.'

My safety? I could not believe it, and yet of course I trusted Price's word. I managed to match his smile with my own.

'Did you truly think after everything you have done here, and everyone you have befriended, that we would abandon you?' he continued.

'In all honesty, I did not know what to think. I am a stranger to the village really, having arrived here so recently.'

'A lot can happen in a short time, my dear,' he said with a gentle pat of my hand, which had finally stopped shaking in his grasp.

'That it can.'

He stood, releasing his grip and giving me a bow. 'I must head back to the village, I'm afraid. I promised someone I would look at a horse that seems to be limping. You are always welcome to join me, you know,' he added hopefully.

Regret threaded through me at his words, knowing that I would perhaps never be able to do such a thing, but I nodded gratefully at the offer.

He reached the door of the parlour before turning. 'Opium,' he said, almost as an afterthought.

'Pardon?'

'The shaking – it is an after-effect of opium, along with the trauma you suffered. It should settle down in the next day or two.'

'Thank you, Doctor,' I said with a light humour I didn't feel. 'Remind me never to touch the stuff again.'

He grinned in reply and straightened the creases in his jacket. 'Take care, Lizzie. I will see you as soon as I am able, and you know the door is always open for you at the cottage.'

I knew that. I also knew that when I visited him and Judith next, it would likely be my last trip to them. The thought twisted in my gut like a corkscrew.

I wandered back up to my rooms to find Marie cleaning out the fireplace. She had almost refused to leave my side since the day of the wedding, vanishing only to fetch me food or tea when I requested it.

'I need to speak to you about something,' I said to her as I entered, flopping down on the freshly made bed.

'Yes, miss?' she replied without stopping in her work.

'I need a girl to go and work for Price and Judith, but I want it to be someone good and worthy of them, ideally with a bit of humour and not averse to their . . . eccentricities.'

309

She straightened and wiped her sooty fingers on a rag. 'I'm not sure if I know the right person, miss,' she said, frowning.

'Well, I do. You. I would have you work for them in a heartbeat if I could, but I wouldn't want you to go unwillingly.'

'Oh,' she replied in surprise. 'Have I displeased you in some way, miss?' she added worriedly.

'No, not at all, Marie. Quite the opposite, in fact.' I propped myself on my elbows so that she could see the sincerity in my face. 'Price has become one of my dearest friends, and Judith, his housekeeper, is desperate for help. I would not want anyone but the very best to work for them, and to me you are unparalleled. I thought that perhaps if you were closer to the village, and with the doctor, you might have more of a chance to see a certain someone . . .' I trailed off, but my mouth quirked in a knowing smile.

'Oh,' she repeated, her big blue eyes widening, her cheeks immediately turning the sweetest shade of pink.

'I will ensure that your pay is matched, of course, and I hope you won't think of it as a demotion.'

'Not at all, miss,' she gushed. 'That is very generous of you.'

I waved a hand and let her leave with the bucket of ashes, a slight spring in her step as she went. I chuckled to myself. It was perhaps my final act as some sort of lady of the house, but one that was entirely necessary. Even if I was sent home tomorrow, I could easily convince the new chief steward to make the arrangements. Geoffrey, Turner's replacement, owed me a favour for his promotion.

After Price's visit, I ventured only between my bed, the music room and the kitchen, sometimes taking my meals there in the warmth of the stove and the company of Mistress Damiani. The older woman had grown friendlier since the wedding; somehow the witnessing of such shock and calamity had brought us together. She still ordered her kitchen girls around, but there did not seem to be such haste to prepare food as there had been when Lord Blountford was in the house, especially since the leftovers from the abandoned wedding feast had fed myself and the staff for a week.

On one occasion I mentioned how much I would miss her cooking when I moved back to London, at which she gave a startled gasp.

'But what about the captain?'

I ignored the emotion I always felt at the mention of him. 'What of him?'

'*Caro Dio, ragazza!*' she exclaimed in what I assumed was some sort of blasphemy. 'Surely he will propose upon his return to Ambletye? You are not going to leave before he has the chance to tell you of his true feelings, I hope.'

I gave a derisive snort in reply. 'Mistress Damiani, the problem is not that I don't know his true feelings. It is that I almost know too much of them.' After all, I had tortured myself by rereading his last letter to Esme over and over, until there was no doubt in my mind that he had wanted to marry her and secure Ambletye. He no longer needed me for that.

'I feel there is something you are holding in, miss,' she said quizzically.

I made a noise somewhere between a groan and a sigh.

'You don't love him?' She frowned at me, disbelieving.

'Of course I love him!' I exclaimed, the truth finally escaping, words running from me like a prisoner tasting freedom. 'I love him more than I knew it was possible to love a man. I had resigned myself to an unhappy marriage and a miserable life with Lord Blountford, but I had no idea that Charles would make me such a fool.' In frustration, I dropped the knife I had been using to butter my bread, the sound of it making her wince. 'For the first time, I finally felt safe in the company of a gentleman. He took all those things I hated about the opposite sex and changed my mind about them one by one. The moment I set eyes on him, it *hurt*,' I hit my fist against my chest, 'it hurt to know that he was not meant to be mine. I have been acquainted with him but a few weeks, and yet I could not imagine a life of which he was not a part.'

She looked not at all alarmed by my sudden outburst, only thoughtful, as if waiting for the rest. I sighed, pinching my nose, my elbows resting atop the table where our half-finished dinner lay. 'It is not so simple. I have nothing to offer him but myself. I know of his feelings for me, but I worry that only a few months ago, he had entirely different affections for . . . another. Someone who could give him what he truly wanted.'

'And what was that, *cara*?' she asked calmly.

I looked around the vast kitchen, my eyes floating upwards as though to indicate the whole house and all within it.

'Ambletye?'

I nodded, too miserable to speak.

To my surprise, she came around the large table and pulled me into an embrace.

'My dear,' she said, as my face pressed into her shoulder, her strong arms around me, 'not every man is only interested in money and heirs. Please don't let this one slip past you without knowing for certain.'

She pulled away, taking with her the scent of spices and herbs, leaving me to finish my meal in stunned silence.

By the following Friday, I had played all the pieces I could find in the music room several times, and knew most of them by heart. I had been tempted to ride into town and find out if Mr Grahame had anything suitable in his vast bookshop, but the thought of being pressed by him for gossip put me off the idea almost immediately. I was grateful for the pianoforte, though, out of tune as it was, for it gave me a way to escape and find solitude without actually feeling lonely.

I should have visited Price and Judith, or even Jordie and his brothers to ease my isolation, but I felt unfit to be in their company. They would only try to make me feel better, and I was not at all ready for that.

I sat at the pianoforte, staring out at the grey clouds hanging over the fields, the gentle patter of raindrops slowly growing louder. It would be quite a storm if the darkening sky was anything to go by. My hands rested upon the ivory in anticipation. There was only one item from my repertoire I had yet to play – the 'Devil's Trill Sonata' – and now it slowly spilled from my fingers, each note louder than the last. The rain seemed to beat in time with the music as I poured myself into it, closing my eyes and forgetting where I was. The piece had a way of transporting me back to when I had first learned it, those days and hours of practice at home, Esme sitting on the floor of the parlour or at her harp as I stumbled through the first chords, and then trying to play along as I became more proficient. Then, at my party, before I knew what was to become of me, the myriad of faces blurring together so that none of them had any meaning at all, save for one.

As I finished, the echo of the final notes ringing through the room, I sensed a presence behind me and my eyes whipped open.

'It is still my favourite piece, ever since I heard you first play it,' Charles said, his shoulder pressed against the doorway, arms folded across his chest. Although his clothes were dry and fresh, his hair was wet, as though he had recently arrived and had changed before coming to find me. He appeared lighter somehow, the tension and worry he had been carrying since I met him gone, along with his uncle.

'I . . . It is mine too. I always felt as though it were written for me, even though I know that not to be the case.' I took my hands from the keys and folded them in my lap, looking down at them. It felt wrong to want to stare at him, to study the planes of his face, when I still had so much to say and so many answers to demand.

'You play it as though it were,' he replied. He walked across the carpet and settled himself on the stool beside the harp some feet away, as though sensing I might protest if he came nearer. 'I have some good news for you.'

From here, I could see how the events of the past few weeks had taken their toll. He was perhaps thinner, from missing meals, but even with the dark smudges beneath his eyes, he was handsome. He must have been up at all hours, riding from here to London and enduring his uncle's trial, all to see that the man met justice. I ached to reach over and trace the angles of his face. I ground my teeth together in an effort to stop myself from acting like an imbecile and throwing myself at his feet.

'Oh?' was all I managed to say.

'It involves some of the arrests made at my uncle's club.' My eyes met his at that, curiosity getting the better of me. 'A certain young Lord Darleston was apprehended for playing faro, hazard and roly-poly.' I started at the mention of the name, and he continued. 'It seems, rather fortuitously, that the young lord was caught in the very act when the constables raided the place, and he now faces fines amounting to the sum of forty thousand pounds.'

'You're sure?' I asked, unable to fathom what I was hearing.

He smiled, a hint of cunning beneath it. 'I made quite sure that he was brought to justice, yes. It will be a long time, if ever, before he is able to host another party or accost any more women, I guarantee it.'

'I cannot believe it. This is truly the best thing I have heard in a very long time,' I said breathlessly, wanting to leap off the piano stool to hug him but settling for an uncontainable grin, my eyes stinging with tears of relief.

His own smile was so genuine that mine faltered for a moment and I averted my gaze. He did not miss the fleeting look of anguish on my face.

'Lizzie, what is it? What troubles you so?' There was nothing in his tone but deep concern, which only made it worse. I swallowed the lump forming in my throat, unable to speak in case my voice betrayed me. 'I promise you neither Lord Darleston nor anyone else will be able to hurt you again,' he said softly.

I shook my head a little, suppressing the agony that coursed through me at just sitting here with him, so close and yet no better than if we were a world apart.

'I'm so sorry,' he continued, standing and coming over to kneel by the stool, trying to read my face. 'I should have asked how you were first. You were so pale and restive after what happened at the church – I wanted to stay with you, but I knew that if I did not return to town, I would regret not seeing my uncle brought to justice. It was selfish of me.' His tone was the same as it had been all those days ago in the summer house, as though nothing had changed. But everything had.

'What is to happen to Ambletye now?' I asked. The question sounded more abrupt than I had meant it to.

He paused for a moment, taken aback. 'Well, my uncle was sentenced to hang, but of course he managed to negotiate with the judge. It seems he will be spending a very long time under house arrest at the magistrate's own manor. It does mean, however, that Ambletye is now mine by right. Everything my uncle owned in London has gone to pay off his fines, but thankfully it was recognised that the house would have belonged in part to my father, God rest his soul, if he had still been alive today.'

'I see,' was all I could reply. I was happy, of course, that Charles had finally gained what he had always wanted, but it also meant that he was more unobtainable to me than ever before. I was, once again, only the poor daughter of a bad gambler and an even worse alcoholic. Even if my father's debts had been written off, I had no dowry.

'Lizzie—'

'Charles, I—'

We both paused, willing the other to break the silence. I steeled myself.

'I wish to speak first, if I may,' I said quickly, before I could change my mind. He nodded, a worried, questioning expression on his face. 'I do not want you to feel obliged to me now that things have changed between us. You . . . Well, your fortune now means that you can afford to be . . . more selective when it comes to choosing a wife, and quite frankly, I do not wish you to think of me with charity.' He opened his mouth to speak, but I cut him off. 'I will return to London as soon as you require it, but I would ask that I be able to say goodbye to Price and Jordie before I leave, if that is acceptable to you.' My voice sounded like a stranger's, curt and achingly polite.

'You . . . you wish to leave?' The hurt in those words hummed through me painfully. 'It is as I feared, then.' He stood when I did not reply, his back ramrod straight as though he were standing to attention. 'I misread your affections,' he continued, searching for the words, 'thinking that you felt . . . Well, it does not matter. You were so quiet after everything that had happened to you. I thought it only an after-effect of the trauma you had endured at my uncle's hand, but had I realised that your feelings had diminished, I would not have disturbed you.'

'You do not need to pretend that this is my own doing in order to preserve my honour, Charles. You can ask me to leave and I would never think badly of you.'

'What is your meaning, Lizzie? I have no intention of asking you to leave,' he said incredulously. 'In fact, quite the opposite. I wanted to ask if you would—'

'I cannot!' I sprang from the seat and turned my back, my fists balling at my sides as I stalked towards the window, unable to confront him. 'I cannot accept your sympathy. I do not wish to become a burden to you simply because you feel obligated, knowing as I do of your affections for my sister.'

'Your sister?'

'Please, Charles.' I turned from the window to face him, confusion creasing a line between his brows. 'I know that you planned to marry her before you were even aware that I existed. I found your letters to her after your uncle sent you away, and it nearly broke me to realise that she was the one originally intended for your affections. That you had called her beautiful.' I twisted my clammy fingers in my skirts, hating every word that came from my lips, despising the truth that I laid before him. 'I thought I could forget that you wanted her, and even wondered if your feelings for me were genuine. But now I fear you have confused love with compassion, knowing what you do of me and of what I told you about my past.' I huffed a frustrated laugh. 'For I have nothing to offer you and I do not think I could ever forget that you loved Esme first. After all, everyone else always did.'

I held myself very still, hoping that if I didn't blink, I could stop the tears from spilling over. But there they were, the ugly facts that had torn me apart these past days, piece by piece.

He was stunned by my honesty, I could tell, his mouth set in an O shape, his hands spread at his sides. That slight crookedness of his nose made him look more boyish somehow, and desire tangled with agony inside my chest. Either he was taking a moment to recover or he was waiting for me to say more, but when I remained silent, he finally took a single step towards me. I had nowhere to go.

'Is this why you have been wound up tighter than a clockwork toy, Lizzie? You think I wanted to marry Esme?' he asked.

'Of course,' I replied slowly, quietly, my mouth turning down at the corners as I held back yet more tears with vicious effort. He took a step nearer and I became rigid again. The weak afternoon light filtering through the rain clouds illuminated his eyes, the emerald irises flecked with amber. 'Your letters spoke of a wedding. Of your honour at being considered for her proposal. And the picture she sent you that you said was beautiful. She even made mention that she had involved you in some scheme . . .' I paused. She had told me that after she died, of course.

'And did she tell you what her scheme was, by any chance?' His face was serious, his voice filled with concern.

'No, she did not need to.'

He shook his head, rainwater dripping from the ends. 'I have been to war and seen more death and destruction in the past few years than most men will see in a lifetime. There were days when a life here in England seemed alien to me. When I not only forgot what love really was, but could not even remember my own name. The letters your sister sent were like stars in the night sky, each one a pinprick of light in the darkness.'

I choked on a sob to hear him speak in such a way, but he seemed intent on going on.

'The picture you refer to? I have carried it with me everywhere since the day I received it.' He reached into his jacket and pulled out a pocket book, prising a weathered slip of parchment from between the pages. Why was he torturing me further? I had not expected him to be so cruel, but without thinking I took it from him, being careful not to brush his fingers. When I unfolded it, the breath caught in my throat.

Three summers ago, the fair had come to the green near our home, and Esme had insisted that we sit for a portrait together. I had forgotten that she had the drawing; it was the only one we'd ever had done of the two of us. And she had given it to Charles.

'Why are you showing me this?' I said, even as a tear slid down my cheek and I wiped it away hastily with the back of my hand.

'Because when I said that the picture was beautiful, I was referring to you.'

It was my turn to frown. 'But you wrote "*You* are beautiful",' I said. ' "If it is even a hint of a true likeness, I would consider myself the luckiest man alive." I know that because I have read that letter a dozen times in the hope that I could make some other sense of it.'

'Yes, I wrote those things, Lizzie, but I meant that you both were beautiful, so as not to do her any disservice.'

'I do not understand.' I fought the quiver in my voice.

'Then perhaps, if you would wait here just a moment, I can clear the matter up once and for all,' he said, holding out a hand as if to gesture that I stay.

He dashed from the room leaving me holding the portrait. I stared at it, Esme's smiling face, my serious expression in stark contrast. I could recall telling the artist that I refused to smile for such a length of time, and so, in exasperation, he had drawn me looking sternly out from the paper. But still my curls framed

319

my face just so, and there was a hint of humour upon my lips. It was a very good rendition. I wished, slightly selfishly, that Esme hadn't given it away. I would have cherished it as much as it appeared Charles had.

He returned, breathless, a moment later with a small bundle wrapped in string, which he placed on the piano top.

'The only way to truly explain my position is for you to see what Esme's scheme really was.' He spoke sincerely, but there was a brightness in his eyes that made me think he was almost laughing underneath.

'You told her to burn the letters,' I said.

'Apparently she and I are both terrible at following advice,' he answered.

Without knowing what to expect, my heart pounding in my throat, I picked up the first letter and began to read Esme's elegant hand, which I knew almost as well as I knew my own.

Dear Captain Blountford,

You do not know of me yet, but I am Lady Esme Blountford, recently married to your uncle, and I have been abiding here at Ambletye Manor since the spring.

I write to you, rather presumptuously, in the hope that you can be of service to me, and I to you.

Please excuse my direct manner, but I have gleaned what information I could of you and your character, and I must say I am impressed. You are of an age where you would be eligible to marry, and you are accomplished enough that I can see your ambition, which I admire. There are servants here at Ambletye who still recall your visits as a boy and young man – only three in your life, yet you seem to have made quite the impression on them. Not one of them can fault your character, and so it is for this reason that I contact you with surety in my mind.

In the hope that the war with Napoleon will be over before too long and you may be returning to England permanently, I have a proposal.

My sister, Elizabeth, is of marrying age and will soon be in need of a husband. Without divulging all of the rather sordid details, we have had a somewhat difficult upbringing, and it is only by fortune and your uncle's devising that I am here at all. Lizzie, however, is not so fortunate as I.

My parents are barely able to keep a house in London and I do not see great marriage prospects for her in her immediate future. This is most undeserved, for she is the cleverest and most talented of all of us, with a modest beauty that she is entirely unaware of.

With the agreement of my husband, I will provide her with a dowry if you agree to ask for her hand upon your return to England. The sooner the better.

I intend to bring her from London to Sussex at the earliest opportunity to live with us here. As of yet, Lord Blountford is unaware of my plans, but I have it all in hand.

All I require is your tentative agreement. I believe she is capable of making a husband very happy, and neither of you shall want for money.

In anticipation, and sincerely,
Esme

The words blurred towards the end of the letter as tears again flooded my eyes, the shaking that had plagued me for days returning with a vengeance.

'Y-you did not want to marry Esme,' I said, stupidly.

'No, Lizzie,' he replied. 'Every letter your sister wrote me included more stories of you. Tales of your character and your charm, plans that you and she had made when you were younger. It was clear to me that if such deep feelings of love could be put down in ink on a page, you must be even more remarkable in the flesh.'

'She p-planned our wedding.' I struggled to speak, to think. I had been so sure that Charles had had deep affection for Esme that I almost could not contemplate that his words of gratitude and love had been for me.

'She tried to, at least. When she died and I returned to England to find her gone and my uncle marrying you in her stead, I was incensed.' He curled his hand into a fist on the piano top, as though the reminder of it still angered him. 'We argued for weeks before we attended your party. It was even worse when I saw you in person, for I had loved only a figment of my imagination until then.' He laughed softly. 'When I met you, I felt nothing but regret for what could never be. You were all the things Esme had said you were and more, and I found myself falling more deeply in love with you every day, even though I told myself it was forbidden, that my uncle might have me killed if he knew of my feelings.'

'He would have,' I said, stunned at this news, my heart ballooning inside my chest so that I thought it might burst. 'He almost sent Canfield to murder you. I tried to bargain for your life by agreeing to go forward with the wedding. Not that you needed my help,' I added.

'You gave yourself up for me?'

I was astounded by his surprise. Did he not know how deeply I felt for him? 'Of course! I could not let them kill you. I would have married him a thousand times over just to make sure you were safe.'

He closed the gap between us, taking one of my hands in his own. That surety, that safety I felt when he was near enveloped me once more. His other hand cupped my cheek, wiping my tears with his thumb as I wept with relief.

'Lizzie, I cannot bear the thought of what might have happened if I had not succeeded in reaching the church in time.' The humour had left him now, the pain on his face clear. 'You must know that I would have done anything to bring him to justice and remove you from his possession.'

'Charles,' I sighed, placing my free hand upon his chest, where I could feel his heartbeat thundering even beneath his jacket. 'All that matters is that you did, and he is gone. I . . . I still cannot believe that I was distraught thinking that your love was for Esme, and that you felt the same way I did about you when we first met.'

'More so,' he replied, his voice rough with emotion. 'For I loved you before you were even aware I existed.'

The echo of my earlier words ignited something inside me, like a spark catching kindling.

The rain battered down outside, drawing the shadows closer, but even in the dim light I could see his eyes, dark and shining, fixed upon mine. He was close enough that I could feel his warm breath on my face, mingling with my own.

He leaned down, his nose brushing mine tentatively, before pulling back again, searching my face as though he were waiting for my permission. I was suddenly very aware of the heat in my cheeks beneath his callused palm, of the subtle curve of his lips, of his hand curled around mine warmly, protectively. My fingers slid up his lapel and over his shoulder to rest on the back of his neck, tangling in his damp hair. He quirked an eyebrow in question, and I gave the slightest of nods, then he leaned forward all the way, our lips touching, tentatively at first, before I felt myself melt into him, drawing him closer so that the kiss deepened. The scent of rain and fresh air filled my lungs as I breathed in, my other hand tugging at his lapel so that he could not pull away.

The elation of knowing that he loved me, that my feelings had not been for nothing, was an explosion within me, a firework of joy.

'Lizzie,' he said, and I knew I would never tire of hearing him say my name. He pulled back breathlessly so that he could take both of my hands in his own. 'Would you do me the great honour of becoming my wife?'

I laughed with sheer delight, a sound I had not heard in too long. 'Charles, the honour would be mine.'

Chapter 23

శ్రీ ◆ ◆

The following morning found the two of us walking through the grounds, wrapped up against the chill autumn air, my arm threaded through his. Without a chaperone for the time being, and knowing that we were weeks from being married, I tried to keep a respectable distance between us, but propriety gave way to staying warm in the end. The sky was a shock of blue above us, and the trees in the woods surrounding the lake and summer house were ablaze with colour. The vivid hues of autumn were so much richer here than in town, where only the plane trees that lined some of the wealthier streets and private gardens marked the passage of the seasons.

I had taken Charles to Esme's purple room, Lord Blountford's study, and the place where Marisa had fallen from her balcony. We had slowly wended our way past the spot where Anne and James had met their end before I pulled him into the woods to where the graves stood, explaining everything that I had learned of the lost wives since I had arrived.

He stood for a long while staring at the headstones. I noted, with no small amount of pleasure, that Mr McMannon had placed pansies at the unmarked grave. I would have the stone properly engraved when I was lady of the house, I decided, with words of his choosing.

325

Charles had said nothing since I'd finished speaking, and I wondered if the admission of my peculiar talent had somehow scared him.

'You mean to tell me that all of this came about because you can see ghosts?' he murmured after a time.

'Yes. It is much to take in, I know,' I replied. 'But I didn't want there to be any secrets between us before we married.'

'Do you know how this ability came about?' he asked, a question I had often pondered on myself but had never known the answer to.

'I'm afraid I don't. It is something I have been able to do for as long as I can remember.'

He nodded distractedly, walking towards the empty grave. With his fists clenched at his sides, I was certain he must be restraining disappointment or disturbance at my confession. He stared into the hole as though it might produce some words, some appropriate response to all that I had told him.

'Remarkable,' he said finally, so quietly that I thought I might have imagined it. A robin sang on a branch nearby, no doubt hoping that we might disturb the earth and provide him with a meal in our wake. I said nothing, wondering if Charles were under some sort of spell.

Finally he fixed his emerald eyes upon me. 'My uncle . . . he did terrible things. Awful acts in the name of greed.' He shook his head. 'It is a miracle that you did not go mad knowing that you were living under the same roof as someone such as he. That you persisted until you had resolved each one of their stories . . . I have seen many things in my time, Lizzie, but you,' he bridged the gap between us in two long strides and cupped my cheek, 'you are the most remarkable of them all.'

A bubble of relief burst in my chest. 'You are not upset? Disturbed that you might be marrying someone peculiar? I've been called many things, including a witch. I would not want you to regret your decision.'

'Lizzie, even if you *were* a witch, I would still love you and still marry you,' he replied, putting my doubts to rest once and for all. 'What you can do is so unique, so wonderful that I wouldn't wonder if we should call you "the ghost tamer" and travel the world solving mysteries,' he added with a chuckle.

I wrapped my arms around him, safe in the knowledge that with Charles I could be entirely myself. No secrets or lies, no hiding my abilities. I relaxed in his embrace, relishing his warmth and the press of his lips on my forehead.

'Not to ruin this moment of tranquillity,' he murmured against my skin, 'but when are we planning to inform your parents of our betrothal?'

I enjoyed the way he said 'we', though I didn't relish the thought of confronting them.

'Soon,' I replied non-committally. 'But not today.'

I stood outside the familiar London town house with its peeling paint and tarnished knocker, rubbing my gloved hands together nervously. The sounds of the city enveloped me, from the clatter of cart wheels to the hawkers calling out on every corner. Children played noisily nearby and there was not a bird chirrup or distant bleat of sheep to be heard anywhere.

'Are you well, my love?' The comforting presence of Charles behind me had me relaxing into him slightly, though not quite near enough to touch out here in public.

'I never realised how cacophonous it was here,' I replied, looking over my shoulder to find the hint of a smile on his lips.

'You've become a proper country lady in the past few weeks, it seems.'

I snorted a laugh in the most unladylike fashion, as though

proving just the opposite. 'Not a lady yet,' I replied with a quirk of my eyebrow. I knew I was deflecting, avoiding the inevitable by changing the subject. Apparently my future husband knew it too.

Something caught my eye behind him in the street – a flash of dark-blonde hair from behind a carriage window, a face turning towards us to give a radiant smile. I raised my hand in greeting as the carriage went past.

'A friend of yours?' Charles asked as his eyes trained on the face of the young woman.

'Jenny Miller. Another one of Lord Darleston's victims,' I clarified, remembering the timid girl who had approached me at my birthday party. She would have heard of Darleston's imprisonment by now, and his consequent ruin. Perhaps that was why she had looked so pleased with herself. I hoped that whatever she did now she found happiness in it; from the looks of things, she would be perfectly fine without the shadow of her attacker looming over her.

As her carriage rolled away, I turned back to the door and sucked in a breath.

'I believe you have to use that brass thing there to alert the household to your presence,' Charles said, pointing to the knocker, which had remained undisturbed while I fought my nerves.

'I don't quite know how to face them,' I admitted, reaching for it before hesitating once more.

'The same way you shall face everything, Lizzie: with me by your side.'

Warmth flooded my body at his words and I gripped the knocker before I could change my mind, letting it drop. The sound was swallowed up by the clamour around us but the door was opened by the maid in seconds, as though she had been waiting on the other side. They would have seen our carriage pull up several minutes ago – it was a wonder they hadn't sent out a search party when we didn't arrive promptly.

My mother stood at the bottom of the staircase, my father just behind, gripping her shoulders. I wondered if he were supporting her or using her to bolster himself. It had been years since I had seen them like this, united somehow.

The silence dragged on for more than a few uncomfortable seconds while I tried to choose my words and failed, creating a peculiar impasse while I read the emotions on my parents' faces. Shame, fear, hope and unmistakable relief, there and gone in a flash. But then the gentle brush of a hand at the small of my back reminded me that I had my own personal support in the form of a handsome naval captain.

'Mother, Father, it is good to see you,' I managed, giving them a tentative smile. My mother broke into a sudden sob and ran forward, pulling me into an embrace, while my father enveloped us both. And with that sudden burst of emotion, my own walls came down as I wrapped my arms around their thin frames and let the moment say a thousand things that couldn't be put into words.

Hours later, after tea and a lengthy explanation of why they had seen Lord Blountford's trial all over the London papers, I took Charles up to see the bedroom I had shared with Esme for years. My parents had offered him their room, but he had insisted he would stay with a friend in town, who would be along later for supper.

I had two reasons for bringing Charles up here – the first was that I wanted to share a part of me that I was ashamed of, a sort of baring of my soul. This was the small space in which I'd grown up, so far from the grandiose halls and rooms of Ambletye. The second was that I wanted to share my peculiar abilities with the person I cared for the most.

I stepped into the room, feeling like a giant who had walked into a doll's house. Little had changed since I had left. I ran a gloved finger over the vanity, pulling the stool out and sitting to stare at my face reflected there. The last time I had sat here, I had been gaunt, my cheeks hollowed, eyes set deep in my skull. I had been a girl haunted by things of the past. Staring back at me now was a full-grown woman, the colour high in my face, my eyes bright with happiness, with only the future to look towards.

'Nice of you to stop by,' said a familiar voice behind me. I turned to find my childhood friend sitting at the end of the bed examining his perfect nails.

'Brisley!' I cried, leaping from the chair and reaching over to him without thinking. Although my hand passed through him, I didn't think that was the reason for his consternation. He spared a glance at Charles standing behind me, his eyebrows raised almost to his thinning hairline.

'Brisley,' I continued, turning to my fiancé, 'this is Captain Charles Blountford. Charles, this is my oldest friend, aside from Esme.' I gave the two of them an encouraging smile. Brisley seemed both fascinated by and slightly wary of my future husband. Charles himself looked slightly lost, but muttered a polite greeting all the same to the empty space I gestured towards.

'My, my, Lizzie, much has changed since I saw you last. A real woman you are now. You do look well for it. But have you been away from me for so long that you have forgotten I am, in fact, unable to be embraced?' His tone was light, but I could sense the smallest inkling of hurt underneath it.

'Not at all, Brisley. I merely forgot myself, I was so happy to see you.'

'Happy? To see me? Are you quite well, dear?' he replied, pretending to lay the back of his hand upon my forehead to check my temperature.

'I am better than ever, thank you very much. I see you have lost none of your sarcasm while I've been away,' I said, narrowing my eyes at him.

'Really, why would I do that? I have had no one to talk to but the cook, and even she does not seem to care for my anecdotes and musings, for she blatantly ignores me at every turn. It is quite disheartening, you know. I have even taken to writing poetry, but she does not seem to appreciate it one bit.'

'Silly you.' I shook my head and rolled my eyes playfully at him. 'I have some news – well, actually I have lots to tell you, but I do not know where to start.'

'Why not try at the beginning?' he suggested. 'I do hope that this news will explain why there is a dashing young man standing here, presumably watching you speak to nothing and managing to hold his tongue.'

'Of course,' I replied, gesturing for the three of us to sit on the bed while I told him all that had happened, starting from the night I had left home, trying to ignore his occasional quips and usual commentary when he suspected that I had done something irrationally stupid. Charles said nothing to interrupt me, apart from adding his own tale of riding to London and finding an investigation under way into Lord Blountford's gambling dens, then assembling a band of naval men and Bow Street Runners to burst in and apprehend everyone. I had heard the tale only once before, but it was just as exciting to hear it again, with Brisley's interjections in one ear.

It might have been an hour, perhaps two of incessant talking before the doorbell interrupted us.

'Oh, I hope you don't mind, but I have a surprise for you,' I said excitedly.

'You know I don't like surprises, Lizzie,' Brisley replied in exasperation, but followed us downstairs when I summoned him all the same.

In the parlour, we found my parents and our guest assembling themselves around the table for dinner.

'Lizzie! That was a lengthy grand tour,' my father said, narrowing his eyes at Charles disapprovingly.

Charles ignored him, pulling out a chair for me before giving the newcomer a hearty handshake. 'Lizzie, you remember Lieutenant Brisley, don't you?'

'It is a pleasure to see you again, Lieutenant,' I replied, greeting him with a curtsey, all while studying my ghostly companion, who had taken up a spot by the window. He gave me a disconcerted frown, a look I was all too familiar with, before he began studying our new arrival.

'Miss Dawson, it is good to see you too, and in such excellent health,' the lieutenant replied with a bow.

I had written to him at the same time as my parents, arranging Charles's accommodations for our visit and asking him if he would take interest in learning if any of his family had lived in the house where my sister and I had grown up. He had, of course, accepted, and there he sat while the maid brought our food, his hazel eyes taking in the room with alert appraisal.

The house was in need of repair, but when I had a little more money to my name, I would insist that my parents use any spare penny to make it presentable for themselves.

'Miss Dawson,' the young lieutenant said as the gravy was passed around, 'thank you so much for inviting me into your childhood home.'

'The pleasure is mine, Lieutenant. I appreciate you making the effort.'

Brisley, who had hung back until the man had spoken, stepped nearer to the table, resting his hands on the back of my mother's chair, puzzlement written across his face.

'How are the wedding plans coming along?' the lieutenant asked conversationally, for the last time I had seen him was that fateful day outside the church, another lifetime ago. Charles and I shared a glance across the table, and my heart did a little flutter, as it often did when he looked at me that way.

'In all honesty, Lieutenant, we have barely begun. The minister will be reading the banns for another two weeks, and there is still so much to do,' I said, eyeing Brisley, who had stalked around the table to eyeball the young man.

'He does look familiar, doesn't he? Handsome fellow,' the ghost said, his nose inches from the unsuspecting soldier.

Charles made small talk with his old friend while I watched mine, seeing the similarities between them. The same mouth, although Brisley's eyes were darker, while the lieutenant had a softness to his features where Brisley had hard lines and angles. But still, I could not shake the certainty that he was a long-lost relative.

'Did you manage to contact your father regarding your family's previous occupancy at this address?' I asked at an appropriate pause in the conversation.

'Oh yes, it is remarkable, actually,' the lieutenant said with enthusiasm. 'Apparently my father's parents and their parents before them lived in this street. I had no idea it was at this address until I mentioned your letter to him.'

Brisley straightened, his face blanching in a way that I did not realise was possible for a ghost.

'Goodness,' my father said, 'what a small world. I bought the house after it had stood empty for a number of years. How remarkable that you should know someone whose family lived here before us, Lizzie.'

'Indeed,' I replied, keeping a watchful eye on my ghostly friend.

'Unfortunately my grandfather passed away quite young, and my grandmother was forced to move out, taking my father, a child then, with her. If Miss Dawson hadn't invited me, I don't think I ever would have known the entire story.'

I felt a twinge of sadness for Brisley, but his eyes were bright with admiration for the boy who it transpired was his grandson. I had never pictured him with a wife or child before, but as I looked at him now, I could envisage it, for despite his often surly attitude, he was just another person who had not had enough time with the ones he loved.

'You wanted me to know that my family lives on,' he said, walking around the table to rest a feather-light hand upon my shoulder.

I nodded almost imperceptibly. My intention had only been to show him that despite having been away so long from him, I had not forgotten, and he was not alone in the world.

And should he wish it to be so, I might be able to help him move on. I didn't say any of this, of course. There would be time enough for that later.

'Thank you, Lizzie,' he said, and I almost choked on my food to hear the words from his lips.

'You are most welcome,' I replied, and although everyone else believed it was in reply to the lieutenant, the ghost knew better. A calm seemed to settle over the room, and I wondered if it had anything to do with the now happy spirit that resided within its walls.

As the lieutenant spoke animatedly of his exploits to my parents, I caught Charles's eye once more across the table and he gave me a knowing smile.

'The ghost tamer' he had called me. The name rang around my head now as though he had said it aloud.

I rather liked it.

Chapter 24

ॐ

We stayed in London for two more days before returning to Ambletye with my mother in tow, bringing her down to act as our chaperone until we were married. Although the house was big enough that an entire London street would fit between our opposite wings, Charles wanted to do everything by the book, and I respected him for that, even if he did make a point of hiding all the alcohol in locked cabinets when we arrived.

The minister read the banns for two more weeks as had been agreed, having barely recovered from the last ceremony. I secretly suspected he needed the time to recuperate before performing another wedding.

It gave me sufficient time to plan, and Marie, who stayed on with me until the very last moment, enough time to make a dress entirely unique for the occasion. She also began training her replacement, a slightly older girl by the name of Edith, who hid her frustration at being ordered around by my no-longer-mousy maid quite well. The two of them did everything, from gathering fabric samples to fittings to presenting me with the final product: a gown of shimmering viridian that turned iridescent in the light, cleverly done by weaving tiny golden threads through the fabric. The colours reminded me of Charlie's eyes. Charlie, because now that his uncle was no longer there to condescend to him and taint his family's childhood name, I was finally permitted to use it in private.

I hadn't wished to wait until the spring to marry, mainly due to Esme's scheming. She had planned an autumn wedding for us before I knew, and it felt only right to abide by her wishes.

I had taken the liberty of inviting the village for the church ceremony, and my father joined us just a few days before, along with Lieutenant Brisley. With Lord Blountford's club closed, and the Bow Street Runners being particularly sharp on all gambling activities, Father had managed to restrain himself from getting into further trouble. For now.

'I must warn you that if you had not been Lizzie's father, I would have had you arrested with the other patrons,' I had overheard Charlie saying to him privately one evening, when the two of them were sitting in the drawing room smoking by the fire. 'You have been given a second chance at life, Mr Dawson, and I sincerely hope you do not throw it away with your habit, for your daughter and I will not come to your aid if you do.'

He had used his captain's voice, as I liked to call it, and if my father was offended by the direct order from a man twenty years his junior, he made no show of it.

Indeed, even my mother was respectfully sober for the majority of their stay, either out of duty to us or because she could not lay her hands on any of her poison. I had my fiancé to thank for that as well.

Ambletye was finally alive with guests and servants milling about, no longer the shell of a home housing only a lonely, embittered man and his secrets.

The morning of the wedding was blue-skied and crisp, the wind picking up the dried leaves and blowing them across the churchyard like confetti. Marie had fitted a light coat over my dress and left my hair mostly down to cover my bare neck, twining strands on each side away from my face and holding it at the back with a heavy comb decorated with brass and precious stones. I suspected, although I did not mind, that she was still dipping into the lost wives' wardrobes when necessity arose, for it was nicer than anything I had ever owned.

The pews in the small church were filled down to the very last seat with friends and acquaintances from the village and beyond. Jordie, in pride of place with his mother and brothers, sat alongside my own mother in the front, Price and Judith in the row behind. Although I couldn't see them, I sensed the presence of others there as well. Perhaps my sister had defied all possible laws to be with me today. I felt the distinct press of a hand over my heart, and I clutched my own to my chest, thinking of how much I loved her and hoping that wherever she was, she knew how grateful I was that she had brought Charles into my life.

Sprays of hollyhocks and white gardenias had been tied with thick green ribbon to the sides of each pew, and candles burned brightly, lighting my path to the altar, where Charlie awaited me.

I had never seen him in his captain's uniform, and the sight stole the breath from me. He looked indescribably handsome in the dark blue outfit with gold trim, and I almost pinched the soft skin on my arm to ensure that I was not dreaming. I was marrying this man. When had my fortune turned so favourable? As his eyes alighted upon me, a smile broke out across his face, so at odds with the austere uniform he stood in. In fact, there were several men in naval dress in attendance – his closest friends, brothers in arms each and every one.

My father offered his arm to me and I took it, steadying myself. This was not the sickening dizziness of a few weeks ago, but a giddy, heady joy that set my legs wobbling. I did not want to close my eyes for a moment. I wanted to remember every detail of this day, every smile, every step and every word of our vows.

'Dearly beloved,' the reverend began, and I turned towards Charles to find his gaze upon me, burning with love and joy.

'Charles Edward Blountford, wilt thou have this woman to thy wedded wife, to live together after God's ordinance in the holy estate of Matrimony? Wilt thou love her, comfort her, honour, *obey* and keep her, in sickness and in health; and, forsaking all other, keep thee only unto her, so long as ye both shall live?'

I did not miss the reverend's emphasis. *Obey?* I looked at Charles, who gave me a flash of teeth, his cunning smile telling me that he had had the vows slightly altered for us.

'I will,' he replied certainly.

'And wilt thou, Elizabeth Anne Dawson, have this man to thy wedded husband, to live together after God's ordinance in the holy estate of Matrimony? Wilt thou obey him, and serve him, love, honour, and keep him, in sickness and in health; and, forsaking all other, keep thee only unto him, so long as ye both shall live?'

'I will,' I breathed, unable to get the words out fast enough.

The ring Charles produced had belonged to his mother; a slim gold band with an emerald set into it. I had never felt more privileged than when he took my hand in his and slipped it onto my finger, and I could see from the brightness in his expression that he felt the same way.

When we emerged from the church an hour later, the register signed, the guests waiting for us, rice was thrown at us all the way to the carriage that would take us back to Ambletye, where everyone would eat and drink and generally be very merry indeed.

Mistress Damiani had outdone herself, producing the most

marvellous wedding breakfast that had ever been, the linen-draped tables filled with platters of breads, fruits, meat and vegetables, all decorated with edible flowers from Ambletye's garden.

'Ah, there you are, Lizzie!' Jordie said when he found me, my arm threaded through Charlie's and surrounded by friends and family. 'I was hoping I might steal you away for a moment,' he said with a conspiratorial waggle of his eyebrows.

Extricating myself from the group, I followed him to a table in the corner, a spray of white roses and buddleia arranged in a tall vase at its centre. Plates of food for guests to choose from had been arranged around the room, and I gratefully picked at a selection of meats as Jordie sat beside me, retrieving an envelope from his breast pocket.

'Have you seen Marie since you arrived?' I asked him, absently peering around the room to see if she was nearby. He blushed and scrubbed the back of his neck nervously.

'Er, sort of. We've been . . . sending each other letters these last two weeks.'

'Indeed?' I replied with a grin. If that was the case, there would be another wedding on the cards before too long, I had no doubt. 'And what did you drag me all the way over here to tell me?'

He looked at the envelope, then passed it over deferentially, as though it contained a letter from the king himself.

'Consider this your wedding gift, Lizzie.' Putting down the plate, I took it from him, careful not to make a mess on the paper. The document inside was several pages long and written in such formal script that it took me a while to appreciate its meaning.

'You're making me joint owner of your stables?' I asked incredulously.

He nodded eagerly. 'Absolutely. I wouldn't want to work

with anyone else, and as your investment paid for it, it seemed only right.'

'Jordie, I can't accept this.' I dropped my voice to a whisper. 'I gifted you that necklace because I wanted you and your family to live well for the rest of your days. I couldn't then take half of the profits.'

'But that's just it, Lizzie. We've enough money left over that Mam, the boys and I will always have a roof over our heads and food on the table. You made sure of that. I wanted you to have something that you could truly call your own.' His eyes were shining so brightly I thought he might burst into tears with emotion, and if he did that, then I certainly would too. So I accepted, pulling him into an embrace.

'Does this mean I get free riding lessons?' I said into his shoulder, and I felt his chest vibrate with laughter.

'Of course. You, and your children, and your children's children,' he replied, and it took all of my willpower not to sit there and cry happy tears at the thought that Jordie would always be in my life, and the lives of all those who came after me.

As the afternoon wound on, I finally found a moment to steal my husband away, taking his hand and pulling him from the circle of friends he had been entertaining for over half an hour. I snuck him to the far end of the dining room, where the fireplace roared merrily, into a corner where the shadows were a little darker than the rest of the room.

'So, Captain Blountford, you will honour *and* obey me, will you?' I asked him playfully.

'In this life and whatever comes after, my dear Mrs Blountford,' he replied, urging me closer with his hand upon the small of my back, the heat of his palm seeping through my dress. I set my glass down at the edge of the mantelpiece and draped my arms around his neck, a thrill coursing through my body at the realisation that I could do this, stand this close to him, share these smiles and quiet moments for the rest of our lives. He bent his head to kiss me, and I wondered if the exhilaration that surged inside my chest when our lips brushed would ever dissipate. I hoped not.

Acknowledgements

ഇരവ

First and foremost, thank you to you, reader, for picking up this book and letting the story be a part of your life, even if just for a little while.

I originally wrote the beginnings of this book in my head when I was about fifteen years old, shortly after I decided I wanted to be a published author when I grew up – the fact that you have it in your hands today is proof that dreams really do come true (even if I haven't fully grown up yet).

Dreams like these don't happen without a team though, and I've had the very best that I could ask for backing me all the way. I'd like to thank my wonderful agent, Vanessa Holt, for championing Lizzie and her story from the get-go, and to the incredibly talented and insightful Kate Byrne, my editor, for seeing exactly what it needed to make it into the book you've read today.

I have so many friends to thank, whether it be in the form of encouragement, cheer leading, reading one or two, or a dozen versions of this book, advice, cups of coffee or grammatical corrections: Roger Ellory, for your invaluable advice and counsel. Gillian Greenwood, for falling in love with my stories and for our shared love of feisty female heroines. Tatiana Gabilondo, for listening to my podcast-length voice notes about plot lines, and for enduring long visits to old houses with me in the interest of 'research'. Olivia Elmiger, for reading the very first draft of this and giving me painfully honest feedback (I know you loved it really) – you really were my first ever editor!

There will never be enough thanks for my Mum & Dad, Tabitha & Tom Hardy. I know you've read all of my stories multiple times, and would be sitting as the co-chairmen of my fanclub if there were such a thing. For your encouragement, validation, inspiration and unwavering belief in me I will never cease to be grateful. (Dad, this is the final, final version – I promise!)

To my husband, Daniele, for being my total rock and supporting me all the way, and to my boys Zack & Damon for being ever so patient with a mother who spends far too much time in front of a keyboard.

And to my grandmother, my Mamgu. For taking me to every historical house and place of historical interest; for dragging me to every 'haunted' castle and watching all those weird ghost programmes on the telly; for spending hours in the library with me and showing me the joys of reading. I dedicated this book to you before the first draft was even finished. I wrote it knowing you would love the story, the history, the ghosts. That you left us so suddenly at the end of last year and never had the chance to read the story I wrote for you broke my heart, but I know that wherever you are now, you are proud, and I'm forever grateful for you. So much of who I am today is because of how you shaped my life.